SANTA ANA PUBLIC LIBRARY
D0408744

THE BARON WAR

BY JORY SHERMAN

FROM TOM DOHERTY ASSOCIATES

The Barons of Texas
The Baron Range
The Baron Brand
The Baron War
Grass Kingdom
Horne's Law
The Medicine Horn
Song of the Cheyenne
Trapper's Moon
Winter of the Wolf

THE BARON WAR

JORY SHERMAN

A TOM DOHERTY ASSOCIATES BOOK
NEW YORK

This is a work of fiction. All the characters and events portrayed in this novel are either fictitious or are used fictitiously.

THE BARON WAR

This book is printed on acid-free paper.

A Forge Book
Published by Tom Doherty Associates, LLC
175 Fifth Avenue
New York, NY 10010

www.tor.com

ISBN 0-765-30255-1

First Edition: January 2002

Printed in the United States of America

0 9 8 7 6 5 4 3 2 1

This one's for the Bell Boys:

Noel and Cohen

There are no men born ahead of their times. There are only visionaries, and there are circumstances; everything else is hindsight.

—"Pellegrino's second law"
Charles Pellegrino,
Unearthing Atlantis

Cast of Characters

The Box B Ranch

MARTIN BARON — patriarch of the Baron family
CAROLINE BARON — Martin's wife
ANSON BARON — son of Martin and Caroline
LAZARO AGUILAR — blind boy raised by Caroline
ESPERANZA CUEVAS — Lazaro's nanny
LUCINDA MADERA — Baron cook
KEN RICHMAN — Martin's friend
ED WALES — publisher of the *Baronsville Bugle*
JIM CALLAN — typesetter
PEEBO ELVES — wrangler
TIMOTEO FUENTES — ranch hand
EDUARDO MEJIAS — ranch hand
MANUEL LAGOS — ranch hand
PACO CASTRO — ranch hand
EMILIO FORTUNA — ranch hand
RAMÓN MENDOZA — ranch hand
CARLOS QUINTANA — ranch hand
JULIO SIFUENTES — ranch hand
CARMEN SIFUENTES — Julio's wife
SOCRATES — freed slave

The Lazy K Ranch

ROY KILLIAN — son of Jack and Ursula
URSULA WILHOIT — Roy's mother
DAVID WILHOIT — Ursula's husband
WANDA FANCHER — Roy's friend

HATTIE FANCHER — Wanda's mother
PLUTO — freed slave
JULIUS — freed slave

The Rocking A Ranch

MATTEO AGUILAR — owner of Rocking A Ranch
LUZ AGUILAR — Matteo's wife
JULIO AGUILAR — baby son of Matteo and Luz
FIDEL RIOS — ranch hand
HECTOR OBISPO — ranch hand
NUNCIO — ranch hand
TOMASO — ranch hand
DAGOBERTO SANTOS — ranch hand
PEDRO CASTILLO — scout

Others

MICKEY BONE — a Lipan Apache
DAWN BONE — Mickey's wife
JUAN BONE — young son of Mickey and Dawn
JULES REYNAUD — a Frenchman
DR. PATRICK "DOC" PURVIS — town doctor
LORENE SISLER — niece of Doc Purvis
NANCY GRANT — schoolmarm
ALLEN OLTMAN — Texas Ranger
MILLIE COLLINS — waitress
KENNY DARNELL — Ranger, Caroline Baron's brother
DAN SHEPLEY — Ranger
JIM-JOE CASEBOLT — Ranger
CULEBRA — chief of Mescalero band
TECOLOTE — Mescalero
OSO — Mescalero
LOBITO — Mescalero
ABEJA — Mescalero
CONEJO — Mescalero

THE BARON WAR

1

MICKEY BONE, THE homeless Lipan Apache, the wanderer of the wild lands of Texas and Mexico, came upon the ancient stone by accident. He had walked away from the little camp he had made in the *brasada*, that thick jungle of mesquite and sand and black loam, to relieve himself, when he looked down and saw it lying half-buried and caught between the trunks of two mesquite trees. It was obvious that the roots of the trees had turned the stone up, for it was tilted on its side, the top leaning against one tree, the bottom jammed at an angle next to the other. A thin shaft of sunlight, stabbing through the leaves of a tree, illuminated the stone as if it were a holy object set upon some primitive altar.

He stared at the stone intently as he sprayed the ground with his urine, listening to the whispering sound of the spattering piss, wondering if he was not hearing the voices of the ancient ones Dream Speaker had told him about more than a week before he had crossed the Rio Grande back into Texas.

When he was finished, he buttoned his fly and bent down to pick up the stone. He had to pull and wrench it from between the two trees and he nearly fell over backward when it came loose. He had seen the odd markings on it, but now he brushed the dirt and moss away from the flat surface and watched the glyphs appear as if by magic. He did not understand the writing, the symbols, but he knew they were old, the way he knew the mountains of Mexico were old and the earth itself was old.

He rubbed and rubbed until all the petroglyphs stood out in stark relief. There were circles within circles, spirals, and strange little stick figures with big round eyes and grinning mouths. There, too, were depictions of stars and round things that had radiating lines encircling them, and a crescent moon among these globes. One of the globes had wings attached to it, feathered wings that were neatly cut into the stone. Next to this was a cross that seemed to vibrate, for its outlines were traced, not once, but three times as if it were a living thing, growing out of the rock.

The stone was not heavy, and the writing was only on one side. Excited with his find, Bone carried the rune back to his overnight camp to show it to his wife, Dawn. As he walked through the thick mesquite jungle, he rubbed the glyphs with the tip of his finger as if to touch the hand of the person who had inscribed the symbols on the stone.

Dawn sat outside one of the old adobe huts that early settlers had constructed and abandoned to nature. She held the baby to her breast, a fold of her open dress over Juan's head to keep the sun out of his eyes. She crooned to the child and rocked back and forth to put him to sleep.

Bone approached and squatted next to her. He lay the stone on the ground, face up, so that they both could see it. He studied the symbols for a moment, wiped away a small clod of dirt lodged in one of the etched grooves.

"What is that?" Dawn asked.

"It is an old stone. Left here by the ancient ones."

"How do you know that?"

"Look at the markings on it."

"Scratches."

"No, look at them. They mean something."

"Do you know what they mean?"

"No."

"Then what good is it?"

"It reminds me of what Dream Speaker told me. He said that the days of the redman are numbered on this earth. He said there had been many tribes here before us and they have all disappeared."

"I do not like such talk."

"This rock is proof that what Dream Speaker said to me is true."

"Who are these tribes?"

"I do not know. Dream Speaker does not know. They were here and now they are gone. This is all they left behind."

Dawn sucked air through her teeth three times to show her disbelief.

Bone picked up the rune, handed it to Dawn. She drew back away from it as if it were an untouchable thing.

"It will not hurt you."

"I do not want it near me."

"I am going to keep it."

"Miguel, you are loco."

He rubbed the face of the stone gently as if commanding it to give up its secrets. He stared at it, tilted it several ways so that the sun struck it at different angles. Dawn turned her face away so that she would not have to look at it.

"When I was carrying this stone back here, I was thinking of what Dream Speaker said and those things I thought while we were riding here. We are not far from Matteo's now."

"I do not like Matteo Aguilar."

"I was thinking that we no longer have a home. We do not have a people. You are Yaqui. I am Lipan Apache. Soon, I think, we will be like those old ones Dream Speaker told me about. We will just disappear and we will never be seen again."

"Do not talk this way, Miguel."

"It was what I was thinking."

"I do not think of my people anymore."

"No, because they are gone. They are lost to you, forever. And, my people are lost to me."

"What about little Juan?"

"He is of another tribe now. He is of mixed blood."

"So, your blood and my blood is now his blood and he will make his own tribe one day."

Bone shook his head. "I do not know. Dream Speaker said nothing of this."

"Well, he is an old man. An old bitter man who has seen too much of life and now sees his own death."

Juan was asleep. He had stopped suckling and turned his face away from his mother's breast. Dawn looked down at him, touched one closed eyelid to make sure. Her touch was light as a down feather. The baby did not stir.

"Blood," Bone said.

"What?"

"Maybe the blood of the old ones is in us, as well. Maybe Dream Speaker was wrong. Maybe the people did not go away, but took their blood to other tribes, bigger, stronger ones. So they disappeared."

"Or they did not disappear," Dawn said.

Bone lay the rock back down between his moccasined feet. He wished he knew what the markings meant. Someone had left a message for him, or for another person, to find. He was sure that whatever was written on the stone was important. It had taken a long time to cut the lines. Perhaps the inscriber had used an antler tip or a piece of hard flint. It was something that was done with care and took a long time.

"Why do you take me to the ranch of Matteo?" Dawn asked.

"I have given this much thought, my woman. We have no home. We have no people. Matteo has said that I will always have a home with him. Our son needs a place where he can grow tall and strong."

"Matteo is Mexican. He is not Apache. He is not Yaqui."

"It is said he has Yaqui blood."

"Who says this?"

"I think his uncle or father told me."

"He killed all of his family."

"Then he has Yaqui blood. Or maybe Apache blood."

"You are loco, Miguel."

"You and Juan will be safe there. It is a big ranch. The biggest ranch in Texas, maybe."

"I will go where you go, my husband. But I do not like this Matteo."

"He gives us money. Did the Lipan give you money?"

"I do not want to talk about this. I am here. I will go with you."

"Good. We will be there before the sun sets this day."

"Take Juan. I will get on the horse, then you will give him to me."

He watched her as she caught up her barebacked horse and climbed on it. She was as lean and lithe as a panther. He liked the way she moved. He got up and walked over to her horse and handed her the sleeping baby. She took the child in her arms and nestled him against her exposed breast. Bone wanted her just then, but he knew this was not the time.

He went back and picked up the stone, and stuck it inside his shirt. It was flat and did not weigh much. Then, he went to his horse and lifted himself up in the saddle.

"Watch out for the mesquite," he said to Dawn. "It is very thick here in the *brasada*."

"I have been here before," she said.

They rode out of the *brasada* and were on Rocking A land. Bone looked up at the blue sky and the thin drifts of clouds that floated on the high winds. He patted the stone inside his shirt. Surely, he thought, the stone would bring him the good luck now that he was coming back to work for Matteo Aguilar.

And Dream Speaker had told him he would not have to kill Martin Baron, or his son, Anson, owners of the Box B Ranch which bordered Aguilar's Rocking A. Perhaps that Frenchman from New Orleans, Jules Reynaud, had already killed Martin, as he bragged he would. Perhaps, Reynaud would be gone from Matteo's ranch by now. Maybe he had killed both Martin and his son, Anson. Bone hoped that was so. Matteo had asked him to help Reynaud kill the Barons, but he told Matteo he would not help Reynaud. But he did not tell Matteo why he would not help Reynaud. Bone would not like to kill them very much, for they had once been friends before Bone had taken Martin's wife Caroline one day when she was near him. And he still did not know if she had been the one to go after him or if they had just come together in a natural way. It did not matter. He had his own woman now and did not need the forbidden loins of another man's wife.

2

THE HOUSE TICKED as the cold wood in its floors and walls began to warm in the heat of the late morning. There was a hollow feel to it as Martin Baron sat next to Caroline's bed, unable to glance another time at her cold, rigid body lying atop the spread, her hands folded across her chest, her eyes closed as if sleeping.

Martin thought it was ironic that Caroline had died in the month of May, a month of flowers and sunshine, a month when the Box B was stretching its legs, with Anson ready to build a herd that would make the Baron ranch the largest in the country, perhaps the world. A month when civil war loomed, after the firing on Fort Sumter just thirty days before.

The hollowness of the house was inside him, too. She had died during the night, with never a whimper, never a chance to say a final good-bye, never knowing, at the end, how much he loved her in those final moments, how sad he was that she was dying.

Esperanza Cuevas made no sound as she applied color to Caroline's cheeks, as she gently brushed vermillion on Caroline's lips and dabbed her eyelashes with wet charcoal she had prepared herself. The blind boy, Lazaro, Caroline's adopted son, sat in a corner, utterly silent, listening with an intensity that furrowed small linear creases in his forehead.

Esperanza had bathed Caroline's body when Martin was out of the room, and had only called him in when she had finished dressing the corpse, folding the hands and straightening the body so that it appeared to be at repose. She had done this because she could no longer stand the sound of Martin pacing the floor outside her mistress's bedroom. Now, she looked at Martin before speaking to him. She did not pity him. He had shown no love toward his wife the past few years and Esperanza had heard them arguing and fighting too much for her to relinquish any of her feelings for Caroline to her widower.

"I am finished," Esperanza said in heavily accented English. "She is beautiful again."

"Thank you, Esperanza. You and Lazaro may go."

"I will help Lucinda with the lunch."

"Yes, yes," Martin said, still dazed by the tragedy that had befallen his household, still caught in the vise of a confused grief that numbed his senses, blurred his thoughts, so that he felt like something not fully human, a being that moved through a half-world in a strange, constricted motion that seemed disconnected from his actual body, as if he were wandering through the world of the dead while still breathing. He felt dead inside, but, oddly, both relieved and ashamed that he was not.

Martin was vaguely aware that Lazaro had arisen and floated across the room on silent bare feet and melted into Esperanza's skirt so that they were a single person leaving the bedroom. He heard the door close, but had to look at it to make sure that his senses were still aligned with some aspect of the living world.

He had seen death before, but none had left him so shaken as Caroline's. First he had seen his parents die horribly; then, he had watched his friend Cackle Jack die slowly from a terrible wound, and then there was Juanito Salazar, shot to death in his prime. Caroline had been dying for a long time, but he had ignored that dying, and her, as well.

He forced himself to look at Caroline's face. Despite Esperanza's care, it looked waxen, the skin darker, as if shadows were emerging from inside the corpse. He could not look at that graven image, and turned away. At least, he thought, I told her I loved her before she died. And he was sure that she had heard him. But he did not know if she believed him or not. Yet he had meant it at the time.

There was a tap at the door.

"Come in," Martin said.

"It's me, Pa," Anson said, pushing the door open. "Doc Purvis should be here in a few minutes. I saw the dust on the road."

"Who's with him?"

"Too far away to tell. I sent Peebo after Purvis, so he's there. I imagine Ken Richman will ride in with them."

"All right. Esperanza, she put some color in your ma's cheeks if you want to look at her."

Anson glanced briefly at the bed. "I—I can't, Pa."

"I know, son."

"I can't hardly believe she's gone."

"Me neither. Let's wait outside. I can barely breathe in here."

Anson was only too eager to leave the room. He closed the door after his father emerged. They stood there, waiting for the doctor who had examined Caroline before her death.

After a brief conversation about funeral arrangements, Anson changed the subject. He didn't want to think about his mother anymore. He mentioned his concerns about Matteo Aguilar.

"He wants our ranch, our land," Martin said.

"My land," Anson insisted. "Ma turned the ranch over to me, and you have no say in it. I'm going to respect her wishes."

"Boy, I sure raised a son of a bitch," Martin said.

"You never raised me, Pa. You left us and that's why I own the Box B."

"I could fight that ownership. Now that your ma's gone . . ."

Anson looked his father straight in the eye. His jaw hardened for a moment. "Pa, I run this ranch. I own it, not you. Now, if you want a fight, you'll get it. And you'll lose."

Martin tried to suppress his anger. He balled up his fists, but he did not throw a punch at his son.

"Go ahead," Anson said. "I'm not afraid of you."

Martin shook his head. "No," he said, "I know you're not."

Before tempers flared, they heard the horses come up. A few moments later, Lucinda let the men into the house. Anson and Martin waited. Then they heard the footsteps on the stairs. Dr. Patrick Purvis walked toward them.

"Doc," Martin said.

"Hello again, Mr. Baron."

"Call me Martin."

"All right. I'm sorry your wife died so suddenly."

"Well, you said she didn't have long."

"I'll take a look if you don't mind."

"Go right on in, Doc," Martin said.

Neither Martin nor Anson spoke as they listened to the mysterious sounds from inside the room. When the door opened again and Purvis came out, they both seemed relieved. The doctor was carrying his satchel and a sheet of paper. He handed the paper to Martin.

"I've filled out a death certificate for your wife, Mr. Baron."

"Thanks, Doc."

"Now, I need to ask both of you a few questions."

"How come?" Martin asked.

"I'm concerned about your health, Mr. Baron."

"Martin."

"Perhaps we should talk privately," Purvis suggested.

"Privately?" Martin looked at Anson, a puzzled look on his face.

"It's a personal matter, sir," Purvis said. "Concerning you and your wife."

"I think my son should hear what you have to say," Martin said.

"It's a delicate matter, Martin."

"Anson's a grown man."

"Very well," Purvis said. "I have to ask you this question because it concerns your own health, your future."

"Go ahead," Martin said.

"Were you and Mrs. Baron intimate the past few years—since she, ah, contracted her illness?"

"No, we were not close. Why?"

Purvis looked relieved. "The nature of her illness, the disease . . ."

"Come on, Doc, spit it out," Martin said. "I know she had the pox."

"Do you know where she got it?" Purvis asked.

"She was violated, Doc. By an Indian. Against her will."

"And, the, ah, man she, ah, who, ah, did this—is he alive?"

"He's alive, as far as I know. Why?"

"Because, if he infected her, then he will also die. You said your wife had the pox, and I suppose that's a good-enough name for a disease we know little about."

"Just what was it that killed my wife?" Martin asked.

"Well, sir, the disease is venereal. That is, it can only be contracted through, ah, intimacy, we believe. I've seen cases like this in Galveston, and the literature is teeming with examples from Europe, centuries ago, until the present time."

"I'm trying to follow you, Doc."

Anson shifted the weight on his foot, feeling more uncomfortable by the moment.

"If you do not have the disease and the person who raped your wife does not have the disease, then she must have contracted it from someone else; someone with whom your wife was intimate."

Anson and Martin exchanged looks.

"You mean," Martin said, "my wife was sleeping with someone who had this disease, right?"

"Yes, Martin, that's exactly right. Now, do you know who this person is? For, as a physician, I am obliged to find this person and treat him. Even if I can't save this person's life, he deserves to know that he, too, is going to die from this particular type of pox."

Martin's eyes blazed with a lambent fury.

Anson dropped his head, closed his eyes, and uttered a soft curse. Then he began to shake his head slowly in disbelief.

3

ROY KILLIAN TRIED to make sense out of the confusion that had intruded, by degrees, into his already complicated life. First, his mother had run away with the surveyor David Wilhoit, married him, and moved onto Matteo Aguilar's Rocking A Ranch. Then his mother had leased his thousand-acre Lazy K Ranch to a strange woman, Wanda Fancher, who, along with her mother Hattie, had moved in with Roy. Now David and Ursula, Roy's mother, had fled the Rocking A and were living in Roy's expanding household. If all that were not enough, Wanda had told Ursula that she and Roy were engaged to be married.

David had brought the news that Matteo Aguilar was planning to attack the Box B and take back his family lands—lands that Martin Baron had paid cash for and which he legally owned. Martin had given Roy a thousand acres of that land to start up his Lazy K and, if Aguilar made good on his threat, that transaction was in jeopardy. And Roy had plans to buy even more land, when he could, and be almost as big as the Box B or the Rocking A. He knew he had a long way to go before he could attain that goal. Texas was big, he knew, and everything in it had to be big, including his puny little Lazy K.

"Things will work out," Wanda said. "You shouldn't worry."

He and Wanda had walked out to the wooded part of the property, well away from the house, so they could talk without interruption. He had been sleeping on the floor of the main house. His mother and David had taken up temporary quarters in the new addition he, Hattie, and Wanda had built onto the main house.

"This is something your money can't buy us out of, Wanda."

"Do you love me, Roy?"

He looked at her, startled by her blunt question. There she stood, a petite, slender, beautiful woman, desirable as any he had ever met: self-assured, dainty, yet tough as a boot. Any man might want such a woman, he had to admit. She had inherited a great deal of money from her father. She was headstrong and knew what she wanted, and knew it when she had found it.

"I—I don't know, Wanda. I sure like you an awful lot."

"I need more than that, if I'm going to help you."

"You've already helped me a heap, Wanda."

"I knew you were the man I was looking for when I first saw you in the Longhorn Saloon. When you went after David that night to beat him up, I saw your passion, I saw the love you had for your mother."

"Well, I still hate David for what he done."

"What he did."

"You've got to stop that, Wanda."

"What?"

"Correcting my English."

"I want people to respect you."

"My English ain't goin' to help that none."

"I know you can speak well and correctly when you want to, Roy."

"Well, I want to talk the way everybody else does."

"But you must set yourself apart, Roy. You must be the leader I know you are."

"I can't hardly think with that house so crowded. I'm not gettin' any work done. And I'm going to have to join up with Anson and Martin and fight Matteo to boot."

"I know," she said. "But first you must settle your differences with your mother's husband. David seems like a very nice man and I'm sure he would like nothing better than for you to be his friend."

Roy kicked at a clod of dirt left by the plow at the edge of the woods. "David worked for Aguilar when he met my mother. He was surveying land here that Martin Baron gave to me. I knew he was a skunk when I first saw him. Then he just grabbed up my ma and took her off to live with the enemy."

"He knows he was wrong, Roy. Give him a chance."

"He didn't give me none."

"Any."

"I just don't like the man."

Wanda stepped up close to Roy and placed her hands on his cheeks. Her touch was gentle and Roy softened. "Do you want to know what I think?" she asked, her voice silken, almost a purr.

"What?"

"I think you were, are, very protective of your mother. From what she told me, your father left her alone to raise you and she was not exactly faithful to him."

Roy's face flushed with embarrassment. "She tell you that?"

"Yes. Your mother is a very honest woman. We stayed up last night, too, you know."

"I can't believe she'd tell you her whole life."

"Maybe that's what's wrong with men," Wanda said. "Maybe that's why they don't get along. They keep too much inside them. A woman can talk to another woman about almost anything and know that her words will be understood."

"I sure ain't goin' to tell no stranger my whole damned life."

"Oh, Roy, Roy, you sweet man, you. Of course you wouldn't. That's one of the differences between men and women. But, surely you can hear David's side of things, try and understand him."

"Oh, I understand him, all right. He sniffed around my mother here like a dog in heat and then swup her up and carried her off without askin' me. Like a sneak."

"Roy, what happened was that David fell in love with your mother. She was the one who didn't want to say anything. She didn't want to hurt you."

"She would have said something."

Wanda let her hands fall away from Roy's face. She laughed and shook her head. "No, Roy. David wanted to tell you. Your mother knew you would be mad, that you would feel abandoned, and she didn't want to spoil what she and David had."

"What was that?"

"The love between them. She knew what a hard time you had growing up without your father. She knew, as a woman knows, what her leaving might do to you. She planned to come back and explain everything to you when everything settled down."

"She never did."

"She couldn't. Matteo Aguilar virtually kept them prisoners at his ranch. He's a tyrant, from what I hear, and made demands on David that he had to meet. David wanted a nice home for your mother, and Matteo was paying him a handsome salary."

"Well, I don't know nothin' about that."

Wanda didn't correct Roy's speech. She smiled and put her arms around his waist, drew herself up to him so that they were touching. Roy began to squirm slightly.

"Roy, I love you. I loved you from the moment I first saw you, and I want to make you happy. But neither of us can hope for any happiness until you make your peace with your mother's husband. And I hope, in time, that you will come to love me, as I love you."

"So many things happening," he said. "So fast."

"I know. Even though I'm eager to marry you, I'm in no hurry. If you're not sure . . ."

"Wanda, I don't know what I'm sure of or not sure of. I feel like every time I start somewhere, I wind up running into myself."

Wanda laughed. A small hawk floated over the trees and out over the plain, its head moving from side to side as it scanned the ground. When it flapped its wings, both Wanda and Roy looked up.

"Hunting mice," Roy said. He kicked at another clod. Wanda let out a breath.

"Are you going over to the Box B this morning?" she asked.

"I should. Martin's wife is pretty sick. I want to find out what Anson and Martin are going to do about Aguilar."

"Do you think Aguilar will really attack the Box B?"

"He's pure mean, Wanda. I wouldn't put nothin' past him."

"Anything."

"Yeah."

"You might get hurt," she said. "Do you have to join the Barons?"

"I'm beholden to them."

"But Anson didn't ask you to fight with him, did he?"

"He didn't have to."

"I admire your loyalty, Roy, but discretion is the better part of valor."

"What's that supposed to mean?"

"It means you should think hard before you get involved in someone else's troubles."

" 'Way I figure it, we're all trying to make a go at raising cattle and what happens to one of us, happens to all of us. I couldn't hardly stay out of any fight Martin and Anson got into."

"What if there's a war, as they say there's going to be—between the North and the South? Would you fight with the Barons no matter which side they were on?"

"I reckon I would."

"That means you have no convictions of your own. You'd follow them blindly into any situation, no matter how foolish."

"You make it sound like I'm stupid," he said, bristling.

"Not stupid, Roy, just misguided. Friends are good to have, of course, but you must not place loyalty to friends above duty to family."

"You sound like a preacher, Wanda."

"I don't mean to." She touched the sleeve of his shirt, squeezed his arm. "I want you to be safe, Roy. I want you to make a go of this ranch. I will help you all I can, you know that."

"I know you will."

"Then promise me you won't make any hasty decisions after you talk to the Barons. At least let me know before you leap into anything."

"Wanda, I knew the Barons long before I met you."

She stepped away from him, looked into his eyes with an intensity that made him want to avert his gaze. But he couldn't.

"Well, you're not going to marry the Barons," she said. "You're going to marry me."

"You sound pretty sure of yourself."

"A woman always knows, Roy. I know what you really want. And I'm the only person on this earth who can give it to you."

She pressed her body against his and wrapped her arms tightly around his waist, drawing him even closer.

Roy became aroused; he blushed.

"I guess you do, Wanda," he said.

"You're damned right I do," she said, and began to move her hips, nudging her loins into his with a grinding motion. Roy's knees turned to mush and his legs quivered. He didn't know if he loved Wanda or not, but at that moment he wanted her more than he wanted anything else in the world.

4

MATTEO AGUILAR KICKED the footstool, sent it clattering into the wall of the empty house. His anger showed in the hard sharp lines of his jaw, the quivering muscle beneath one of his high cheekbones, and in the crackling fires that lit his black eyes until they shone like polished obsidian.

"Puta. Pendejo. Chingaderos." He spat the words out as if they were bitter bits from some vile seed he had cracked with his teeth. "The ungrateful bastard and his whore wife."

Jules Reynaud stood in the doorway, slouching against the jamb, a thin smile on his lips. He admired passion and exulted in seeing another man's anger displayed so visibly. It made him calm inside, and that calmness had been a benefit in many a brawl in New Orleans' seedier dens of iniquity. Reynaud was a schemer, a planner, and he seldom flew off the handle when his rage rumbled inside him like the thunderous voice of an erupting volcano.

"You hired the man, Matteo," Jules said. "You gave him your trust."

"I hired the bastard, but I never trusted that fucking gringo." Matteo turned to look at Reynaud, his eyes still smoldering with fury. "I gave him this house for his bitch, and he runs away in the night, stealing two of my best horses."

"You hired a horsethief."

"I hired a surveyor. *Un mentiroso.* I think he lied about the survey where the whore's son is squatted."

"Roy Killian?"

"Yes. Roy Killian. That Ursula, his *puta* mother, is *una bruja,* a witch."

"I think you are angry because she did not spread her legs for you, Matteo."

"Shit. I could have had her."

"You wanted her."

Matteo waved a hand at Reynaud, turned, and began to survey the room. He walked around it, poking here and there, examining what the Wilhoits had left behind. "He did not take his surveying instruments."

"Perhaps he means to return."

"I will kill him if he shows his face here."

"Yes. Then you could have his woman."

"Do not speak of his woman. I do not want her."

Reynaud smiled. Matteo disappeared into the bedroom and was gone for several moments. Reynaud stepped outside, began to roll a smoke. He heard noises from inside and knew that Matteo was kicking things around to vent his anger.

Matteo came outside, slammed the door behind him.

"Did they steal anything else?" Reynaud asked. "Besides your horses and your pride?"

"Reynaud, you have the fast mouth and the filthy mind."

"I thought Wilhoit a poor choice for a gun when we tried to move those slaves up north."

"And you were not such a good choice, either, eh?"

"We were outnumbered."

"Well, we will see how you do when I take my men, my soldiers, and attack the Baron rancho. Come, let us walk back to the house. I want to tell you my plan."

The two started walking toward Matteo's house, passing the large barn where some of his hands were grooming the horses, doling out lead and powder for the upcoming raid on the Box B. It still galled him that Martin Baron had bought so much land from his forebears, land that had been granted to the Aguilar family by the Spanish—hundreds of thousands of acres—and now, Roy Killian, even, owned part of it. If Matteo did not stop the gringos now, they would someday own every piece of land from the Nueces to the Rio Grande. Matteo waved to the men, and they saluted him but said nothing.

"I think you are making a big mistake, Matteo."

"Eh? Why do you say that?"

"Wilhoit obviously warned Martin Baron about your planned raid. If you go against him with your little army, he will be waiting for you. Do you remember what he and his cannon did to the Apaches who attacked him?"

"Yes," Matteo said.

"Well, you don't want to run up against a four-pounder. He'll cut your men to pieces."

"I have been training my army for a long time, Reynaud."

"Ah, have you trained them to be bulletproof?"

"There is no need for sarcasm."

"Perhaps there is. The only way to beat Baron is to outsmart him."

"I intend to outsmart him. And to outshoot him, too."

"How?"

"I keep my plans to myself until the last moment."

The two reached the back door of the house. Inside, the new baby born to Luz Aguilar was squalling at the top of his lungs. Matteo rolled his eyes and leaned against the wall of the house, unwilling to go in and face the noise of the newborn.

"I think it would be better if I take on Martin as originally planned," Reynaud said. "Give me two of your best men, Luis and Paco, perhaps, and I will see to it that Martin comes to town. I will call on him to fight. Your two men will be hidden and when I face Martin, we will cut him down."

"You were going to do that months ago, Reynaud."

"Ah, but you wanted to make money in the slave trade, my friend. That was a distraction from my mission."

The baby stopped yowling and Matteo turned, opened the back door. The two men walked through the empty kitchen to the front room, which was also deserted. Matteo sat in his favorite chair, one covered in cowhide, soft, comfortable. Reynaud took a seat on the leather-covered sofa, next to a small table. He picked up the clay *cenicero*, saw that it was clean, and dug out the makings from his shirt pocket. He offered the pouch to Matteo, who shook his head. Reynaud rolled a smoke, struck a *fosforo*, and inhaled the warm smoke.

The room was spacious, cool, with all the windows open and a light breeze blowing. It was a man's room, a rancher's room, with spurs and dueling pistols on the wall, a set of polished longhorns above the mantel over the fireplace, with its forged andirons and small bellows all neatly stacked next to a firewood cradle. Apache scalps decorated one corner where there were also bows, arrows, quivers, lances, and medicine pouches taken off of dead Indians.

"How would you make sure Martin came to town looking for you?" Matteo asked.

"I would send him a message, reminding him of how he defiled my sister in New Orleans, and that I had come to challenge him to a duel."

"And he would come?"

"Martin has never run away from any fight that I know."

"But, a duel?"

"If he is a man of honor, he would take up the challenge."

"It might be worth my consideration, this plan of yours, Reynaud."

"With Martin dead, you would have little trouble taking over his rancho, *n'est-ce pas*?"

"Do you know Martin's son Anson?"

"No. I have never met him. Why, is he to be considered?"

Matteo smiled without showing any of his teeth.

Reynaud blew smoke into the air, waiting for a reply.

"There are some who consider him more dangerous than his father."

"And are you one of those, Matteo?"

"I have respect for Anson. The stories about him are too many and too reliable not to be true."

"Then perhaps I should challenge Anson to a duel, as well. After I have taken care of Martin."

Matteo laughed out loud. Reynaud, discomfited, sat back on the divan, stiffening as if slapped.

"I do not think Anson would be such a gentleman as his father. He grew up here in the valley. He is as wild as an Apache, I hear, and when he has the blood in his eye, he is like the savage wolf with the fangs."

"Hmmm." Reynaud took another puff on his cigarette. His face was wreathed in blue smoke, but he relaxed and crossed his legs. "Then I shall have to think of this pup and how we might, ah, do him in, as well. Perhaps he drinks the whiskey in the saloon?"

"Anson is, as I have said, a wild thing. He seldom goes to town, I have heard. You are more likely to find him out with the wild cattle or trailing after Apaches in the mesquite."

"I am an expert shot with the long rifle, Matteo."

"You would hunt him? Then you would have to be very smart, like the Apaches, who have done the same and Anson is still alive."

"He is a man, is he not? Then he can be killed, the same as any other."

"If you kill his father, Reynaud, you would have to kill Anson. How you do it is your business."

"And I am very good at my business, Matteo."

"Claro que si." Matteo shook his head. "I do not know if you can do any of this. I have the army. My men are ready to attack the Baron rancho. I think we can win."

Reynaud finished his cigarette, ground it out in the ashtray. He was about to speak when there was a knock on the front door. Matteo looked around, but there was no *criada* present to answer the knock. He arose and walked to the door, opened it. Reynaud sat there, listening to Matteo speaking to one of the Mexican hands in Spanish. He thought it was Fidel Rios, but was not sure.

Then the door closed and Matteo walked back into the room, stood looking down at Reynaud. "Did you hear what Fidel had to say?"

"I *thought* that was Rios. I heard some of it. Bone? Mickey Bone?"

"Mickey Bone. He has returned. Fidel said he was riding in with his wife and perhaps a baby. This might change everything, Reynaud."

"I do not like Mickey Bone and he does not like me."

Matteo smiled. "I know. But you asked for two good men. If Mickey would go to town with you . . ."

"He has already refused once, remember?"

"Yes, I remember. But perhaps Mickey has more at stake now than before. If he has a child . . ."

Reynaud shrugged, stood up. "I do not trust Bone," Reynaud said.

"Then you are a pair. He does not trust you, either."

"Did not Bone once work for Baron?"

"Yes."

"Maybe he still has loyalty for him."

"Maybe. Maybe we will find out, eh?"

With that, Matteo walked to the front door, gesturing for Reynaud to follow him. Reluctantly the Frenchman fell into step behind Matteo as the rancher went to meet Mickey Bone, riding in from God-only-knew-what hell on earth.

5

LUCINDA FANNED THE coals in the firebox, opened the lid and put more kindling inside as the fresh shavings caught fire. She leaned over and blew on the flames until the small sticks of wood burst into flame. She closed the lid and opened the breather on the side. Then she turned to Esperanza, who was seated at the table, holding the young blind boy Lazaro on her lap. Both women had been crying. Their eyes were red-rimmed, their cheeks streaked with the tracks of tears.

"Why did my mother die?" Lazaro asked.

"God took her," Esperanza said. "Took her to heaven."

"Where is heaven?"

"In the sky. Far beyond the stars."

"I wish I could see the stars."

"One day, you will."

"How?"

Esperanza choked. "When you see your mother again."

Lazaro squirmed on Esperanza's lap. He had not cried, because he had not been able to see his mother. But he had touched her face and felt the rigidity. He knew that she no longer breathed because he had listened for such a sound and there was none. Esperanza had tried to explain to him what death was, and that he would never see his mother again, but he was still wrestling with the concept.

Lucinda looked at Lazaro, her face stitched up with a worried frown.

"You ought to take Lazaro to your rooms, Esperanza. There is going to be trouble."

"You heard something?"

"There will be questions asked."

"What did you hear?"

"The disease."

"The pox?"

"Yes. There are suspicions."

"Suspicions?"

"Esperanza, do not question me. I do not want to speak with many ears listening."

Esperanza looked at Lazaro, knowing he could not see her. Her expression changed, softened as if her facial muscles were liquid. Then she looked into the eyes of Lucinda and saw the answer there.

"Yes, yes," Esperanza sighed.

"Go. Go quickly."

"They have been talking about my mother," Lazaro said.

"Shhh," Lucinda warned. "They will be talking about you, soon. Go, Esperanza. Take Lazaro from this house."

Esperanza rose from her chair, her features broken by scrawls of worry that added and deepened the lines already there. She set Lazaro down with a sudden jar to his feet.

"Protect him," Lucinda whispered.

Esperanza nodded and scurried for the back door, dragging Lazaro behind her. Lucinda sighed when she heard the back door shut softly.

Lucinda began to place the warming dishes on the hot stove, the freshly made tortillas, the beans, the beef. Then she began to chop tomatoes from the garden, and an onion that made her eyes moist with their stinging.

Footsteps outside the kitchen made her turn in the direction of the door. The men she had heard talking in the front room walked in and she nodded to them. She knew the one better than the other, for he had been to the Baron house many times. The younger man she had met only recently, when he had started to work for Anson. The man with the funny name, Peebo.

"Lucinda," Ken Richman said. "Smells good."

"Yes," she said, and continued to chop the onion, her fingers deft with the knife and the onion.

"Howdy, Lucinda," Peebo Elves said.

"We're early, we know," Ken said. "But I think the others will be down shortly. Mind if we sit down?"

"Sit," Lucinda said.

"Where'd Esperanza and Lazaro go?" Ken asked.

"They go to her casita."

"Aren't they staying for lunch?"

"I do not know," Lucinda said quickly, and started herding the chopped onions into a pile before placing them in a wooden bowl.

"Why'd we come in here, Ken?" Peebo asked. "I'm right starved and the smell of the food is clawin' at my innards."

Ken laughed. "You were hungry out in the front room. We'll eat in here, when Martin, the doc, and Anson come down."

"You didn't want to hear what they were talkin' about upstairs, right?"

"Right," Ken said.

"It was you who sent for Doc Purvis."

"Yes."

"Me 'n' Anson met him and his niece when they were headed for Baronsville."

"That wasn't the only reason I sent for Doc Purvis."

"Oh, yeah?"

"Baronsville needs a doctor. I'm hoping I can get Purvis to move his practice here."

"From what I saw of the town, it didn't look all that crowded."

"It's growing. But there are ranchers to the north and west and east of us, and they have from a dozen to several dozen families living on each ranch. I want them to bring their business to Baronsville. It's the only way the town is going to grow bigger."

"Anson said the town was pretty much your idea."

"Mine and Martin's. And Juanito's."

"Well, if you get Doc Purvis to move there and if his niece stays with her uncle, then you'll sure as hell make Anson happy."

"Lorene?"

"Yeah. Lorene. A mighty pretty gal."

"Yes. I think she would stay. I've already offered her a job."

"What doin'?"

"Helping me in my office. The work has gotten to be too much for me to handle alone."

"And you got a gal, I hear."

"Nancy Grant. The schoolmarm. Yep."

"You got a gal for me, Ken?"

"Well, we'll just have to look into that, won't we? I'm sure there's someone your age in or around Baronsville."

Peebo grinned wide. He stretched his legs out under the table and tipped his hat back on his head.

"I see I got to spend more time in town," Peebo said.

"You're always welcome. But what's this I hear about you and Anson chasing after some rogue longhorn bull?"

"Yeah. The white bull. Mexicans are scairt plumb shitless over it and the Apaches give it a wide loop. Anson thinks he can get some big cows with that bull in his pasture."

"You've seen it, then?"

"Yeah, we saw it, all right. It's big and mean. Tore up some Apaches pretty good and done in a horse of mine. It has horns wide as a pair of barn doors. White as a bedsheet."

"El Blanco," Lucinda said, thoughtlessly.

Ken turned around to look at her. "You've heard of this bull, too?"

"I am sorry. I did not mean to . . ."

"No, that's all right, Lucinda. This bull seems to have quite a reputation."

"It is a devil," Lucinda said. *"Un diablo blanco."*

Lucinda's face seemed to blanch with fear as Ken stared at her. Then she turned away quickly and began to wipe off the cutting board, clearing away the scraps of tomatoes and onions.

"Such a bull is a menace," Ken said. "It ought to be destroyed. It certainly can't be caught with a rope."

"That's what I've been tellin' Anson. But he thinks he can catch it."

"He can find better breed-bulls than that one."

"I don't think it's worth it to try and catch that white one alive," Peebo said.

"I'm surprised you've even seen it. A bull like that usually is too wild to even show itself. I think that's why the Mexicans are superstitious about it."

"Well, even if he caught it, I told him, where in hell would he put it? It's a pure killer, that's all it is."

"Let's hope the damned thing dies of old age before either you or Anson gets hurt."

"Or killed," Peebo said.

Out of the corner of his eye Ken saw Lucinda move. When he looked at her, she was crossing herself and her lips were moving in a silent prayer.

6

ED WALES, THE new publisher of the *Baronsville Bugle*, parted the batwing doors of the newly built Longhorn Saloon and stepped inside, letting the doors free to fan on their hinges until they stopped back in place. He blinked his eyes to adjust them to the lesser light of the saloon from the glare of outdoor sunlight. When his pupils had opened wider, he scanned the room until he saw the man he was seeking, sitting in a far corner, his back to the wall, as expected.

Ed tucked the folded newspaper he held in his hand under his left armpit and walked across the room, avoiding the tables occupied by diners as if walking through an obstacle course. Dishes clattered, glasses tinkled, and eating utensils scraped and clanged on porcelain plates. Some men sat or stood at the long bar to the left of the entrance; waiters and waitresses flowed in and out of a second pair of batwing doors to the rear; while busboys piled empty dishes in wooden bins, pulled soiled tablecloths from deserted tables.

Allen Oltman did not rise when Wales approached. He touched a finger to his wide-brimmed hat and nodded. Wales knew enough to take one of the side chairs, affording Oltman an unobstructed view of the saloon and its entrance. The two men had met before.

"Al," Wales said. "Glad you asked me to lunch."

"My pleasure," Oltman said. "This is quite a town you've got here. You can still smell the green lumber, the fresh sawdust. Quite a town. And the bar is new, too, from the looks of it."

Ed, hatless, rubbing the balding spot on his pate, plucked the newspaper from under his arm and slid it across the table to Oltman. "Hot off the press," he said. "Ink's still damp a mite."

Oltman unfolded the paper, holding it by its edges. He read the large headline in 72-point Bodoni Bold: UNION TROOPS FLEE TEXAS.

A subhead declared, "State Militias Formed."

Oltman read the first two paragraphs, snorted, then looked Wales square in the eye.

"Looks like we won't be invaded from the north, but the Rio Grande is going to be a problem."

"Yes. The Union troops are still there."

"At least we cleaned out San Antonio."

"The Texas Rangers are confiscating arms, taking prisoners."

"I wish Houston was still in Austin."

"He did all he could."

"The Union is broken up for good, I fear."

"Texas is a border state. Maybe we won't have to cross the Mississippi and fight in Virginia."

"Texas will fight to preserve the Confederacy."

"I know, Al, but this will be a bitter war and it could tear Texas apart just as it already has torn the nation apart."

Oltman lifted his hand, caught the eye of the waitress a few tables away. She was the prettiest one in the place and he had kept one eye on her the whole time he'd been waiting for Ed Wales.

"Hungry?"

Ed nodded. "I worked all night putting this paper to bed."

"Maybe you need a drink."

"I want a drink, but I don't need one. I need some food in me."

"Aw, one drink to loosen you up. Your neck's so tight it's about to bust a strap."

"Well, I guess one won't hurt. I am pretty wound up."

Oltman smiled. "Whiskey?" he asked lightly, but he and Ed passed a look of understanding between them.

"Do you read minds?"

Oltman laughed. "I read men."

The waitress appeared magically at their table, slate in hand. "Hello, Ed. Need a bill of fare?"

"No, Millie. Do you know Allen Oltman? Allen, this is Millie Collins, the best waitress in Texas."

"Just in Texas?" Oltman asked. "I'm pleased to meet you, Millie. We'll have two whiskeys. You can leave the slate here."

Millie set the slate beside Oltman, brushed away a wisp of hair that was caressing her cheek. Oltman almost overreached the slate, but she slid away from his hand in a practiced glide that offended no one.

"I'll be right back with your drinks," she said, and gave Oltman no less a smile than he deserved.

"Mighty pretty gal," Oltman said.

"I wouldn't try and write my name on her just yet."

"Oh? She got a feller?"

Ed licked his lips as if he could taste the whiskey yet to come. "Not exactly, but the gossip in town is that she has her eye set on a man."

"Who?"

Ed looked around him, then bent over the table and whispered to Oltman. "No less than Martin Baron."

"But, he's . . ."

Ed sat back, a smile playing on his lips. He was close to gloating. "Ah, you forget, Al. Martin's a widower as of this morning."

"Anything going on between . . ."

"Oh, I doubt it. But Martin's met her and she made her play. He didn't back down."

"Well, it doesn't sound to me like she's all hogtied and branded."

"True, but if I were you I'd step careful. Especially if you want Martin to join you and the Rangers."

"Good point, Ed."

Millie brought their drinks and Al told her they'd order lunch in a few minutes. She batted her eyes coquettishly at Oltman and lingered at the table for a moment until he dropped his gaze, breaking eye contact with her.

"Now, a few questions, Al, if you don't mind?"

"Go right ahead."

"Officially, there are no Texas Rangers, right?"

"Officially? No. Unofficially, we're still in business. And getting bigger by the day. Nobody to stop us, really. Except the army, and it's too busy hiding its head in the sand."

"Why?"

"The damned army doesn't like us. And it doesn't like to fight Indians."

"Know why?"

"Sure. The settlers in Texas are howling over the Indian raids, the killings, stolen stock, burnt ranches and farms. They scream to Washington and the government does nothing. It sends in troops who say the Indians are not their problem. They say the settlers have to settle it themselves."

"So the Rangers fight the army's battles."

"That's the way we look at it, Ed."

"Mmm. Interesting."

"I wouldn't print any of this right now, if I were you."

"Oh, I don't intend to. I just wanted some background. But why? Doesn't the army know about you?"

"Sure, they know. But if there's going to be a war, the Indians will damned sure take advantage of the situation. When the men go off to fight the North, they'll run roughshod over the whole country."

"You may be right," Ed said, a thoughtful cast to his freckled face.

"You're worried, aren't you?"

"Yes. For several reasons."

"Well, so am I. If war comes, and it will if Lincoln beats out Calhoun, then this whole country's going to explode like a room full of powder kegs. The army will be running around chasing its tail and the Apaches and Comanches will have a field day in all the empty spaces."

"Christ."

"There are a few of us looking into the future. Rangers. We're going around trying to sign up good men in key places. To keep the bloody peace when war erupts."

"So, you came after Martin Baron."

"Martin, some others, here and there."

"Won't the army try and stop you?"

"Which army? The Southern or the Northern?"

"Um, I see. You sound like a militia group."

"Allowed by the Constitution of these United States."

"Soon to be un-united, maybe."

"The Constitution will stand, Ed. No matter what."

"Sounds like you, or someone in your organization, has it all figured out."

"Well, we have good advice from a very good man."

"I could take a guess," Wales said.

Al smiled knowingly. "And you'd probably guess right."

"Sam Houston?"

"He's one. Maybe the only clearheaded man in Texas right now. Not many up in Austin, that's for damned sure."

"God. It's going to be a horror, isn't it? This war."

"Yes, Ed, it's going to be a horror. And right at the center of it stands a black man who won't even know why everybody's shooting at everybody else."

"Oh, the Negro will know. Martin freed some slaves not long ago, brought them to his place, town, some other ranches."

"I know. That's one reason I want him on my side. On the side of Texas."

"Is that what Sam thinks? That the North will win and the slaves will be freed?"

"That's what most of us think. We don't cotton to slavery, Ed. It ain't right and there are going to be some mighty soreheaded folks who don't agree."

"You think Mr. Lincoln will free the slaves if he becomes president."

"Either that, or someone will come after him with a gun in hand."

"Maybe someone will if he does free the slaves," Ed said.

"Could be," Al said. "That's what I meant when I said the black man won't even know the trouble he's caused. Not through any fault of his, mind you, but the Negro is liable to have a worse life as a freeman than he ever had as a slave. That's why the Rangers are going to be important."

"You're going to be bucking against a mighty hard foe—not only the U.S. Government, but whatever government Texas has left."

"I know. But we're Texans, Ed. And we mean to keep the peace. And, when this is all over, there will be peace. A peace to keep."

"God, I wish the legislature had listened to old Sam."

"Oh, don't worry, Ed. They'll hear him good and loud when we get through doing what we have to do. I guarantee it."

Al lifted his hand and motioned to Millie. Then he finished his drink and set the glass down.

Ed looked at Al Oltman with intensity. He sighed and finished his own drink as Millie approached. He could hear her footsteps on the hardwood floor of the saloon.

"I think, Al," Ed said softly, "that Martin will want to join up with you. I'll put a word in Ken's ear when he returns."

Al grinned wide.

"That's what I was hoping you'd say, Ed. We need Martin Baron if the Rangers are to stay alive beyond this moment in history."

"Gentlemen?" Millie said. "Have you decided?"

Ed looked up at her and smiled. "Yes, Millie, I think we have. Al?"

"For sure. We have decided a whole hell of a lot."

Millie wrinkled up her face in puzzlement as she looked at the two men. She had the feeling that she had stepped onto foreign soil where nobody spoke her language. For a brief moment, she felt as if she were standing there stark naked, without a stitch of clothes on her back. She blushed and batted her eyes in confusion.

And, as the two men looked at her, she opened her mouth and found she could not utter a word.

7

MARTIN READ THE death certificate without much comprehension. The doctor's scrawl was difficult to read and he did not know the Latin words. Doc Purvis was speaking, but he didn't hear him clearly. He heard Anson speaking, too, but the words were like wet cotton in his ears.

"You want to know who was close to my ma beside pa?"

"I think it's necessary," Doc Purvis said.

"Why?"

"She caught her disease from someone. Someone with whom she had intimate contact."

"I don't follow your drift, Doc."

"Your mother had an infection, Anson. She got it from someone who was infected. It doesn't appear to me that either you or your father were the source of her illness. So, it has to be someone else and that person might infect others. He or she would have to be warned of the danger."

"If Pa doesn't know, then you'd have to talk to Esperanza and Lucinda. They saw Ma every day."

Martin snapped out of his mild reverie when he heard the names of the two *criadas.*

"Huh? What's this about Esperanza and Lucinda?"

"Doc Purvis wants to talk to them," Anson said.

"Why?"

"Something about Ma."

"It's important," Purvis said.

"Something to do with Caroline?" Martin asked.

"Yes."

Martin scratched his head. "Well, let's go downstairs. Lucinda ought to have lunch about ready. I reckon we can scare up Esperanza right quick."

The three men walked downstairs and into the kitchen. Martin nodded to Peebo and Ken, spoke in Spanish to Lucinda.

"She and Lazaro are outside," she said.

"Bring them here," Martin said.

Lucinda nodded, looked at the doctor with worry etched on her face. "The lunch is ready," she said. "If you wish to serve yourselves."

"We will," Martin said, waving Anson and the doctor to chairs that had been set out for them. Lucinda had put dishes on the table, and more on the sideboard. She went out the back door as Martin walked to the stove.

"Martin, I'm sorry about Caroline," Ken said.

"Me too," Peebo said, his voice soft as glove leather.

Martin grunted and lifted a pot from the stove.

"I'll help you, Pa," Anson said, and walked over to the stove. Doc Purvis pulled out a chair and sat down at the table. Ken passed forks and plates to Peebo and the doctor.

"Anyone want water?" Anson asked. "We don't have milk or anything else."

"Water's fine," Purvis said. Peebo nodded, and so did Ken.

The men began eating, passing the warm tortillas, scooping up beans, and Anson filled water glasses and set them before each man there and at his own place.

Halfway through the meal, Lucinda returned. She stole into the kitchen from the back door in a furtive manner, a dark scowl on her face. Martin looked up.

"She does not want to come," Lucinda said in Spanish.

"Why not?" Martin replied, in her tongue.

"She has fear."

"Why has she fear?"

"I do not know."

"I am not going to hurt her."

"She has fear for Lazaro."

"I am not going to hurt him, either."

"She will not come."

Martin slid his chair away from the table. "I will speak to her," he said.

"Pa, I'll go with you," Anson said, scooting his chair out from under him.

"Ken, I'll be back. Finish your meal. Doc, you'd better come with us," Martin said.

"Peebo, you stay here," Anson said. "I'll meet you out at the barn later."

Ken and Peebo looked at each other as Martin, Purvis, and Anson strode toward the back door. Lucinda smiled wanly and began to clear the dishes from the places where father and son had sat.

"Trouble?" Peebo asked.

"I don't know," Ken said, his brows furrowed. "Could be."

"Family stuff."

"Yeah, likely."

They heard the back door slam and both men jumped at the noise. Neither began eating again, but sat there picking at what was left on their plates as Lucinda began to scrape the plates she had taken away. She muttered under her breath and Ken listened to her but could not tell whether she was praying or cursing.

Ken dropped his fork with a clatter, turned in his chair to face Lucinda. "What passes?" he asked in Spanish.

"I do not know," Lucinda said.

"Yes, you know. What passes with Esperanza and Lazaro? Why will she not come into the house? Do not lie to me. Answer my questions."

Lucinda looked down at her hands. She was rubbing them together, a look of anguish on her face. She wrung them hard as if trying to remove a stain. Then, her face clouded up like a thundercloud and the tears began to leak from her eyes.

"Hurry up," Ken said. "I do not have patience."

"Pues," Lucinda began. "Esperanza has fear for the blind boy, Lazaro. She believes he is in danger from *el patrón*."

"Martin?"

"Yes."

"But Martin is not *el patrón.* Anson is the owner of the Box B."

"I know. But Martin is the husband of Caroline. It is he who will be angry."

"Martin will be angry? Why?"

Peebo was following the conversation with an intense interest. He knew enough Spanish to understand what Ken and Lucinda were saying.

"Because it is Lazaro who brings the disease that kills my mistress into this house. And it was Esperanza who brought Lazaro here. That is why she has fear."

"Jesus," Ken said.

"Please do not curse," Lucinda said. "Have you no respect for the dead?"

"I'm sorry," Ken said. "So, Esperanza knew that the blind boy has the disease that kills?"

"My mistress knew, as well. I knew. All but Martin and his son, Anson."

"I do not see that Lazaro is to blame. He did not know. He was a small child when he came here. He was Pilar Aguilar's son."

"No, the boy did not know. And Caroline did not want her husband to know."

"Then, surely, he could not blame Esperanza or Lazaro . . ."

The look on Lucinda's face told Ken all he needed to know. A look of surprise brought a blankness to his eyes, a stare that fixed on nothing in the immediate world.

Peebo looked from Lucinda to Ken, wondering what he had missed in the conversation. But when he saw the look on Ken's face he knew it was something important.

Peebo was wise enough not to ask what it was, but suddenly he wanted to be anyplace else than where he was at that moment. A cloud passed before the sun and he saw the kitchen darken as the sun was blotted out. He felt a twisting in his gut that made the food inside turn raw and acid and he gulped in air to keep from being sick.

"Jesus," Peebo muttered, and Lucinda crossed herself and buried her face in her hands.

8

BONE SAW ALL the Mexican vaqueros around the Rocking A barn and knew that Matteo was planning something. The men did not greet him, but he knew they had seen him and Dawn ride up. He had seen most of them before, conducting military maneuvers in secret, marching and shooting at Matteo's orders.

Dawn uttered a word in Yaqui that Bone knew was the equivalent of the Spanish *caca,* and he knew she was not happy to be brought to this rancho. He rode on past the barn where the men were gathered and then saw Matteo and Reynaud walking toward him. Reynaud strode with an arrogance that was mildly irritating, but at least he didn't wear that oily smile, or that condescending smirk, of a man who thought he was superior to all others.

Matteo lifted a hand in greeting and Bone reined up his horse. Dawn settled next to him with her mount, and drew the baby to her breast protectively as Reynaud and Aguilar approached.

"You come to stay," Matteo said.

"Yes."

"That is good, my friend. As you can see, we are getting ready to make war on Martin Baron."

"You will not fight Baron, will you, Bone?" Reynaud asked.

"Are you going to fight him?"

"I am going to kill him."

"You have said that before. Martin must still be alive."

"I asked you a question, Bone."

Matteo stood silent, regarding both men with interest.

"I come to work for Matteo. I work with cattle. That is what I want to do. If Matteo asks me to fight Martin Baron, then I will fight him."

"Eh? I thought Baron was your friend."

"No, he is not my friend. But he has done me no harm."

"Enough of this," Matteo said, interrupting. "We will talk of this later. Miguel, you and your woman have a baby."

"Yes. A boy. He is called Juan."

"Good. Do you know the little *colonia*? Over past the pond?"

"Yes. I do not want to live there. Dawn does not want to live there."

"Ah, then you have another casita where you wish to live?"

"Yes. Where I lived before."

"The old adobe. It is not clean. No one has lived there since you left."

"I will live there," Bone said.

Matteo nodded. "That is good. Go, and when you have made your little family comfortable, come to the house. If you need food, there is plenty."

"I will come," Bone said.

Matteo nodded to Dawn, who drew herself up like a proud woman and did not speak to Matteo. Nor did she look at Reynaud, who now wore that knowing smirk of his when he looked at her.

"I hope you're ready to fight Baron," Reynaud said, as Bone and his family rode away, past the barn and the corrals.

Bone did not answer. He heard Matteo say something to the Frenchmen but he could not hear the words.

When he had passed the barn and turned at the corrals, Dawn spoke to Bone. She rode up next to him and looked into his face. It was like looking at something made of stone. It was like looking at Death.

"I do not like this place," Dawn said. "I do not like Reynaud. I do not like Matteo. They have bad faces."

"We have no other place to go," Bone said.

"We could look for my people. They would take us to their hearts."

"Your people are scattered like the leaves that die in the winter. All of my people are gone from this earth."

"But why must we live with these white men? They are not our people."

"We do not live with them. We keep ourselves apart. You will see. Here there is food, there is plenty. In Mexico there is only starvation and death. Be patient."

They rode past the little adobe houses and beyond all signs of a rancho and into a place where trees grew and there was quiet. Then there was a path, and beyond, a small adobe house in a small clearing, all by itself.

"We will live here," Bone said. "None of the Mexicans will bother you here."

"Is this where you lived before?"

"Yes. I did not want to live with the others. Matteo understands."

"You are a strange man, Miguel. Or should I call you by your white man's name, 'Mickey'?"

"You can call me what pleases you, my woman."

"I will call you Miguel."

"Even that is a white man's name."

"Yes, but it is Spanish and I like it better than 'Mickey.' "

"You see. They have even taken away our language. They give us Mexican names or American names and we forget the tongue we heard as children."

"Yes. I have forgotten a lot," Dawn admitted.

There was a small barn out back with a leaning roof and Bone rode there, dismounted. He held little Juan while Dawn got off her horse, then she took the baby and walked to the house while Bone put up the horses, unsaddling his own and setting out grain for them that he kept in a wooden cupboard. He saw that they had water and then he walked to the house.

"Did you build this?" she asked, when Bone entered the dwelling.

"Some of it. Do you like it?"

"It is better than a cave."

"The bed is soft and you can cook here. I will bring food when I go to see Matteo."

She roamed the two rooms and the small storeroom made of wood and adobe bricks. She saw that there were cooking utensils and coffee, flour, sugar. She tasted the sugar, put a few grains in Juan's mouth. The baby smacked his lips until the sugar had all dissolved.

"The rooms need sweeping," she said.

"There is a broom."

"I saw it. Did you sweep it when you lived here?"

"Sometimes," he said. He sat in a rustic chair made of wood and cowhide. It was big and solid and dusty.

"I will need a cradle for the baby."

"I will bring you a cradle."

Dawn poked around, looking for things she might use, things she needed. Bone sat there like a stoic for several moments, searching the room with his eyes, then he arose and walked over to his bedroll and unwrapped the ancient stone he had found. He walked to the wall by the door and placed the stone near the center. The light from the window streamed directly at the stone, illuminating it.

"Is that where you will keep the old stone?" Dawn asked, shifting the baby to her other arm.

"I will place it there for now. I am going to build or get a box to keep it in."

"It is worth nothing, that stone."

"What is worthless to one is a fortune to another."

"Rock is rock."

"Rock with such writing on it is something else."

"What is it, but stone?"

"I do not know. I know this, my precious. I did not find that stone. That stone found me."

"Has the hot sun taken away your senses, my husband? Have you gone loco?"

"I am not crazy. There is a reason that the stone found me. Perhaps it is a message from those who lived before and who have gone away. The ones Dream Speaker told me about."

"Dream Speaker had hunger. His mind was addled like the cow that eats the crazy weed."

"No, he was not crazy. He knew much. He knows much."

"Do you think he is still alive?"

Bone turned away from the stone and looked at his wife and son.

"He is alive for me. He will always be alive for me."

She shook her head and rolled her eyes backward. The baby stirred and opened its eyes. It began to whimper, then to cry. Dawn went to the other chair and sat down. She lifted up her tunic and exposed one of her full breasts. The infant closed its eyes and found her nipple with his mouth. He began to suckle as Dawn swung him to and fro in her arms, slowly, gently.

Bone looked at the two of them and then sat down in his chair once again. He looked over at the stone, still struck by a thin lance of light that streamed through the window in the opposite wall. He saw the ancient markings and knew that they were meant to be read and understood by someone, perhaps by him, or another, who found it. The one who had etched the symbols into the rock did not do it for his own tribe, Bone knew, but for those who would come after his own people had gone from the earth forever.

He closed his eyes and saw the symbols there, flashing with colors, the colors of the rainbow, and he knew they were mystical signs, magical signs that had great power for one who could understand them.

"Someday," he said, "I will know what the stone says."

"What?" Dawn asked, her attention drawn away from her infant son. "What are you saying?"

"Nothing," Bone said. "I was just thinking and my mouth spoke by itself."

"Tsk, tsk," Dawn clucked. "You had better go and talk to Matteo. Bring back some food and a baby cradle."

Bone did not move right away. He looked at the stone again and saw the band of light shimmer and move ever so slightly as the sun changed position in the sky. It seemed to him that the archaic signs were moving, dancing, running, jumping. He strained to see if they rearranged themselves in a way that would make him understand them. But the light faded and moved away and the stone fell into shadow, and he could no longer see the etched figures.

Finally, Bone got up from the chair. He left the house without speaking to his wife, who had dozed off with the baby suckling at her breast. He did not saddle his horse, but walked to the house of Matteo, taking his time. He kept thinking about the carvings on the stone and how they moved as if they were living things, as if they were trying to speak to him. As if they were trying to tell him something important.

9

WANDA FANCHER AND her mother, Hattie, finished inspecting the little house they had helped build on a corner of Roy Killian's property. It sat in a clearing not far from the main house, in full view, but had its own privacy since they had left oak trees standing at intervals in front of it and had trimmed back some mesquite trees that formed a kind of shrub on one side.

"All it needs is a coat of paint," Hattie said.

"We'll get some," Wanda said. "Pluto, can you paint?"

The young black man grinned and shook his head.

"How about you, Julius?"

"No, I ain't never seen paint what wasn't already on a house."

"Well," Wanda said, "we'll go into town and I'll buy some paint and teach you. You can paint your own house. Do you like it so far?"

"Yes'm," Julius said, "I likes it just fine. So does Pluto."

"Do you, Pluto?"

"Yes'm. It's a right fine house. But it ain't our'n."

"Yes it is," Wanda said. "You helped build it and it's yours as long as you work for Mr. Killian."

They had taken in the two slave boys after Martin had brought them back to the Box B from the Aguilar ranch. They were hard workers but it was obvious to Wanda and Hattie that they had known nothing but slavery and ill treatment all their lives. They still could not believe they were truly free and Roy had given up trying to convince them. But not Wanda and not Hattie.

"Is you going to grow cotton here, Miss Wanda?" Pluto asked.

"No, I don't think so. Why?"

"That's 'bout all we knows how to do, Miss Wanda. Grow cotton and pick it."

"Now that you're a free man, Pluto, you can learn how to do new things. Mr. Killian will show you how to raise cattle that will feed you and your wife, when you get married, and your children."

Pluto and Julius looked at each other with wide, white-rimmed eyes.

"Yes'm," Pluto said, "but we's scared to death of them cattle. They look mean."

Wanda laughed. "Mr. Killian will teach you how not to be afraid of them, how to be boss over the cattle."

"Boss?" Julius asked.

"That's right. Didn't your people in Africa raise cattle?"

"Yes'm, but not as big as these here and not with them big long horns."

"Cattle are cattle," Wanda said. "Just like people are people."

Again the two young men looked at each other. Finally Julius grinned and so did Pluto. Hattie and Wanda smiled at each other.

"We'll buy some paint and brushes the next time we go into town," Wanda said. "Now, let's get back to our house and get to work."

"Yes'm," the two men chorused.

Roy waved to Wanda, her mother, and the two new hands as they walked up to the Killian house. He had begun digging a well and stood, naked to the waist, sweat glistening on his tanned skin, and leaned the shovel against a rock. He was already four feet down and had begun to see seepage. Rocks and dirt lay strewn around the hole.

"Where's your mother?" Wanda called.

"Inside."

Wanda set Julius and Pluto to work finishing up the spare room, asking them to put dirt around the foundation and tamp it down hard. Hattie went inside the house and the two black youths went to work with small shovels. They soon shed their shirts in the hot sun.

Roy looked over at the outhouse as the door swung open and David Wilhoit, his mother's husband, stepped out.

"I thought you had fallen in," Roy said.

"Reading," David said, with a slight grin.

He walked over to Roy and picked up another shovel that lay on the ground. He looked into the hole. "You're getting to water."

"How'd you know I'd find water here?" Roy asked.

"I looked at those trees growing yonder, and yonder," David said, pointing, "and figured they'd send their biggest roots just about here."

"Bullshit."

David laughed.

"I saw you walking around here with a forked stick last night. I thought you had lost what little sense God gave you."

"Divining rod."

"Huh?"

"One of the tricks I picked up as a surveyor. An old man used to take a willow branch and walk over the ground, holding the two forked ends. When the straight end bent to the ground, he knew there was water at that spot."

"I never heard of such," Roy said.

"This man said the branch had memory and smartness and when it sensed water, it just naturally bent down toward it to take a drink."

"Trees can't think."

"Well, that's how I found water, not only here, but in other places."

Roy grunted and lifted a lump of dirt out of the hole, threw it a few feet away. David stepped in and dug more dirt out and flung it.

"Next you'll tell me trees have brains."

"They might," David said, smiling.

The two men dug deeper and more water seeped up out of the ground, in a muddy, cloddy soup. Nearby, flat stones they had gathered lay stacked neatly, as if to build a fence. The pile represented several days of work by the women, David, and Roy. They would be used to shore up the walls of the well after the men dug two feet past where the water would gush freely. They would lay the stones as latticework to keep the dirt out, but let the water from the aquifer seep through and keep the well filled. Wanda and Hattie had told Roy how to dig the well, but David had told Roy where to dig that very morning, after going over the ground with that divining rod like some crazed alchemist plucked from another century.

"You don't like me much, do you, Roy?" David asked.

"I don't like you at all."

"Why?"

"For one thing, I don't like the way you took advantage of my mother."

"How did I take advantage of her?"

Roy leaned on the handle of his shovel, stared David straight in the eye. "She was a widow woman and I was lookin' after her. You just come up and stole her from me."

David stepped back away from the hole and leaned on his shovel handle. He sighed and rolled his eyes in his head. "I didn't take advantage of her. From what she told me, your father ran off and left the two of you in Fort Worth."

"He come back."

"That's not what your mother told me."

"What in hell did she tell you?"

"She said he came back and took you away and then he got killed."

"So?"

"So, damn it, you both left your mother. I know you brought her here, but the damage was done. She needed someone dependable to take care of her."

"You?" Roy put a sarcastic twist to the question.

"Yes, me."

"And, so you took her over to Aguilar's and worked for that Mexican bastard. Now my mother's homeless again. You call that 'dependable'?"

"Look, Roy, I admit things didn't work out. But I did honest work for Matteo Aguilar. I gave your mother a home. I put bread and meat on the table."

"And now you don't have no job. You don't have nothin'."

"I just couldn't stand by and see those Negroes sold into slavery by Matteo."

"You didn't do nothin' to stop him. Martin Baron got those slaves away from Aguilar. The night we come and got them slaves loose from ya'll, I was hopin' you'd be in my sights. I'd have dropped you like a sack of meal, sure enough. But I didn't get the chance. You was going to take them Negroes up north and sell 'em for Aguilar. You should have been shot."

"There wasn't much I could do. If I didn't go along, Matteo would have killed me, and probably your mother, too."

"Then you run off, and now my ma's got nothin'."

"She has me."

Roy glared at David. "And that ain't much, is it?"

"I intend to get our things away from the Rocking A and set your mother up in a nice home again."

"Shit. How're you gonna do that? Matteo will shoot you plumb dead if you step foot on his ranch. And you don't have no job, no land, no home."

"I thought it was best to come here and warn you of Matteo's plans to make war on you and the Barons."

The muddy water gurgled in the well hole as an air bubble rose to the surface. The two men looked down at it, then at each other once again.

"Mister," Roy said, "you made two bad choices. You went and married my ma, then you took her to the Rocking A and put her in danger. Them's two good reasons why I don't like you."

"We all make mistakes, Roy. I love your mother. And she loves me."

Roy's neck swelled with rage. He gripped the shovel handle tightly and it appeared as though he would pick it up and swing it at Wilhoit. "Look, Dave, I don't want to hear no more about you and my ma. You keep your damned feelings to yourself, hear?"

"I'm sorry you feel that way, Roy."

Roy's face darkened as he glared at Wilhoit. He relaxed his grip on the handle of the shovel and his hand began to quiver as his rage subsided.

"Let's get to diggin', Dave, before I think of something else to do with this shovel."

David shrugged and began digging again. Roy picked up the beat and they dipped their shovel faces into more water and mud as the hole kept filling up.

Both were so intent on digging the well, that neither noticed Ursula walk up. She came over to David and put her arm around his waist.

"My, it's nice to see my two boys working together," she said, a pleasant lilt to her voice.

Roy's face turned pasty with a sheepish look as if a thin layer of cream had been poured over it from the eyes down to his chin. He summoned up a thin smile that stretched his lips, but did not show his teeth.

He tried to quell the anger that rose up in him, but suddenly he felt almost suffocated by it, felt as if the whole world were caving in on him. And in that instant, he knew it was not just David Wilhoit who spurred the fury inside him, but it was his mother strangling him—his mother, and Hattie and Wanda, the three of them, crowding him into a corner, all nagging him to do this or that. And Wilhoit somehow a part of it, on their side, not his, and Roy felt shut out and cut off from who he was, pressured by all the women in his small house and that smug son of a bitch David, sleeping with his mother and filling her ears with lies. He was a traitor who had surveyed Roy's land for Matteo Aguilar and found that the land Martin Baron had given Roy might not be his after all. It was like having a rug jerked out from under his feet.

"I ain't your boy, no more," Roy said, a surly, nasty tone to his voice.

"What?"

"As long as you're married to this turncoat rascal, you ain't my ma," Roy said.

Ursula drew back as if struck. David started to step forward, toward Roy as if to strike him.

"Come on ahead, David. Just throw one punch and I'll stuff your sorry hide in that hole there and dig me a well someplace else."

"Roy," Ursula exclaimed. "Whatever's gotten into you?"

"I don't like your husband, for one thing. I don't like him bein' here and moochin' off me."

"Roy, you'd better shut up," David said.

"Make me."

"Roy. David. Stop it this instant. There's no need for you two to quarrel. Roy, you have no call to be mean to David. He's done you no harm."

"I don't like the son of a bitch."

"Oh, you're just like your father, Roy. Now, let's not hear any more talk like that. If you don't want us here, we'll leave."

"That's right," David said. "We wouldn't want to stay where we're not welcome."

"Well, you ain't welcome here, Mr. Wilhoit. So just pack your bag and get your sorry ass out of here."

"Roy, stop that," Ursula said. "I won't have you talking that way to my husband."

Roy threw down his shovel and stalked off. He walked away from the house as David and his mother stood there shaking their heads in disbelief.

"Will he get over it?" David asked.

"I don't think so. He's stubborn, like Jack was. And he's mad. His father stayed mad all his life."

"Why?"

"I don't know. Maybe Jack hated me and maybe my son does, too."

David took Ursula in his arms. "I don't believe that," he said.

His words only made Ursula break into tears. She clung to David, sobbing so loudly Wanda heard her and walked over from the house.

"Is there anything I can do?" she asked.

"You can marry my son," Ursula said. "Maybe he can learn to love and not hate."

Wanda sighed. She looked at Roy, who was still walking away, and frowned. "He loves you, Ursula," Wanda said. "It's your husband he hates. I think he's jealous of David."

"Why?"

"Maybe you loved your son too much," Wanda said. "And maybe his father didn't love you enough. Roy will have to work all that out for himself. And he will, given time."

"I hope so," Ursula said. "I don't want him to hate me. Or David."

"Just be patient," Wanda said, and then she left them and started walking after Roy.

"David, I'm sorry this happened," Ursula said. "I don't want you hurt."

"I think it's time we moved into town and let Roy solve his problems."

"Perhaps you're right. I hope Wanda can help him see how wrong he is."

"If she can, she'll make him one hell of a wife," David said.

"She's the strongest woman I've ever known," Ursula said.

"No, you're stronger than she is," David said. "You've stood up to two very tough men. Jack and Roy both."

At that, Ursula broke into tears again. David held her very tightly against him and slowly began to lead her away from the unfinished well and toward the house.

ESPERANZA DREW AWAY from the window of her casita, floating from it on tiny sandaled feet that left faint impressions in the dirt floor. Lazaro heard her move and turned his head toward her as if he had eyes to see.

The small house had one large room which served as a place to sleep and eat. There was another small room that Esperanza used as a kitchen, even though she took most of her meals at the big house. But she had a small iron stove on which to cook and it kept the rest of the house warm in winter. There was another small room that she used for storage of her few things. She and Lazaro had spent most of their days and nights in the Baron house, but this was her retreat, her safe haven, a place where she and Lazaro could go to stay out of the way of others, a place where he could play his guitar and they could speak to one another without prying eyes and ears. It was a modest little house, but she kept it neat and clean and she cherished it as something that belonged to her.

"What passes?" he asked, in Spanish.

"Martin is coming. And Anson. Do not say anything. If I tell you to go, leave this house. Do you understand?" Her voice was a raspy whisper in the quiet of the small front room.

"Have you fear?"

"Yes. There is much to fear when Martin begins to ask the questions. You close your mouth and keep quiet."

"Yes," Lazaro said, and he listened for the pad of boots outside. He turned toward the door and heard the men coming. He could tell they were angry by the way they walked, by the sound of their bootheels. "I hear them coming. They are very angry."

"Your ears have the sharpness to hear much," she said.

"There are three men," Lazaro said.

"Three?"

"Martin and Anson and one other I do not know."

Esperanza shuddered. She wanted to go to the window again and look out, but she was afraid. Instead she shuffled across the room and stood in front of Lazaro as if to protect him from any who came through her door.

The knock made both Esperanza and Lazaro jump.

"Esperanza," Martin called through the door.

"What is it that you want?" she said in English.

"I want to talk to you. Now."

"Enter," she said.

The door swung open and Martin filled the small doorway. He ducked his head and walked in, followed by Anson and Dr. Purvis. The room grew smaller with the presence of the three men.

"I have but two chairs," Esperanza said.

"That's all right. We won't be here long."

"Hello," Lazaro said, an innocence to his soprano voice that lingered in the silence that followed, like some haunting fragment of lyric one can never put a name to or keep from running incessantly through one's brain.

"Lazaro, maybe you'd better go outside," Martin said. "I want to speak to Esperanza privately."

"Is it about me?" Lazaro said.

"You ask too many questions," Martin replied. "Outside. Please."

Lazaro hesitated, then put out a hand and grabbed a handful of Esperanza's dress.

"I want to stay," Lazaro said. He clung to Esperanza's dress and pressed up against her leg, fastening his body close to hers in a desperate attempt to avoid being sent away.

"I'd like to examine the boy," Purvis said.

"Examine? Why?" Esperanza asked.

"I think he may have a disease. Does he have a disease?"

"He is blind," Esperanza said, a note of desperation in her voice.

"I can see that. Does he have sores on his body?"

"Sores?" Esperanza was wild-eyed.

"You know what he means, Esperanza," Martin said. "Let the doctor examine Lazaro."

Lazaro began to whimper softly.

Doc Purvis swept the room with his gaze, saw the other two *salas.* "Perhaps I could take the boy into one of the other rooms and have a talk with him?" Purvis directed his question to Martin.

"Yes," Martin said. He nodded to Esperanza. "Lazaro, go with the doctor."

"I do not want to," Lazaro said.

"Go, or I'll take my belt to you," Martin said.

Anson looked at his father with surprise. In all the years of growing up, his father had never made such a threat, nor taken a belt or any other punishment tool to him.

Lazaro tugged at Esperanza's dress. She pushed him away. "Go with the doctor," she said, her voice soft-toned but firm.

"Come," Purvis said to Lazaro, and started toward the little room that served as a kitchen. Lazaro released his grip on Esperanza's dress and followed on shaking legs.

"Now, Esperanza," Martin said. "Take a chair and we will talk."

Esperanza sat in a chair. Martin pulled one toward him and sat down opposite the woman. He looked straight into her eyes without flinching.

Anson stood by, his weight shifting to one foot. He could hear the doctor speaking to Lazaro but could not understand what he was saying. He could barely hear Lazaro's replies. But, a moment later, he heard the rustle of clothes and knew that Purvis had asked the boy to strip for the examination. He avoided looking into the room, although he was curious.

"Esperanza," Martin said, "I am going to ask you some questions, and you'd better—by God—answer every one of them. Do you understand?"

"I will try."

"You will damn well answer me. I want to know how my wife got the pox. I think she got it from that blind boy in there."

"I do not know," Esperanza said, but her voice was quavering and she dipped her head as she sighed. "Truly."

"Yes, you do know. Did Lazaro ever sleep in Caroline's bedroom? Did she sleep with him in her bed when I was not there?"

Esperanza's lips drew back on her teeth and quivered. "Yes," she said. "Sometimes the boy sleep with his mother in her bed."

Martin swore under his breath.

"Pa," Anson said, "you don't want to go any further with this. Let it be."

Martin whirled to face his son, his eyes blazing with the fire of anger and madness.

"Goddamn you, Anson. Stay out of this."

"No," Anson said, the flesh on his face tautening as his eyes narrowed to thin dark slits. "Whatever happened in Ma's bedroom with that blind boy is between him and her. It ain't rightly none of our business."

"It's my business, by God, if that blind boy is responsible for her death."

Esperanza shrank away from the anger in the room, her eyes moving antically in their sockets.

"Lazaro ain't any more responsible for Ma's death than you or I are. And if he is, then so are you."

"What?"

"You heard me plain," Anson said, his voice steady, without rancor. "You turned your back on her a long time ago. If she found comfort in sleeping with Lazaro, then you're as much to blame as he is for what happened to her. But you've got to leave this alone. She's dead and gone and that boy in there was like a puppy to her. She doted on him and he loved her as if she was his own mother."

"Damn you, Anson. Do you know what I'm talking about, here? Do you know what that little bastard did to my wife?"

Martin balled up his fists as if to strike Anson. Anson did not back away, but stood firm on his spot, his narrowed eyes masking whatever feelings he had at the moment.

"You can curse all you want to, Pa. You ain't going to bring her back, and if you mean to punish Lazaro, you'll have to whup me first."

Martin took a half-step toward his son. Anson did not move. His arms hung at his sides; his hands stayed open and fistless.

"I ought to, by God. I ought to beat the living shit out of you and Lazaro."

"You ain't layin' a hand on Lazaro," Anson said. "I mean it. Let this be. If you find out what you are bound to know, it'll only eat at you like what ate Ma up."

"Where in hell do you get this? From Juanito?"

"I learned some things from him."

"Like what?"

"He taught me that the first mark of a civilized man is his ability to forgive."

"You forgive your mother for what she did? You forgive Lazaro?"

"I don't judge, first off," Anson said. "And if I know someone wronged me, I find a way to forgive it so whatever it was don't eat me up."

"You sound like some pious preacher, son."

"Maybe."

"You don't want to know what your mother did?"

"No. Whatever she did, she has been punished enough. She died young."

"And no damned need to."

"That's not for you or me to say."

"There you go again, Anson. Preaching like a goddamn Bible-thumping parson."

"Look, Pa, you can't go back and fix what went wrong, no more'n I can. And you can't see what's going to happen tomorrow. All you have is what's right now and that's what you got to live. Just this one moment. Don't go spoilin' it."

"Now you don't make any sense at all, you sanctimonious whelp."

Anson shrugged. He caught Esperanza's glance out of the corner of his eye. She was watching him raptly, her mouth frozen slightly open, her eyes glittering like a pair of agates shot with sunlight.

Martin turned back to Esperanza. "So, are you going to tell me what that boy in there did to my wife when he was sleeping with her?"

"No, señor. I do not know what Lazaro and the señora did when they were alone together. I did not stay in her room with them."

"But you know, don't you?"

"Pa—Martin," Anson said, "leave her alone. She did no wrong."

"She let it happen. She knew what was going on."

"Leave her alone," Anson said again, and this time there was iron in his tone, and menace.

Martin turned around again to look at his son. "I got things to say, things I want to know."

"You don't have any say in what goes on at this ranch no more."

"Why, you ungrateful—"

"If you keep on with this, I'll have to take you down. I don't want to do that. You're still my father, but now you're laying the quirt to a woman who works for me, who works for the Box B."

"I'll be a son of a bitch," Martin said.

Anson again heard the rustle of clothes in the next room, and Dr. Purvis came into view, followed by Lazaro, who had a sheepish look on his face.

"Well?" Martin asked, directing his question to Purvis.

"Maybe we'd better talk outside, away from the boy."

"Why? Lazaro can damned well hear it."

"Not from me, he can't," Purvis said.

"Are you turning against me, too, Doc?"

"No, it's just a matter of protocol. And ethics. The boy is very young. What I have to say can't help him, and it might do him harm."

"Esperanza," Anson said. "You take good care of Lazaro. We're leaving."

Anson stepped over and grabbed Purvis's arm and led him toward the door.

"Shit," Martin said, but he followed the two outside.

"We'll go on back to the house," Anson said. "We can still eat some lunch."

"I want to hear it from the doc," Martin said. "Did the boy have the pox?"

Purvis scowled, kept walking. "He has lesions on his loins."

" 'Lesions'? What's that?"

"He has the disease. I would see to it that he has no further sexual content with anyone, male or female, in the time he has left."

"Huh?" Martin caught up with Purvis.

Purvis stopped, looked the elder Baron straight in the eye.

"Look, Mr. Baron, there's no way to sugar over any of this. Both your wife and that blind boy got them a dose of what they've started to call by a fancy name: syphilis. You get the disease by sexual coupling."

"You mean . . ."

"I mean you shouldn't think about how your wife got it, but I'm sure it started out innocently enough. Some mothers and sons . . . fathers and daughters . . ."

"Jesus Christ," Martin said.

Anson grabbed the doctor's arm and dragged him on toward the house.

"Let it be, Pa," Anson said. "For the last time, let it damned be."

"You knew about this, Anson?"

"No. I did not know."

"Christ."

Martin had to walk fast to catch up, but he said no more as they neared the house. Anson turned to look at him and saw the stricken look on his father's face. It tore at him to see his father in pain, but he had his own anguish to deal with. His stomach was knotted up and he felt queasy with the knowledge he had now, of his mother and Lazaro.

Still, he knew Juanito had been right. You could not live your life with anger, nor take vengeance on those who wronged you. If you were to live and grow, you must first forgive.

And it was a damned hard thing to do. He wanted to do what his father wanted to do with Lazaro: kill him in his tracks with knife or gun and wipe the slow smile off the blind bastard's face.

WHEN MARTIN BARON buried his wife, Caroline, the whole town of Baronsville came to the funeral. Many of the neighboring ranchers attended the services held on the Box B Ranch, including Roy Killian, his mother, Ursula, and her husband, David Wilhoit. Also from Roy's new ranch, the Lazy K, were his partners, Wanda Fancher and her mother, Hattie. Doc Purvis was there, along with his niece, Lorene Sisler, who could not take her gaze away from Anson Baron. Al Oltman stood near the back of the ground, a tall, lean figure of mystery, chewing on a grass stem while studying the faces of those who turned to look at him. Noticeably absent was Matteo Aguilar, who owned the Rocking A. Neither he nor his wife, Luz, who had just given birth a week or two before Caroline's death, nor any of his hands—including Jules Reynaud, who did not work for Matteo, but was staying with him for another reason: he had vowed to kill Martin Baron.

Ken Richman, newly elected mayor of Baronsville, delivered the stirring eulogy. He brought along his special gal, Nancy Grant. Also present was the waitress from the Longhorn Saloon, Millie Collins, who had taken a shine to Martin shortly before his wife's death. Now she wept profusely, along with everyone else, as Ken told of Caroline's grace and beauty and bemoaned her short life. There was no mention of what Caroline died of, and nobody in town really knew, but it was whispered that she had succumbed to a venereal disease, which was true.

There was one man who watched the somber ceremonies from a distance, however. And he had been sent there by Matteo Aguilar. No one saw him, for he did not want to be seen. Mickey Bone had ridden to the Box B the night before the funeral and had found a place where he could observe everything without being detected. He sat in a large oak tree he had climbed early that same morning, and he sat very still so he would not give his presence away. He was close enough so that he could hear every word, see the faces of those who came to pay their last respects to Caroline Baron.

Bone studied the tall man at the rear of the assemblage, the only man there who did not take off his hat when the prayers were said by the preacher, a thin bony man whose name he did not know, but who was dressed in black except for his white shirt.

He also watched Anson because the young man he had known for so long was no longer a rangy boy, but a man grown and Anson kept looking his way. Bone knew he could not be seen as long as he did not move, but Anson seemed to sense his presence, as if he was one who had unusual abilities, as if he knew without knowing that someone was watching him. He took his gaze off Anson for a time then quickly glanced back to see if Anson was still looking at the preacher and the wooden casket.

But no, Anson looked toward the oak tree as soon as Bone fixed his gaze on the young man. So, Bone thought, Anson has the gift. He is a hunter, a man who has a sense beyond the ordinary senses, a man who knew when things were wrong before anyone else did.

Bone sat very still until Anson stopped looking in his direction. Then he methodically began to count the entire crowd. He made a mental note of the number of people. Next, he counted the able-bodied men and remembered that number. Finally he began backing up on the limb, pausing often to remain still. When the coffin was lowered into the ground, Bone slid down the tree and kept it between him and the crowd. He bent over and smoothed away his footprints, kept backing away, rubbing his hands on the earth and placing twigs and leaves over his tracks. When he was far enough away from the tree, he hurriedly walked to his horse, hitched to a mesquite nearly a mile away. He mounted and rode off in the direction of the Rocking A.

Anson watched as his mother's coffin was lowered into the ground. He felt a rush of sadness that flooded him until his eyes brimmed with tears. He looked at his father and saw that Martin was overcome with grief. Martin's head was bowed and he had a hand to his face, two fingers pressing on his eyes.

Ken Richman stepped forward then, carrying a Holy Bible in his hands. He bent over and picked up a handful of the dirt piled by the open grave and tossed it onto the casket. Then, he opened the book and began to read the twenty-third chapter of Psalms:

> "The Lord is my shepherd; I shall not want.
>
> "He maketh me to lie down in green pastures; He leadeth me beside the still waters.
>
> "He restoreth my soul; He leadeth me in the path of righteousness for His name's sake.
>
> "Yea, though I walk through the valley of the shadow of death, I will fear no evil, for Thou art with me; Thy rod and Thy staff they comfort me.
>
> "Thou preparest a table before me in the presence of mine enemies; Thou anointest my head with oil, my cup runneth over.
>
> "Surely goodness and mercy will follow me all the days of my life; and I will dwell in the house of the Lord forever.
>
> "Amen."

Many in the crowd, including Martin, intoned, "Amen."

"Thank you all for coming," Ken said. "There will be refreshments served at the Baron house. Won't you all stop by and share in Martin Baron's hospitality?"

The crowd began to break up and drift away, walking toward La Loma de Sombra. Martin stepped up to the grave and looked down at the wooden casket. Then he began to weep. Anson walked up behind him and put a hand on his father's shoulder.

At that moment, his feelings toward his father changed from those he had held just the day before and all that morning. A great sadness enveloped him as he heard his father sobbing out his anguish and grief.

Anson thought about the discussion he and his father had had the night before. They had talked about where Caroline should be buried. Anson thought she should be buried with her parents, to the south.

"We got a cemetery already started," Martin had said.

"Where . . ." Anson said.

"We'll bury her out where Juanito and Jack Killian are. It's a cemetery, I reckon."

"Yeah, I reckon. . . . Peebo, Roy, and I talked last night," Anson said, after several seconds of silence.

"What about?"

"Matteo Aguilar."

"That son of a bitch."

Anson remembered that he and his father had argued about the land.

"We got to take him on, Pa," Anson said.

"I know. Your mother told me to bring the cannon back out here."

"It's in town, ain't it?"

"Yeah, stored at the livery. Your ma hated it."

"She wasn't right in the head."

"You shut your mouth, Anson."

"I didn't mean anything. She . . ."

"I know. It's just not right to speak ill of the dead."

"I didn't mean any disrespect."

"Well, she hated that cannon, all right."

"Yeah," Anson said, dropping it. "Want me to get some boys and bring it back out?"

"I'll take care of it."

"You know Matteo's going to go all out," Anson said.

"Likely."

"He knows about the cannon."

"Yeah, but he doesn't know where it'll be when he comes."

"There aren't too many places to hide it."

"It can't go in the barn. He'll expect it to be out there."

Anson nodded.

"Where, then?"

Martin sighed. "I reckon I'll set it up in the house."

"In the house?"

"Yeah. Either right at the front door, or at one of the windows."

"You've got it all figured, I reckon."

"No, not all of it. You got any ideas?"

"I thought you didn't like my ideas."

"Not every one of 'em."

"Not many."

"We better skip all that, Anson. I'm talking about the damned cannon."

"I know what you're talking about."

"So?"

"I'll have to think about it. It's going to be a hell of a mess, having it in the house. You've got to have it far enough back from the door or a window so's we can load the damned thing."

"It would be used as a last resort," Martin said.

"You mean if Matteo and his men come storming into the house itself."

"Yeah. Unless . . ."

"Unless what?"

"Unless we wanted him to storm the house."

"Hell, he'd see through that right away. He's not stupid, you know."

"I know. But if we kept retreating, drawing him back . . . toward the house . . ."

Anson pictured it all in his mind. He could see Matteo and his men circle that hill where the Apaches had attacked from, staying to the low ground, using the barn for cover. He'd come right straight toward the house. But would he hit the front, the side, or swing around in back? One cannon, a couple of doors, front and back, several windows. It was not a simple problem, he could see.

"You know, Pa, I think you can work this out yourself. You don't need my advice."

"Oh?" Martin's eyebrows arched and his eyes flickered wide. "Am I hearing you right? You think I can actually make a decision?" Sarcasm clung like frost to every word in Martin's last sentence.

"You're a fighter. You beat Cuchillo and his Apaches without me. You and Ma. You can beat Matteo."

"Matteo knows too damned much about La Loma de Sombra.

And he's got a passel of Mexicans trained like soldiers to fight. According to Dave Wilhoit."

"You're going to have to do it, Pa," Anson said. "Me and Peebo have got to get the branding done. We've got strays all over that basin below the Nueces. Soon as Ma's buried, we're heading out."

"You won't even take time to grieve for your mother."

"I can grieve anywhere I am."

"You sound like you're running off because you don't want to be around me. Aren't you afraid I might put a bullet in Lazaro's head?"

"I don't really give a damn. If you did that, you'd have to live with it," Anson said.

"I ought to, that bastard."

"Then do it. Just don't torture him before you kill him."

"What in hell do you mean by that?"

"I think you'd like to beat the shit out of that blind boy just to rid yourself of your own sack of faults and blame that you're packing around with you."

"You think you're smart, don't you, Anson?"

"I don't think anything."

"No, ever since you took up with Juanito, you've been riding a high horse, thinking you're smarter than anyone else. Hell, I knew Juanito a long time before you were even born. He wasn't nothing but an Argentine cowboy."

"Juanito was more than a cowhand," Anson said, his voice dropping to just above a whisper.

"He had brains, some, but his were full of crazy ideas."

"You treated Juanito worse than any man deserves. Worse, because you treated him as no friend would ever treat anyone."

"I made a mistake, that's all."

"And now you want to make another one, with Lazaro. Blame him for Ma's death, when he had no more part in it than I did."

"Lazaro caused your mother's death."

"Not on purpose."

"He ought to know the difference between right and wrong."

"He worshiped Ma. Whatever he did with her, she told him to do."

Martin's face swelled with anger, turned as red as if it had been scalded with boiling water.

Anson looked at his father as though Martin were his son, and he the father. To think that he had once respected his father, before Martin had run away, back to the sea, before he had driven Juanito away, falsely accusing him of raping Anson's mother, tearing the family apart, ruining everything and everyone that Anson had held so dear. He had tried to excuse his father for his past behavior, but now he saw that nothing had changed. Martin had lost his way along the path of life, had lost those nearest and dearest to him, and now wanted to blame a poor blind boy who was just as much a victim as any of the Barons.

"Anson, I don't know if you can count on me anymore. I just don't have the heart to fight for this place with your ma gone."

"You'll fight for it, Pa. You'll do it for Ma and you'll do it for yourself."

"Did you meet that Ranger, Al Oltman?"

"Yes."

"He says there's going to be a war if Lincoln is elected in November. He wants me to join up with his bunch."

"Are you going to?"

"I'm thinking hard about it. I just don't think I can go on here, staying in that big, empty house."

"Peebo thinks Texas is going to secede from the Union if Lincoln abolishes slavery, and that all of us will be fighting the North."

"There's a lot of hatred to go around right now. North and South. Slavers and non-slavers. White and black. Mexican and gringo. I don't know why we can't just let those other folks fight it out among themselves and let us be. My hunch is to just tell Oltman to go to hell."

"You think we could stay out of war?" Anson asked.

"We damned sure ought to. I don't give a damn about other people's quarrels. I've got all I can handle right here. With you."

"I'm not fighting you, Pa."

"We came close this morning."

"And if we had fought, do you think that would have ended our quarrel? Do you think everybody else around here would have stayed out of it?"

"I don't know. I didn't think about it that way."

"Beyond the fight between you and me, you mean?"

"Yeah," Martin said.

"Well, I did. I saw this ranch, all the work you've done and I've done, just getting taken over by Matteo or whoever comes along, and us left with nothing."

"You thought that?" Martin looked at his son as if seeing him for the first time.

"And more," Anson said.

"More?"

"Pa, whatever you think about Juanito, he taught me a hell of a lot. About life, about myself, about this ranch, big as it is, just being a small part of bigger things, part of the whole world."

"Juanito didn't always think straight."

"I think he did. Like now. Like this war we might get ourselves into without wanting to."

"What about it?" Martin asked.

"Just think of everything we do, you and me, in miniature for a minute."

"I don't follow you, Anson."

"One man fights another, is the same as a war between nations. Only in miniature."

"Huh?"

"Whatever one man does is a reflection of what all men do. All over the world. All the time."

"I'm trying to understand what you're saying, Anson."

"I mean you and me, all of us here on the Box B, in the whole Rio Grande Valley, we're all just a pale reflection of something a whole lot bigger. It's like those slaves Matteo was going to sell. You freed them, but they're only a handful of the slaves in this country. But, when you freed them, you started something that Mr. Lincoln might finish. He might free all of them."

"He might. But that has nothing to do with what I did."

"What we do, big or small, as men, a nation does, for good or bad. So we better make sure we do the right thing. You and me, all of us here, make the nation what it is, good or bad."

"The Union doesn't give a damn what we do down here. They don't even think about us. The men in Washington, or in Austin, for that matter, don't even know we're here, don't know what we're doing."

"They may not know they know, but something inside them knows. It's like chunkin' a pebble in a pond. It makes ripples and the ripples spread through the water and cover every inch of the pond. And, if the ripples are big enough, they spill over the edge of the pond. If a pond, a lake; if a lake, an ocean; and the waves in the ocean can swamp every boat on the sea all over the world."

"Seems to me you're stretching a pebble in a pond to an ocean too far away to even notice you chunked a rock into a little old pond."

"Well, that's what I think, Pa. I'm going after that white bull, yes, because I want to build the best herd of cattle, not only in Texas, but in the world. I aim to brand every stray, every maverick I find while I'm huntin' that big bull and we'll see what happens with that little chunk of rock."

"You've got big ideas, son. But you leave Matteo Aguilar for me to fight."

"Only because you are the man to fight him. You bought this land, fair and square. I know Ma gave it to me and I own it, on paper, but it's your land and you're going to fight for it."

"And you're not."

"I'm trusting that you will beat Matteo and let me fight for the future. If you don't have any more children, I'm the last of the Baron line. I want to marry and have children and leave them something, something solid, something bought and paid for, in cash or blood."

Martin sighed. "I thought I knew you, Anson, but I don't. You've grown up way beyond what I expected."

"I've followed your path, Pa."

"Mine?"

"That's right. Even if you turn the wrong way, I learn from it."

"I reckon you've got me there."

"Let's put away our anger right now, Pa, and let Ma rest in peace. We'll save what we can, and begin to build a future."

"I'm willing, if you are."

Anson smiled and embraced his father. He felt Martin stiffen for a moment, but he loosed his hold on Martin before it got any more awkward. Now, he looked at his father in another light and knew that they would go on from this place of death and loss and overcome any obstacles in their paths.

It was very quiet after the crowd left. Three of the Mexican hands stood with shovels a short distance away, their backs turned so that they did not have to look at Martin. Finally Martin stopped shaking and sobbing. He wiped a sleeve across his eyes and turned to his son. Anson let his hand fall from his father's shoulder.

"I miss her so much," Martin said.

"I know, Pa. I do, too."

"Are you still going to go out on the range with Peebo?"

"I reckon."

"Then I guess I'll have to stay here and fight Matteo."

"I guess so."

"What if war breaks out and we have to fight?"

"We'll fight if we have to, but not against each other."

"No. We wouldn't do that, would we? What about us being a reflection of the bigger world? If North against South, why not father against son?"

"That's what makes the difference in the world. Pa."

"What?"

"We can learn and make choices. What you and I do will eventually spread like those ripples in a pond. The war will end and people will begin to learn what they should have known before it started."

"I hope you're right, son."

"I hope I am, too, Pa."

The two men walked toward the house, side by side. The Mexicans turned around and walked over to the open grave. They began shoveling more dirt over the casket. Martin winced at each plop of dirt striking the coffin as if the dirt were striking his own flesh with terrible force.

12

DAWN CRADLED LITTLE Juan in her arms as she sat near the crude table in the casita, feeling the pleasure of his lips on her nipple as he suckled at her breast. His eyes were closed and his tiny hands cupped the curves of her breast, his fingers light and soft, adding to her pleasure. She crooned to him, trying to remember the words to the ancient cradle song that eluded her memory.

Mickey had gone off on an errand or something for Matteo, she knew, and she felt a longing for him, a wish to share these moments with their son. But since they had come to the Rocking A Ranch, she had seen little of Mickey. And, when he was home, late at night, they seldom spoke. He would have taken his supper with Matteo and Luz and the oily Frenchman, Reynaud, and so she had eaten alone, chewing disconsolately on the dry corn tortillas and the watery *frijoles,* and the stringy beef that had gone almost rancid from the heat.

There was a sharp rap on the door that startled Dawn. She sat up straight and cupped a hand around the baby's head to protect it. "*Quien es?*" she asked.

"Luz. *Puedo entrar?*"

Dawn's eyes widened. She glanced around the room as if to

straighten all that was out of order, or to see if anything she owned needed to be hidden from view.

"Yes, come in," she said, her senses bristling as if she were in danger.

The door opened and a flat sheet of light stretched into the darkened room and stayed there, a trapezoidal shape that illuminated the hard-packed dirt.

Luz entered, carrying her child in her arms. She wore a thin shawl that shielded her hair from dust and shaded the child from the bright sunlight.

"Oh, you are feeding your baby. I came to see him and to show you my little one."

"Yes. I am called Madrugada. In English I am called Dawn."

"I know. Matteo told me. I am called Luz."

"Yes, Mickey told me you were called Luz."

"May I seat myself?" Luz asked.

"At your orders."

"Please, let us not be formal." Luz sat down in the chair that was used by Mickey. Her child was asleep, as was Juan.

"What do you call your son?" Luz asked.

Dawn told her.

"I call my son Julio. He sleeps."

"Yes. Juan sleeps too. He is almost full of my milk."

"Julio drank himself to sleep." Luz wiped a trace of milk from her son's lips.

The two women stared at each other, both protecting their sons while attempting to show them off to the other. They feinted in silence and in motionlessness for several seconds. They measured each other with their eyes and with their minds and Juan finally stopped pulling on Dawn's nipple and his mouth fell from its perch and was slack and open as he breathed long breaths deep in sleep.

"You do not like it here," Luz said. "You are away from your people."

"I do not like it here. My people are all dead."

"Sometimes I think this is a place for the dead," Luz said. "It is far away from my own people."

"You have a house and land," Dawn said.

"An empty wild land. An empty house much of the time."

"I was happy in the mountains."

"Why? What did you have there?"

"We had nothing. We had hunger. We had each other to share that hunger."

"I understand."

"Do you?" Dawn asked.

"Yes. The house is big and I have no cousins or aunts with me. I have no grandmother or grandfather."

"They are all dead?"

"I do not know. They are in Mexico, perhaps."

"I would not complain if I were you," Dawn said. There was no rancor or admonition in her voice.

Luz turned her head to study the room. Her gaze fell on the rune stone leaning against the wall and lingered there for a moment, then shifted to take in the bare walls and dirt floor, the spartan furniture, the bed mats, the few visible cooking utensils.

"We do not have much, as you can see," Dawn said, without defensiveness in her tone.

"Would you like to spend more time in my house? With me and my baby? We could talk, drink tea, and sew clothes for our little boys."

"Miguel says I must stay here."

"Not all the time."

"No. He did not say that."

"Why do you not come with me to my house and I will show you how we live? I have some clothes that should fit you, if you would accept them."

"Charity."

"No, not charity, Dawn, little gifts of things I have no use for."

"I have shame," Dawn said.

"But why?"

"I have shame that I do not speak Spanish as well as you. I do not know the tongue very well."

"You speak well enough, I think."

Dawn lowered her head. "Thank you," she whispered.

"Do not have shame about yourself or the way you speak. I can teach you. I am alone in the house. I have no companions."

"You have a maid, do you not?"

"Yes, but she is dumb and sullen. I do not like her."

"Perhaps you will not like me."

"I like you. I want to see more of your baby. Perhaps our sons could grow up together, learn together."

"You and I are so far apart. I mean to say, our places in the world are different."

"Yes, but that need not be. I would take you in my home during the day and you could be with your husband at night." Luz's glance swept the room again, and once more she stared at the strange stone for several moments. "If you do not like it there, you can always go out the door and stay here."

Dawn drew in a deep breath and let it out slowly. She, too, looked around the barren room, and the walls seemed to close in on her, shrinking the room to an even smaller size. Sometimes, she admitted to herself, she felt trapped in this little house. Here, she could not see the sky, nor smell the trees, nor hear the birds call clearly, could not see the green land or feel close to it as she once did.

"Perhaps I could go with you and stay awhile this day."

"And any other day you wish," Dawn said.

"Good. I will go with you now, then?"

"Yes. That would please me."

Luz stood up. Again she looked at the stone. This time, she walked closer to study it, cradling her baby in her arms.

"Where did you get this stone?" she asked Dawn.

"My husband found it in the *brasada*. Why do you ask?"

"Those markings on it. My husband has a piece of stone with similar cuts in it. He keeps it in a little box."

"What does he say of it?"

"Only that it is very old and may have been brought here by the conquistadores, the Spanish conquerors, a long time ago. But a man told him that it was made by a tribe that no longer is, the Tegua. Indians. He found it over by El Paso where there are many such drawings on large stones. It is a mystery, I think."

"I do not like that stone in my house," Dawn said.

"Why?"

"I think it has curses written on it."

"Why do you think that?"

"The old people of my tribe speak of those ancient ones who were here before and who left the earth because it was a bad place. They say that these ancient ones left curses behind."

"Matteo thinks it is just a code used by the conquistadores. He thinks it may be a map to where gold is hidden."

Dawn got up from her chair and stood next to Luz, looking down at the leaning stone. "I will tell Miguel this when he returns," she said. "Perhaps it is a map."

"It is nothing for which you must have fear," Luz said.

"No. I just do not like it. It does not belong in this room, in this house."

Luz laughed. "You have reason," she said, and Dawn laughed, too.

"Come," Luz said. "Let us go to my house and we will look at clothes and some other things I have which I do not need. I want to hear about your people and, if you wish, I can tell you about mine."

"It is good to talk about our people," Dawn said.

"Yes," Luz said, her voice slightly off-key, "for we may never see them again."

For a moment, Dawn hesitated. Luz sounded so sad when she said that about their people, and it brought back dim memories of her own people, those she knew before she was captured and taken away from them. She did not like to feel sad. But then she realized that she and Luz were not so very different, after all. They were women, with newborn sons, and they were married to men who were puzzling to live with, and they were both lost from their parents and the people they had loved once a long time ago.

Dawn followed Luz outside the casita and felt the warm breeze of afternoon, felt the wind build as it always did when the sun began to fall away to the west, and she felt suddenly alive and freed from that dark, dirty room and that old stone leaning against the wall.

"I am happy you are coming with me," Luz said, turning to Dawn. She smiled.

"Yes, I am happy, too," Dawn said, and there was a springiness in her step and she pulled the light covering over Juan's head to shield him from the sunlight. She felt like dancing as she walked next to Luz toward the big house with its pretty shade trees all around, so green-leafed and friendly in the heat of the burning day.

13

PEEBO SAW ANSON steal away from the people who had stayed after the funeral, and he broke off a conversation with Al Oltman to go after him. Martin was surrounded by people as he stood under a live oak tree holding a drink in his hand. Ken Richman, Doc Purvis, his niece Lorene Sisler, and a girl whose name Peebo did not know, were trying to comfort the elder Baron in his grief.

"Where you goin', Anson? That girl, Lorene, has been askin' about you."

"I'll be back. There's something I want to check."

"What?"

"Nothin'. Go on back and drink some wine."

"Damn it, Anson, don't brush me off. I seen that gal look at you and you hardly paid her any mind."

"I don't have time for sparkin', Peebo. Now go on."

"I'm comin' with you, old son."

"Fine, suit yourself."

Neither of them noticed when Lorene turned around just in time to see them leave the assemblage. She slowly drifted away from her uncle and the others, then changed course and began to follow Peebo and Anson at a discreet distance.

" 'Curiosity killed the cat,' " she chided herself, then smiled at the thrill of what she was doing.

She stepped casually through the crowd, every muscle in her legs quivering, her stomach fluttering with the tickling sensation of small beating wings. Her throat constricted with apprehension and an invisible lump seemed caught in her larynx so that she began to breathe with difficulty.

No one noticed that Anson and Peebo had left, nor had anyone seen Lorene evaporate as she drifted out of sight.

The three Mexicans looked up as they saw Anson and Peebo walk toward the fringe of trees bordering the small cemetery. Anson did not acknowledge them, nor did Peebo, and the men went back to work, filling the grave with dirt from the diminishing mound a few feet away. Moments later Anson and Peebo disappeared from view. Then they saw the American girl following after the two young men. They said nothing, at first, but shook their heads in wonder at the strangeness of *"los gringos locos,"* an epithet they muttered as the girl passed on by and vanished in the clump of trees.

"What in hell did you come way out here for?" Peebo asked.

Anson stopped, looked up into the leaves and branches of the big oak tree. He circled the tree, staring upward.

"You aim to squirrel-hunt?" Peebo asked, as he stood there watching the odd antics of his friend.

"I had the feeling somebody was over here during the funeral ceremonies," Anson said. "Watching us from this tree."

"Well, son, they ain't nobody up there. Probably never was."

Anson circled the tree, looked down at the ground around it, careful where he stepped. He did this twice, as Peebo looked on in puzzlement and scratched the back of his head as if viewing a creature gone suddenly mad.

"Aahh," Anson breathed, and stopped his pacing. He knelt down and with a delicate stroke of his index finger, pushed aside a twig and a tablespoon-sized mound of dirt. He pinched some of the dirt between two fingers.

"You like playin' in the dirt, son?" Peebo asked.

"Well, Peebo, this dirt is damp. It hasn't yet been warmed by the sun. It didn't pile up here all by itself."

Peebo walked closer, bent down to take a closer look.

"See?" Anson said, pointing to the dry dirt next to the small mound he had disturbed. "Somebody went to a lot of trouble to cover up a footprint."

"It ain't no deer scrape, that's for sure."

Anson stood up, looked at the bark on the oak tree. He pointed to a bare spot where a chunk of bark once had been. "And that ain't no deer rub, either."

Peebo examined the tree where the bark had come off. "Nope, you're right. Looks to me like somebody climbed that tree."

"Right recent, I'd say."

"Son, you've got a keen eye."

Anson stepped away from the tree, began looking down at the ground again. He stepped very slowly and carefully along an imaginary line, scanning each parcel of ground, taking in sections three or four feet wide along the path he walked. Peebo saw what he was doing and followed him on another tack, bent over like a prospector searching for a hidden vein of ore on a surface of solid rock.

"Why are you walkin' this way, Anson?" Peebo asked.

"Whoever was here, probably kept that tree between him and the graveyard. Seems likely this'd be the direction he'd come."

"Got any idea who?"

"Not yet." Then Anson stopped and squatted. He stirred a patch of earth with his finger, moving aside dirt and leaves and twigs. Soon a bare spot appeared and Anson cleaned the debris away until a clear image emerged underneath. Peebo was still walking aimlessly along just ahead when he realized Anson was no longer beside him. He turned and Anson looked up, caught Peebo's eye.

"You find something?" Peebo asked.

"Come take a look."

Peebo walked back to the place where Anson was squatting. He knelt down and looked at the spot Anson had cleared.

"Moccasin track?" Peebo said.

"Clear as day."

"Damn, but you got a tracker's eye."

Just then, both heard a branch crack. The two men stiffened and looked back down through the trees along the way they had come.

"Don't you just wish we had strapped on our pistols?" Peebo whispered.

"Shhh," Anson said, holding a finger to his lips.

It was very quiet for several moments, then they both heard a rustle of leaves.

Anson reached over and put his hand on Peebo's back, forcing him even lower to the ground. Then Anson stretched out to diminish his own silhouette.

Peebo eased himself forward until he, too, lay flat on the ground. They waited, listening. They heard nothing more for several seconds, then a sound made them both stiffen. Then they heard more sounds: the scrape of a shoe across leaves, the rustle of twigs, the faint clack of small pebbles, then distinct footfalls.

Anson peered along his line of sight as if he were looking down the rounded blue top of a gunbarrel. He saw a flash of something dark, then heard a small tearing sound, followed by a muffled exclamation, a cry just above a whisper.

Peebo heard, too, and strained his eyes to see what was moving toward them.

Lorene stepped out from behind a tree into full view, a look of bewilderment on her face. She bent down to brush something from her dress. One of the sleeves of her black blouse was torn, dangled like a fragment of tattered crepe bunting from her arm.

Anson cursed under his breath and pushed himself off the ground. Peebo blinked owlishly and slowly got up. Anson stood his ground and called out to Lorene.

"Hey."

"I get it," Peebo said. "Now I know why you didn't want me to come with you."

Anson turned to look at Peebo. "Huh?"

"You don't need to hit me over the head, son. I'll go on back. You and Lorene have your fun."

Anson spluttered a protest that never made the transition into coherent language as Peebo strode on past him. He watched as Peebo nodded to Lorene and disappeared. Lorene turned her head to watch him go, then looked again at Anson.

"What in hell are you doing here?" he asked.

"I—I followed you. Wondered where you were going. Now, I—I'm lost."

"You aren't lost. Go catch up with Peebo and go on back to the house."

A moment before, Anson had heard Peebo crashing through the woods, trampling the brush, but now there was only silence. Lorene appeared bewildered and stood there in confusion.

"He's gone," she said.

Anson shook his head in disgust and hesitated. He rubbed his chin as if trying to decide what to do next. Lorene started walking toward him as if in a trance, stepping carefully, with all the hesitancy of a doe stealing through the woods.

"What are you doing way out here?" she asked.

"Nothin'," he said.

"Nothing?"

"I'm lookin' for something. You better find your way back to the house."

"Anson, I—I'm lost. I don't think I can find my way back there."

She looked around her, cringing as if afraid.

"That damned Peebo," Anson said.

"What?"

"Nothing."

"Is everything nothing to you?"

"Huh?"

"Well, you said you're doing nothing out here and then you said something and I asked what you said and you said 'nothing.' "

"Lorene, you shouldn't have come out here. You don't know what's in these woods."

"You're here," she said, as she came near and Anson became aware of a strange feeling coming over him. He could smell her faint perfume, like lilacs, he thought, or honeysuckle, but unlike anything he had ever smelled before.

"I belong here. You don't."

She smiled, stepped close to him, and began brushing the dirt from the front of his shirt. "You got yourself all dirty, and you looked so nice at your mother's funeral."

Anson felt his throat swell and clog up with a lump as her hands thrummed at his chest like the beating wings of a bird. He had never been this close to a woman his own age before, never so near a young, beautiful woman such as she, and he felt his nerves give way and turn to tatters.

"I hope you haven't ruined this shirt. It's going to need a good wash and a good ironing."

"Lorene," Anson croaked.

She stopped brushing him off but did not move away. Instead, she looked up into his dark eyes and smiled. "I like the way you say my name," she said. "You've got a husk in your voice."

"Christ."

"Oh, you musn't swear. Especially in front of a lady."

"No'm."

"I forgive you." Her voice was like a soft song in his ear, a croon that left him limp all over, helpless.

"Are you going to go back?" he asked, now that he had found what was left of his voice.

"Can't I go with you? It's so sad and awkward back at your house. And I really don't know your father all that well. My uncle says he's stricken with grief and you must be, too."

"I got me something to do," he said, and started to step back from the closeness of her.

"Oh, I won't get in your way, Anson. I'll just keep you company."

"I don't need no company."

"I won't say a word," she said, and there was a twinkle of merriment in her eyes. "Please don't send me back there. Let me stay with you. I'm dying to know you better, Anson."

Anson stifled a curse and gulped in a deep breath. Exasperated, he shook his head and slumped his shoulders in surrender. Her skin was so soft, her touch so delicate, yet he could feel her hands through his shirt as if she had burned his skin when she was brushing him off and now, even though she was farther away than before, he felt enclosed by her, trapped by her in some invisible web of desire.

"All right, I guess. You can come along with me, but keep quiet and don't ask me no questions."

"I won't," she said.

To shut out her image, he turned so that he could break the line of vision and he began to look at the ground as if trying to regain his bearings. He took several steps, then picked up the track again. He could feel Lorene behind him, could hear her footsteps rustle the leaves and stir the twigs, disturb the small stones.

Anson soon determined the walker's direction by the signs of the path he had already discovered. Each person, each animal, he knew, had a purpose when moving. Once one could fathom a creature's purpose, the tracking became easier. The man who had made the impressions in the earth, who had tried to conceal his presence, was in a hurry, Anson now knew. Whatever he had come for, whatever he had been looking for, had been found, and now his purpose was to get away as fast as possible. The earth was less disturbed now. The man had dragged part of a branch behind him and used it like a broom, sweeping away his tracks in a general way. But, to Anson's practiced eye, he could see the marks the leaves attached to the small limb had left and, beneath, he saw the faint outlines of a moccasin track, just enough shape to these that he knew a man on foot had made them.

Anson became so absorbed in the tracking, that he all but forgot about Lorene. She was still there, in the back corner of his mind, but she was no longer the dominant presence. Instead he found himself totally absorbed in the spoor, his focus so intense that he blocked out almost all other thought.

Some thirty yards behind a clump of wind-stunted oak trees, he came into a clearing and his gaze caught the branch the walker had tossed aside. Then, two or three feet away, he saw a clean set of moccasin prints. He saw where they were headed, toward more brush on the other side of the bald spot of land, and he hurried to close the distance. He did not look back, but he could hear Lorene running to keep up.

A few feet beyond the fringe of grass, he saw where the man had tied his horse. The grass was beaten down in several places, and when he bent over to look more closely, he saw the chopped grasses where the horse had grazed. In another place, he found clear hoofprints and these he examined carefully, cataloguing each track in his mind until he had all four separate.

Anson huffed a breath in and out and stood up straight, listening. There was not a sound, but he already knew that the rider had long gone. He took a few more paces and saw where the man had mounted and ridden off to the south, toward the Rocking A, the nearest ranch. He stood looking in that direction for several moments until Lorene came up close behind him and touched his arm.

Startled, he turned and came face-to-face with her, so close she took his breath away.

"Did you find what you were looking for, Anson?" Her voice was pitched low and it was soft and lyrical and twisted into him like a skewer and he felt impaled on the sound of it.

"Yeah," he croaked.

"You were tracking someone," she said. It was a flat, factual statement, not a question.

"Yeah, somebody was watching Ma's funeral."

" 'Somebody'?"

"A man I once knowed. Knew," he corrected himself.

"Who is he?"

"An Apache named Mickey Bone," he said, and the voicing of Bone's name set his blood to racing. Yes, he knew it was Bone. He knew his moccasin track, knew the track of his horse. One moccasin had a crease in it near the heel, the other had a nick in it just under the big toe. And the horse was even easier to identify. Its shoes were worn down and one heel was uneven. He knew both tracks well, having seen them before.

"An Indian?"

"He used to work for my pa."

"Is he dangerous?"

"I reckon he could be," Anson said.

Lorene feigned fright and stepped so close to him, her breasts pressed into his chest and her nipples burned him where they touched. "I'm scared," she said.

His arms hung by his sides then, without volition, arose and wrapped around her. He pulled her close to him.

"No need to be scared," he said. "Bone's already miles from here."

"How do you know?"

"He saw what he came to see and now he's riding back to the Rocking A. I reckon he's working for Matteo Aguilar again."

"I heard my uncle and your father talking about Aguilar. He is a bad man?"

"I reckon so," Anson said, and he felt her burrow into him until his chest was on fire from the pressure of her soft breasts, and he felt the sky close in on him and the earth rise beneath him until he was snared in that small place where the grass was high and the brush thick and the outside world a vanished presence known only to memory, and that dimming by the second.

"I'm frightened again," Lorene said.

"There's no need." Anson's voice was gruff, with gravel in it, barely audible even in the hush of the moment.

"I feel safe with you," she said.

"Uh, we'd best get on—get on back, I mean."

"Can't we stay awhile?"

Anson felt himself melting inside, for her words were charged with meaning, stirred his manhood, and he was drawn into the heat of her, the fire in her loins as she pressed closer to him, rubbed his leg with her hand, stroked it until he no longer needed to hear her speak to know that she wanted him. She pushed her loins into his and jolted his flesh with a surge of electricity and he felt the blood drain from his brain and swell in his manhood until he could feel his member throb against her, against that secret place between her legs and the sky that was close began to spin and his knees turned to jelly, no longer able to support him.

They sank to the ground and her weight atop him was light and of no consequence and he drew her even closer to him and found her mouth with his and she responded with a savage eagerness that surprised him while his body turned to fire and his manhood to stone.

"I want you," she breathed, and her words were like a firewind tearing through him as he found his hands and they were searching for the buttons on her garments and her hands were severing his shirt from his body and the rustle of cloth was the sound of great walls tumbling, opening a breach into a city of pure gold, a treasure beyond human imagination, and he raced through the opening on a plundering quest and they coupled like lovers in a garden, joining together in desperation as if they were the only two people on earth left alive after some cataclysm that had claimed all else, leaving them to seed the earth so that their kind could spread to all corners of the land when all others were dead and gone.

And they each saw wonders in their minds and hearts that day and they explored each other again and again until the sun began to fall away in the vault of the sky that had gone back into its dimension all blue and flocked with white clouds like some distant peaceful ocean where sails billowed full and haughty before the windy breaths blown by the gods themselves.

14

REYNAUD SAT IN a chair in one corner of Matteo's room, cleaning one of his fine pistols. Matteo leaned over a small desk, scribbling notes, drawing lines and diagrams on a sheet of foolscap with the quill gripped tightly in his hand. The feather moved like part of a broken wing as he formed geometric-like icons: rectangles, squares, triangles. He stippled in small dots along certain lines and showed movement by inscribing primitive arrows pointing toward the geometries drawn from memory and the words of those who had been where he wanted to go.

"Bone give you all the information you need, Matteo?" Reynaud set the cleaned pistol aside for a moment, wiped his hands with a clean cloth, and reached for a snifter of brandy on the side table.

"He has very good eyes and he told me much of what I needed to know."

"I don't trust him."

"He does not need your trust, Reynaud."

"I mean he favors young Anson Baron. Maybe he did not tell you all that he saw."

Matteo twisted around to look at Reynaud. "You are a man who is like a spider, Reynaud. You sit on the far edge of a web and wait for something to get caught in it. And, when nothing is caught in it, you begin to doubt the web and wonder whether it is working or not."

"That is not a fair call on who I am, Matteo. I wait when I should wait. I move when I should move."

"You have not moved very much."

"You are calling the play, my friend."

"I am calling the play because you have done nothing since you came here. You lost the contraband to Martin and you did not go and kill him as you said you would."

Reynaud finished off the brandy and arose from his chair, so smooth and silent, Matteo thought, like a snake. He continued to look at Reynaud's eyes and Reynaud did not flinch from his gaze, but held his eyes on Matteo.

"Let me see what you have fashioned there," Reynaud said, walking toward Matteo. "Is this your plan for attacking the Box B?"

"You are like those lizards from South America that change their colors when they slither from tree to leaf to stone."

"A chameleon? You compare too many creatures, Matteo. Does that give you satisfaction?"

"It gives me a picture of who you really are, Reynaud."

"Ah, first I am a spider, then I am a lizard. What next, pray tell?"

"Soon I will see if you are a coward as well," Matteo said.

"Let me see what you have drawn," Reynaud said, and Matteo marveled at how he could slide away from a subject and never blink an eye. It was a gift he had probably used effectively in New Orleans, dealing with other thieves and scoundrels. Luz had said that Reynaud was "oily" and he had wondered if she was talking about Reynaud's speech or his appearance or his smooth manners around women. She was right, of course—Reynaud was oily, in the sense of being slippery and hard to tack down. He slid from one guise to another so that one talking to him never quite knew who he really was, nor what sincerity he possessed, if he possessed any at all.

Reynaud looked down at the drawing, pointed to a large square on the foolscap. "Is that the Baron house?"

"That is La Loma de Sombra where Martin lives."

"Are those lines the roads? And those little triangles?"

"There is one road, and some trails. The triangles are the houses of the vaqueros."

"And the dots are your men?"

"Yes."

"You have split your forces," Reynaud said. "Is that wise?"

"You are interested in my plan of attack, Reynaud?"

"Of course, Matteo. Am I not willing to fight by your side? I have a stake here, as well. After all, Martin Baron is my enemy, too. I will have his blood for sullying my sister."

"I hope I can count on you to follow my orders and help lead one group of men."

"I am at your service, Matteo."

Matteo pointed to a rectangle he had drawn next to the large square. "This is the barn. Martin has a cannon in here, or did. He used that cannon when Cuchillo's Apaches attacked La Loma de Sombra. The Apaches came at him from this small hill here." He pointed to some squiggly lines he had drawn opposite the square and the rectangle. "The Apaches thought they had caught Baron by surprise. They had a short distance to ride, down this slope, and they were met by cannon fire. The Indians were chewed up and cut to pieces."

"A cannon?"

"Yes, four-pounder. The Apaches had no chance. They were slaughtered as they came across the flat, here." Matteo stuck a finger at a place on his map between the top of the hill and the barn. "He and his men shot those that scattered. With only a small force, he was able to defeat the Apaches and they have not visited the Baron rancho since that day."

"So, you want men to attack the barn and some to attack the house?"

"Those dots I put behind, along that line of small triangles, are men who will come along and burn the houses of the vaqueros and then attack the house from behind, while these dots here," he pointed, "are men who will attack the barn from the rear and the house from the side."

"Humm," Reynaud said. "It appears you have a good plan, as long as the cannon is inside the barn and facing the front."

"That is the way it was with the Apaches."

Reynaud stroked his chin and walked away, toward the window. He stopped, looked outside for a long moment, then turned back to face Matteo. "I, too, know Martin Baron, although not as well as you. He is not a stupid man."

"No, he is not stupid."

"He would find another place to put the cannon."

"But where? There is only the barn."

"And the house," Reynaud said.

Matteo looked down at the foolscap with all of its diagrams and lines. His eyes narrowed to dark slits, then the lids drew back and he scowled. "Yes, he might put the cannon inside the house to fool me."

Reynaud walked back over to the desk and pushed his outstretched index finger down onto the square that represented the Baron house. "I do not see any windows or doors here. He could put that cannon at any one of them."

"Claro que si," Matteo said. "That is true. But where?"

"You have to think like Martin does," Reynaud said. "Where will he expect you to attack? If he does put the cannon inside the house, he will sacrifice the barn, perhaps. He will either let your men storm the barn and then wait until they come out to shoot them down, or he will just wait for you to rush the house."

"Yes, Martin might do that."

"I would say he would not worry about the back door. He could defend that, if necessary. But he will expect you to come through the front door to kill him."

"So, he will put the cannon at the front door."

"Or just inside. He would be waiting. When your men came through, he would touch off the powder and blow them to pieces."

Matteo let out a breath and stood up. He paced the floor for a moment, back and forth in front of the desk. Then he stopped and looked at Reynaud. "If we had men waiting to come in the back door, they could rush it after the cannon first fires. Martin would not be able to get off a second shot. We would be on him like the locusts, like the swarming hornets."

"He would not have a chance," Reynaud said.

"I think this is a good plan," Matteo said.

"You should have another group of men ready to charge the front door after the cannon fires, as well. They would keep him from reloading. It might be hand-to-hand combat at that point."

"My men have been trained for all kinds of situations."

"Then you have nothing to worry about," Reynaud said, his lips crinkled in a faint smile.

"We would lose a few men, no more than half a dozen, eh?"

"If that," Reynaud said.

"It would be worth it to kill Martin and take back the land my family gave away."

"Martin did not pay for the land?"

"That is beside the point. My people should never have sold our land to a gringo."

"There is still the boy, Anson, to worry about. You cannot count on Bone to help you there."

"If Anson is stupid enough to be inside the house, then he will die, too."

"Then you must ask yourself another question, Matteo."

"What is that?"

"Will Anson be in the house with his father?"

"I do not know," Matteo said. "Perhaps he will not be there at all. Bone said that he was away branding wild cattle most of the time."

"If he is not there when you attack, then what will you do when he returns to find that you have killed his father and have taken his home?"

"He will have only his friend, the blond-haired man, and a few vaqueros. There is nothing that he can do. I will squash him like a bug."

"Ah, then there is nothing to worry about with Anson," Reynaud said.

"I do not worry about him." Matteo walked back to the desk and picked up the foolscap, held it up so that the light shone through it. "If you cut off the head of the snake, the body will die."

"When do you plan to attack the Baron ranch?" Reynaud asked.

Matteo let the paper fall back on top of the desk.

"Within a week. At night."

"You will attack in the night?"

"Yes. With luck, that cannon will never be fired. We will catch Martin when he is asleep. He will never wake up."

"If that is so, then you might want to consider a better way."

"What is that?" Matteo asked.

"Have your men sneak up in the dark and surround the house. Set fire to it. Then, as Martin and his men run out, shoot them down. They will be lit by the flames."

"I have thought of that. I want that house, as well as the land."

"Then you have to make a decision, Matteo. If you want a victory without the blood of your men being spilled, you must sacrifice the house."

"Yes, Reynaud, that is something I will have to decide."

"And when will you do that?"

"I will sleep on it tonight. By tomorrow morning I will know what I will do."

"Good. I look forward to seeing Martin's corpse lying on the ground. It will give my family in New Orleans much satisfaction."

"Not as much satisfaction as it will give me," Matteo said. A moment later, after being silent, he looked at Reynaud. "I will have a drink of that *aguardiente* myself, I think."

"It is good brandy, Matteo."

"We will drink to our victory, Reynaud."

"Yes." Reynaud walked to the sideboard and picked up a snifter. Then he took the bottle and filled his and Matteo's glasses. Matteo picked up his glass, held it up to the light.

"It is clear," he said. *"Muy fino."*

"To victory," Reynaud said, clinking his glass against Matteo's.

"A la venganza," Matteo said.

"And what is that?" Reynaud asked.

" 'To vengeance.' "

The two men drank and smiled at each other.

Matteo's cowled eyes seemed to hood his other thought as he drank. No matter what happened, he wanted to see Reynaud laid out on the ground alongside the body of Martin Baron. He wanted no witness riding back to New Orleans bragging about their victory. Reynaud would not be drinking brandy in celebration after the battle. A bullet in his back would wipe the smile from Reynaud's face. Forever.

15

MILLICENT COLLINS STOOD a few feet away from Martin, watching him with a cowled intensity. She dipped her head slightly so that her gaze did not show to the casual observer. She was turned slightly away from him so that she could give him a sidelong glance without his knowing it.

Martin stood under a thick, leafy oak, speaking to Doc Purvis and Al Oltman. Millie could just barely hear what Martin was saying.

"Caroline has a brother, Ken Darnell," Martin said. "I sent word down south to him, but I guess he didn't have enough time to get here for his sister's funeral. Her parents are both dead. I haven't seen Ken in some time. My man, Tomasito Herrera, has not returned, either."

"You did the best you could," Purvis said.

"I know Kenny Darnell," Oltman said.

"You do?" Martin asked.

"He still has his ranch, but he joined up with the Rangers four months ago."

"Where is he, then?"

"He was in Austin last week."

"Is he married?" Martin asked.

"No. And he has no plans. He's a dedicated Ranger. Wants to fight Indians. Because of his folks."

"Well, then what is he doing in Austin? He might lose his scalp there, but I doubt if he'll run into any Apaches."

"You probably did not hear Houston's farewell speech," Al said, "but he was a dying man when he spoke it and he ordered us Rangers down to the border. He wanted to start a fight with Mexico to preserve the Union."

"I didn't know that," Martin said.

"But, since Lincoln got elected by the skin of his teeth, there are greater issues at stake. J. D. Throckmorton and Sam did their best to stave off a secession vote, but they lost. The Germans around Austin all voted to preserve the Union. Now General Twiggs has ordered the Union flag to come down on all Texas forts and military establishments. That has been done, as of last month, so I hear. When I rode to some of them they were flying the Lone Star flag of Texas."

Purvis nodded somberly. Martin's mouth dropped open in surprise.

"Seems to me," Martin said, "somebody already made up my mind for me."

"There's not a government office, nor a fort, nor any federal building in Texas flying the Stars and Stripes," Purvis said. "The Lone Star of Texas waves over all those places where the Union flag once held dominion."

"Our independence was official on March second," Oltman said.

"And this is already April of 1861," Martin said.

"Not only that, but Austin had formed a delegation to apply for membership in the Confederacy," Purvis said, "but before they could even get to Montgomery, Alabama, the Confederacy accepted Texas as a member."

"Lincoln's not going to stand still for that," Martin said.

Oltman grinned wide.

Millie moved closer to the three men. Out of the corner of her eye, she saw people still gathered at the tables laden with roast beef, potatoes, beets, beans, and other foods. Roy Killian was hemmed in by three women: his mother, Ursula, Hattie, and her daughter, Wanda. He looked lost, Millie thought, or, more properly, trapped.

David Wilhoit stood a few feet away from that group, eating from a tin plate that Lucinda had just refilled for him.

Socrates was helping out, carrying plates over to the refuse barrel and scraping them clean, before handing them to Julius, who carried them into the kitchen where Esperanza and Lorenzo were washing them. Millie had been inside the house to look around, curious about how Martin lived, and Esperanza had given her permission to go upstairs to the bedrooms. It was a man's house, except for Caroline's room and a couple of others. She saw his stamp everywhere she looked, feeling like a spy, but delighting in every new discovery.

Ken Richman was sitting on a nail keg in the shade, talking to Nancy Grant, who was sitting on a small wooden chair. Ed Wales was drinking whiskey at a table made from boards stretched across two sawhorses under a shade tree. He was talking to other convivial townsmen and there wasn't a woman within ten yards of the outdoor bar.

"I can't believe Sam Houston would just stand by and let this happen," Martin said. "He's a Union man through and through."

"And a very ill man," Purvis said. "But he stepped back, let this happen."

"Sam said that to oppose Texas becoming part of the Confederacy would lead to civil unrest and he loves Texas too much to see it torn apart," Oltman said. "Look, Martin, Houston is a great man, but he saw the handwriting on the wall."

Millie stood behind a small tree, listening to the conversation. She could see Martin, but not Purvis or Oltman, and she watched him in rapt fascination.

"Sam told me he had two choices," Purvis said.

"You spoke to Houston?" Martin asked.

"Yes. We are good friends. He moved to Corpus Christi, you know. I suggested he do so."

"What two choices?" Martin asked.

"He could either fight to retain his office under the United States Constitution, or he could, as all of the officials were required to do, embrace the Confederacy and swear allegiance to it."

"And which did he decide to do?"

"Neither," Purvis said. "He said he could not swear an oath to the Confederacy since it would violate his allegiance to the Union. And he did not want to be one who had a hand in starting a civil war."

"That must have started a ruckus in Austin," Martin said.

"The committee voted him right out of office," Oltman said. "They put in Clark and Houston was out of a job."

"Just like that," Martin said.

Purvis chuckled. "Not quite. President Lincoln offered to send Houston federal troops to help him hold on to his office, but Sam declined the president's offer."

Martin let out a low whistle.

"Houston," Purvis said, "refused to be responsible for shedding any Texan's blood. He believes too much in Texas and the United States. He is a sad, dying man, I'm sorry to say."

"It's a damned shame," Martin said.

"That's why we need you to join the Texas Rangers, Martin. Houston believes that we can help both sides through this mess."

"He does?"

"Yes. The Rangers will have to keep order if the South erupts in war. We will see to it that Texas does not suffer and that Texans are treated fairly."

"A tall order," Martin said.

"And it will take some tall men to fill it," Oltman said.

"You wouldn't be pushing, would you, Al?" Martin asked.

Oltman suppressed a grin. "You read men, Martin. That's good."

"And you don't answer questions real good."

"Oh, I answer those that need an answer. You know why I came. The Rangers, right now, *are* Texas, and Texas is in bad need of them. This war talk isn't just talk. It's like a fire burning through the whole country, consuming everything, and everyone in its path. When it boils up high enough, there will be federal troops crossing our borders, and men you and I know are going to fight those troops and a lot of them will get killed."

"So, what are the Rangers going to do? Just sit back and wait until it's all over?"

"No, we'll fight, too, but we'll fight what needs fighting, not our brothers and uncles and cousins from the North. We'll fight to keep Texas a republic, if that's what's to be. After the war, Houston, and

I, think that whoever wins, be it South or North, they'll want to lay waste to all that reminds them of the war. There will be lawlessness and that's no good for anyone. The Rangers will uphold the law."

"Even if the Union wins?"

"Absolutely," Oltman said. "Houston fought hard to get us into the Union. And, we think, when this trouble is over, Texas will once again be part of a great nation, the United States."

"You sound like a politician," Martin said.

This time, Al grinned. Wide. "Well, if I do, I caught the disease from old Sam, sure enough."

Martin smiled. "I'll think it over, Al. Right now I don't feel much like warring with anyone, even though I'm likely to have one on my hands right quick."

"Oh? Would that be Matteo Aguilar?"

"You heard?"

"Ken Richman told us something about that, and I talked to Dave Wilhoit, who worked for Aguilar, I gather."

"Well, it's something I have to take care of myself."

"This is just the kind of situation the Rangers are bound to discourage. If the law is on your side, we'll back you all the way. Sam thinks the war, if it happens, will flush out a lot of land-grabbers like Aguilar. We want to prevent that from happening."

"In the meantime," Martin said, "I'm bound to have a little war of my own. It's between me and Aguilar. I don't expect the Texas Rangers to fight my battles for me."

"And what if you're defeated?"

"I guess Aguilar would own the Box B. Not legally, but if he has my land, who's going to take it away from him?"

"That's just my point, Martin. If Aguilar could get away with this, then Texas would be wide open to other land-grabbers. What a man works for and pays for, would no longer be his to keep."

"You make a good point, Al," Martin said.

"I'm going to throw in with you, Baron," Oltman said. "I'll get a message back to Corpus Christi asking for more men, but I'm siding with you in this."

"I wouldn't ask any man to fight my battles for me."

"It's not just your battle, Martin. The future of Texas is at stake here. I've already checked on your deed. You bought this land fair and square from the Aguilar family. From a previous generation, to be sure, but that doesn't mean Aguilar has the right to take the land back his family once owned. Not this way, not by force."

"Matteo doesn't see it that way."

"But Texas does, and the Rangers were formed to fight for Texans. Against all enemies."

"Does that include the Yankees?" Martin asked.

"All enemies."

"Fair enough. I could use you if it comes to a fight with Aguilar."

"And you have your son, Anson."

"No, Anson will be away on ranch business, branding stray cattle."

There was an awkward silence as Oltman and Purvis digested this scrap of information.

"I see," Oltman said finally.

Purvis interrupted. "Allen, I think it's time we returned to town. Have you seen Lorene around? I wonder where she went."

"Martin, I'll be back tomorrow," Oltman said. "Can you put me up?"

"We have a bunkhouse."

"Fine. So long, then. I hope I can be of help."

Oltman walked away, but Doc Purvis lingered for a moment.

"Martin, about that blind boy. I wouldn't make too much of it. He's probably perfectly innocent of any wrongdoing."

Martin's jaw stiffened and his hazel eyes flashed sparks of various hues. "It is not something I want to dwell on, Doc."

"I understand. Please accept my sympathies for your loss. Good-bye."

"I hear you're going to stay in Baronsville, practice there."

"Yes, I think I'll enjoy the challenge. The town is growing and you have no physician."

"I hope you do well. Thanks for all your help with Caroline."

Purvis nodded and walked away in Oltman's wake. Martin bowed his head and fought back the tears. His body shook with the spasms of grief.

Millie walked over to him and put a hand on his shoulder. Her touch was light and warm. Martin looked up, his eyes wet.

"Huh?" he asked, startled.

"I'm Millie, Mr. Baron. From the Longhorn. I just wanted to tell you how sorry I am that you lost your wife."

"Millie? Oh, yeah. Millicent. Connors, wasn't it?"

"Millicent *Collins*, yes. I waited on you at the Longhorn."

"It was nice of you to come."

Her hand lingered on his back, slowly slid downward until she let it fall away. Martin turned to her as if to obtain a better look at the pretty young woman.

"I know what it is to lose someone very dear," she said, her voice low. "Grief is a terrible thing to bear alone."

"Yes," he said. "I'm sorry to hear you lost someone, too. Your father? Mother?"

"My husband," she said.

"You look too young to have been married."

"I was married young," she said. "My husband was older."

"Did you know Caroline?"

"I met her once, in town. She was very nice. A lady."

"Yes."

"If there's anything I can do . . ."

"I can't think of anything," Martin said quickly.

"I know you have servants. A cook, a lady who cleans the house. I met them today."

"Yes, Lucinda cooks for me. Esperanza does the housework. Did you—I mean, were you, ah, looking for work?"

"I have a job," she said. "Mr. Richman was kind enough to hire me when I came to Baronsville, having just been widowed recently."

"Recently?"

"Six months ago," she said.

"Did you come here to . . . I mean, the memories . . ."

"No, well, maybe. Partly. My husband had no family and I wanted to start fresh. Someplace new."

"And you heard about Baronsville?"

"No," she said, "not at first. I heard about you, about what you were trying to do out here."

"Me? Raise cattle, is all."

Millie moved still closer to Martin, even though she was no more than a step away when she did so. Martin's back was all but scraping the oak tree and he did not try to move away.

"Oh, you may not know it, Mr. Baron, but people talk about what you've done here, what you're going to do. Everyone says you're a man to watch, a man with a vision."

"Who says that?"

"Charlie Goodnight, for one. Others I've met."

"You know Charlie?"

"Yes. Not well, but I met him. My husband worked for him now and again."

"Well, Charlie's the man with a vision. He's given me some good ideas."

"He said you would someday be the backbone of Texas. That you would be king of all the cattle ranchers."

"Charlie said that? Well, I'm surprised."

"You shouldn't be. I've been in town long enough to know that Charlie was right. I know you've had troubles, and losing your wife like this is harder than any of them, so I just wanted you to know that I know what you're going through and to tell you that you should not give up hope, but go on and succeed in your plans."

Millie looked into Martin's eyes without wavering or blinking and she saw that he did not avoid her gaze. But the look on his face had changed, from open curiosity to genuine interest. She smiled at him, encouraging that interest.

"I have a hunch there's more to you than meets the eye, Millie. You're not only a waitress, are you?"

Millie blushed. "The truth is, Mr. Baron, that I have been schooled in numbers, arithmetic, and I am a keeper of books and ledgers."

"Books and ledgers, eh?"

"Yes, sir. I worked for an accounting firm in Austin, Balcom and Reynolds."

"I've never heard of them."

"They handled a variety of accounts, sir, which included banking, businesses, such as mercantile and hardware, and for various vendors and traders, not only in Texas, but in other states and territories."

"Why did you leave there?"

"They wanted to transfer me to Denver to manage an office there."

"Doing what?"

"They wanted me to manage the books for a number of sheep ranchers."

"You didn't want to do that?"

"Oh no, I would have loved it. But I love Texas, and, like you, I think cattle will be the future of big business in the West. Not sheep."

Martin laughed. "Sheep? No. This is not England or Scotland. And we grow cotton. Who needs wool?"

"I think you're exactly right, Mr. Baron."

"So you came to Baronsville," Martin said, "and are working as a waitress."

"Well, sir, this is not the time . . ."

"The time for what?"

"I wanted to manage your ranch accounts, Mr. Baron. Did your wife do that for you?"

"Yes, yes, she did. I never even thought of that. Caroline handled the money—what came in, what went out. I never had to bother with that."

Millie did not tell Martin that, while inside the house, she had looked at Caroline's small office where she kept the ledgers. All of the figures were there, neat and tidy, and the Box B was barely holding its head up above water.

"Well, I'm sure you can find someone . . ."

"No, let me think," Martin said quickly. "I don't know if I can understand all that, uh, accounting and such. Would you do me a favor?"

"Why, surely, Mr. Baron. What is it you would like me to do?"

"Could you, say, in a few days, come back out here and look over Caroline's books? Maybe tell me how I stand and all. I'll gladly pay for your time."

"Mr. Baron, time is cheap. Everyone has the same amount. If I do look at your books and have any recommendations, you will be paying me for my knowledge, my brains."

"Hey, hold on, Millie. I didn't mean . . ."

"Accounting is a specialized skill, Mr. Baron. Some might even say it's an art. I'm proud of my ability and my accomplishments. I just wanted you to know what you're paying for, that's all."

Martin's face creamed over with a sheepish look. He appeared as if all the blood had drained away from his visage and left a pasty complexion.

"Okay, Millie. Let me go through everything in a couple of days and I'll send for you when I'm ready. You see how I stand and let me know how much I owe you."

"All right, Mr. Baron. I'll wait to hear from you in a few days."

She held out her hand. Martin looked at it in surprise. Then, as if he realized that she wanted to seal the bargain, he took her hand and shook it.

She squeezed his hand extra hard and Martin's eyes widened. She smiled at him.

"You know where you can find me," she said, and pulled her hand away.

Before Martin could say anything, Millie had turned on her heel and walked away, toward the buggy that had brought her and some others out from town.

She could feel Martin's eyes on her and she put a little extra sway into her hips. She hid the smile that was playing on her lips, for she did not want to look too cheerful at a funeral and raise questions in anyone's minds as to her reason for attending the solemn ceremony.

But inside, she was grinning wide and wanted to jump and shout for joy.

I'll be seeing you soon, Martin Baron, she said to herself. You don't know it, but you need me.

As if Millie's leaving were a cue, the crowd began to break apart and people starting leaving, saying good-bye to Martin. Martin looked around, but he didn't see Anson.

Doc Purvis was the last to stop by. "If you see my niece Lorene, will you see that she gets to town, Mr. Baron?"

"Oh, do you know where she went?"

"I believe she is with your son, Anson. According to that man over there." Purvis pointed to Peebo Elves, who was picking over the food at one of the tables.

"I will surely do that, Doc. Thanks for coming."

"You take care, Mr. Baron."

Martin watched as Purvis joined Al Oltman. Al waved good-bye and soon all that were left were Roy, Wanda, Hattie, Ursula and David, Peebo, and the two black men. He walked to the house alone, feeling oddly detached, as if none of what had happened this day or the previous ones, was real.

And he wondered where Anson had gone with that niece of Purvis's, whose name he could not remember.

All he could think of was Millie. Millicent Collins. And he tried to remember everything she had done when she had waited on him in the Longhorn Saloon, every move, every word she had spoken, every inflection in her voice.

And he cursed himself for not thinking only of Caroline, already cold in her grave.

16

ANSON KNOCKED LIGHTLY on the door to his father's room. He heard a muffled voice, but could not make out the words. He lifted the latch. It was free and the door swung open on leather hinges.

"Pa?"

"Anson?"

The room was dark, but Anson could make out the silhouette of his father. Martin was sitting on the edge of the bed, his back to Anson, facing the star-filled window to the sky. The stars flickered like the far-off lights of a city and the wind that had sprung up in the afternoon was whispering through the branches of the trees outside.

"I come to say good-bye," Anson said. He heard a series of sobs from his father and something caught in Anson's throat as he realized Martin was weeping. He had never seen his father cry before, except at the funeral, and that wasn't really crying, not out loud, like this.

"You goin' somewhere?"

"Yeah, me and Peebo are headin' out toward the Nueces in a while."

"Christ, it's darker'n the inside of a coal pit."

"And by sunup, it'll be boilin' hot."

"I wish I were going with you."

"Come on."

"You know I can't. That bastard Matteo."

"Yeah."

"You get that gal back where she belongs?"

"I rode her into town, packin' double on Jake."

"That old horse?"

"He's slow, all right." Anson grinned in the darkness.

"I miss your mother, Anson."

"I miss her too."

"There's a big empty place where she was. I can't go into her room without breakin' down. I keep thinkin' she'll be in there."

"I know. You've got to get over it, Pa."

"I don't know if I ever will. I keep thinkin' of all the things I wanted to say to her; all the things I should have said."

"You can't go back. You can't go back and undo things. You have to go on ahead."

"Yeah, true. I hope she's happy where she is."

"She was happy where she was. She put a lot of stock in you, Pa. You can't help who you are and neither could she."

"I keep thinkin' . . ."

Anson cut him off. "You can't do that no more, Pa. Look, I come to tell you something before I ride out."

"What?"

"You talk to Esperanza. No, you go see her, first light, and listen to what she has to say."

"Esperanza?"

"I done had a talk with her. She's got something on her chest she wants to tell you."

"Excuses."

Anson shook his head. "No excuses. She knows somethin' you got to know."

"Can't you tell me?"

"I think you better hear it from her."

"Why?"

"From me, it'd be secondhand, Pa."

Martin stirred on the bed. He stood up. Anson could see him touch a pair of fingers to his eyes, rub them downward. "I can't talk to her right away, son. I've got too much in my craw about that blind boy."

"That's why you got to talk to her."

"I—I'll think on it."

"Pa, you're carryin' too much on your shoulders right now. She can help you get rid of some of it."

Martin walked over to Anson. The room was still pitch-dark. Anson could not see his father's face, his eyes. He wanted to leave before he said anymore, before he said too much.

"Anson, you've got a good heart and good sense. But this is somethin' you can't help with none. I know your ma was not right in the head a long time before she died and I can forgive her. But I can't . . ."

"Pa, I've got to go. I know how Ma was. You don't have to forgive her for nothin'. You have to forgive yourself for a lot, though. A hell of a lot."

"You're mad, aren't you?"

"No. I just think you're letting something eat at your innards that ain't doin' you no good. You got to . . . well, I ain't goin' to tell you what you got to do. I gotta be goin'."

"Are you going after that white bull?"

Anson sucked in a breath, let it out slow. "If I see him, I aim to bring him down. He's good stock."

"Is that white bull more important to you than the Box B, Anson?"

"Huh?" Anson's head jerked backward in surprise.

"If Matteo beats me, you could lose this ranch."

"He won't beat you. Unless you let him."

"What in hell is that supposed to mean?"

"If you mean to beat Matteo, you will, and my being here won't make no difference."

"Two extra hands might make a hell of a difference. I don't know how many men Matteo is bringing with him, but I'm sure it's a sight more'n I have here."

"Peebo says that Ranger feller is throwin' in with you."

"Oltman? That's one man, and I don't know if he can fight as well as you. Or Peebo."

"I'm sure the Rangers didn't pick him 'cause he was a hand at growin' pansies."

"That's not the point, Anson. A man fights for what is his, for what's rightfully his. Your ma turned the ranch over to you while I was away that time, and now you're walking away, turning your back on it."

"Pa, we've gone over all this before. If I didn't think you could handle Matteo, I'd stay here and pin his ears back. I'm not walking away; I'm doing ranch business, and the business of the Box B is raising cattle. I'm not going to let Matteo stop me from doing my business."

"You might come back with that white bull and there won't be any ranch here to keep him on."

"Do you really believe that, Pa?"

Martin did not answer for several seconds. He stood there, his face invisible to Anson, like some shadowy presence, mute, unfathomable as stone.

"I don't know what I believe anymore, Anson. When Caroline died, it felt like the whole world caved in on me. I guess I'm not handling it very well. I mean, when Cackle Jack died, I was heartbroken, but I watched him die, like I watched my own pa die. And I saw my own ma killed by Shawnees and, at the time, I wished they had killed me, too. I couldn't bear losing my ma, and it was torture watching my pa die, slow, like Cackle Jack. And I grieved when Juanito died, too. I hated myself because I had wronged him and he was a good man. But there were reasons I could see in my mind why Ma and Pa, Cackle Jack and Juanito died. Reasons I could see plain. But with your ma, it seems like she was taken away so quick and so young and for no good reason. And I couldn't see it coming."

"Or else you just didn't look," Anson said.

"Huh?"

"She was your wife. You should have been close enough to her so that she would have told you she was dying."

"I don't think she knew."

"She knew, Pa. She had to know."

"She say anything to you?"

"Not directly. But I knew she was scared, deathly scared of something. Something she couldn't see, neither."

"Oh Christ," Martin said, and his voice was full of anguish and bewilderment and anger. "Oh sweet Christ. I couldn't see it coming. I just thought . . ."

"You thought she was addled. Or worse."

"I—I guess so."

"Well, she was. And now we know why. Doc Purvis said that the disease affects the brain in its final stages."

"It must have been horrible for Caroline. I can't stand to think of her dying like that and me not being able to help."

"You can't help what can't be helped. Stop blaming yourself."

"I know who to blame."

"No, you don't. Pa, I've got to go. You talk to Esperanza. Then you'll know who to blame for Ma's death."

"Why won't you tell me?"

"Because you wouldn't believe me."

"Why should I believe a Mexican maid?"

"She's a person, Pa. And Esperanza doesn't lie. She's very religious and she would not tell such a lie. She's very upset and worried about you."

"All right. It's the least I can do, I reckon."

Anson saluted his father and turned to leave. "I'll be seeing you, Pa. Good luck."

"Good-bye, son."

Anson hurried out of the room. He was wringing-wet with sweat, his palms clammy. He had wanted to put his arms around his father and give him a good squeeze, but he felt that was not the manly thing to do. But he could feel his father's grief in that room, thick as a hair coat, scratching his own hide, threatening to envelop him. He had had to get away from Martin before he broke down himself and shouted out all he knew about his mother's death and all the blame still at his father's feet, even so, and some at his own. But none of that would have done any good; none of his own feelings would have helped his father through this bad time.

Anson needed air to breathe after being in the claustrophobic room with his father, and the wide space of the sky to clear his thoughts and his head. Juanito had told him that he would always find peace away from people, out on the plain or in the woods, with nature.

"Look to the sky," Juanito had said. "Know that you are part of it, and that it is part of you. That is where you will find comfort when the times are bad."

Outside, in the dark, he looked up at the stars and felt the breeze wash his face, warm it like a soothing hand.

"Come on, Anson," yelled Peebo from the darkness near the barn. "We need to be burnin' daylight, son. I thought you was never goin' to come out of that house."

"Hold your horses, Peebo. You'll wish you were back here before this day is done."

"Son, I can't wait to see that white bull again. I want to measure them horns with my own two hands."

Anson saw Peebo's silhouette emerge out of the shadowy dark of the barn. He was holding their horses by the bridles, and they were tossing their heads and stroking the ground with their forehooves.

"I hope you filled those boys with water," Anson said.

"They ain't camels, son. They drank what they wanted to drink."

"Well, let's go find that bull, then."

"We've got enough rope to stretch from the Rio to the Nueces, that's for danged sure."

Anson took his horse from Peebo and mounted him. He had to hold him in to keep the animal from going into a spate of bucking. Peebo climbed aboard his horse and had the same problem.

"Frisky, ain't they?"

"Peebo, these horses are plumb tame for this time of day."

"Why, sure," Peebo said, and Anson could see his grin in the dark, like a miniature picket fence, all whitewashed and dazzling.

"Packhorses ready?" Anson asked.

"They're hobbled up on the flat, loaded down with grub and such, a pair of branding irons, water."

"You done good, Peebo."

"Just the two of us?"

"No, we'll need other hands. I told Lucero to get five other hands and meet us at a place he knows. We put up a lean-to there last year and some of the boys made it into a right good jacal. So we got us a line camp this side of the Nueces, not far from where we last saw El Blanco."

"Sounds as if you thought of everything."

Anson didn't say when Lucero and the other men would meet them. Nor did he tell Peebo he had something else to do before they rode out to the line shack.

He ticked his horse's flanks with his spurs and felt the surge of power between his legs as the horse jumped into a fast trot. He closed his eyes so that he would not look at the house to see if a lamp was burning in the upstairs bedroom where his father and he had talked.

When the horse started to climb the slope in front of the house, heading east, Anson opened his eyes, and it seemed, as they topped the rise, that he was riding into a field of stars, and he felt his spirit rise to the heavens, to safety and a calm peace that was almost beyond comprehension.

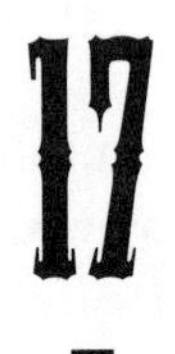

THE LONGHORN SALOON was nearly deserted at that early hour. Yet Ken Richman had given orders that the restaurant be opened at dawn every morning to serve those early risers like himself. But he was not there that morning after the funeral at the Box B. There were only one or two diehards at the bar, two Mexicans at one table near the front window, a drummer who had arrived the night before on the stage from Galveston at another, three unshaven men of unknown reputation at one of the back tables, and, in the center, three women and two men who had been there at first light.

Roy Killian pushed his chair away from the table in the Longhorn Saloon. He was the first to finish his breakfast and he'd hurried so that he would be. Wanda looked up from her plate, fixed Roy with a withering stare.

"You gulped your food down, Roy."

"I've got a lot to do."

Hattie, a forkful of *frijoles refritos* suspended in midair, glared at Roy in defense of her daughter. Ursula lifted her head as if roused from sleep by the sudden conversation that had sprung up around her. David worked a half-eaten biscuit through the beef drippings on his plate. He had eaten his food nearly as fast as Roy.

"If you ask me," Hattie said, "you're messing in something that's none of our business, Roy."

"Mama," Wanda said.

"No, I mean it. Roy's got better things to do than get involved with Martin Baron and his affairs."

"David, you comin' with me?" Roy said.

"Yes."

"You too?" Hattie said. "My, it seems everyone in this country kowtows to Martin Baron."

"Mama," Wanda said again, "Roy promised, and David wants to help. Ursula doesn't mind, do you, Ursula?"

"We owe Martin a lot," Ursula said, looking at David for support. He avoided her gaze.

"You've got your own ranch to look after, Roy," Hattie persisted. "What happens with Martin Baron is not of your concern."

Wanda opened her mouth to say something, but Roy spoke first. "What happens to one of us, happens to all of us, Hattie. Martin needs some things done and I told him I'd do them. Now, you and Wanda and Ma can have the whole day to yourselves to shop and whatnot. Good-bye, Ma."

Roy leaned over and gave his mother a peck on the cheek. David, sallow-faced, merely nodded at Ursula and the other two ladies.

"Well, I swan," Hattie said. "Roy didn't hear a word I said."

"He heard you, Mama," Wanda said. "I'm sure he agrees with you, but a promise is a promise."

"Roy's as good as his word," Ursula said.

"Hmmph," snorted Hattie, and glared after the two men as they left the Longhorn.

"Ursula, how do you feel about your husband and son helping Martin Baron fight his battles?"

Ursula, caught off-guard by the question, hesitated. She dabbed at the corners of her mouth with a napkin and then put her hands below the table, on her lap, so the others could not see that they were starting to tremble.

"Martin got my first husband killed," Ursula said.

"What?" Wanda leaned over the table toward Ursula.

"Jack was a drifter," Ursula said. "Always riding off somewhere. I had to practically raise Roy by myself. I guess my husband didn't always obey the law, but, deep down, he was a good man. And I loved him."

"So, what happened?" Hattie asked, all aflutter with eagerness. "What did Martin do to your husband?"

"I don't know the whole story," Ursula said, "but somehow Jack wound up on the Box B, working for Martin Baron. Jack came to see us, Roy and me, in Fort Worth. He took Roy with him back to the Baron spread. Next thing I knew, Jack was dead and Roy was under Martin's thumb."

"You don't think Martin killed your husband, do you?" Wanda asked. "I mean . . ."

"I—I don't know. I've heard that Martin took a dislike to Jack. Perhaps . . ."

"Perhaps what?" Hattie said, an insistent tone in her voice.

"Well, maybe Martin put Jack in harm's way. You know, just to get rid of him. I mean, Jack was pretty smart and I sometimes thought he might wind up being hanged for horse-thieving, but Martin said Apaches killed Jack."

"You believe him, of course," Wanda said.

"I've had my doubts of late."

"Well, Roy said Martin's own son is not going to help him fight that Mexican, Aguilar," Hattie said.

"Makes you wonder, doesn't it?" Ursula said.

Hattie looked away as something caught her eye. "Here comes that haughty waitress, Millie," she said. "I saw her batting her eyes at Roy and David when they left."

"Oh, Mother," Wanda said.

"I mean it. Did you see her clinging to Martin at the funeral yesterday? She ogles every man she sees. If you ask me, she's nothing but a hussy."

"Mother, be quiet," Wanda said. "She's almost here."

Millie walked up to the table and smiled at each woman. "Is there anything else I can get you ladies?" she asked.

"We're just fine," Hattie snapped.

"I'd like more water," Wanda said.

"I would, too," Ursula said.

Millie looked at their glasses. "I'll send someone over to your table to fill your glasses," she said.

"I'll have you know, Miss Collins," Hattie said, "that Roy Killian is taken. You keep your hands off him."

Millie took a step backward and a look of surprise suffused her face. "I beg your pardon?" she said.

"You know what I'm talking about, young lady," Hattie said. "I saw you batting your eyes at Roy and David a minute ago."

"You have good eyes, then," Millie said. "I smiled at them and thanked them for their patronage, as I do with all our customers. If you saw me bat my eyes, then I must have been having a fit."

"What?" Hattie asked.

Millie smiled. It was an indulgent smile such as one would use with the simple, or the very daft. "I'm saying that I normally do not bat my eyes at anyone, madam. So I must have had a severe tic or a mild case of Saint Vitus' dance that affected my eyelids. I'll see that your water glasses are filled, ladies."

With that, Millie turned and left the table. Hattie's mouth sagged open. "Was she making fun of me?" she asked.

Both Ursula and Wanda suppressed giggles, which nevertheless seeped out of their mouths as titters.

"Now you're both making fun of me," Hattie said, squirming like some large bird ruffling its feathers.

"No, Mother," Wanda said. "It's just funny, that's all."

"What's funny?"

"Millie. Her tic. Her eyes with the Saint Vitus' dance."

Ursula began to laugh aloud. She covered her mouth with a napkin, but the damage was done.

"I will not sit here and be mocked," Hattie said. "Wanda, you ought to be ashamed of yourself."

Wanda looked at Ursula and burst into laughter. Ursula could no longer hold back her mirth and she began to laugh louder. Hattie glared at both of them and shoved her chair away from the table with a loud scraping noise.

"I'm leaving," Hattie said. "When you two get over your girlish cruelty, I'll be outside."

Wanda looked at her mother and tried to speak, but only doubled up with laughter. Hattie shook herself into a tight turn and clumped across the room and out the door.

"It *was* pretty funny," Wanda told Ursula. "Wasn't it?"

"Hilarious," Ursula said, still chuckling.

"I mean, what Millie said."

"Yes. What Millie said. Very funny."

And the two continued to laugh until the boy came with a pitcher of water and poured their glasses full.

"Seriously," Wanda said, "I don't believe Millie is any threat to me, with Roy and all."

"No, I don't think so, either."

"But, she does have her eye on Martin Baron."

"Now that he's a widower," Ursula said, "isn't he fair game?"

Wanda drew a breath and, as if withholding more laughter, let it out and said, "For any woman with an eye tic." Then Wanda leaned back and laughed until tears seeped from her eyes.

"Or the Saint Vitus' dance," Ursula said, and they both laughed so hard, everyone in the Longhorn turned to stare at them.

Later they drained their water glasses and wiped their eyes dry, and when they left, they strolled like two ladies of dignity who would never behave in a silly manner for any reason whatsoever.

18

ROY STOPPED AT the counter and paid Millie for the breakfasts.

"Be careful, Roy," Millie said, handing him his change.

"Oh, I don't expect much will happen today, ma'am."

"You never know," Millie said.

Outside, Roy let out a long breath. " 'Egods, them women are a caution," he said.

"They've got you pretty well hemmed in," David admitted.

"I don't blame them none, but I wisht, sometimes, they'd just leave me alone."

"They care about you, especially your mother."

"They're smotherin' me, Dave, for danged sure."

The two men walked to the livery stables down the street. They could hear the hammering inside, but it was mild compared to the din they heard when they opened the door and walked in. Ken Richman waved to them and said something they could not hear. Five men surrounded an oversized wagon that consisted of a large bed and struts of planed boards on each of the four corners. Two other men worked on wide flat boards that they were hinged together with wood screws.

"Is that it?" Roy asked, when he got close enough to yell into Ken's ear.

"Just about finished. What do you think?"

"It might work," Roy said.

"It'll damned sure work. Martin's counting on it."

"His idea?" David asked.

Ken nodded. His face was oiled with sweat, florid from the heat inside the stable. Stains spread from his armpits onto the shirt that was plastered to his back. He reached into a pocket and pulled out a folded sheet of paper. He unfolded it and showed David and Roy a set of drawings.

Roy whistled and David smiled and nodded as he looked over each picture.

"When in hell did Martin draw this?" Roy asked.

"Yesterday. Right after the funeral, when we went to the house. He just sat down in Caroline's office room and drew it all out and said he needed the wagon built by today. Some of these men have been working all night."

"What are those boards jutting out from under the wagon bed for?" Roy asked. He pointed to the drawing and then to the wagon itself, where he saw that the boards were actually poles.

"Come on over here," Ken said, "and I'll show you how it'll all work."

David and Roy followed Ken over to the wagon. When they looked inside, they saw that there were boxed-in places all around the bed, and nails driven every two inches, twenty-penny nails, at that.

"Those poles are wide enough so that two men can grip each pole and carry, or turn, the wagon," Ken said.

"Why did he box the bed on all four sides?" David asked.

"Those open from the inside," Ken explained. "We'll put sandbags inside. For protection against rifle and pistol fire."

"And the nails sticking up from them?" Roy asked.

"To hold more sandbags, with spaces in between for rifles to poke through."

"Like a fort on wheels," Roy said.

"Not only on wheels, but the whole shebang can be lifted up by sixteen men and turned on a dime."

"And what are those panels with hinges?" David asked.

"Those will enclose the entire wagon," Ken said. "And I'll rig ropes through eyeholes, so that all four sides can come down when the fighting starts."

"Hmm," David said. "Let me see those drawings again." Ken handed him the sheet of paper. Roy and David both studied it.

"I see," Roy said. "When it's all set up, it will look like a chuck wagon or such."

"That's right," Ken said. "Nothing will show. There will be men inside, and underneath. There will be skirts hanging down from the wagon bed to hide those men who will man the poles. The skirts will drop like veils when a single rope is pulled and the wagon will still be supported by the wheels."

David walked over to one of the poles in the center of the wagon. He leaned over and pretended to lift it. "Damned ingenious," he said. "The poles are placed just right so the wheels can be lifted off the ground."

Roy stepped away and looked at the wagon again, then closed his eyes. In his mind he saw the men hunkered down inside, and the men bent over, huddled beneath the skirted wagon. Then he saw the men emerge from underneath and grab the poles, move the wagon 180 degrees, then swing it in another direction. He saw the cannon mounted atop the wagon, manned by two Mexicans, and those at the sides, front and rear, aiming rifles and shooting at charging attackers.

"Slick," Roy said. "When will it be ready?"

"We're just about finished," Ken said. "Al will be over here any minute now and ride back with you boys."

"What about the cannon?" David asked.

"It's already at the Box B. That's the last thing to be mounted, and Martin wanted to supervise that himself. I'm sending along several kegs of black powder and some ball shot. He'll have everything he needs."

"I hope it works," Roy said.

"It'll work," Ken said. "Martin will make it work."

"Did you know Anson left the Box B this morning?" Roy asked.

"Martin said he wasn't going to stay there and fight Matteo."

"How do you figure that?"

"Anson is his own man. He and Martin don't get along too well sometimes."

"But it's Anson's ranch, not Martin's."

Ken shook his head. "On paper, maybe. But that's Martin's ranch and Anson knows it always will be, no matter whose name is on the deed."

"It don't make sense," Roy said.

"Martin's blood was on that land long before Anson's was, Roy. Both men know it. Anson is stubborn, but he's smart, too. He knows Martin wouldn't give up that ranch without a fight. Maybe he left because he wanted Martin to play out the hand."

Roy and David exchanged looks. David shrugged. "I don't know the man," he said. "Anson, either."

"Anson runs deep," Roy said.

"Well, Martin sure isn't any shallow ditch," David said.

Ken laughed. "You'll never figure it out, if you live to be a hundred years old. Anson has a deep respect for Martin, and Martin, I think, doesn't really know what makes Anson tick. There were too many years when Martin was gone and Anson was growing into a man. Big gap there that Martin hasn't yet figured out."

"Funny," Roy said. "Martin gave me my land but I always thought the gift came from Anson. In a roundabout way."

"Maybe it did," Ken said.

"I sure thought Anson would be right up there in front if anyone tried to take the Box B away from him."

"Well, the bad blood is between Martin and Matteo. Anson hardly knows anything about the Aguilar family. Martin knows it all."

"Hell, *I* don't even know much of it," Roy said.

"And you don't want to," Ken said, turning back to supervise the finishing touches on the wagon.

Just then Al Oltman entered the livery, followed by Ed Wales. Al's face was contorted with worry and Ed's complexion was ashen.

Ken looked up from one of the wheels and straightened when he saw the faces of the two men.

"Something happen?" Ken asked.

"Fort Sumter was fired on," Wales said. "Confederate forces."

"Lincoln's calling for volunteers," Al added. "It sure as hell looks like war."

"When?" Ken asked.

"A couple of weeks ago, April twelfth," Wales said. "I just got the news from a rider who came in from Austin. Throckmorton's now a brigadier general."

"Where in hell is Fort Sumter?" Roy asked. "Somewhere in Texas?"

"It's in South Carolina," Wales said. "Close enough. There's going to be a civil war, for sure."

"Sumter's a federal garrison," Al said. "Lincoln wants volunteers to preserve the Union. It's war, all right."

"Jesus," Roy said. "And Texas *is* the Confederacy, right?"

"Right," Al said. "But there's hell to pay in Austin and Fort Worth and everywhere else. People are already choosing up sides. Some want the Union to stay put; others want the Confederacy to break away. Throckmorton's a secesh, and so is most of the government."

"We'd better tell the womenfolk," David said.

"They already know," Wales said. "I'm getting out an Extra, but the whole town is buzzing with the news."

"That wagon ready, Ken?" Al asked.

"Two minutes," Ken said.

"Well, we'd better get it rolling pretty quick. When Aguilar gets this news, he's liable to start war on Martin Baron quicker'n you can blink your eye."

"Lopez, you got that wheel set?" Ken asked one of the Mexicans.

"It is ready, I have give it the grease."

"You can take this to Martin now," Ken said. "Tell him I wish him luck."

"I've got to get back," Wales said. Nobody paid him any attention as he scurried from the livery.

The Mexicans brought mules out of stalls and hooked up the wagon. When it was all boarded up and skirted, it looked like a box on wheels.

Roy took the lead, with David and Al as flankers. They rode through the town and not a soul showed any curiosity whatsoever. The people were gathered together in clumps and some were waiting by the *Bugle* offices for the paper to come out. Roy looked everywhere for his mother, Hattie, and Wanda, but he didn't see them. David looked, too, and his face was wooden as they left Baronsville behind in a spool of dust.

Roy's heart quickened. If there really was going to be a war between the North and the South, he might have to fight for the Confederacy. He looked back at David and wondered where his loyalties might lie. There was something exciting about the prospect of war, he had to admit. But there was also a feeling of dread that filled his heart like a dark shadow drifting across the face of the land as a black cloud obscured the light of the sun.

19

PEEBO LOOKED UP at the Big Dipper for the sixth time. His gaze swept the constellation, fixed on the polestar once again. He shook off a touch of giddiness and lowered his head to readjust himself to level ground.

"Just where in hell did you stake out them packhorses, anyway?" Peebo asked.

"Back there," Anson said, his curt tone cryptic as the night itself.

" 'Back there'? Back where?"

"Yonder."

"Well, son, there's all kinds of 'yonder's and I'm wondering why we're heading south instead of east all of a sudden."

"Oh, you noticed that, did you?"

"Well, I ain't blind. I can see that North Star same as you, and we're headin' south of it."

"We're going to cut west in a while," Anson said.

"West?"

"Somethin' I want to show you, when the sun comes up."

Peebo looked to the east and saw the horizon paling, turning a lighter color than the stygian blackness of the sky overhead.

"Seems to me you'd be ridin' in circles, son."

"A half-circle, really."

"Mind tellin' this old son why and what for?"

"Reckon I can, now," Anson said, and he turned his horse to the west and they rode through clumps of mesquite glistening with starshine and ducked under branches until they came out in the open plain turning pewter in the soft eastern glow that spread skyward behind them. " 'Member when I took off after the funeral and followed Bone's tracks?"

"Yeah, and then you and that Lorene . . ."

"That ain't got nothin' to do with what I'm tellin' you, Peebo," Anson snapped.

"Well, you said those were Bone's tracks, I recollect."

"He come over to the Box B for a look-see and then he rode back toward the Rocking A. I aim to track him on back and see what's going on there. Bone had a reason to come over that day, and that means Matteo Aguilar probably sent him to spy on us."

"So?"

"So I'm thinkin' that Matteo must be mighty close to makin' his move. If Dave Wilhoit was right and Matteo plans to run us off the Box B, I want to make sure he doesn't get very far."

"Your pa know about this?"

"No."

"That's what I thought. You told him he had to fight this battle without you and here you are going after Matteo toe-to-toe. How come all the secrecy, son?"

"Coupla reasons," Anson said, so low Peebo had to strain to hear him above the scrape and plod of the horses' hooves. "He's got a lot on his mind, already, with Ma's death and his grief, and Aguilar breathin' down his neck. And if he thinks I'm gone, he'll fight all the harder to keep the ranch from that Mexican bastard Matteo."

"There ain't no packhorses waitin' for us back yonder, are there?"

"Nope."

"Any other surprises you got, Anson?"

"A couple, maybe."

Peebo kept silent and so did Anson as they doubled back toward the trail Bone had left two days before. Then Anson turned to the south again, and as the dawn broke, Peebo was amazed to see that they were right on track. He could see the hoofprints of Bone's horse going in two directions. The wind had blown dirt into them, but he knew they were the same tracks as the ones Anson had found after his mother's funeral.

Then Anson halted his horse and held up his hand to stop Peebo from riding on.

"What's wrong?" Peebo asked.

"Nothing. Just wait." Anson whistled like a meadowlark, a curly, high trill that sounded remarkably like the bird itself.

In a moment, there was an answering call.

"I'll bet a Dixie dollar that warn't no meadowlark callin' back," Peebo said.

Anson merely smiled and kicked his horse in the flanks.

The Mexicans were waiting in a copse of trees, mixed mesquite and scrub oaks, wreathed in veils of blue-gray smoke from their cigarillos that smelled, on the morning air, like burning rope. There were five of them, none of whom Peebo recognized, although he thought he might have seen one of them the evening before, talking to Anson when it was getting dark.

"Listo?" Anson asked.

The man apart replied. *"Estamos listos."*

"Follow me and Peebo, Timo."

The lone man nodded. Four cigarettes went out like winking sparks. Peebo saw that the men carried rifles and all wore two pistols in their belts, old cap-and-balls, that rode high on their hips. The rifles were short-barreled carbines, single-shot muzzle-loaders jutting out of handmade scabbards, with large trigger guards and single triggers. He could see, even in that early light, that some of the rifles were rusted and had long since lost their bluing. They appeared to have been made in Mexico, but they could have been manufactured in Spain, Peebo reckoned.

"You don't need to know all their names, Peebo," Anson said. "The head man is Timoteo Fuentes. They're all dead shots."

"Where in hell did you find them?"

"They have been working for me for over a year. I keep them away from the others because they double as guards and hunters. But everyone is a true vaquero and can rope and ride with the best of them."

"Were these the hands you were going to take to go after that white bull?"

"They're about the only ones who aren't superstitious about *el diablo blanco.*"

"Christ, you mean business, don't you?"

"I always mean business, Peebo."

Peebo snorted and looked back at the men who were following him, Anson, and Timo. Their faces bore no expression. They were dark Mexicans, more Indian than Spanish blood in their veins, he guessed, with high, florid cheekbones and oriental eyes, no moustaches or beards, bandannas lazed around their necks, ball-and-powder pouches were slung to their shoulders, and each kept one hand on his rifle stock, ready to jerk it free of its scabbard.

The wind stayed down and the sun rose in the sky until it beat down on them like Vulcan's hammer, and Peebo felt the sweat run down his sides and legs and into his boots. He slapped at flies without making any noise and listened to the swish of his horse's tail as it drove off the ones he missed.

When they reached the edge of the property around the Aguilar ranch house, Bone's tracks veered off to the west and Anson followed those until he sighted the casitas surrounding Matteo's home. Voices drifted to their ears from an unseen location beyond Matteo's house. Anson held up his hand, halting the small column.

"We go on foot from here," Anson said to Peebo. He spoke to the Mexicans in Spanish, telling them to dismount. All of them slipped their rifles from their scabbards and stood waiting for their orders. Peebo slid his rifle from its boot and checked the flint and pan. There was a thin haze of powder in the small bowl and he closed the frizzen. "I told the Mexicans to spread out and lie flat on the ground," he said to Peebo.

"I heard you. I speak a little Mexican myself, you know."

"Yeah. Well, you and I are going to sneak up to Matteo's house and see what all the jabbering's about. Think you can stay low and keep quiet?"

"Son, just think of me as a piece of stone rolling across a thick old rug. I won't make a sound. You goin' after Bone?"

"No. I just wanted to make sure he was spyin' for Aguilar."

"Lead on," Peebo said, with a wave of his hand.

Peebo followed Anson's movements as they hunched over and started moving through cover toward the main ranch house. The voices grew louder as they approached. They went from tree to tree and then Anson lowered himself to the ground in a squat, and duck-waddled closer. Peebo began to see an opening and the silhouettes of men walking back and forth. As they came to the edge of the clearing around the house, Peebo's eyes widened.

Matteo was barking orders to marching men, a dozen, while others were taking positions behind wagons and trees, going after one another in mock attacks. Reynaud stood beside Matteo. Mickey Bone was some distance from the marchers, watching them with narrowed eyes from his perch on the top rail of a small corral.

The marching men stopped at a command from Matteo, and scattered, threw themselves headlong and aimed their rifles at imaginary targets. Then a half-dozen Mexicans rode up on horseback and pointed their rifles at the concealed men. These riders flared out and circled, flanking those on the ground. It was a beautiful, smooth maneuver, worthy of any execution on horseback by the best plains Indians.

"Jesus God," Peebo said softly.

Anson kept silent, looking at each man, and holding his gaze for several seconds on Reynaud, who wore a brace of pistols on his belt and was dressed in clothes more suitable for a parlor social than a rough ranch with dozens of Mexicans playing war.

Matteo barked an order and the marching men broke formation, encircled the house as those on horseback formed another, moving ring around them, mock-firing at the house as they rode. Peebo watched this maneuver, his scalp prickling at the precision the Mexicans demonstrated. The Mexicans on the ground ran in zigzag patterns, staying low, presenting difficult targets to anyone who might be besieged within the house.

"It doesn't look good, Anson."

"No. Those men are well trained."

Matteo whistled and the men withdrew from their positions, gathered around him and Reynaud. Two women walked around the corner of the house, from the front, and headed toward the assemblage.

"Who are they?" Peebo whispered.

"One of 'em's Matteo's wife. I don't know who the other'n is."

A moment later Dawn walked over to stand by Bone, and Anson nodded.

"Bone's wife," Peebo said.

"Looks like."

They could not hear what Matteo was saying, but the fighting men all were listening, leaning on their rifles, but not fidgeting. Peebo strained to hear, but Matteo spoke in rapid Spanish and he could only catch parts of certain words. At the end of his speech, Matteo raised one arm and made a fist with his hand.

"To victory!" he shouted in Spanish.

And the Mexicans all cheered and two or three among them began to order them to disperse. Soon the yard was empty, except for Matteo, Reynaud, Bone, and the two women.

"Looks like they're just about ready to march on the Box B," Peebo said, sotto voce.

"I heard Matteo say they would leave tonight," Anson said.

"Son, you've got good ears."

"I just caught part of it. I didn't get the time. Could be right after dark, or just before dawn."

"Yeah. Let's get the hell out of here. What are you going to do? Warn your pa?"

"No time for that."

The two men slithered backward, careful not to make any noise, and when they were well out of earshot of Matteo and the others, they stood up and started walking back toward the place where they had left their horses with the Mexican hands. Peebo looked at Anson every few minutes. Anson seemed to be mulling over something in his mind, and Peebo kept silent, not wanting to break into his friend's thoughts.

Instead Peebo thought about what he had just witnessed, while feeling an elusive sense of deep dread. Matteo's band functioned like an army in miniature, responding to commands, executing precise maneuvers, moving swiftly and decisively on their targets with cunning and craft. He wondered if Martin and his small group of Mexican workers and friends could withstand the onslaught of a trained army such as Matteo had.

Anson stopped to relieve himself and Peebo unbuttoned his fly to stand alongside him under the shade of a mesquite tree. They watched their yellow streams roil the dirt and pock it with small holes such as doodlebugs make in the earth.

"It looks right bad, Anson. I don't think your pa realizes what he's facin' up to with Aguilar."

"No, I reckon not," Anson said, sliding the buttons on his fly through the fastening slits. "That's why we've got to even up the odds some."

"What are you aimin' to do?" Peebo shook the dew from his penis and tucked the organ back in his trousers.

"I've been thinkin' about that."

"And?"

"The most reasonable thing to do would be to ride back and tell Pa what we seen and give him some help with our guns."

"But you ain't goin' to do that, are you, son?"

Anson sighed. "Nope. We might not make it back in time to warn Pa, and even if we did, it would only cause confusion. Some of the hands might just light a shuck and leave us short on fighting men."

"Well, we can't stave off a bunch that size. Hell, they'd overrun us like cattle in a stampede, trample us to dust without so much as a howdy-do."

"Yeah. True. We can't go at them in any regular way. Matteo's done a good job with his men. They act like damned soldiers."

"We can rag their heels," Peebo said. "Cut 'em up, scatter 'em, maybe."

Anson looked at Peebo with a rigid intensity as if trying to read his mind.

"Just a quick suggestion," Peebo said, after those moments of silence.

"Might slow 'em down some," Anson said. "But it might get us killed, too. No, I think Matteo has probably thought of such a situation. He'll have men front and back on the march and flankers. We wouldn't have much of a chance."

"Yeah, we might get off one shot apiece before he was down on us like stink on a skunk's ass."

"Let's go," Anson said. "We can talk along the way. I don't want my hands to get jumpy."

"Hell, they ain't got nothin' to be jumpy about. They didn't see what we seen."

As they approached the waiting Mexican hands, Anson stopped suddenly and Peebo almost bumped into him.

"There might be a way," Anson said.

"To stop Aguilar?"

"Yeah."

"I'm all ears, son."

"What's the best way to kill a snake, Peebo?"

"Hell, I don't know. Chop it up into a dozen pieces. Stomp it to death."

"Or cut off its head."

Peebo thought about that for a moment. "You mean, kill Aguilar right off?"

"He's the head of that snake back there."

"I reckon."

"You don't like the idea," Anson said.

"No, it makes sense. If you could get him off by hisself. But there's something you're not thinkin' about, 'pears to me."

"What's that?"

"That snake's got two heads. The Frenchie. Reynaud."

"You think so?"

"Or maybe three heads."

"Three?"

"Yeah. Bone."

Anson drew in a breath as if to clear his mind. Peebo regarded him with solemnity.

"I almost forgot about Bone," Anson said.

"I don't know if them greasers would foller him, but 'twixt him and Reynaud, they might just get mad as hell if we kilt Aguilar, and come after us like hornets on fire."

The Mexican hands started to walk their way, as if wanting to hear what the two men were saying. Peebo grinned at them, but they did not look as if they were fooled.

"Well, you got any better ideas?" Anson asked quickly.

"Nary a one," Peebo said. "I just wisht we was chasin' after that white bull instead of standin' out here talkin' about how you, me, and these here Mexicans are going to stop a damned army."

"Well, we're going to damned sure do something," Anson said, as the Mexicans came up on them.

"Que pasa?" Timo asked.

Anson did not answer. Timo looked at Peebo, his eyebrows arched like caterpillars in midstride.

"You boys ready for a fight?" Peebo said, grinning as if he were inviting them to a fiesta on the president of Mexico's manicured lawn.

20

URSULA SWAM THROUGH layers of sleep, struggling upward from the dream of drowning, fighting off suffocation. Shreds of scenes from the dream began to fray at the edges and fall off, like articles of clothing, and sink back down into the depths, out of memory, blurring as they fell until they vanished. The faces of people in the dream twisted and corkscrewed until they lost all identity and floated off like misshapen blobs of oily substance and the names attached to them no longer made sense.

But one of the dream people resembled her son, Roy, or represented him, while another seemed to be Martin Baron, and she was sure that another man had to be her dead husband, Jack Killian, for it was he who kept trying to hand her a rifle and when she finally took it, it came apart and she kept trying to put it back together, but the parts were all crooked, and the one who seemed to be Roy in a different guise, kept running away from her and when he stopped, he was using the broken rifle as a cane and he hobbled away and the man who seemed to be Martin took the cane and made a box out of it and the box kept getting bigger and bigger until it was a maze of boxes that became a house on a hill that was surrounded by faceless men carrying pitchforks and knives that flashed like lightning in a black stormy sky, and she wandered through the rooms of the house looking for her son and her dead husband and saw Hattie and Wanda sitting down at a table and they seemed to be praying in a foreign language that she could not understand and then she saw Roy sitting in the middle of the table. He was tied up with ropes that wriggled like writhing snakes and Wanda gave him a fork that, instead of tines, had four barrels that leaked smoke as if they were pistols that had been fired, and when she tried to enter the room, a man who looked like Matteo Aguilar appeared out of nowhere and barred her way and his face turned black and his eyes blazed red and he changed into David, who was crying red tears that filled the room and covered the table and the women ran away into a large box that closed up behind them and became a large empty field that bordered a stand of corn. As she approached, the cornstalks became rifles and they belched green smoke and bent their barrels to face her, and they boomed like thunder and she felt herself falling down, down, into a house that was like the one she and David lived in on the Rocking A and then it became a wagon filled with dead men who nevertheless cried out to her and seemed like lifeless beggars asking for money and they all disappeared when she was about to land in their midst and she moaned in terror as the dream broke off and left her breathless.

She gasped for breath as she bobbed up like a cork in her bed, drawing precious air into her lungs as if she had actually been underwater and had suddenly surfaced. On waking, the last dregs of the terrible dream crumbled into dusty fragments that made no sense and dissolved into powdery scraps that blew into nothingness like smoke before a high wind.

She sat up, bewildered, felt beside her for David, knowing he was gone, had been gone all night. She looked down at the empty place where he should be and fragments of the dream began filtering up into her consciousness. She tried to hold the images steady in her mind so that she could study them and determine their meaning. She knew that they meant something. Then, she let them all go and slid over to the edge of the bed. She leaned down and felt under the bed for her slippers.

She put them on her feet and stood up. It was very early in the morning. The sun was not up, but she heard the clank of plates in the main quarters where her son lived with Hattie and Wanda. She smelled the fragrant aroma of coffee and the smell stirred still more memories of the dream.

She walked to the small dresser and looked down at the bowl of water she had filled the night before. She leaned over and dipped both hands in the bowl and splashed her face. The cobwebs lacing her brain began to dissipate, but the subtle portions of her dream eluded her, yet some crumbs still remained.

She heard voices through the walls as she dabbed a small towel at her face to dry it off. She pushed her hair back with both hands and walked to the wardrobe David had built for her. It had no door on it, but her clothes hung there neatly on wooden pegs. She put a light wrapper on and padded toward the door.

She stepped outside and walked to the other door that led into Roy's house. She knocked on it loudly, peering around in the darkness as if expecting to be attacked by some wild animal. More of the dream pushed up in her mind, disturbing little bits and pieces that still made no sense.

"Come in," Wanda called. "Ursula, that you?"

"Yes," Ursula said, pushing the door open. She was glad that it was not latched. She shuffled through the main room and into the kitchen and dining area where the lamps dispelled the gloom and dark from the other room. Wanda and her mother were sitting at the table in their robes, sipping coffee from tin cups just like cowhands.

"Good morning, Ursula," Wanda said, in a cheery voice. "We couldn't sleep."

" 'Morning."

Wanda had her hair tied in curls and she looked as if she had fallen into a sack full of cotton and bolls had stuck to her hair. Hattie had her hair wrapped in a bandanna, but a few tufts stuck out and these were tied with white cloth, as well. Both women were red-eyed from lack of sleep and looked haggard, with bags under their eyes that looked like the shadows of mice.

"Coffee?" Wanda asked.

Ursula sat down and nodded. She cleared her throat of nightsand and waited while Hattie arose and got a cup from the cupboard and poured it full of steaming coffee. There was sugar on the table, but Ursula did not spoon any into her cup.

"Bad night?" Hattie asked, as Ursula stared down into the black pool of coffee in her cup.

"I had bad dreams," Ursula said.

"Dreams are cautions," Hattie said. "Portents."

"I don't know," Ursula said.

"Ma, you don't know anything about dreams," Wanda said. "Don't you go scaring Ursula."

"Dreams don't scare me," Ursula said, "but this one disturbed me." She finally picked up her cup and tipped it to her lips. Steam frosted her mouth for a moment as she blew on the liquid to cool it.

"What was the dream about?" Hattie asked, a quiver of excitement in her voice.

"I'm not sure. It's all so confusing. But I know this dream means something. At times it seemed so real. I know my boy was in it. And Martin and David."

"See?" Hattie said. "There's meaning to that there dream."

"Pshaw," Wanda said. Then she tried to change the subject. "We thought we'd string beans today. Pick them first, of course. It's so quiet around here with the men gone."

"What do you think the dream meant?" Hattie asked. Her eyes glittered like beads of sorghum.

"I don't know," Ursula said, "but I have the feeling there's some meaning there. That there's something I must do."

"You can help us string up the beans," Wanda said, an airy lilt to her voice.

"There were signs in that dream, Ursula," Hattie said. She licked her lips like a cat yearning for a feast.

"When I left my room, I had the overpowering urge to go over to the Baron ranch, be with David and Roy. I think the dream had something to do with going over there."

"You mean . . ." Wanda said, suddenly interested.

"I mean, maybe we should help Martin. Or something."

"That could be it," Hattie said.

"What do you think of Martin Baron?" Wanda asked point-blank.

"Me?" Ursula said. "Well, I don't know him very well, of course. He seems good-hearted. He gave Roy this piece of property."

"Don't you blame him for the death of your husband?"

"I had some resentments. But Jack was a wild one. I was sometimes surprised he lived as long as he did. He was a horse thief and he had killed men."

"What about Martin's son?" Wanda asked. "Do you like him?"

"Anson? I don't really know him. Roy sets a great deal of store in him, I guess."

"I don't know him, either," Wanda said, "but I think it's terrible that he's run off and left his father to fight for the ranch by himself."

"I heard that, I guess," Ursula said. "Roy didn't say much about it. Said that was the way Anson was."

"But I heard Anson really owns the ranch," Wanda said. "So why wouldn't he fight for it?"

"He's a strange one, that Anson," Hattie said.

"Mother, you don't know him, either," Wanda said.

"I know he doesn't respect his father."

"No you don't.

"He didn't even cry at his mother's funeral."

"Who?" Wanda asked. "Anson or Martin?"

"I think Martin cried," Hattie said. "I know Anson didn't shed a tear. He's a cold one. Hard-hearted."

Ursula sighed. "He does seem distant, at times. I noticed that girl, the doctor's niece, staring at him all during the funeral."

"Then she went chasing after him after he left. He didn't even come to the condolences," Hattie said. "Uppity, that's what he is."

"Mother, don't go judging people," Wanda said.

"He's cold, that one," Hattie said again. "Cold as ice."

Ursula leaned back as if exhausted from thinking and picked up her cup again. She blew on it and let coffee trickle into her mouth. Now, after uttering those words about going to the Box B, the dream seemed to resurface in her mind, and parts of it became more clear all of a sudden.

"Well, we could go over there," Wanda said, musing aloud.

"We should go over there," Ursula said. "In fact, I am going over there. As soon as I get dressed."

"I'll go with you," Wanda said.

"We'll all go," Hattie said, caught up in the others' enthusiasm. "Better than sitting around here, stringing up beans."

"I think Roy and David would want us there," Ursula said. "I'm not afraid of a fight. Lord knows, I had enough of them with Roy's father."

"Neither am I," Wanda said, sitting up straight. "I can shoot a rifle or pistol with the best of any man."

"Me too," Hattie said.

Ursula smiled. "I've shot mad dogs and meat myself. I still have a pistol my father gave me. I'll get it out."

"We have pistols, too," Hattie said, "and we keep them loaded. We'll show that Aguilar a thing or two."

Ursula looked at the other two women and beamed. Then she began to think of the enormity of her decision, and theirs. But she knew her thoughts had been guided by the dream of moments before. She knew, in her heart, that she was supposed to fight alongside her men. Mixed with the resolve, though, was a growing fear that she might be interfering with destiny, with fate. She began to feel faint and she sat back in her chair and blinked her eyes as Hattie and Wanda began to waver out of focus.

"What's wrong?" Wanda asked.

"Are you all right, Ursula?" Hattie started to get up out of her chair.

"I just wonder if we're doing the right thing. I mean, Roy didn't say anything yesterday in town, and neither did David."

"You don't look well," Hattie said.

"I'm all right."

Wanda finished drinking her coffee and arose from her chair. Hattie sat there, looking at Ursula.

Ursula touched a hand to her forehead as if to steady herself. She found she was able to focus and she stared back at Hattie.

"I think I'm frightened of this war everybody's talking about," Ursula said.

"You mean with this Aguilar feller?"

"No, I mean the war between the South and North."

"I just hope Roy doesn't have to fight in it," Wanda said, finally leaving the room. Then, "Or David, either."

"What's the world coming to?" Hattie asked of no one. "If you ask me, all of this trouble can be laid right at President Lincoln's doorstep."

Ursula was no longer listening. She got up from the table and turned away from Hattie, started for the door. After she left, Hattie muttered to herself, then spoke aloud.

"Some people are just downright rude and ungrateful," she said, and poured herself another cup of coffee. Outside, the eastern sky began to lighten and she leaned over and lifted the chimney on the lamp and blew out the flame.

21

MARTIN RUBBED THE granules of sleep from his eyelids and turned on his bed to look out the window. It was still pitch-dark outside, but he heard noises downstairs, noises that had awakened him: the clank of a pan, the scrape of chair legs, the light patter of footsteps. The crickets had gone silent, but he heard the leathery flap of a whippoorwill's call and the far-off bawl of a cow lowing for its calf.

"Damn," he said. "Shoulda been up already by now."

His voice sounded strange to him in the hollow room. Caroline's room. He had slept there, after debating with himself about it the night before. He had felt strange coming into the room; its emptiness shrieked at him through the empty silence and when he smelled the cloying scent of Caroline's perfume still clinging to her clothes and her bed, the tears had welled up unbidden in his eyes. It had taken him a long while to slip into sleep. He kept hearing her footsteps on the hardwood floors, and hearing her whispers in the darkness, whispers that he was certain called out his name.

He finally realized that he was just hearing things, that his memory was playing subtle tricks on him, and had fallen asleep to the soothing orchestras of crickets and the soft sough of the wind sniffing at the eaves and brushing gently against the windowpanes.

Martin had not dreamed, or if he had, could remember none, and he was grateful for that. His mind was cluttered enough as it was, with worry over when Matteo might attack, and how he should make ready for such an event. He did not want to be kept prisoner in his own house, nor did he want to cry wolf if Matteo was not coming. But he had to be ready, and he had to make sure he was not caught by surprise.

He left Caroline's room and walked to his own. He slipped on a clean pair of trousers and a shirt, brushed his hair and rubbed his beard to see if he needed to shave that morning. There was stubble, but he could go another day. The aroma of coffee wafted to his nostrils and he left his room to go downstairs, drink a cup to clear away the last of the cobwebs in his sleep-silked brain.

The house was dark except for the stream of yellow-orange light that leaked around the closed kitchen door. Martin walked toward it, his boots ringing loud on the hardwood flooring. The noises in the kitchen stopped as he drew closer and when he opened the door, he saw Esperanza rising from the table as if to leave. Lucinda stood by the stove, frozen there, while Lazaro had ducked his head under the table as if to hide.

"Good morning," Martin said in Spanish.

The women replied in kind. Esperanza bowed slightly. "I am going," she said.

"No, do not leave," Martin told her. "I wish to talk to you."

"To me? Why?"

"Anson said that I should. Is Lazaro going to stay under that table? What is he afraid of?"

"He is afraid of you, my *patrón*," Esperanza said.

"Well, there's no need. Finish your breakfast, Lazaro. Esperanza, have you finished eating?"

"Yes," she said quickly.

"Sit," Martin commanded. Esperanza sat back down in her chair. Martin sat down and looked at Lucinda. "Just coffee."

"Yes, *Patrón*," she said, and went to the cupboard for a cup.

"What is it you wish to speak to me about?" Esperanza asked.

"In a moment. I do not think we should speak about this while Lazaro is here."

"I will go," Lazaro said. He had slithered back in his chair without making a sound.

"No, finish breaking your fast," Martin said. "I will speak to Esperanza after I have finished my coffee."

"I do not have hunger," Lazaro said. His plate sat before him, and Martin could see that he had not eaten much of his beans or beef. There was a half-eaten tortilla there, too. Esperanza had not finished her meal, either.

Martin looked at Lazaro's dark, closed eyes, the way the lamplight emphasized the dark shadows that lined his closed lids. Lucinda had three lamps burning, the wicks turned up high, and whichever way Lazaro turned his head, his sightless eyes carried with them the darkness of his blindness.

"More coffee, Esperanza?" Lucinda asked, as she set a cup before Martin. Esperanza, her lips pursed tight, shook her head.

"What passes, Esperanza?" Martin asked.

"The vaqueros are already awake," she said. "They have eaten. Roy and David are up, too, and they are in the barn where the cannon is. The blacks are helping them with the heavy wagon."

"You see much," Martin said.

"The noise of the men awakened me," she said. "I am getting ready to leave."

"Leave?"

"I thought I would take Lazaro away from here and go back to Mexico."

"Why?"

"I just think it would be better now that the señora is gone. We do not feel at home here without Señora Caroline."

Martin cleared his throat, sipped at the hot coffee. Lucinda stood by, watching him as one would watch a man drinking poison. He looked at Esperanza and tried to smile.

"You and the boy are welcome here," he said in English. "There is no need for you to leave just because my wife is not here. You will be paid as always."

"I think I will be more happy if I take Lazaro away and go to Mexico. *Queremos salir.*"

Martin saw the stubborn jut of her jaw, heard the finality in her words. "Wait until after we talk, then decide what you wish to do."

"Our things are packed up in bundles. We are ready."

Martin turned to Lucinda. "Don't stand over me like that. Sit down, Lucinda. Eat. Drink some coffee."

Lucinda jumped as if sparked with a jolt of static electricity. Her hand flew to her mouth in embarrassment.

"No. I am sorry. Do you not have hunger? There is much to eat."

"No," Martin said, as Lucinda walked toward the stove. "I will drink my coffee and speak to Esperanza before I go to the barn."

"Very well," Lucinda said, and added a stick of wood to the firebox of the stove.

Esperanza sat there, looking stony-faced at Martin. Lazaro seemed frozen in his chair, listening to every sound. Martin couldn't swear to it, but he thought he could see the boy's ears twitching like a rabbit's. But, he realized, it was only an illusion.

Martin drank his coffee and drummed his fingers on the table. Lazaro cocked his head slightly as if trying to decipher the sound. Lucinda wiped the counter with a cloth. Esperanza stared at Martin and beyond him, seemingly lost in her own thoughts.

"I will go outside and fetch water," Lucinda said, grasping the handle of a pail on the kitchen counter. Martin nodded, but no one said anything. Her sandals made soft sounds on the floor and the back door opened and banged shut, deepening the thick silence in the kitchen.

Martin finished his coffee. Esperanza jumped up from her chair. *"Mas café?"*

"No," Martin said. "Do you wish to talk here or outside?" he asked Esperanza.

"We will talk here. Lazaro, go outside and tell Lucinda to wait until I come out."

Lazaro, without a word, shot out of his chair and fled the room. The back door cracked like a rifle shot when it slammed closed, and Esperanza's body seemed to jump as she stood there.

"Sit down," Martin said.

Esperanza sat down again and folded her hands in her lap. She was wearing a thin cotton dress dyed a light brown. She wore a small crucifix on a chain around her neck. Her hair was bunned in the back, with not a stray hair poking from its raven mass. Her dark eyes glittered like obsidian beads in the glow of the lamplight.

"What is it you wish to talk about?" she asked.

Martin squirmed in his chair, avoiding her piercing gaze while he composed himself. He stopped tapping his fingers on the table and then didn't know what to do with his hands. He sighed and drew in a deep breath, held it for a moment before he spoke.

"I reckon there's no way to pussyfoot around it," he said in English. Esperanza's eyebrows arched as if she didn't understand. "Might as well just come out with it. Anson said that you might tell me about Lazaro and my wife."

"Did he says that?" she asked in broken English.

"Yes," Martin said tightly.

"Well, I do not know what it is he wanted me to tell you."

"I think Anson believes that Lazaro did not give my wife the infection, the disease, that killed her."

"That is true."

"But did you not tell me that my wife took Lazaro to her bed at night?"

"Only to comfort him. And he gave her comfort, too."

"I do not understand."

"*Patrón*, your wife was given the disease before Lazaro was even born."

"What? How?"

"I do not know if you will believe me or not."

"Tell me. I will judge the truth of what you say."

"Then you must listen with care. What I tell you now is the truth. The señora did not want me to tell you this while she was alive. She knew it would make you angry. She knew that you would want revenge."

"I will not be angry. Tell me."

"It will do you no good to be angry now. The thing that happened to her was a long time ago."

"Are you going to tell me?" he asked.

"Be patient. It is difficult to tell, but it is the truth."

"Tell it. I am listening."

"One day, Señora Caroline and I were alone here in the house. Lucinda was in town buying the groceries. Augustino Aguilar rode up and gave the knock on the door. I let him inside the house as I was told to do. The señora was upstairs. She was not yet dressed. Augustino called up to her and she told him to wait, that she would soon come down."

Martin felt a cold chill down the back of his neck, but he felt warmth as his blood turned hot and rushed to his throat and face.

"Go on," he said, with a tightness in his voice, as if the words were hammered out of iron slabs.

"I asked Augustino if he wanted a cup and he said that he would take one. I went to get the whiskey and when I returned to the front room he was gone. I heard his boots striking the stairs as he ran up them. I stood there with the *copa* in my hand and I heard the door slam shut. I did not know what to do. I truly did not know what to do."

"Then what happened?" Martin asked.

Esperanza sighed deeply and went on with her account. "I heard footsteps. I heard voices. The voices became loud. I heard Augustino's voice. It was very loud. Then I heard a sound that was like a blow from a fist. I heard the sounds of hands slapping."

Martin stiffened as Esperanza paused to catch her breath and search her memory. He waited until she had composed herself, then nodded for her to continue.

"I heard the señora scream. I dropped the glass of whiskey. I listened some more. I listened very hard."

"And?" Martin interjected.

"It was quiet for a few little moments and then I heard the grunting from Augustino and I heard the señora weeping with loudness, with great fright."

"What did you do?"

"I lost all reason," Esperanza said. "I ran up the stairs and I went to the señora's room. The door was closed, but I pushed it open. I went inside and saw a most terrible thing, a most shameful thing."

"What did you see?" Martin asked, his voice full of a dry husk as if his throat was lined with parched gravel. "Speak English."

"The señora was on her bed, lying on her back and Augustino was mounting her. His trousers were wadded up at his ankles and he was between her legs. His body was rising up and down and I could see his stiff mast going in and out of the vagina of Caroline."

"What was she doing?" Martin's voice was so faint he could barely hear himself ask the question, and the question tore at his heart like the sudden jab of a locust thorn.

"She was fighting him. She was beating his shoulders with her fists and her face was wet with tears and her sobs sounded like the cries of a wounded animal."

"Jesus," Martin breathed.

Esperanza crossed herself.

"Tell me the rest of it," Martin said.

"I will try, *Patrón.* It is hard, remembering it. They did not see me and there was the heavy lead in my feet. I could not move. It was as if my shoes were nailed to the floor. Augustino kept slapping Caroline and she moaned and cried out and still she beat him with her fists but the blows only made Augustino go faster and then he yelled loud and fell on top of her. I knew that he had spilled his seed inside the womb of the señora. He smothered her with his body and she lay very still and stiff, like wood."

Martin fought to suppress his anger, clenching his teeth until they ground together to the point of cracking. His neck swelled with engorged blood as his anger crescendoed to a boiling rage. His bone-white lips quivered, and his brown eyes seemed to flash light even as they darkened in their sockets. He clenched his fists so tightly the knuckles blanched.

Esperanza drew back, away from Martin, as if repelled by his anger. Her eyes began to mist as she took in a breath that swelled her lungs so that her breasts pushed against the cloth of her dress.

"Augustino," she continued, "spat in the señora's face. Then, he lifted himself from her body and pulled up his pants."

"Did he see you?" Martin asked, his voice a raspy whisper.

"No. He leaned over and said to her in English something."

"What did he say?"

"He say, 'Now you got the pox, you bitch, and you and Martin are going to die like me.' "

"Christ."

Esperanza made the sign of the cross on her forehead and chest.

"Then I run away, but I don't make no noise, and I go downstairs and pick up the broken glass when Augustino he come down the stairs and walk past me and out the door. I wait until he go away on his horse and then I go upstairs."

"Damn. Why didn't Caroline tell me? I would have killed Augustino, the bastard."

"She say she don't want you to know what happened. She is crying and she want to take a bath. Her face is, *como se dice,* all puffed out and she is talking crazy talk. She say she wants to kill herself and I give her a bath and put some leaves on her face and the cold water and the swelling she goes down."

"Did Lucinda know what happened to my wife?"

"She don't know," Esperanza said. "Nobody know. The señora, she tell me don't say nothing and I don't say nothing to nobody."

Martin hung his head for a moment, shook it before he looked up at Esperanza.

"Thank you for telling me this. Don't tell anyone else."

"I don't tell nobody."

Martin got up from the table. "Tell Lazaro I am not angry with him, will you?"

"I will tell him," Esperanza said.

Dazed, Martin stalked from the room, went out the back door. He shook off a giddiness that made him nearly stumble on the last step of the small back porch. He walked toward the barn, gripped by an anger that nearly blinded him. He did not see Lucinda or Lazaro and he was glad that they could not see him.

Before he reached the barn, he heard a sound, then, out of the darkness, he saw Wanda Fancher's buggy rolling toward him. He ducked his head and walked on quickly. He heard Ursula call his name, but he did not answer, pretending not to hear her.

He heard sounds from inside the barn, but he waited outside for several moments, leaning against the outer wall. He let his anger subside as he thought about Caroline carrying that terrible secret with her to her grave. He felt suddenly alone and sad that he could not talk to her, could not tell her how much he loved her and missed her at that very moment.

He looked up at the sky and the stars until they blurred with the sudden tears that welled up in his eyes. Then he turned and drove a fist into the side of the barn. He did not feel the pain as his fist came away, the knuckles cracked and bleeding.

It was too bad, he thought, that Augustino was already dead, for he wanted to kill him at that moment, kill him with his bare hands.

"God damn the whole Aguilar family," he said. "God damn them all."

22

MATTEO LOOKED DOWN at the ground, his forehead creased with furrows made by worry wrinkles. One of his men, Hector Obispo, pointed to the tracks that led to the shallow wallows he had discovered. A moment later Mickey Bone walked up, following the line of tracks to that place.

"Well?" Matteo asked.

"Two men," Bone said. "They walked here less than two hours ago. Then they returned to a place with at least half a dozen horse tracks."

"Do you know who they were?"

"No," Bone said. "But they rode in from the direction of the Box B. I did not follow the horse tracks."

"Why?"

"Because I was on foot and because I was outnumbered."

"Shit," Matteo said.

"They did not go far, I think," Bone said.

"What else do you think?" Matteo asked, a sarcastic tilt to his words.

"I think one of those tracks there," he pointed to the ground, "belongs to Anson Baron."

"Why do you think that, Mickey?"

"Because I know his boot."

"So, it was Anson Baron."

"Or someone wearing his boots."

"Don't you act the *sabio* with me. You know damned well it was Anson Baron."

Mickey said nothing. Obispo's face bore a sheepish look. He had been patrolling the outer edges of the land bordering the ranch when he discovered the tracks less than a half hour before. He had left right after finishing the maneuvers the onlookers had apparently witnessed.

"I will have to think about this," Matteo said, more to himself than anyone there, and there were three other Mexicans and the silent Reynaud standing nearby. Reynaud had said nothing the entire time they had been there. Instead he had watched as Bone left to follow the tracks and listened to Matteo conjecture on who might have been spying on them.

"It seems obvious to me," Reynaud said, finally breaking his silence, "that you have lost the element of surprise, if you wish to leave for the Box B tonight."

"I have not lost anything," Matteo said, a stubborn brunt to his words. "I think maybe we have the opportunity here."

"Ah, an opportunity," Reynaud said. "Pray tell, what might that be?"

"How many were with Anson, Bone?"

"I counted at least six horse tracks. No more than eight."

"See?" Matteo said to Reynaud. "Eight, only. And we have many more men than has Anson. If we leave now, we can catch Anson and there will be eight less men at the ranch."

"You'll have to hunt them down," Reynaud said. "And you'll have to kill them all."

"And that is what we will do, eh? Mickey, you will track these men for us?"

"A blind man could track them."

"I want you to track them."

Bone said nothing.

"He will not track Anson," Reynaud said.

Matteo fixed Reynaud with a hard look of disapproval, his eyes flashing a dangerous brilliance. Reynaud lifted his shoulders in a Gallic shrug.

"Even if he does, he will not fight him," Reynaud said.

"Shut your mouth," Matteo said.

Reynaud shrugged again, as if none of this was any concern to him.

Matteo turned to Bone. "You will track for me, Miguel?"

Bone nodded. His face, an inscrutable mask, bore no expression.

"Reynaud, take ten of my men and go with Bone. I will follow with the rest along the same trail. Leave markers if you go off the trail. If you get into a fight, we will be right behind you."

Reynaud nodded, without comment. He turned to go back to the house to gather the men he would take with him. Bone watched him go, with hooded eyes.

"Bring Bone's horse back with you," Matteo called to Reynaud.

"I ought to make him walk," Reynaud said before he walked out of sight.

"Watch him, Miguel," Matteo said to Bone.

"I cannot watch him and do the tracking, too."

Matteo turned to Hector Obispo. "Then you go with Bone and watch the Frenchman."

"What will I do?" Obispo asked. "What will he do?"

"I do not know. I do not trust him."

"Then why do you send him?"

"I send him because Miguel will not kill Anson. Reynaud will kill him."

"Then why do I watch this man?"

Matteo looked over at Bone. He sighed and dipped his head, then looked Obispo straight in the eye. "I think Reynaud might want to shoot Bone in the back."

Obispo sucked in a breath, then looked at Bone. "He would?"

"I think that is true," Matteo said.

"Then you should not let this Frenchman go with Miguel."

"It is a problem, is it not?" Matteo said. "But, it is a problem that may solve itself, true?"

"I do not know how, truly."

"If you have two men who do not like you, and these two men do not like each other, then what does one do, eh?"

"Truly, I do not know the answer to this. You are a smarter man than I, Matteo. You are more wise than I."

"You send those two men into battle against an enemy. If one or the other kills the other man, then what is lost? If only one of these men comes back alive, it is very simple."

"It is?"

"Yes, you kill the one who comes back, and then both of your enemies are dead. Is that not a simple solution to the problem?"

"Yes, Matteo, I see it. I see it now. It is very simple. And this is what you will do with Miguel and the Frenchman."

"*Por suerte.* Then I do not have to worry about either man doing the job he is sent to do. In this way, one may eliminate three or more enemies with but a single bullet from his own pistol."

"*Tu eres muy sabio,* Matteo. You are a very wise man."

Matteo indulged himself in just the flicker of a smile as he turned from Obispo and looked kindly at Bone. Even though he knew Bone could not hear him, Matteo wanted him to feel at ease. Bone, however, was impassive and this was disconcerting to Matteo. He had the feeling, for just an instant, that Bone could read his mind, that he knew, somehow, what he had said to Obispo.

They all heard the sound of hoofbeats, and when Matteo looked back toward the ranch house he saw Reynaud riding toward him, followed by several men, all on horseback, all carrying rifles.

Reynaud halted his horse and those following him did so, all in a line. Matteo looked at them and nodded his approval.

"You have chosen your men well, Reynaud. Then, you are ready?"

"I am ready."

"Then go. Follow Bone and bring me back the head of Anson Baron."

"He is as good as dead."

"No, he is only dead when he is dead and I know he is dead."

"As you wish, Matteo, but he's not the fish I want to catch."

"I will follow you and you will have Martin Baron in your sights by tomorrow's dawn."

"I always kill better on an empty stomach," Reynaud said.

"You will be good and hungry by the time we arrive at the Box B."

"Tell Bone to get moving, then. I am impatient."

Matteo looked over at Bone, who still stood there. "Did you bring his horse?"

Reynaud looked down at the last man in line and nodded. The man rode up, leading Bone's horse. He gave the reins to Bone, who mounted up without a word.

"Satisfied?" Reynaud said.

"No todavía," Matteo said.

"You will be. How close do we follow Bone?"

"Let him ride for ten minutes. Then take the men and follow his tracks."

Reynaud tilted his head back and looked up at the sky, marking the sun. He looked down then, and turned his head to talk to the other men. *"Diez minutos,"* he said, and the men nodded.

"Come," Matteo said to Obispo. "Let us make ready to ride out within the hour."

Matteo did not look at Reynaud as he started walking back toward the house through the narrow clearing, Obispo following in his wake.

"Don't go to the Box B without me," Reynaud called after Matteo.

Matteo cursed the Frenchman under his breath.

"That filth," he said aloud. "I hope he gets his balls shot off."

"You do not like that Reynaud?" Obispo asked.

"He has the reputation as a backshooter. I thought he would be just the man to kill Martin Baron, but he is *un cobarde, un cabrón sin huevos.*"

Obispo laughed. "If he has no *huevos,* how can they be shot off?"

"You have reason, Hector. The man has no balls, therefore there is no need to shoot them off."

And they both laughed at that wry observation.

23

Martin finished inspecting his creation, the walled caisson, checking every hinge, latchstring, board, and beam. Men stood waiting next to the cannon, awaiting his orders. Al Oltman walked into the barn, blinking to adjust his eyes to the comparative darkness after leaving the realm of bright sunlight just outside. Martin saw him come in, and nodded to him as he made one last walk around the wagon.

Oltman walked over and touched one of the sideboards. They were all down, so that the bed of the wagon was visible, and it was still on the wheels used to haul it to the Box B. Four folding beams braced it so that the wheels could be removed when the time came.

"Looks like you're pretty well set," Oltman said.

"Not quite. We've still got to batten down the cannon and put on some more sandbags."

"Ken was telling me about this invention of yours. Think it'll work?"

"We won't know until we try it."

"Where's Anson?"

"Hunting wild cattle," Martin said, with no bitterness in his tone.

Oltman's eyebrows lifted into twin arches. But he made no comment.

"Ken said to tell you howdy," Oltman said.

"Okay."

"Anything you want me to do?"

Martin stood up straight as if jolted by a shock. "Matter of fact, you *can* do something. Pretty thankless."

"I do a lot of thankless things."

"I've got a couple of hands riding back and forth to the south of here. One of 'em's supposed to come riding back if he sees dust or hears anything coming from the Rocking A."

"Sounds like a smart idea."

"The reason I sent them down there is because neither one can shoot worth a bowl of *frijoles* and I can't use 'em here. One is very old and the other is just downright timid. But I figure they can ride well enough if they see anything."

"You want me to add a pair of eyes to that situation."

Martin smiled wanly. "If you wouldn't mind."

"If you think I'd be most useful there."

"Right now I need your eyes, Oltman. I've got a lot to do here. If you don't see anything by nightfall, all of you come back in. I'll have guards posted around the house and barn here."

Oltman grinned. "I'll see you sometime after sundown, if not sooner."

"Thanks, Oltman."

"Call me Al, will you?"

"Al. Much obliged."

"Glad to be of help."

Oltman left the barn and Martin called in the men who were waiting for his instructions. He explained how the cannon would work and asked certain ones to help lift the four-pounder onto the wagon. As they did this, he picked up some large bolts and nuts from a sack he had set aside earlier. A half hour later, the cannon was mounted and anchored.

Next he assigned the men who would lift the wagon and two others who would lie on top as riflemen. "I'll fire the cannon," he said.

For the next two hours, he and his men walked the wagon in and out of the barn, practiced putting up and letting down the sides. Some wanted to practice shooting, but he said he didn't want to waste powder and ball. The men carrying the wagon did not complain about the weight.

"You won't have to carry this far or very much," Martin told them. "Mainly we'll use it to turn the cannon at my orders."

When he was satisfied, Martin set the wagon up behind the house, with the sides up. It looked, from a distance, like a small shed without a roof. However, the overhanging tree branches threw a shadow that could, at first glance, be taken for a flat roof. He fastened a tarpaulin around the bottom to hide the wheels and folding supports.

"You men will have to stay in the barn, out of sight," he told them when he was satisfied with the placement of the cannon wagon. "I'll have food sent in to you. No smoking. Stay alert. Keep your rifles and pistols primed and ready to shoot. When I give the signal, those of you who are going to work on the wagon, come running. Understand?"

The men all nodded. Some translated for the slower ones, speaking in rapid Spanish.

Martin looked over the men, started counting. They waited, their expressions laden with curiosity. Finally he picked out one man with his gaze, Eduardo Mejias. "Eduardo, *ven pa' 'qui,*" he said.

Eduardo left the group and walked over.

"Where in hell is Timo Fuentes? And some others I don't see here. They're the best shots with a rifle."

"I do not know," Eduardo said.

"You don't know where they are?"

"I do not know where they are, I think."

"Did you see them this morning?"

"No, I do not see them this morning."

"Damn it, Eduardo, don't lie to me. If you know where they went, tell me."

"I do not know where they went," Eduardo said, and Martin knew he had to wear him down, ask the specific questions so that he would answer truthfully. He knew that Eduardo wasn't lying—not exactly—but he wasn't telling the truth, either. He was surely not telling what he knew about the missing men.

"Bueno," Martin said. "I believe you. Did you see Timo last night?"

"I see him last night, yes."

"And did he say he would not be here today?"

"He say he was going somewheres, I think."

"Did he and the others just run off? Were they afraid of a fight?"

"No, I don't think so. They were not escared of no fight. I think they go somewhere with Anson."

"Christ. With Anson?"

"That is what he say."

"Where?"

"He do not say."

"Now, what in hell is Anson up to? He took my best men with him. Did Timo say anything about going after that white bull, the one you all call *el diablo blanco*?"

"No, he do not say anything about *el diablo blanco.* He just say he is going to go with Anson somewheres."

"Bastard," Martin said. "All right. Go on now. We'll just have to do this without them."

"I think so, *Patrón.*"

"Damn," Martin said, after Eduardo went back to join the others. He squeezed his hands into fists and drew in a deep breath. He watched the men disperse, start traipsing out of the barn to take care of the chores they had to do before he would need them again. When they had gone, Martin climbed up on the wagon and poured powder into the cannon's breech, loaded the barrel with thin pieces of jagged metal he had collected over time. He wiped the brass barrel until it shone and then he climbed down and boarded up the back after slipping the small ladder onto the bed.

"All ready?"

Martin turned at the sound of the woman's voice.

"Yeah, Ursula. I thought you'd be inside, helping the other women with the food for my men."

"I wondered where David and Roy were. I didn't see them when you had all the men working with that contraption."

Martin walked over to her. "See that line of trees to the south of the big pasture?"

"Yes."

"I've got those boys stringing rope and chain across the road there. That's where I figure Matteo will come in from. That road leads right to the Rocking A."

"Lucinda said you sent your Negroes to town. I was curious about why, when you need every available hand to fight Matteo."

"You really want to know?"

"I thought maybe you didn't trust them to fight as good as the Mexicans."

"No. I just thought that if Matteo saw them here, he must kill them just for spite. They were his slaves, before I got them."

"Stolen slaves."

"Right. I'd feel real bad if they got hurt in this fight."

"I didn't know you gave one whit what happened to those Negroes."

"What did you think?"

"I thought you just wanted some slaves of your own."

"Where'd you get that idea?"

"I guess I thought that's what most men would do."

"Well, I'm not most men."

"No. Jack told me as much. When—when he was alive."

"Jack didn't know as much as he thought he did."

"No, I suppose he didn't."

"Look, Ursula, is that all you've got on your mind? I'm kind of busy right now."

Ursula stepped close to Martin and grasped his hand, gave a slight squeeze. "I wonder how you're managing to do all this, Martin. You're packing around a heap of grief."

Martin felt his hand burning, but Ursula did not release it. He closed his eyes for a second and then opened them. They were wet. "Maybe this is a way to work through the grief," he said. "I keep thinking about the good moments we had."

"Those are the memories I keep of poor Jack. I didn't know Caroline very well, but you must have loved her very much, and I know she loved you."

"Yes, I think she did love me. Even after all I put her through."

Ursula squeezed his hand again. "Men like you and Jack put their women through a lot, Martin, but you can't help it, no more than we can help loving you."

"I keep thinking of all Caroline had to endure when I wasn't around to help her."

"Maybe that's part of what a woman must bear when she loves a man—the absences, the hurts, the misunderstandings."

"It's hell thinking on it."

"Then don't. I don't, any longer. I know Jack had to go his own way, and that was part of his man-ness, why he was Jack and nobody else. I even knew that when he was alive."

"You did?"

"A woman knows her man. She may not act like it. She may fuss and want to punish, but deep down she knows a man can't give back the kind of love she has to give him. Men and women just love different, that's all. There were times when I wanted to beat Jack with my fists, and times when I cried because I thought he didn't love me. But I know he loved me in his own way, and that should be enough for any woman."

"Did you think he was cold? Caroline thought I was cold to her. Mean, even."

"Yes, I thought Jack was cruel at times, that he didn't give a whistler's whit about me. But we lived in two different worlds. There's one thing I do know, though."

"What's that?" Martin asked.

"I know that Jack was always thinking of me when he was away, and that everything he did, he did to make me happy. He just never knew that I would have been happy with him even if we were poor. He thought he had to lay riches at my feet, that this was the only way I could love him. But even that told me how much he loved me. He wanted to please me, as I'm sure you wanted to please Caroline."

"I wanted her to be happy. She was so sad in her later years."

"A part of her was happy," Ursula said, and released her grip on Martin's hand. Even that loosening was a comfort to him and the heat of her touch stayed in his flesh and warmed him.

"I sure as hell hope so."

"Trust me, Martin. It's true. I saw the way she looked at you. I heard the way she talked about you when you were not around. She couldn't hide her love for you."

"You are a comfort, Ursula. I'm much obliged."

"Now, you go on and do what you have to do, but you think back to when you first met Caroline and what sparked you and what made you want her for your wife. And you'll know that she wanted you just as much, if not more, and that's something nobody, not even another woman, or time, or death, can ever take away. What you and she had together . . . that's what's worth remembering."

Martin sighed. "I feel a heap better," he said.

"Good. Now I'll get back to helping fix food for all you rascals and when the time comes, me and Wanda and Hattie will fight right alongside you and your men."

Ursula walked away before Martin could say anything, and he watched her go in a new light. He thought of Caroline and knew that if she were alive, she'd be right there with those other women, cooking, fixing the food, and, when it came to a fight, she'd be right alongside them, loading and shooting her rifle. His heart swelled with the thought, and he turned away from the wagon and walked over to the barn, feeling considerably lighter on his feet than before.

24

TURKEY BUZZARDS WHEELED in the sky, spiraling upward and downward on the hidden wires of air like leaves swirling around in a clear glass funnel. Every so often, one or two buzzards dipped down low and disappeared below tree level. Then another pair would rise up from the ground and join the circling birds in a mysterious cycle of falling and rising. All this in a dead silence, as if the sound had been sucked up in that vortex of invisible air.

The line of riders approached that place where the buzzards fell out of the sky like giant autumn leaves and others rose up as if swept there by an equally large broom. The riders were naked except for rags of tanned deerskin drooping over their loins, and boot moccasins laced with thongs. They rode their horses bareback and were so attached to their mounts they might have been centaurs, half horse, half men, joined in some odd alchemy of evolution and chemistry as to seem single animals in procession.

They passed in and out of the trees and small clearings, their horses walking so slowly they did not raise the dust and their unshod hooves made only the smallest thudding on the baked earth; as if the earth, too, soaked up all vagrant sounds in order to deepen the silence across the land.

The riders rode through the flapping buzzards surrounding the carcass of a longhorn cow, and did not regard the cloud of flapping buzzards that scattered to the sky and the trees as the men passed, leaving behind the ravaged skeleton the buzzards had fed upon, the rib cage dripping with shreds of blackened meat and shreds of tattered skin. Coyotes had gnawed the eyeless skull, leaving tooth marks on the skinless visage that resembled ancient cuneiform wedges from some lost and forgotten book of the dead. A few wisps of reddish hide still clung to the skull clogged with dirt and dried blood, matted there like dyed wool glued to a broken bust of some slain beast of burden left behind on the sands of time.

The men rode on and, as they left, the buzzards returned, one by one, and strutted like martinets emerging from a military haberdashery in mourning coats, shifting their shoulders as if to make their clothes fit. They returned to the remains of their feast, supplicants at a supper for homeless beggars on an empty plain.

Culebra, chief of the small band of Mescalero Apaches, raised his hand to call a halt to the column of his followers. Neither he nor his braves were painted for war, but were scouting a trail that had grown cold since they had last traveled it. Still, they could read the signs unbrushed by the wind and the few rain sprinkles, and they had the landmarks in memory.

"We will stop here," Culebra said. "We will rest and smoke."

The remains of the burned jacal lay strewn around them, the stench of wet burnt wood still strong on the air. The skeletons of burned tumbleweeds lay against stumps of buried posts that had burned almost to the ground, and pieces of charred rope were scattered like the bones of the dead in a ravaged graveyard.

"We have hunger," Tecolote said, pointing to the pair of jackrabbits dangling from the thong around his waist.

"We have thirst, too," Oso said, shaking an empty wooden canteen.

"You are like whining children," Culebra said as he slid from his horse, demolishing the centaur. "Your bellies are full from eating the Mexican food; you have grown fat like the women in the mountains. Cook the rabbits, then, and eat. Maybe you will not be able to cry with your mouths full of meat."

The men grumbled no more as they stepped from their mounts and drifted toward the shade of a mesquite grove, leading their horses in silence. Culebra tied his horse to a small mesquite where the grass grew sparse in shadow and sat down first. His followers sat surrounding him in a semicircle and began opening their leather pouches, bringing forth the little clay pipes they had traded for. Culebra fished a packet of tobacco from his fringed pouch and dipped his pipe inside, then passed the tobacco to Lobito, who was sitting next to him.

Tecolote got up after lighting his pipe and began gathering small pieces of deadwood and dried grass. Oso got up, too, and began doing the same, while the other men smoked their pipes in silence.

"Do you not have hunger?" Lobito asked of Culebra.

Culebra did not answer right away. He let the smoke curl from the pipestem into his mouth, let the warmth seep through him as his thoughts drifted far away from that place. He could almost feel the smoke rise up through the little noseholes above the roof of his mouth and drift into his brain. He closed his eyes and saw the smoke swirl in his mind like the mist that cloaked the *brasada* early in the morning before the sun came awake, and then the smoke thickened like the fog that sometimes lay along the ocean shore at Trespalacios, so quiet, so silent, he could hear the singing of the sea, the melodious lapping of the soft waves driven shoreward by the dawn tide.

Through the swirls of mists and smoky fog in his mind he could see the old trails he and his father and the brothers of his tribe had ridden over the long sad years. He saw the place where his father, Cuchillo, had been killed by one of the Barons, his body left to the vultures and coyotes and worms. He saw the trails they had traveled from the mountains in Mexico and the rivers they had crossed, rivers that ran with the blood of his people over the centuries, rivers that knew the sweat of their horses and carried their urine to the Gulf and their footprints left on the banks all the way to the sea.

He felt the smoke flow through his nostrils and saw their tendrils float out in twin spirals into the air and then he went back into the darkness of his mind and watched the fog and mist part once more and show him the trail leading away from this place to another where brothers had died, and he could smell their blood as it soaked into the grains of dirt and sand and the patterns it left on the cactus and mesquite, like warpaint daubed on the face of the earth itself.

In his mind Culebra saw the faces of those who had gone to the stars, they floated in and out of the swirling darkness like masks glowing in the firelight, and their ghostly visages seemed to be trying to speak to him, for he could see their mouths move, opening and closing, as if they had words to say but could not bring them to life, for they had no throats, only faces that wavered and shrank and stretched and grew as if they were painted on moving water.

A great sadness came over Culebra as he sat there, dreaming in the shade. He opened his eyes to see the sunlight dapple the leaves on the trees and closed them again to see if he could find his way back to that place in his mind where he could see the spirits of the dead, see their faces float out of the smoke. Perhaps he would see his mother's face and his grandmother's this time, for he had not seen them before when he was dreaming like this.

Culebra let himself float up with the smoke to his mind and he waited as he would wait by a grave for some sign that the spirits were there. He closed his eyes tight and looked and looked, but he saw only blackness and the afterimage of sunlight and shadow on the leaves of the mesquite trees and these waved away the quaking smoke and trembling mist in his mind and he saw only the bleakness of the land, the vast emptiness that had been his world for so long.

"Culebra does not have hunger," Oso said finally, to break the terrible silence of the shade and still leaves on the trees.

"Not for food," Abeja said, chuckling. "He sleeps as if he had spent himself with a woman in his blankets."

"Smell his mouth, Oso," young Conejo said, joining in, "and see if he does not sleep from the drinking of the *aguardiente*."

"I will close your mouth, Conejo," Oso said. "Nothing comes out but the shit in your bowels."

The others laughed and Culebra opened his eyes.

"I have hunger," Culebra said, and put his pipe to his mouth and drew on it until his lungs filled with warm smoke. He let the smoke out slowly and watched it curl in the windless air like a coiling spirit. "I have hunger for the blood of my enemies. I have hunger for the land that is empty of the white-eyes. I have hunger that might make me eat all of you up so that I do not have to listen to you prattle like the quail in their wallows."

The others sniffed the air and turned to look at the rabbits roasting over the fire. They all licked their lips and looked sheepish when

Culebra glared at them. He did not look at the rabbits or seem to hear their juices boil and their small leg bones crack from the heat.

"We only talk this way," Oso said, "because we wonder why we have come back to this place. There are no horses here. We have taken them. There are no white-eyes here. We have driven them away. There is nothing here in this place but the buzzards and the burned jacal. We have ridden our horses until their tongues grow long. We have seen no cattle or deer. We have seen only jackrabbits and lizards. Not even the snake hunts in this country. Even the flies have hunger in their bellies."

"You want to go home, eh, Oso?" Culebra asked. "Back to the safe place in the mountains? Back to your woman's blanket where she will play with your pecker until it gets mad and turns into a stick?"

The others laughed at that, but Culebra made the mirth die in their chests as he looked at them with a withering contempt. "And you, Conejo, do you want to live like the rabbit you are and hide in the mountains from the hawk and the eagle?"

Conejo looked as if he had been bitten by the snake, Culebra. He did not answer, but pressed his lips together and frowned.

"Go and eat the rabbit, all of you," Culebra said. "You will need the strength its meat gives you. Oso, you eat the heart for courage, and you, Abeja, eat the liver so that you have the bravery of a mouse. Eat, eat, eat, all of you. Eat the bones to make your peckers stiff and eat the marrow to quench your thirst and eat the eyes so that you can see in the dark when the owl flies from its roost to pluck you from your blankets and carry you off in its talons like the baby chickens you are."

None of the men moved until Culebra arose and put out his pipe and walked away to relieve himself.

"Come, eat," Tecolote said, and the men got up and put out their pipes and squatted near the fire and passed the rabbits around until there was nothing left but cracked bones sucked empty of marrow.

Culebra did not return until the men had finished eating and were acting sleepy and looking for shady places to lie down and close their eyes.

"If your horses are not too tired," Culebra said, "ask them to come with us. I am ready to leave this place. Did you leave me any of the rabbit to eat, Tecolote?"

"I did not think you had hunger."

"You are like the goat, Tecolote. You eat the grass down to the ground and leave nothing for the deer or the cattle."

"I had hunger; I ate."

"I wonder that you all did not go where the buzzards were feeding on the dead cow and shoo them away so that you could eat that carrion as well."

"Are we to go hungry because you do not eat?" Oso asked.

Culebra walked to his horse and loosened the rope reins. He slid atop the mount and rode up to the others. "No, Oso," Culebra said. "I want you to fill your bellies for the long ride ahead. We are going far this day and we will not stop until the sun has gone to sleep."

"Where do we go?" Tecolote asked. "To the ranch of the white-eyes?"

"No, we do not go there," Culebra replied. "We go to the place where the white bull killed our brothers. We follow the track of the white bull and when we find him, we eat when he grazes and we sleep when he sleeps."

"But why?" asked Tecolote. "Will you kill the white bull?"

"The white bull is a devil," Oso said. "Bad spirit."

"The young white-eye, the one called Anson, the young Baron . . . he will come after the white bull," Culebra said. "And we will be waiting. I will kill Anson. I will carry his scalp back to our camp in the mountains and I will hang it in my lodge."

"Ahhh," the others said, and walked to their horses.

Culebra rode away, knowing they would follow. He looked at the sky and marked the sun's place as it arced toward the west, and smelled the air, knowing it was the same air that the sun and the stars breathed, and when he saw the floating hawk, he breathed deeply and nodded to it.

"We are one, my brother," he said. "You hunt in the sky and I hunt on the earth, but we are one. We are the same."

When the other men rode up, Culebra spoke no more but he felt as strong as if he had eaten one of the cattle with the long horns all by himself.

25

Anson found just the place he was looking for, some five or six miles north of Aguilar's Rocking A ranch. A large mesquite forest flanked the road on both sides. The trees grew thick through there and anyone venturing inside the dense grove could become lost quite easily. No one had chopped the mesquite away from the road for many years and it had grown back, leaving a narrow defile for nearly three-quarters of a mile.

"Timo, you and your men get some grub," Anson said to his foreman. "Then, you take both sides of the road here, where you won't be seen."

"I think this is a good place," Timo said.

"Matteo will have to ride right through here."

"He will have many men?"

"Yes, but I'll explain how this is all going to work after you and the others have had some grub. Leave your horses back in the trees while you eat so they can shade and graze."

"I will do this," Timo said, giving Anson a salute with his right hand.

Timo rode over to his companions and spoke to them in rapid Spanish. He and two others rode their horses into the mesquite on one side of the road, and the others disappeared into the forest on the other side.

"Looks like Timo knows what the hell he's doin'," Peebo said.

"He don't take a lot of tellin' to get the idea."

"So, you'll flank this road and when Aguilar comes through, you'll light into him. Then what? He comes into that mesquite like a bunch of mad hornets and we end up maybe chasin' our tails."

Anson stripped the bandanna from around his neck and wiped his forehead. Then he lifted his hat and ran the cloth around the sweatband inside. "Maybe you think I didn't think this all through, Peebo."

"It come to me that you might not have."

"There's somethin' Juanito told me once that stuck with me."

"Everything Juanito said stuck to you, son."

"Maybe."

"Well, what was it this time?"

"He said that a great general going into battle never gives himself an escape route."

"Jesus, son. You mean to make this godforsaken place your last stand?"

"No. He also said that the smart man, who is outnumbered, always leaves himself a way to get the hell out and run like the devil."

"I like that suggestion," Peebo said.

"Better than the first?"

"A whole hell of a lot better."

Anson stopped studying his hat and put it back on. He retied the bandanna around his neck and dug spurs into his horse's flanks as he reined him into a tight turn. He rode off the road and into the mesquite just as Timo and three hands, Manuel Lagos, Emilio Fortuna, and Paco Castro, came walking out. The Mexicans crossed the road, carrying a single saddlebag full of tortillas wrapped around beef and beans, and these wrapped in cloth that had started out the day being damp. Peebo followed Anson into the brush.

"Boy, you get in here and you can't see ten feet in any direction," Peebo said. "I don't even know where them boys tied up their horses."

"I've ridden all through this country as a boy and as a man, Peebo. Follow me."

Peebo and Anson rode single file through the thick mesquite forest, ducking their heads, to keep from being knocked from their horses. They passed the place where Timo's horse and the others were tied, not far from the road, but invisible from there, even so.

Anson seemed to follow some hidden trail through the brush and he did not look back. But he could hear Peebo behind him, his horse rubbing against tree limbs, trunks, Peebo's hat-scraping low-hung branches. It was like riding through an emerald world and Anson remembered how, when he was a boy, he sought out such places where he could be alone and live in a world that was of his own making, a world of fantasy and dreams, inspired by his book-reading with his mother.

Anson was fascinated by the tales of knights and castles, of King Arthur and the Round Table, of Merlin and Sir Galahad. After he read these books, he would saddle his pony and become a knight. He rode into the wilderness on a stallion draped in gold-and-velvet raiment to do battle with the enemies coming to storm the castle. He rode into the *brasada* and there he could imagine himself back in that place and time so long ago. He had built forts out of mud, surrounding them with moats, and pretended he was a king at court with his subjects.

His mother read history to him, and he liked the stories of long-ago battles and wars and he carried these with him into the mesquite thickets and played them out while hidden away from the real world that seemed so harsh to him. There, in the woods, he did not have to hear his parents argue and fight. He did not have to hear his mother weeping alone in the bedroom and hear his father storm out of the house to be gone for days. It was easy, at such times, to steal away and ride his pony into the mesquite jungles and pretend that he was grown and wearing silver armor. He made swords out of tree branches, cutting them to size, making them flat and sharp and tying a crossbrace on for a handguard. Then he would pretend to engage in swordfights with imaginary enemies. He made lances and threw them at pretended attackers, or charged at trees and unseated knights vying for the favors of the beautiful princess.

He remembered those times now, and recalled all the secret trails he had made, trails that only he knew, and how he had been able to find his way through the mesquite, through the many mazes, and find his way out again. He had read about the Minotaur and he pretended the mesquite forests were mazes, and there he fought dragons and monsters and escaped every time.

Anson rode up to a place he had visited as a boy, and he stopped his horse. The memories flooded in on him when he saw the boxes he had hauled there in his little wagon. He had built a fort at this place and the boxes, weatherbeaten and bleached of their oils, had all collapsed. He remembered he had gathered stones, too, and stacked them as breastworks. These were now scattered, though he saw some still piled up there. But there was his wooden rifle and part of a bow he had made that had never worked right. He remembered that this had been his last fort, built when he was eight or nine, and he recalled sitting in it, and fending off Indians, shooting them dead as they charged him in imaginary battle.

Peebo rode up along Anson and stopped. "What's all this, you reckon?" he asked.

"Nothing," Anson replied. "A child's playhouse."

Peebo glanced hard at Anson, but said nothing. Anson swallowed hard. "Let's go," he said.

They rode on and the forest began to thin. Not long after, the trees stopped and they rode into a wide, flat open plain.

"God," Peebo said, "I never thought we'd get out of that jungle yonder."

Anson pointed across the plain to another mesquite forest. "This is our escape route on this side of the road. If we ride across this open place and into those woods yonder, Matteo will never find us."

"Is there a way out of that one, too?"

"Yes, but it runs all the way up to the Box B and there's an old cow trail right through the middle of it."

"How do you know about all this?"

"It's all Baron land, Peebo."

"Yeah, but how do you know the lay of it so damned well?"

"I rode every goddamned mile of it."

The two turned their horses and followed their return path through the mesquite. "Looks easy once you do it," Peebo said. "Oncet, anyways."

"Matteo wouldn't know about this place," Anson said. "Nor any of his men. Bone might, though. In fact, I'm sure he knows this land better than I do."

Just before they reached the road again, Peebo rode ahead and stopped, turned his horse. "Mind tellin' me what that was back there?"

"Back where?"

"In that mesquite. Them rocks and boxes. You been there before."

Anson made a sound in his throat, pulled in air through his nostrils. "Looks like a place where some kid once played," he said.

"You?"

"I don't remember."

"Look, Anson, you don't have to tell me nothin', but if we ride together, we better not have too many secrets between each other. I run away from home when I was a skinny youngster. That time was for good. But I run away more times before that, to a place where I wouldn't be bothered none."

Anson tried to ride around Peebo. Peebo blocked his way. "Peebo, that's what you did and it's damned interesting."

"Didn't you do that?"

"What?"

"Run off to be by yourself when you was just a tadpole."

"Run off to where?"

"This here mesquite grove."

"I never run off," Anson said tightly. "I left that to my pa."

"Jesus, you're a hard damned nut."

"Come on, we got plenty to do before that sun goes down."

"Okay, Anson, keep your damned secrets. I just thought we might have had something in common."

Anson said nothing. Peebo tried flashing his smile, but it didn't work. He glummed up and switched his horse's rump with his reins, turned it back toward the road.

Anson looked at Peebo's back as he rode off, and he clucked to his horse and ticked the flanks with his spurs. What he had done as a boy, he thought, was nobody's business but his own. If it was a secret, then that's what secrets were for—to keep, and he meant to keep this one. Once you let another person get inside you, you could get hurt. He didn't want Peebo to know what he did as a boy. It was none of his business. It wasn't anybody's.

They met Timo and the other Mexicans. Anson told them where he wanted them to wait. He showed them all the path through the mesquite and the open plain and left Peebo to watch the road.

When Anson, Timo, and the others returned, Peebo was sitting behind a tree where he could watch the road. His horse was ground-tied a few yards away. Peebo was munching on a dry tortilla fat with beans and beef. His canteen rested against his leg. "All's quiet," he said.

"Good," Anson said. "You and I will take the other side of the road. Timo and the rest of the bunch will spread out along this side."

"Any escape from the other side?" Peebo asked, just after swallowing the last of his food. He stood up and drank from the canteen in his hand. He reached for his rifle, which was leaning against the tree.

"Do you really want to know?" Anson asked, looking down at Peebo from his saddle perch.

"I reckon you're going to tell me there ain't none."

Anson turned to Timo and spoke to him in Spanish. "Go gather up your horses. Spread out along here, in the trees," he said. "One hundred paces between each man. Stay on your horses."

"Do you think Matteo will come soon?" Timo asked.

"I think he will come after the sun falls in the sky."

"In the night, then."

"Yes. Near the dawn maybe. I think he will want to attack the house at the ranch just as the sun rises."

"You know this Matteo well?"

"I know if he is not here now, he will want to fight at dawn."

"You are a smart man, Anson. *Muy sabio.*"

"So is Matteo. *Ten cuidado.*"

"I will be careful," Timo said.

"I told your wife I'd bring you back. Alive."

Timo laughed. He had crooked teeth and these were stained with the tobacco he kept tucked in the pouch of his cheek. All of his teeth showed when he laughed—all ten of them, none of which touched each other.

"I think she would like you to bring her back a younger man, one more handsome than I."

"That is not what she told me, Timo. She said that you broke her bed last night, as you do every night, and that you must come home and fix it."

Timo laughed again.

"*Ai,* that woman," he said. "It is she who breaks the bed. She is a tigress. And she has claws. My poor back will never heal, I think."

"Do not brag, Timo. You do not have to boast. There are five children in that house and each one is as ugly as you are."

"That is true. I am trying to make one that will look like my Lila."

"Well, Lila wants you back so you can keep trying. Now, think of this when Matteo comes. You shoot and run. I do not want to stop him. I just want to slow him down."

"I will slow him down," Timo said, and drew himself up proudly and grinned crookedly, for emphasis. The grin, in his mouth, was an absolute leer, as obscene as any smile Anson had ever seen.

Anson watched the Mexicans ride off. He wanted them all to come out of this alive, and if they followed Timo's orders, they would. He knew he was no match for Matteo's small army, but he wanted him to think long and hard about riding on the Box B, and if he could cut some of Matteo's numbers, Matteo would have something to think about while he completed his ride to the north.

"You're mighty chatty, son," Peebo said. "Can't them Mexicans find a way to cut their talk shorter?"

"It always sounds longer when you don't understand it."

"I savvy enough of it."

"Enough to get you into trouble south of the border."

"I have enough trouble right here. I don't have to go to Mexico to find it."

"Let's ride on up to the edge of the mesquite so we can get off the first shots, warn Timo and his men when Matteo comes."

"Why don't we just get some sticks and pie plates and bang 'em together? That ought to give our position away enough and we'd save some lead and powder."

"Let's see how funny you find all this when the shooting starts."

"Hell, Matteo might not even ride out today. We could starve to death waitin' up yonder."

"Oh, he's coming, all right. Otherwise all those men would be out working cattle, not marching like soldiers."

Peebo said nothing. Anson nodded to him and rode across the road and into the thick mesquite on the other side. He knew he was right, and he knew Peebo knew it now. Sometime that night, toward morning, Matteo and his army would come riding up that road.

He wondered what his father was doing at that moment. He wondered if he had spoken to Esperanza and found out the truth of how Caroline had gotten sick and died. He thought about his mother, too, and wondered if he would ever get over her death. He was sure his father would not. But, maybe, they each could turn some of their grief under, plow it beneath the hatred they carried for the Aguilar family.

Maybe, he thought, that was why men fought each other, fought wars. This war between the states. Neighbor fighting neighbor. Why? Because men hated. But why did they hate? Because they wanted what another man had. Because, he thought, they coveted what the other man had. Maybe that was it. They hated what their neighbor had and if they had been wronged, then they carried grudges, like he was carrying for Matteo and his family. Well, if that was the way it was, he was no different.

But, he thought, a grudge is a terrible thing to bear. A grudge eats at a man's innards and keeps eating at his guts until it eats his very soul.

By the time he and Peebo reached the edge of the mesquite forest, Anson was sick inside. Sick in his heart, sick in his belly. He found a spot where he and Peebo could wait for Matteo's army and he slid out of the saddle and promptly threw up all that was in his stomach.

"You sick?" Peebo asked. "Or just scared?"

Anson looked up at the grinning Peebo and saw him through watery eyes, like some imaginary figure rising out of a mirage.

"Both," Anson said, and gagged again.

Maybe, he thought, it would be easier to kill in the dark, and he prayed for the sun to go down so he could hide his feelings and his thoughts and he would not have to see the faces of the men he would kill. And maybe the killing would wear down some of the grudge before it ate him alive.

26

MARTIN HEARD THE rumble and jouncing clatter of the wagon long before he saw it. He fingered the trigger guard on his flintlock rifle for several anxious moments as he stood in the shadows next to the wagon bearing the cannon.

It seemed to him that the Mexican hands around and underneath the wagon were all holding their breaths and then he realized he had been doing the same thing.

"Who comes, *Patrón*?" Ramón Mendoza asked. In Timo's absence, Ramón was Martin's *segundo,* in charge of those who would lift the wagon and turn it on Martin's command.

"I do not know, but the wagon is coming from town."

"Yes, that is good, maybe."

"Ojalá que sí," Martin said. "I hope so."

The two men listened as the wagon drew closer. On the still night air, the sound carried from a long way, Martin knew. He looked up at the sliver of moon and then back into the darkness, hoping to catch a glimpse of the wagon before it was too close to the house. He wondered if the women upstairs had heard it. Wanda, Hattie, Ursula, Esperanza, and Lucinda were all in the house, upstairs, sitting by windows in front, back, and the south side. Only Esperanza and Lucinda did not wait with rifles in their hands. The two Mexican women were to hand loaded rifles to the other three and reload the empty ones when the fighting started.

"It is not a wagon," Martin said, his words an abrupt intrusion into the silence between him and Ramón. "It is a buggy."

"A buggy?"

"Yes. Hear it. It creaks like the joints of my knees in the morning."

Mendoza laughed. "Yes, I hear it."

"Two wheels," Martin said. "One horse."

"Yes. I know it."

"Wait here. I will go and see who it is."

"Have your rifle ready."

"I do not think I will need it."

"It could be a trick."

"You listen good, Ramón."

"I will listen. I will be ready."

Martin walked around the side of the house. He stepped with care so that he would not make noise. There were men in the barn, there were others flanking both sides of it. They would know he was there, but they would not be alarmed if he did not hurry.

The buggy pulled up to the front of the house. Martin waited in the shadow of the porch.

"It's so dark," someone said. A woman's voice. Martin did not recognize it.

"Shh," said another, a man's voice, lower in register.

"Doc?" Martin called.

"Is that you, Martin? We can't see you." The horse pulling the buggy, snorted and blew steam through its nostrils, a silvery spray by the thin light of the carved-out moon.

"Light down," Martin said. "Quiet as you can. Walk over here slow. By the porch."

Doc Purvis set the handbrake. He stepped down from the wagon and walked to the other side. Martin saw someone else get out, a woman by the shape and size of her, and then another got out, taller than either Doc or the woman.

"Where are you?" Doc asked, as he walked toward Martin.

"Just keep coming. Keep your voice down."

"My niece insisted on coming," Purvis whispered when he

saw Martin. Behind Purvis, the tall man stopped short. "It's Lorene," the doctor said lamely.

Martin stepped out from the porch shadow and saw that it was indeed Doc Purvis and his niece. He peered at the tall man behind them.

"Socrates?" Martin said. "What in hell are you people doing here?"

"Well, I thought you might need a surgeon if there was a fight. Socrates wanted to come. And Lorene."

"Jesus Christ," Martin said.

Lorene tittered.

"Shh, Lorene," Doc said.

"I come to fight with you," Socrates said, his accent thick with the twang of his African roots.

"This isn't your fight, Socrates."

"You done made us free, Mr. Martin. I want to fight with you."

"Can you shoot a rifle?"

Socrates stepped forward, close to Martin. He raised his hand into the air. A stream of moonlight glinted off the blade of a machete.

"Holy Christ," Martin swore. "Socrates, you're crazy. You go into a fight with that machete and they'll cut you down before you could lift your arm."

"Yes, suh. They calls me 'Sox' now. I wants to fight."

"Well, we'll see about that. Doc, you and your niece come into the house. You'll be safer there. But I wish you'd both get in that buggy and go right back into town."

"I think you may need me," Purvis said.

"Where's Anson?" Lorene asked.

"He's not here," Martin replied.

"Oh."

"Socrates, uh, Sox, maybe you ought to drive the young lady back to Baronsville."

"No, suh, I'se stayin' right here."

"Doc. Are you sure you want your niece to be here?"

"She has assisted me on many operations."

"All right. Into the house, then, both of you. Sox, you wait out here. And I mean *don't move.* You might get shot. I'll be right back."

"Yes, suh," Socrates said.

Martin led the doctor and his niece around to the front steps and up to the door. He knocked loudly. After a few moments he heard footsteps.

"Who is it?" Wanda asked through the door.

"It's Martin. Open the door."

The latch rattled and the door swung open. Wanda stood there with a rifle in one hand.

"Make sure Doc and his niece have a safe place to wait," Martin said.

"My name's Lorene," Lorene said.

"Yes, I know. Inside, both of you. And do what Wanda tells you."

"It's awful quiet," Wanda said.

"Pray that it stays that way," Martin said.

"Won't you come in?" Wanda said to Doc Purvis.

Martin left before the door closed behind him, and walked back to where Sox was waiting.

"Come on," he said. "Stay close and don't wave that damned blade around."

"Yes, suh," Sox said.

Back at the wagon, Martin told the other men that Sox would be there to help. "If any man falls, you take his place, Sox."

"I wants to fight."

"You'll probably get more fighting than you want. Now, just find a place to sit and be quiet. And put that machete someplace where it can't hurt anybody."

Sox drew the blade close to him. "I'll be careful," he said. He sauntered over by the tree and sat down cross-legged. He laid the machete across his lap.

Martin walked away far enough so that he could not hear all the men breathing. He wanted a smoke more than anything, but he had given orders that no man should light a pipe or cigarette and give away their positions.

He looked up at the star-sprinkled night sky and breathed deeply of the warm air. At least the wind was down, he thought, and they wouldn't have to fight dust and the noise while they were waiting for something to happen. He listened intently for any distant sound. He was counting on Roy and Al to fire warning shots. He knew they would carry on the still night air and give him time to climb up in the wagon and maneuver the cannon for a shot.

He had gone over the battle scenario in his mind dozens of times, but he knew that things never worked out the way they were planned. He had no idea of Matteo's strategy. He had tried to work out his plan of defense for any contingency, but he knew Aguilar was smart and would probably attack in some unexpected fashion for which Martin had not prepared.

Martin shifted the rifle in his hand to the other, then laid it on his shoulder for a while. He waited and listened and knew it was going to be a long night. He wondered if the men could wait that long without speaking. As if reading his thoughts, he saw one of the Mexicans leave the wagon and walk a few yards away then stand stock-still. Then he heard the swooshing sound of the man urinating. He was sure that such a sound could be heard by Matteo, no matter where he was. It sounded like a cascading waterfall, like a cow pissing on a flat rock.

Martin sighed and watched the man walk back to the wagon. Then two others arose and walked to the same spot and relieved themselves. It was contagious, he thought, and now he had to piss, himself. But he waited, and sure enough he could hear men get up, walk a few steps, and piss into the silence of the night.

A moment later Martin heard the sounds of violent retching. He turned and saw a lone dark shape doubled over like a horseshoe. The man was vomiting up everything in his stomach and the fluid gushed forth in a hideous flood of sour liquid and food chunks that stank to high heaven.

Martin walked over and saw the man drop to his knees and gasp for air. He slapped the man's back.

"Socrates, what the hell's wrong with you?"

"I'se sick."

"God, man."

"I'se scared, suh."

"Scared? Then why in hell did you come out here? Why didn't you stay in town where it was safe?"

Socrates stood up. He was trembling, and Martin could see the whites of his rolling eyes. He waited while Socrates regained his breath.

"I'se all right, suh. I just got me a wrigglin' in my stomach."

"But you're scared."

"No, suh, not no more. It was just sittin' there, thinkin' and so awful quiet. And dark. I got scared thinkin' somethin' might come at me out of the dark."

"Well, something might."

"No, suh. I got my machete."

Martin looked at Socrates' hands. They were empty. "You better forget about that damned machete."

"No, suh. I aims to fight."

"Well, you just stay out of my way when the shooting starts. If you get in front of that cannon when it goes off, you'll be blown into a thousand pieces."

"No, suh, I won't get in the way of no cannon."

"Go on back and be quiet. You've already made enough racket to wake the dead."

"Yes, suh. I'se goin'."

Socrates walked back to the wagon and disappeared from Martin's sight.

Martin breathed in deeply, caught the smell of the vomit, and himself nearly threw up. He walked far enough away so that he could handle the acrid taint that lingered on the air.

Yes, he thought, it was going to be one long goddamned night.

27

LAZARO SAT BY the back window in Caroline's bedroom. He had lifted it a crack so that he could hear the men talking by the wagon below. But they were silent. He only heard Martin's voice and another's, the black man, Socrates. He heard the other noises, too, and pieced them together in his mind so that he could see through his blindness, could see Socrates throw up his food, and then he could smell the sour aroma of chilies and the half-digested musk of corn tortillas and the acidic fermentation of pinto beans, all mingled together, wafting toward him like messages from another world, another civilization.

He heard the women whispering in the other rooms and he could identify their voices. Hattie and her daughter, Wanda, were across the hall, at a front upstairs window. Ursula was with Lucinda in the bedroom next door, and Esperanza was in her room down the hall, alone. But he knew she would be looking for him. He had sneaked away while she dozed in a chair, a rifle across her lap.

He heard the clunk of Martin's bootheels as he walked back toward the wagon. The black man, Socrates, was making noises in his throat and then louder ones as he dry-heaved. Martin's voice floated up from near the wagon. Lazaro strained to hear his words.

"What in hell did you have to eat tonight?" Martin asked.

"Mexican food."

"Chili peppers?"

"I don't know. Somethin' real hot."

"I can smell the chilies."

"Yes, suh."

"Stop making noise. Go in the house if you have to do that."

"I'se over that now."

Then it was quiet once more. He heard Martin walk away again and his hearing followed Martin until the footsteps stopped.

He wondered what Martin was thinking as he stood out there in the dark. Lazaro knew there was going to be shooting, like there was before, when the Apaches came. He could still hear the sound of the cannon's roar when he thought about that time. He could still hear the screams of the Indians as the pieces of metal tore into their bodies, and he could still smell the blood, scent the death that had lingered over the courtyard for a long time afterward. And he longed to touch the sleek metal body of the cannon again when it was cool and had not been fired. Caroline had let him touch the cannon before and he still remembered how it had felt, the solidity of it, the coolness of the brass, the shape of the barrel.

Lazaro heard footsteps down the hall and he followed them closely with his ears. He heard a door open and then close a few moments later. The footsteps continued down the hall and he heard them go down the stairs. He recognized the footsteps as belonging to Esperanza. Then he heard voices from downstairs. She was talking to the doctor and his niece. Lazaro had known when they arrived and came into the house, and he knew they had stayed in the front room, talking in whispers. Then he knew they had fallen asleep down there.

"Have you seen the blind boy, Lazaro?" Esperanza's voice carried up the stairs and into Caroline's room.

"No, I've been dozing," Doc Purvis said.

"He has not been downstairs," Lorene said, and Lazaro let out his breath.

Esperanza would come looking for him, he knew. She must have thought he had gone downstairs. He did not want her to find him. He was sleepy, but he wanted to stay up and listen for the cannon's roar if Martin fired it off. He wanted to know what the men were saying while they waited through the night for the attack by Matteo Aguilar.

He heard Esperanza's footsteps on the stairs, and he shrank against the wall beneath the window. She walked on past his mother's room and went to the one where Ursula was sitting with a rifle. He knew that Lucinda was with her, too, and had another loaded rifle across her lap, for he had made Esperanza tell him where the women were and where they were sitting, and about the rifles. He wished he had a rifle and wished he could see to shoot it, or at least hear enough to point it at the sound of an enemy and pull the trigger.

Lazaro heard whispers floating down the hall. He could not make out the words, but he could associate the voices: Esperanza, Hattie, and Wanda. The whispers stopped and he heard no sounds for several seconds. Then the slap of Esperanza's sandals broke the quiet and he knew she was once again walking down the hall.

The footsteps stopped at the door to Caroline's room. Lazaro held his breath. He waited, his ears attuned to every nuance of sound. Then he heard the latch lift on the door. The door opened. It did not creak, but sounded like a brush sliding across a rough surface.

"Lazaro?" Esperanza called in a loud whisper.

He did not answer.

"Lazaro, are you here?" Esperanza asked in Spanish. "You answer me. Are you in this room?"

Lazaro felt as if his lungs would burn up with his held breath.

"Answer me, Lazaro."

Lazaro let out his breath slowly so as not to make any sound. He began to tremble as he drew in a slow breath.

"I know you are in here, Lazaro. I do not want to light a lamp. Answer me."

"I am here," Lazaro whispered.

"Where?"

"I am by the window."

"Come here," Esperanza said. "With hurry."

Lazaro stood up. He walked toward the door with measured slow steps.

"I want you to come to bed, Lazaro."

"I want to sleep here, in my mother's room."

"You will not sleep here."

"Why?"

"Because it will displease *Don Martín.*"

"Why?"

"Because I say so." Esperanza reached out and took Lazaro's hand. She led him from the room and closed the door. Lazaro dragged his feet all the way to the room down at the end of the hall, the room where Esperanza slept when she stayed at the house.

Inside her room Esperanza bolted the door. Lazaro heard the bolt click, but it didn't matter. He knew how to lift the latch and slide the bolt.

"Go to bed," Esperanza said.

"I do not have sleepiness."

"You will sleep. The night will be long."

"I want to be awake when Matteo Aguilar comes and the shooting starts."

"He will not come this night."

"Then why is no one else sleeping?"

"You ask too many questions, Lazaro. Go to your bed."

Lazaro lay on his bed, but he could not sleep. Esperanza had the window open, so he could hear the noises from outside. He heard her breathing and knew that she was getting sleepy.

"I know you are not sleeping," Esperanza said, after a while.

Lazaro twitched in the bed because she had startled him. He said nothing and held his breath.

"Lazaro, listen to me," Esperanza said. "You must never mention the señora Caroline as your mother again, especially when *el patrón* is present or can hear you."

"Why?"

"Because it would not be good to remind him of her."

"I do not understand."

"He is stricken with grief and he will carry his sorrow with him a long time."

"But I carry sorrow for my mother with me, as well."

"I know. But he will wish to keep his sorrow private and would not wish to share his grief with anyone else. And you are not of his blood."

"I know that."

"Then you must keep your mouth closed about my mistress. Do not speak her name except to me. Will you do that?"

"I will try."

"You must promise."

"I promise, then."

"Good. I do not want trouble here. I wish to raise you as my own son and teach you what I know. If we anger the Baron family, we will have to leave."

"Where would we go?"

"I do not know. I am old and my family are all dead. We would have to go back to Mexico, and that is a very hard place to live. We would be beggars."

"What are 'beggars'?"

" 'Beggars' are those without homes who have to ask for money, for food, for clothes."

"I will not be one of the beggars, then."

"No, you will not be a beggar."

"I could play my guitar and people would give me money."

"People would still pity you. I do not want people to pity you."

"What is 'pity'?"

" 'Pity' is when you feel sorry for a person who is lower in class than you are. It is a shame to be one who is pitied. I would not want you to have shame. I want you to be proud."

"And what is 'proud,' then?"

" 'Proud' is when you hold your head up high and keep your shoulders straight and do not have to bow and scrape for any man. 'Proud' is when you feel God's hand on your shoulder and know that he has blessed you in a special way."

"Am I proud, then?"

"Yes, you are blessed. God did not give you sight, but he gave you other gifts, and your task in life will be to find these gifts. Perhaps you will play the guitar better than anyone else. Perhaps you will do some great thing that others will admire and praise you for."

"But what?" Lazaro asked.

"I do not know. But God will show you the way. You must listen to your heart and you must be patient."

"You are always telling me to be patient. That means waiting, does it not?"

"No, it means that you must be always ready for more gifts from God. You must keep your heart pure and know that you are blessed by the Almighty."

"I do not know who God is. I cannot see Him in my mind."

"Nobody can. That is why God is God. He is not seen, but He is everywhere and He is in every living thing."

"I do not understand how God can be everywhere."

"In time you will, Lazaro. Be patient. God is a spirit, and spirit cannot be seen with the eyes—only with the heart. God will come into your heart and you will see Him."

"Will I really see Him?"

"Not as you imagine, but as a spirit, as a force inside you, as power. When you are older I will tell you of miracles performed by God and by His son, Jesus."

"Why do I have to be older?"

"Because you will be ready to understand; you will know that truth when you see it and hear it."

"I wish I were older now."

"Go to sleep, Lazaro. You will be a little older when you awake."

She walked over to the bed and put her hand on Lazaro's forehead. Then she closed the lids over his sightless eyes and held her hand there.

He could feel sleepiness overtake him. It was so soothing to have her hand on his eyes. She did not say anything, but he thought that she was singing a lullaby to him as she used to do when he was a baby. He could hear the words in his mind, and he could hear the melody and the hearing brought a great peace to his heart, and he felt himself falling away into that deeper blackness that he called sleep, and just before he lost consciousness, he thought he heard Esperanza humming that little lullaby she used to sing to him and it was the sweetest sound he had ever heard.

28

BONE HAD KNOWN that Reynaud and ten men were following him. Gradually, he had been widening the distance between him and them. He knew why Matteo had sent the Frenchman Reynaud, and ten others, to follow him. The Frenchman was to kill Anson Baron. But, if Bone had anything to say about it, Reynaud would not do that.

He had left the road several times to confuse Reynaud and those who rode with him. They would spend time trying to find his track, and time was what he needed to gain, along with distance.

There was something inside him that had hardened after he left Matteo. Something that had been working inside him for a long time, something he had not been able to put a name to, but something that was attached to an old hate, a hate that also could not be named quickly or easily. But he thought it arose out of being back with his people again, after realizing, when he had returned, still again, that he had no home, no people, anymore. There was only Dawn and his son.

He had thought he might find a home with Matteo Aguilar, but that man wanted only those around him who were like the slaves that were stolen from him, men who did what they were told and did not ask questions. Bone had seen the look in Dawn's eyes when he told her he was leaving again, that he was riding after a man Matteo wanted killed. He had seen the shadows in Dawn's eyes and those shadows had spoken to him more clearly than any words she might have said.

The hatred inside him was formless, but it was like a river seeking a bed, cutting through him to carve a way to run to some ocean where it could be swallowed up, where it could fill a basin inside him that was like a reservoir gone dry.

The old ones had told him that he would be homeless, that the tribe was dying out to make room for new people, just as the ancient ones had died off long before the Lipan sprang from the earth. The old ones had told him that the earth was alive, and all things on it, but, like the leaves of the trees, people died off and others came to take their places, like new leaves that would also die one day.

He had thought long and hard about the stone he had found in the *brasada*, and felt that it had been left behind by the ancient ones, perhaps just to say that they had been here on earth and were leaving it behind.

With the anger, there was a sadness in Bone, too. He had taken Dawn away from the mountains, away from the dying old people, hoping to find a place for her and their child, hoping that, with Matteo, he would find a home, peace, new roots in soil where his son could grow to be a man. But now he thought that perhaps he could not outrun time, that he could not be the lone Lipan to survive and raise his son to begin a new generation. The people were scattered and their bloodlines wiped out by Spanish and mestizo blood and his son would never find a Lipan mate, and even if he could, he was no longer pure Lipan, but had his mother's mixed blood in him.

He was weary thinking about it, thinking about the anger and living with the sadness. He was not old, but he felt old, sometimes. Dawn was young, and he wanted her to be happy. She liked Matteo's wife, Luz, but she did not like Matteo, and she hated the Frenchman Reynaud. She hated that she and Bone lived on Matteo's land and not their own. But they had no land; they had no people.

Where could he go? Bone wondered. Where on earth was there a place for him, Dawn, and their little son?

He did not know, and the anger grew in him along with the sadness, and he felt like a blind man groping his way through a darkness that had fallen upon the earth and surrounded him, cut him off from the sun and all his brethren.

But he could not just go away and leave no trace of himself. The ancient ones did not do that. They left behind memories and stones inscribed with words of their own language. They left behind skeletons that spoke of their passing to those who could read the stories of the bones—like the tracks he was following—like some could read books.

Mickey Bone had the uncanny ability to read sign and figure out, after a while, where the person he was tracking might be headed. Now, as he followed the tracks of Anson and Peebo, his thoughts roamed over the country ahead. He saw the land beyond unfold in his mind and knew, in that instant, not only where the two riders were headed, but what Anson's plan for ambush was to be. He knew the country, and he knew how Anson thought, for he had taught the boy some things about tracking and concealment.

Bone turned his horse off the path, for there was no longer any reason to look at the hoofprints that were so plain, so fresh. As he rode to the west, he pondered what he might do, what he must do, when he came upon Anson. He already knew the size of Anson's small force, to the man, and now he had to figure out where Anson would deploy his companions, what spot he would pick for himself while waiting to ambush Miguel and his men.

A roadrunner streaked across an open patch of land in front of Bone, its legs scissoring the air as if it were cutting through a bolt of tan cloth. A lizard lay sunning on the bright side of a rock, catching the late-afternoon rays of the sun. A jackrabbit froze against a stalled tumbleweed, nearly invisible against the striations of the skeletal plant. Bone judged the distance he would have to ride the semicircle to come up on the west edge of the mesquite forest as he rode through the waning afternoon. His mind teemed with thoughts of what he would do when he found Anson. He had not talked to him in a long time and he knew the boy had grown into a man and was no longer the youth he had once known.

The sun was slipping over the distant horizon when Bone rode up to the beginning of the huge mesquite forest. He rode a hundred yards before he turned his horse into the thicket. A covey of quail burst into flight in front of him and scattered through the trees like flung featherballs. His horse skittered under him, but did not bolt.

It was darker inside the grove, but he could see well enough to follow a course he had set in his mind. If his timing was right, it would still be light enough to see when he reached the edge that bordered the road. But he would know where Anson waited, a few minutes before he reached that point.

Shafts of sunlight penetrated the leafed-out mesquite as shadows gathered and striped the ground, puddled up in the heavier growth. The sun's warmth began to dwindle as Bone followed his eastern course. Every so often now, he stopped to listen. It was deathly still inside the green garden of mesquite, but he listened intently, even so.

He looked at his shadow and his horse's moving on the ground in front of him, constantly changing shape like some inky sea creature floating and flapping just beneath the still surface of the sea.

As the mesquite woods darkened, Bone's horse slowed as it encountered deep pockets of shadows that sometimes bore frightful shapes, and some that resembled hollows and holes in the ground, pits into which man and horse might fall and disappear in the bowels of the earth.

A small deer arose from its dusty bed and ran off, making little sound. Bone passed the bed and smelled the musk of the deer. A crow flew through the trees and began cawing after it had seen him. Soon he heard answering caws and heard the flapping of wings, as others of their kind took wing and announced his presence.

It could not be helped. Anson would know he was coming, if he judged the man right. The din blotted out almost all other sound and Bone prodded his horse's flanks, putting him into a lope through the mesquite. They followed a deer trail that wound through the trees and coursed the more open places.

Bone knew he was not far from the road when he reined his horse in. At that moment, he heard the snicking sound of a cocking hammer and knew that he was no longer alone in the woods.

He started to reach for the rifle in its boot, but stopped before he moved his hand. Bone knew that if he tried to pull his weapon free, he would be a dead man before he drew another breath.

29

ANSON HEARD A crow caw deep in the woods behind him. A few moments before, a small deer had run across the road into the mesquite forest on the other side. The deer flashed the white of its tail like a warning flag and then disappeared.

Peebo sat his horse a few feet away, his rifle across the pommel of his saddle. He looked as if he were dozing, but Anson knew he was wide-awake and as alert as he was.

"What you reckon scared that there deer?" Peebo asked.

"Same thing that made that crow caw," Anson said.

A few minutes later another crow took up the chorus, then a series of caws rang through the woods. Anson stiffened in the saddle and shifted his own rifle until its stock lay across his right leg. He put a thumb on the hammer and turned his horse to face the woods behind him.

"Jesus," Peebo said. "What a damned racket."

"Yeah, you stay here. I'm going to find out what's got those crows a-yammerin'."

"Sing out if you need help."

Anson nodded and clucked to his horse as he ticked its flanks with blunt spurs. The horse glided into the deep shadows of the mesquite under a rapidly graying sky.

Crow calls filled the air and Anson heard the flapping of wings as birds left their roosts somewhere up ahead of him. He rode with care, moving from copse to copse, then waiting a few seconds before continuing on, deeper into the woods.

Then he heard the muffled sounds of an animal moving very slowly through the trees. He stayed behind a group of three trees, listening. The sounds came closer and Anson did not move a muscle. He laid a hand on his horse's withers to keep him from whinnying, while pulling gently on the bit to keep his mouth occupied.

He recognized the horse when it came into view, then saw Bone. Anson's blood quickened as he remained motionless. Still, Bone came on, about thirty yards away, at an angle where Bone could not see him unless he turned his head and looked directly at Anson.

Anson waited until Bone had passed him on a parallel course, then, when Bone's back was to him, Anson thumbed back the hammer of his flintlock. Bone halted and stiffened in the saddle.

"Mickey."

"That is you, Anson."

"You trying to sneak up on me?"

"I was looking for you."

"Just sit there. Don't go for your rifle. I'm going to ride up behind you."

"I mean you no harm."

Anson said nothing. He held the rifle in his right hand, pointed at Bone's back, the reins in his left hand. He prodded his horse forward and rode up behind Bone.

"Why are you looking for me, Mickey?"

"Matteo sent me to follow your tracks. I think some of his men will be along soon. Matteo means to kill you and your father."

"Did Matteo send you to kill me?"

"No."

Anson believed Bone, but he continued to be wary.

"How many men are coming?"

"I do not know, but I would bet many pesos that the Frenchman, Reynaud, is among them."

"I don't know the man."

"No, but Martin does. Reynaud is very dangerous, I think."

"Why would you warn me?"

"I told Matteo I would not kill you."

"He must have really liked you to say that."

Bone said nothing.

Anson rode up close enough to shove the barrel of his rifle into the center of Bone's back. Bone did not move.

"I want to believe you," Anson said.

Bone still said nothing.

"Why in hell would you work for Matteo?" Anson blurted out.

"It was a mistake."

"So, are you going back to him if I let you go?"

"I will go back and get my wife and son."

"You have a son?"

"Yes."

"Hmmm. Well, maybe you want to live, then."

Bone stayed silent.

"Can I trust you?"

"That is up to you, Anson."

"Well, I want to hear you say it." Anson poked the barrel into Bone's back, kept the pressure on the spine.

"I was coming to warn you."

"So Matteo is riding to attack the Box B?"

"Yes. He and his men will be there in the morning."

"At dawn."

"Yes. That is what Matteo says."

"You saw my tracks at the Rocking A."

"Yes. So did Matteo. He sent me to track you."

"Does he know I'm waiting for him?"

"I do not think so."

"What are you supposed to do? Tell him where I am?"

"Yes."

"But you will not. Not now."

"I never would have."

"Then why did you track me?" Anson asked.

"Are you going to shoot me in the back, Anson?"

"Maybe not."

"It is hard to make talk with a gun in my back."

Anson pulled the barrel back an inch.

"I will answer," Bone said. "But let me turn around so that you can see my eyes. So you can see if I speak the truth."

Anson backed his horse. "Turn around. Real slow, Mickey."

Bone turned his horse. The crows began to fall silent. Only one or two still cawed and they were far away. The shadows in the mesquite forest began to deepen and the sky began to darken, its grayish cast turning to slate.

"I'm listening," Anson said.

"I thought if I tracked you, I would find you. And then I would tell you that Matteo is coming to rub you and Martin out. If someone else had tracked you, I do not know what would have happened."

"Matteo is still coming. I mean to slow him down."

"When I left the road, I wiped out your tracks for some ways. Then I rode back and forth, leaving my tracks all crossing each other. This might slow down those who follow. For a little while. Then Matteo, Reynaud, and many men will come. They carry many weapons."

"Now that you've found me and warned me, what will you do?"

"I will go back to the Rocking A and get my wife and son. We will leave this place. I will not work for Matteo."

Anson considered what Bone had told him. He could still see his eyes, but he could not tell if a man was lying just by watching his eyes. He could only tell what a man might do in the next instant. He kept the rifle barrel level on Bone's gut while he thought over what he had said.

"Matteo will come after you, if you do that," Anson said.

"I do not think so. And, if he does, he will not find me."

"Where will you go? Mexico?"

"I do not know."

"There is a war now. Coming to Texas maybe."

"I have heard this."

"You might be hunted down by others. By soldiers."

"We must follow the paths we choose."

"You sound like Juanito."

"He was a man *muy sabio.*"

"Yes. But you have the chance to choose the path. You chose Matteo."

"And I am leaving that path."

"To follow a more dangerous one, perhaps."

"Perhaps. But I speak the truth. I will go away from the Rocking A. That is not my path."

"I wish you well. *Buena suerte.*"

"Buena suerte a ti, también."

Anson hesitated. He did not want to leave, but he knew he must. Once, he had wanted to ride with Bone, to go with him to Mexico when he had left the Box B, but he had stayed behind because Juanito Salazar had told him not to go with Bone. But he was still fascinated with the man, and he had learned much from him when he was a boy growing into a man.

"I got to be going," Anson said. But he did not move, nor did he change the aim of the rifle in his hand.

"Yes. There is not much time. You will not be able to stop Matteo, you know."

"I just hope I can slow him down a little."

"He has many men. You have only four."

"I know."

"Watch out for the Frenchman."

"I will."

"Are you going to keep that rifle pointed at me? Or are you going to shoot me dead?"

Anson looked down at the rifle as if realizing for the first time that he had it in his hand.

"No. You go, Mickey. Maybe I'll see you sometime. Again."

"Maybe."

Anson pulled the rifle back, but he did not uncock it.

"I want to give you something before I go," Bone said. "It is in my saddlebag."

"If you go for a pistol, Mickey, I'll shoot you out of the saddle."

Bone smiled. Anson could barely see it in the gathering gloom of the grove.

"Get it real slow, Mickey."

Mickey leaned back and twisted in a turn to lean over his left saddlebag. He reached inside and brought out an object that Anson could not see. But he knew it was not a pistol. It was flat and could have been a package of tortillas, for all he knew.

"I want you to have this," Bone said. "I found it in the *brasada.*" He leaned toward Anson and handed him the flat rock.

"What is it?"

"It is a stone with very old writing on it. I do not know what it means."

"Why are you giving it to me?"

"I do not know. I have thought about it much. I think you might one day know what it says."

"I cannot see the writing," Anson said, as he took the stone, held it closer to his eyes.

"It is very strange writing. Pictures. I think it belonged to the old ones who came before—who are no longer walking the earth."

"I will keep it for you, Mickey. It means a lot to you?"

"It means that I, too, will pass on, and my family, and there will be nothing but stones to mark where our bodies once were."

Anson put the stone in his saddlebag. It was growing darker by the second.

"Mickey, *ten cuidado.*"

"You take care as well, Anson."

Bone turned his horse and rode away, into the mesquite shadows. After a moment Anson was alone, as if Bone had never been there.

"So long, Mickey," Anson breathed softly, and wondered if he'd ever see Bone again.

He turned his horse and started riding back to where Peebo was waiting.

The darkness overtook him and when he rode up on his friend, Peebo swung the rifle toward him.

"Jesus, you scared the shit out of me, Anson."

"Jumpy?"

"Listen. Somebody's comin' down that there road and it ain't no solitary soul, neither."

Anson realized his rifle was still on cock. He left it that way and listened.

The hoofbeats were muffled, but Peebo was right. There were a bunch of them and they were riding slow, following his tracks, most likely. In a few minutes he and his men would be up to their necks in trouble.

"That's them," Peebo said.

"Part of them, anyway. You take one shot and then turn tail and follow me. Hear?"

"You want me to aim at any particular party or thing?"

"Don't get smart. You take out the front man. I'll get whoever comes after him."

"God, I hope there's time for two shots."

"You won't even hear mine, Peebo. Just remember to get the hell out of here."

"I hope your hands drop a couple."

"They will. They'll shoot at those in the rear. That ought to set the whole bunch to milling like a bunch of turkeys."

Peebo didn't say anything after that; for now they could see dark shapes in the road, coming from the direction of Matteo Aguilar's Rocking A.

In the darkness, the riders looked like phantoms. Anson could have sworn they all had death's-heads atop their shoulders, skulls that were grinning at them as they came on, saddles creaking, rifles sticking up, all of them silent, like men hunting wild game before time had begun to be counted on the earth.

30

REYNAUD RODE ON the right flank of the small column for as long as he could see open country. He changed flanks when the cover got too close, so he constantly rode back and forth through the column, watching the lead riders with an intensity that made the two men up front nervous enough to turn their heads every so often to see who was staring at their backs.

Those around Reynaud, those closest to him, portrayed their nervousness, too, often slowing their mounts so they could keep their eyes on the Frenchman.

The nervousness among the men was contagious and the line of men became ragged and spread out until finally Reynaud called a halt.

"You men," he said, "keep a horse-length of distance between you. You're too spread out."

The Mexicans shrugged and several muttered the timeworn phrase used by their kind to ignore English commands: *"No sabe,"* which Reynaud knew was not even good Spanish. But Reynaud understood what they meant, and his facial features contorted with rage and the veins in his neck stood out like purple worms bulging under a scarlet scarf.

"You understand me. Close up, close up."

The Mexicans bunched up, but as soon as Reynaud started roaming, they began to thin their ranks, letting gaps form between them until they were strung out again, offering no show of force, or any protection for Reynaud.

"Que pasa?" Reynaud shouted, for at least the tenth time. "Nuncio, *que estas haciendo*?" he yelled to Nuncio, the point man. That was the only name Reynaud knew him by and he didn't know the names of many of the other men.

"We are following," Nuncio said in Spanish. *"Siguiendo, no mas."*

"Malditos," Reynaud shouted. " *'Cerca. 'Cerca,"* which he hoped meant for them to close up. He did not see that the Mexicans were smiling and grinning at one another. But he saw that none made a move to close up the gaping holes in the column.

Reynaud, it seemed, had reached the limits of his patience. He was about to draw his pistol and offer to shoot the first man who refused to obey his orders, when the column stopped abruptly. When he looked toward the front of the line of men and horses, he saw Nuncio holding up his hand to halt the procession.

"Now what?" Reynaud said, to no one.

He heard the men talking in rapid Spanish and then those in front of him began trotting their horses to the head of the column, leaving Reynaud by himself at the rear. He swore under his breath, but did not draw his pistol. He tried to make out what Nuncio was saying as he prodded his horse to catch up with the others.

The Mexicans milled around, chattering among themselves as Reynaud rode up. He knew they were excited, but he didn't understand why until he looked down at the ground in front of Nuncio's horse.

"Many tracks," Nuncio said. He was a dark-skinned man with a heavy moustache that covered his upper lip and most of his lower as if he had a black bat stuck to his face.

"So?" Reynaud said.

"They go this way and that way."

Reynaud studied the ground. The sun was just brimming the western horizon so that there was enough light to see. But in a few moments they would lose the light, he knew.

Should he follow Bone's tracks, Reynaud wondered, or those of Anson Baron and his men? Reynaud knew he didn't have much time. He had to make a decision, and make it fast. He looked again at the tracks, marveling that he had made sense of them, that he had actually been able to read the marks on the road and decipher them.

But what did they mean? Why had Bone ridden off the road? And where had he gone? Reynaud had never trusted that half-breed son of a bitch. Bone was up to something, that much he knew. But what? Had he warned Anson Baron, then ridden off to God-knew-where to hide while Baron waited in ambush just ahead?

Reynaud looked at the tracks again. He thought, for an instant, that Bone and Baron might have ridden off together. But no, there was only the one track leaving the road. Bone's. Christ, he thought, what in hell was going on?

Suddenly Reynaud was gripped with a sense of panic. His palms began to sweat, turn clammy. He rubbed one, then the other on his trousers as if they were stains that marked him for a coward. In the distance he heard the raucous calling of crows. They sounded like the cries of terrified children.

He looked toward the setting sun. The rim had disappeared and now the shadows filled in all the hollows of the earth around him and the road turned sullen and mysterious in both directions.

"Nuncio, Obispo, come here," Reynaud called, as he faced the Mexicans still bunched down the road. *"Andale, andale."*

The Mexicans did not hurry as they rode their mounts toward Reynaud. He could see that they were deliberate in their slowness, but he knew there was nothing he could do about it. The more he harangued them, the slower they would be. He wished now, as he had for the past several days, that he had never gotten involved in that slave deal with Matteo. He wished he had never told Matteo that lie about Martin Baron when he said that Baron had defiled his sister and gotten her pregnant. It was not a lie so much as an exaggeration. Martin had come to their home, and Reynaud's sister had been smitten with Baron, but, in truth, it was merely an infatuation and Martin had not taken advantage of the girl's lovesickness. But his sister had wept for days after Martin had left, and later she had thrown herself at another man, who had gotten her pregnant. That man was now dead, his skeleton at the bottom of a bayou. But his sister had named the son she had birthed "Martine," since she was still infatuated with Baron. So he had not lied too much to Matteo. And he still hated Martin Baron for reasons he could not clearly define. He had seen Martin's effect on his sister and her subsequent confusion, the loss of her virginity, and that was enough, in Reynaud's eyes, to blame Martin for what his sister had done, gone and given herself to the first scoundrel she happened to meet.

He knew that Matteo hated Martin Baron, and it had been easy to devise a scheme to meet the man and do some business with him; all he had had to do was pretend that he and Matteo had a common enemy: Martin Baron. At first he had just wanted to sell Matteo slaves, slaves that had cost him nothing but time to steal. Then he had thought he could use Matteo's greed to his own advantage, perhaps help the Mexican regain the lands his forebears had sold to Martin and thereby gain either a monetary benefit or land for himself. Or both.

But, as it was turning out, Martin Baron was a more formidable foe than he had realized. The land was bigger than he had imagined, and much of it unfit for human habitation. And, as he had discovered, Matteo was cash-poor. He had paid for the slaves, of course, but only partially. Since the slaves had not been sold at market, Aguilar hadn't paid the remainder of the money due Reynaud.

And now Reynaud was chasing after Martin's son, Anson, whom he did not know. He had known Martin in New Orleans, of course, seen the money he had made driving cattle there, had heard the talk that Baron would one day be rich, as the market for cattle grew. Now, with the nation entering a civil war, he doubted if Martin would ever be able to develop Northern markets.

In those moments, as Reynaud was waiting for the Mexicans to ride up to him, he saw his schemes vaporize into air as the land darkened around him. He knew, then, that he had made some serious mistakes in his plans, mistakes in judgment. He had thought Matteo would back any move he made, but instead he had been sent on a wild-goose chase with a bunch of sullen men who did not take orders. He wondered now if there was any way out of his predicament. That man who had been watching him, Obispo—had Matteo sent him along for a some nefarious reason? Was Obispo to be his assassin if he failed to find and kill Anson Baron?

The thought not only crossed Reynaud's mind, it planted itself there and bloomed like some poisonous flower.

In the next instant, just before the men came up to him, Reynaud made his decision.

"You have found something?" Nuncio said. "What have you found?"

"The Indian, Bone," Reynaud said, "is trying to fool us. He rides off here, is that not so?"

Nuncio and the others all examined the tracks for several seconds. They uttered exclamations and nodded their heads in agreement.

"It is so. Bone rode that way, toward the setting sun."

There was a quiet then. Reynaud no longer heard the cawing of the crows. He looked at the men in the gathering dusk. He sought out the eyes of Obispo and when he found them, he stared directly into them.

"Obispo and I will follow Bone. Perhaps he is running away; perhaps he knows where the other riders are going. You, Nuncio, take the others on down the road and shoot anyone you see."

Nuncio turned to look at Obispo. Obispo nodded to him.

"I will take the men and find where the tracks go on the road," Nuncio said. "And where will you be if we find them?"

"We will hear the shots and come to you," Reynaud said.

"Bueno," Nuncio said. *"Vamanos."*

He and the others rode on, while Reynaud and Obispo stayed behind.

"You lead out, Obispo," Reynaud said.

"Why?"

"Because you are a better tracker than I. Go ahead."

Obispo hesitated. Reynaud fixed a steely gaze on Obispo.

"Go on," Reynaud said again.

"I think we should go with Nuncio and the others."

"I'm in charge here. You will do what I say or turn back to the Rocking A."

Obispo sucked in a breath. Then he shrugged his shoulders. *"Bueno,"* he said. "We will follow Bone and see where he goes."

Reynaud nodded.

Obispo turned his horse off the road and began to read the ground, following Bone's tracks.

Reynaud rode a horse-length behind him. He kept his eyes on Obispo's back.

The sun disappeared over the horizon, leaving a last long blaze in the far sky. The bottoms of the clouds looked as though they had been forged of gold just before they turned to ashes as the furnace died out beyond the western rim of the bleak land.

31

PEEBO SPOKE FIRST. "That them?" he said in a thin whisper.

"Nobody but." Anson eased the hammer back on his rifle, pressing the trigger slightly so as to lessen the metallic noise of the cocking mechanism.

Anson heard the faint scrape of the sear on Peebo's rifle locking into place as he cocked it. The riders came on, dark shapes in an indistinguishable mass. Peebo lifted his rifle to his shoulder.

"Wait," Anson whispered.

"You start the ball, then."

Anson drew his own rifle to his shoulder and drew a bead on the dark mass of men. At that angle there was but a single shape. He waited, tracking the progress with the muzzle of his rifle, moving it slowly as the group drew closer. He knew that once they completely rounded the short bend in the road, he would begin to see single figures.

As the men riding toward them began to separate, Anson began counting. When he had counted six and saw more coming, he took a bead on the second man. He figured the first would turn around if Peebo didn't drop him, and the men behind the second man would scatter for cover.

Mentally Anson figured yardage, and it was difficult in the dark.

There was no moon up as yet and judging distances was tricky. He relied mostly on memory—memory gathered in daylight.

"Well, fuck," Peebo whispered rhetorically, and Anson wanted to strangle him. But he had his man picked out and he led him just a hair and squeezed the trigger when the buckhorn front-sight eased away from the Mexican's chest. The flintlock whispered a spark into the pan and the pan flashed. Flame shot through the hole and ignited the powder grains and the rifle belched flame and lead. White smoke billowed from the barrel and obscured not only Anson's target, but the entire procession. He heard the report from Peebo's rifle right on the heels of his own and knew that Peebo had fired while he could still see.

A man screamed through the billowing cloud of smoke and then his scream was cut off as if the sound had been sliced by a guillotine. Other men shouted in Spanish, cursed in two languages. Anson shoved the smoking barrel of his rifle into its boot and turned his horse.

"Let's light a shuck, Peebo," Anson said, loud enough for his friend to hear. As he rode into the mesquite wood, he heard Peebo's horse pounding the ground behind him.

Other shots sounded from across the road and more men screamed. Anson dodged through the trees, huddled over his horse's neck so that he wouldn't be knocked out of the saddle by a low-hanging bough. He hoped his men had gotten away; in fact, he was counting on it. They had the advantage. Matteo's men would be shooting into the woods at shadows, blinded by darkness and fear.

Anson heard more firing from the road, and then an awful quiet descended on the forest as his horse twisted through the trees, surefooted as a dancer. Anson slowed, so that Peebo could catch up to him. He didn't want to wear out his horse and he was sure they had gotten far enough away so that none of Matteo's men could track them through the mesquite thicket.

Peebo rode up alongside as they reached a small clearing.

"We done spilt blood, son," Peebo said.

"Maybe."

"Hell, I saw that second man in line throw up his arms just as I shot number one clean out of his rockin' chair."

"Did you get shot at?"

"Hell, I don't know. Right after I started chasin' you, I heard rifles poppin' off like New Year's from acrost the road."

"You count how many there was?"

"I seen there was more'n enough to go around."

"That's why we're going back."

"Huh?"

"Follow me," Anson said, and cut his horse hard to the left, following an arc that would bring him and Peebo up into the rear of the column. He stopped just before reaching the road again and slid his rifle down until he gripped it close to the muzzle. He began pouring powder down the barrel directly from the horn slung over his shoulder.

"You're crazy as a damned hoot-owl, Anson," Peebo said, when he pulled up alongside.

"Reload your rifle. Got any buckshot?"

"I got some."

"Put a patch over the barrel once you've got the powder poured and drop about six or eight buck balls down on top."

"You are plumb loco."

"Hurry up. We can catch 'em by surprise."

"Or they can catch us."

Anson leaked a half dozen balls of buckshot down onto a greased patch, then rammed the load home. He poured fine powder from the small horn into the pan, and blew away the excess. He adjusted the flint, made sure it was tight and closed the frizzen.

Peebo finished loading his rifle. "Can't see a damned thing," he said. "Don't know if the powder went down the barrel or down my pants-leg."

"Let's go," Anson said, and he eased his horse toward the road.

There was nobody there. He and Peebo kept to the shadows along the right side as they headed toward the Box B. Then Anson heard a rustling ahead and reined in his horse.

Peebo stopped also, right next to Anson. The two stood staring down the road. Anson saw a dark lump that resembled a body. The shape was less than fifty feet away, and beyond, he thought he saw another body lying in the road. But it might have been a tree shadow or just a peculiar shade of chiaroscuro in the landscape of the night itself.

The rustling sound continued, sporadically, but neither man could determine its source.

"What is it?" Peebo asked.

"I don't know. That could be a body yonder on the road."

"I make it out a dead man, son."

"Can you see what that is just beyond it? Another ten, fifteen feet."

"Nope. It looks like something, though."

"Yeah, it looks like something," Anson said, a sarcastic twang to his voice. "Every goddamned thing looks like something."

" 'Specially at night."

"Don't get smarty now, Peebo."

"That sound might be coming from off in the woods."

Anson turned his head to the left, then to the right. He kept doing this until he located a place where the noises might be coming from. They didn't last long enough for him to be sure, but he pointed off to the right. "I think those rustlin' noises are comin' from over yonder," he said.

Peebo stared in that direction. "Yep, seems likely. Some animal, maybe, rustlin' around."

"Or a man," Anson said. "A wounded man."

Before Peebo could reply, Anson rode slowly forward, closing in on the first lump in the road. When he drew parallel to it, he stopped. Peebo rode up.

"That's one dead man, I reckon," Peebo said.

"He's not moving. And it's a man, all right."

"I don't hear that sound no more."

Anson listened. It was true. There was a silence around them now except for the thundering deadness of the body lying in the road. Anson felt his skin ripple as if it was trying to crawl off his back. He could smell the scent left by the man, as he had voided just before death. Anson turned his face away as if to avoid the scent of the man's bowels.

"There," Peebo said. "There it is again."

Anson looked down the road. Another body lay some fifteen or twenty feet away. He was sure it was a body now. A rifle lay next to it.

He figured these two men might have been shot by Timo and his companions. If so, the men he and Peebo had shot should be a short distance ahead. He heard the rustling sound again. And, then, he heard a man moan.

"Over there," Peebo whispered, loud enough for Anson to hear.

"I hear it."

"That's a human yonder."

"Maybe," Anson said.

"No 'maybe.' Ain't no critter makin' that sound."

Then they both heard it. A single word. *"Ayudame. Help me."*

Anson felt the hackles rise on the back of his neck, like the faint silent tatter of a spider's legs prancing on his spine.

"I heard that," Peebo said.

"You watch the road," Anson told him. "I'll see what's what."

Anson rode toward the moaning sounds. He was wary, but he already had a sickening boil in his gut, a swirling that told him what he might find. He saw movement out of the corner of his eye and veered toward it, his rifle leveled at the figure on the ground from hip level.

"Anson," groaned the man. *"Ayudame. Please help me."*

"Quien es?"

"*Soy* Paco."

"Paco?"

"Yes."

Anson quickly dismounted. He tied his horse's reins to a small mesquite and dashed over to the wounded man. He bent down and looked into the face of one of his own men, Paco Castro.

"Where do you hurt?" he asked Paco in Spanish.

"In my stomach. I took the ball in my stomach."

"What you got there, son?" Peebo called.

"Come on, it's Paco Castro."

Peebo rode up as Anson was knifing away Paco's shirt, his sharp blade ripping through the fabric. He felt hot sticky blood on his hands. He could not see in the dark, so when Paco's belly was exposed, he felt around it, probing with his fingers, the size and depth of the wound.

"Ai, de mi," Paco bleated.

"It is bad, Paco. Very bad."

"I know. Can you get the lead ball out? I can feel it still in my stomach."

Peebo dismounted and walked over to the two men. He knelt down and felt Paco's forehead.

"He's hotter'n a two-dollar pistol," Peebo said, wiping his sweat-stained hand on his trouser leg.

"Calmate," Anson said to Paco. He gently lifted the man at the small of his back and felt underneath. He felt more blood and what felt like the shattered ends of two or three ribs. The ball had gone straight through Paco and he was bleeding out pretty fast.

"Do you feel the *galena?*" Paco asked.

"Yes," Anson lied. "I will take it out."

"I do not want to die, Anson. I have a wife . . ."

"I know. Wait." Anson let the man down gently and pulled back his bloody hand from underneath him. He did not look at Peebo for fear he would give it away that Paco did not have long to live.

But Peebo must have understood, for he spoke to Anson for Paco's benefit. "Lucky you could feel that ball. Should be easy to get out."

"Yes," Anson said. "It is near the skin. In a good place."

"Ai, duele mucho, tanto," Paco said.

"I know," Anson said in Spanish. "*Esperate pocos minutos,* eh?"

Paco closed his eyes but his face was contorted in pain. He seemed to be gathering his strength so that Anson could dig the ball out of his back, or stomach.

Anson looked at Peebo then, and shook his head. Peebo nodded.

"Dios mìo, el dolor, el dolor," Paco chanted in a weak voice. *"Hace mucho dolor."*

"I have to tell him, Peebo. He is very religious," Anson said.

"Yeah, I reckon."

"What? What?" Paco asked.

"Paco, you are dying," Anson said in Spanish. "Pray. I will tell your wife you died a brave man."

"Did you take the ball from me, then?"

"Yes," Anson lied. "I am not able to stop the blood."

"Is there nothing you can do?"

"No, there is nothing."

"Jesus, Mary, and Joseph."

"Yes, you pray," Anson said.

Paco began to pray in a soft voice. He reached out and grabbed Anson's hand, then squeezed it. He held that tight grip until his voice faded away and, finally, he sighed and released his last breath. His hand relaxed and fell away.

Anson choked on something in his throat and stood up, gasping for breath. "He's gone, Peebo."

"May he rest in peace."

"Peace? What is that?" Anson asked bitterly.

Peebo kept his mouth shut. After a moment, he remounted his horse and waited for Anson to leave the body of the dead cowhand.

Finally Anson turned and walked to his horse.

"I can't see your face, son, but I'll bet you got blood in your eye."

"You're damned right I do. Come on, let's ride. I might not know what son of a bitch killed Paco, but I'll damned sure know when I'm finished."

"How's that?" Peebo asked.

"I aim to kill every one of those men who rode by here."

"All by yourself?" Peebo asked.

"If necessary."

"Lead on out, son. I reckon I'll surely foller you."

Anson slapped his horse's rump with the trailing ends of his reins and the horse bucked from a standstill into a trot that grew into a gallop.

Peebo had to put the spurs to his mount to catch up with Anson. They rode along the side of the road so close to the mesquite trees they felt the slap of the limbs on their legs and shoulders.

Anson only slowed when they came upon more bodies in the road. Riderless horses stood hipshot next to the woods like frozen statues, and none whickered when Anson stopped to examine the brands to see if he had lost any more men.

"I count four, so far," Peebo said.

"Well, you're going to count a hell of a lot more before daylight, Peebo."

Then Anson was off again and Peebo rode hard to catch up.

Peebo felt as if he was chasing after a madman and he hoped the blood in Anson's eye didn't blind him to the danger that lay ahead on this dark and solemn night.

32

BONE WAITED. DEEP in the shadows of a mesquite grove, he sat his horse without moving a muscle, a shadow within a shadow, invisible to any eye but the owl's. For some time now, he had been listening to the sounds coming from the nearby road, and the sounds told him much, but not all.

He had heard the Frenchman's voice and the liquid sounds of the Mexicans talking among themselves, then had heard Reynaud order Obispo to follow the tracks off the road, his own tracks. He had seen the two pass by moments ago and wondered if Reynaud meant to shoot Obispo in the back. Or perhaps Matteo had sent both men to kill him, and that was why they were following his old trail.

If Obispo was a good-enough tracker, he would find the new trail and come back to this place. Bone wondered whether he should just wait for them or ride on, back to the Rocking A, where he planned to get Dawn and take her away, to another place.

All this time, since he had left Anson, he had been thinking of Dream Speaker and the many things the old man of the tribe had told him. Riding through the dark it had seemed to him that he was the only man alive on the earth, that he was the last of all human beings, and he tried to imagine how it must have been for those Dream Speaker had told him about, those who had lived long ago and then vanished, like smoke on the wind, never to be seen again.

He had given the strange stone to Anson and he wondered why, but deep down, he knew. He felt that Dream Speaker had wanted him to find the stone and to give it to someone, to Anson, perhaps, so that the talking signs in the stone could finally be heard by someone alive in another time.

Dream Speaker was dead, Bone knew. Gone to the dust that claimed all living things. But his spirit lived on and Bone could feel him now, near him, whispering in his ear, so soft he could not make out the words.

The sound, however, took Bone back to a time when Dream Speaker was alive, when they sat together on the mountain, smoking the pipe and looking at the sky.

Dream Speaker had picked up a handful of dirt. He held it in his open right hand, then poked his left index finger into the mass, spread it around on his palm. "Do you know what this is, Hueso?"

"Dirt."

"Yes, it is dirt, but where did it come from?"

"I do not know, Dream Speaker. Perhaps it was always here."

Dream Speaker had looked up again at the sky. He extended his left arm and pointed to a floating white cloud. "It came from beyond that cloud, beyond that part of the sky you can see now with your eyes."

"How do you know this?"

"Many, many winters ago, the old ones knew all this and they told their children and their children told their children and I heard it from my grandfather."

Dream Speaker closed his hand and tipped it. The dirt started to pour from his half-open fist and trickle back down onto the ground. "So it is," he said, "that the dust from the stars settled on the earth and we humans were created from this same dust. That is all we are. That is all that anything is, in the sky, on the earth, and in the sea."

"It is not much, I think," Bone had said.

"No, it is everything."

"Why?"

"Because we can see it and think about it, that is why. And it can see us and think about us. This is what my grandfather told me and he had heard it from his grandfather. All is nothing and nothing becomes all, over and over, ever and ever."

"It does not make sense."

"Perhaps we come from the stars and we go back to the stars one day."

"No sense to that at all, Dream Speaker."

"Life is endless. That is the sense of it. It becomes and then it goes away. It comes back changed. This is what we must see as we watch our bodies grow old and wither. This is what I see. I see myself becoming as the babe again, no teeth, no hair, no sense. All a circle, all life a circle, and the sky a circle. We see ourselves going away and we meet ourselves coming back."

"Coming back?"

Just then a golden eagle had floated over them, floated on the sky itself, its wings outstretched, unflapping, and it had soared and floated in a wide circle. Dream Speaker had looked up at the eagle and so had Bone.

"Who is that eagle, Hueso? Is that your father? Maybe it is my father, or your mother. Maybe it is my grandfather."

"It is an eagle. It is a bird."

Dream Speaker had smiled then, and his wrinkled face resembled the rugged mountains with their creases that were valleys, their hard ridges that were the color of rusted iron.

"It is us, too. We are no different. He is of dust as we are of dust. The dust is just put together in a different way, like the sand paintings of the people who live to the west of us. I am that eagle and you are that eagle and that eagle is you and that eagle is me. We are all one thing. Look, I breathe, and I breathe the sky into my body and the sky is endless and it fills me with the spirits that have gone before and will come again some day."

"All of this is a big mystery to me, Dream Speaker."

"Yes, it is a mystery. It will always be a mystery because all life is a mystery. Ghosts are a mystery. That is as it should be."

"Why do you tell me these things if I cannot understand them?" Bone asked.

"Because then you will know that when my body is dust, I am not dust. That I am alive and with you. I will be the air you breathe and the thoughts you think. I will be the ghost who leaves no shadow, but is like the shadow that you see out of the corner of your eye, the shadow that when you turn to see what it is, is no longer there. I want you to know that, although I die, I yet live."

"How will I know?" Bone had asked.

"You will know." Dream Speaker closed his right fist and struck his chest over the heart. "You will know here."

"In my heart?"

"Yes, and here." Dream Speaker tapped a bony fingertip on his forehead.

"I will look for you," Bone said, but he knew he was saying it only because he thought that was what Dream Speaker had wanted him to say.

"No, do not look for me, Hueso. But, when you are not looking for me, when you are all alone and death is near, you will know that I am there, beside you and in your heart and in your head."

As it was now, Bone knew. Death was near. And so was Dream Speaker. He drew in a deep breath and thought of what Dream Speaker had told him. He looked up at the night sky and knew his breath had come from there, had traveled all that far way through the stars and the night and was now in his lungs, and he felt strong and alive. He felt alive in two ways, as if he were two beings, as if he were himself and the one watching himself. It was a good feeling, a strong feeling, and he saw a flitting shadow out of the corner of his eye and knew it must have been Dream Speaker, the ghost of the old man passing by.

Bone turned suddenly to see if the shadow was real. He turned very quickly as if to catch it and make it reveal itself. But the shadow was not there and he thought, at first, that it must be a trick of the light from the stars, or something caught in the corner of his eye, but then he listened to his heart and knew that Dream Speaker had been there and when he turned back to look in the direction of the hoof sounds, he knew that Dream Speaker was still there, not as a ghost or a shadow, but inside him, part of him, like the eagle they had seen that day, floating in the sky and seeing them as they were seeing him.

Bone rode out from the bower in the mesquite and began to follow Obispo and Reynaud. He wanted to see what these two would do, and he was not afraid, because he knew Dream Speaker was with him and that he would be watching, too, to see what would happen.

33

ANSON MADE A hasty examination of the body in the middle of the road, feeling like a grave-robber invading a private tomb. The face, a frozen bronze mask, told him that it was one of Matteo Aguilar's men. He and Peebo found two more dead men farther on.

"That one's yours," Peebo said, pointing to the farthest one. "That other is the one I shot out of the saddle."

"How do you know?"

"See that bandanna pokin' out from under his hat?"

"I see it." There was a hole right through it which Anson could see when he leaned over and looked close.

"That's what I aimed at."

"Pretty good shot."

"He didn't suffer none too much."

Anson rode on and looked at the man he had shot. It made him sick, not just from the smell, but he could see where his ball had entered the man's chest, right at the heart, and there were bone-white ribs, splintered into darning needles, sticking out around it. He must have hit the man at an angle, because of the size of the hole, and the man's right arm was smashed, bent at a sharp angle. There was a large hole in the side of the man's chest and a pool of blood big enough to float a toy boat.

Anson's stomach heaved and he turned his horse away from the stench, gulped in air that bore no taint, held it until his lungs burned. He let his breath out and pulled his stomach in to keep from vomiting.

"Gets you, don't it, son?" Peebo said, as he rode up a moment later.

Anson gasped.

"A man don't die pretty when he dies sudden like that."

"Shut up, Peebo."

Anson stopped his horse a few strides farther on to let the queasiness in his stomach pass. Still the bile threatened to rise up in his gullet and strangle him or spew forth. Peebo waited patiently alongside, listening, his ear cocked to pick up any sound.

Anson gripped the saddlehorn tight and took deep breaths until his stomach settled. He tried to think of something other than the man he had shot, but he couldn't make the image of the man's dead body vanish.

"I guess you don't never get used to it," Anson said, a few moments later.

Peebo said nothing.

"Damn you, Peebo. Don't you have nothin' to say?"

"You told me to keep my mouth shut."

"There are times when you talk too much, that's all."

Still, Peebo kept silent.

The image of Anson's mother, Caroline, crept into his consciousness, unbidden. Anson thought of her lying there in her bed, in death, and it was not like that dead man on the road. He could smell the scent of the cloying perfume that had drenched her room and her bed, and that was just as gagging to him as the odor of the dead Mexican. It was not natural, that overpowering smell of perfume, but it was better than the other. But he could not keep from connecting the two deaths in his mind and it bothered him that he would think of his mother at such a time and in such a context.

"And there are times when you don't say enough," Anson said.

Peebo did not respond. He pretended not to hear and that irritated Anson even more than his tar-baby silence.

"Don't it bother you none?" Anson asked.

"What?"

"That goddamned smell."

"What smell is that?"

"You know damned well what smell I mean."

"No, I reckon I don't."

"I ought to pop you one."

"Go ahead. If it'll make you feel any better."

"I feel just fine, Peebo Elves."

"When you use both my names like that, I know you're pissed off."

"I'm not pissed off."

"Well, you want to pop me?"

"I asked you a question, damn it."

"I forgot what it was."

"That dead man. That one I killed. He stank to high heaven."

"I didn't notice it none in particular."

"Be damned if you didn't."

"Well, son, when a man dies sudden, everything inside him lets go. I mean *everything*."

"It's god-awful."

"Mine must have gone without lunch. He didn't smell hardly at all. Maybe a little piss smell."

"You're being a little too smarty now, Peebo."

"Well, you asked me and I done told you."

"It don't bother you? That smell?"

"I try not to let it."

"You must have a stuffed-up nose," Anson said.

"Look, Anson, if you're going to kill a man, you got to expect he ain't goin' to be pretty to look at, and he might stink up things some. You got to put it all out of your mind."

"It's hard."

"No it ain't."

"How do you do it?"

"Son, I don't look at their faces and I hold my breath when I come up on anything that's dead, no matter whether it be critter or human."

"You've seen a lot of dead men?"

"I've seen a lot of dead things. Likely you have, too."

Anson's irritation sprang up. He wondered if Peebo was talking about his mother. "What in hell do you mean by that?"

"Hold on, son. Don't you go shootin' the messenger. I just meant things die—people, critters big and small. You, me, everybody. You go to thinkin' about it too much, you'll go plumb loco."

Peebo was right, Anson decided; he had made too much of it. He was only curious about how Peebo could just ride on by those dead men and not be affected by them. The sight of them tore things inside him, tangled up his mind like twine in a sticker patch.

"I reckon I let it get to me, all right."

"It'll pass, son."

But Anson wondered. He had buried his grief when his mother had died, held all his emotions inside him like a balled-up fist. And now he grieved for her, but it was a quiet, slow grieving, like a sadness that was just out of reach, a sadness that had no shape or form and could not be defined in simple words or handled with simple thoughts. The grieving was filled with a grayness like an autumn sky, a bleakness that was like the sad bare trees in winter, a fleeting scent in his nostrils like the brief smell of a crushed rose.

There was a big hole in his life where his mother had been, a vacancy that he knew could never be filled, and that was sad, too, because he missed her, missed hearing her voice and seeing her lean over his bed to wake him on dark mornings when the earth was still and the cock had not yet crowed. He even missed hearing her argue with his father, for that was her life, too, and his, and the longing in him deepened in that soft moment of reflection and he had to struggle to keep from weeping with the memory of her and the terrible moment when he had known, finally, that she was dead, the life and love gone from her body and nothing left of her but the clothes in her wardrobe and the jewelry in her jewel box, the books she had read to him, lying on a table, and the faint sound of her feet on the hardwood floors still lingering somehow among the creakings and mysterious stirrings in the silent and sleeping house.

"Anson?" Peebo said. "You okay?"

Anson shook his head to clear it, bring himself back to the moment. "Yeah, I'm okay."

"Do you still want to chase after them other Mexicans?"

"I think we ought to. They might not be expecting us."

"Lead on out, then."

Anson spoke to his horse and turned it.

They had not ridden a hundred yards when they heard the sharp crack of a rifle up ahead of them.

"Uh-oh," Peebo said.

"What the hell . . ."

Then they heard the crackle of more rifles firing, and Anson was the first to see the blue-orange muzzle-flashes.

"Looks like . . ." Peebo started to say, when a lead ball whistled past the two men, so close it set the hairs on their necks to bristling.

"Get the hell off the road," Anson said, and wheeled his horse toward the woods on his left.

The firing stopped as men reloaded their rifles. Anson slid from the saddle, cocking his rifle. He let his horse stand free as he ducked and scrambled toward the nearest mesquite tree. Peebo ran his horse into the woods and came up behind Anson.

"What do you figure?"

"Damned if I can figure it. Those men up there are sure as hell shooting at something."

"Well, we'd better fish or cut bait."

Anson started skulking toward the sound of the rifle fire, the orange images of the last muzzle-flame still burning as a glowing afterimage in his brain.

He saw the hulk of a dead horse lying in the center of the road. He knew it was dead because it was not moving, and something next to it was. He stopped and tried to make out what was moving, staring hard into the dark as if to shred it and bring light upon the object. Seconds later he saw a hat in bare silhouette, scarcely visible, and then what he took to be a rifle slid across the pommel of the saddle. As he stared, the rifle steadied on something off in the woods and the rifle barked, spewed flame from its muzzle. From the woods a split second later, another rifle spat with a noise like a breaking branch and he saw the muzzle flash. He heard the ball *thunk* into the horse and the hat disappeared.

Anson got down on his belly and crawled toward the fallen horse and the man lying prone behind it. He could hear the clack of a powder horn on metal and, later, the hollow metallic sound of a ramrod sliding down the barrel.

"Timo?" Anson called, then hugged the ground. He was close

to the horse now and, with one eye, he looked for movement. Two rifles fired at him from his side of the road and he heard the hiss of a ball as it sped by, and the harsh, scything sound of the other ball spewing through the grass next to him.

The man next to the horse turned and trained his rifle in Anson's direction.

"Over here," Timo shouted, and Anson marked the place where he had seen answering fire moments before. Anson kept his eye on the man next to the horse, hoping he could not be seen if he did not move.

The man raised up to look for Anson, but Anson could not bring his rifle up without being seen. He held his breath as his gut knotted with fear.

The man behind the horse carcass rose up slightly, took direct aim at Anson. Anson had started to roll away when he heard a hammer strike the frizzen, followed by a puffing sound and an explosion. He heard the ball whistle over his head and saw the Mexican in the road twist upward for a moment, then fall sideways. Anson looked around to see Peebo reloading his rifle.

"Damned good shot," Anson said.

"He looked a lot like a turkey, I thought."

"Where are the others who were shooting at me?"

"Up yonder. I think they had that dead horse staked out, let that bastard in the road draw all the fire."

"Pretty smart."

"Damned smart. Was that Timo what hollered?"

"Yeah. He's over on the other side of the road."

"Thought he was supposed to light a shuck."

"Matteo's men must have caught up to him."

"Reckon he's by hisself?"

"I don't know. I could walk over there and ask him."

"You do that, son."

It was quiet for a few moments. Peebo finished reloading his rifle and crawled up next to Anson. They both lay there and listened for several moments. Neither heard anything worth commenting about and then they saw someone crawling across the road. Peebo lifted his rifle to his shoulder. Anson grabbed the barrel and pulled it down.

"That might be Timo," Anson said.

"Yeah, could be. Let me keep a bead on him, will you? Just in case."

"Don't shoot him until . . ."

"Until I see the whites of his eyes?"

"Don't get smart, Peebo. I'll know if it's Timo soon enough."

Peebo brought his rifle back up and followed the man's progress with the end of the barrel. A rifle cracked the air up ahead and the man on the road froze.

"They've spotted him," Anson said.

"Looks like."

"Wait, here he comes, crawling pretty fast."

"Can't tell who it is," Peebo said.

The man came closer and Anson let out a sigh of relief. "It's Timo."

There were no more shots and Timo kept coming, using his elbows to pull him forward, cradling his rifle in his arms. There were no more shots as he reached the side of the road.

"Do not shoot the rifle," Timo said, when he had crawled within earshot. "Do not shoot."

"I am not going to shoot you," Anson said.

"No, do not shoot at those men who are by the road."

"Why?"

"Because they will see the fire from the barrel and shoot you."

Timo stopped crawling. He panted for several seconds.

"Are the others all dead?" Anson asked.

"No, only one, I think. The others have gone back to the rancho."

"Why did you stay here?"

"They shot my horse. The horse, she is dead. She is in the *selva.* The woods."

"Did the others leave you behind?"

"No, I told them to go. Don Anson, we have killed all their horses, the horses of the men of Matteo. They have to use the feet and they do not go. They try to kill me."

"We can't just stay here, Timo," Anson said. "We've got to either shoot it out with Matteo's men or get to the other side of the road and ride to the plain."

"I know. We can kill them, I think. Look, Don Anson, there are men on the road. They wait to see the rifle make the fire. Then they shoot, eh? So, we make them come here. Then we shoot them."

"Why would they come here?"

"I will tell them that we wish to surrender."

"That won't work."

"It will work. They told me. They say if I surrender they will not shoot me. They say they will let me go if I throw them the rifle."

"So? If we throw down our rifles, Timo, they will shoot us dead."

"I know. We will throw the mesquite stick. We will tell them it is the rifles," said Timo.

"Peebo?" Anson said.

"I don't think it will work no more'n pourin' coal oil on a campfire."

"What do you think we ought to do? It's darker'n the inside of a coal pit out here," said Anson.

"Moon'll be up soon."

"So Matteo's men won't need rifle-flashes to see us. We're outnumbered."

Timo stopped panting. He crawled around the other side of Anson, closer to the trees. He started picking at his clothes.

"What are you doing, Timo?" Anson asked.

"I pick the cactus from the clothes."

Peebo suppressed a titter.

"Well, Peebo," Anson said, "any ideas?"

"We could cut into the woods here and head on back."

"We could get lost, too. The mesquite on this side of the road runs a good two or three miles wide to the west and some ten miles north."

"Yeah. Not good."

"We could get behind them, maybe," Anson said.

"No," Timo said. "They sit in a circle and there is one man, he is in the tree. He took the machete and cut the limbs. He can see all of the road. He can see much."

"Shit," Anson said.

"We shoot that bird first," Peebo said.

"How?"

"Maybe I could crawl over to that dead horse yonder and get him to shoot at me. Then I'd know where the son of a bitch was and drop him outta that tree."

"He'd shoot you before you got halfway across the road," Anson said. "I'm not going to risk it."

"I'd be the one to risk it."

"No," Anson said.

"There is another way, I think," Timo said.

Peebo and Anson turned their heads to look at Timo. He was still prone on the ground, clutching his rifle.

"What way?"

"I will go in the mesquite and shoot the man in the tree."

"You mean, go through the mesquite here and crawl around behind? But you said they were in a circle. They could hear you coming. They would shoot you the minute you got close enough to see the man in the tree."

"That is true," Timo admitted.

Anson looked up the road. Beyond the dead horse it appeared deserted. He thought of Matteo's men up there, all sitting in a circle. And one man sitting on top of a mesquite tree, the branches cut away. He looked back at his horse, and at Peebo's. Two horses, three men. Going against a half-dozen or so of Matteo's. All of them sitting there, waiting. Their rifles loaded, their eyes peering into the dark. All listening for the slightest sound. He supposed that he, Peebo, and Timo could all make a dash across the road and then ride to the plain. They'd probably draw fire, but they might make it. *Might.*

Anson sighed, looked up the road again.

Maybe, he thought, there was another way—one with less risk. Was it better to run? Or was it better to attack? They were outgunned. Matteo's men had pistols, and so did he and Peebo.

"You got a pistol, Timo?"

"Yes, I have the pistol."

"Loaded?"

"It has the six balls in the cylinder, yes."

"What are you thinking, son?" Peebo asked.

"Firepower," Anson said.

"You aim to just walk up there and blast away with our six-shooters?"

"No," Anson said. "I'm just trying to think of every contingency."

" 'Contingency.' By Jesus, there's a six-bit word. What in hell does it mean?"

"Possible things that might happen if we jump those men up yonder."

"Well, I'll tell you one damned contin—one damned possibility. We'll get our asses shot off."

"Maybe not," Anson said. He looked at Timo. "How far away are Matteo's men?"

"They are not fifty paces from the dead horse in the road. And you can not see them. They are behind the trees and they have cut the wood and they make the walls."

"Breastworks?" Anson asked. He had read of such barriers in books.

"I do not know," Timo said. "They stack the wood and they hide like chickens behind the wood."

"Not wood, Timo. Just cut branches. They have leaves, do they not?"

"Yes, they cut the branches; they pile them up, I think."

"So, not breastworks, just concealment."

"Son, you goin' to just jaw all night? What the hell difference does it make? If we can't see them, we can't shoot them. But they sure as hell can shoot us."

"Exactly," Anson said. "But if they can't see us, they can't kill us, can they?"

Peebo let out a long breath he had been holding in his lungs. "You got an idea, son?"

Anson said nothing. But a plan was beginning to form in his mind.

Before he could speak, though, one of Matteo's men fired at them. He saw the flash and ducked, from instinct. He heard the whiff of the lead ball as it passed harmlessly overhead. Then he heard the man who had shot at them move to another position.

It grew very still, but in that instant Anson made up his mind. He knew what they must do and he prayed it would work. He looked up at the sky and a sinking feeling came over him. Just topping the trees to the north, he saw it, the moon, rising like a giant glowing eye in the sky. In moments it would shed its light on the road and on their position off to the side.

If he was going to act, he thought, now was the time.

34

Reynaud heard the crackle of rifle fire and his finger on the trigger of his rifle tightened as he watched Obispo pull his horse to a stop in front of him. Obispo turned in the saddle.

"There is shooting," Obispo said.

"I hear it."

"It comes from the road."

"I know that, too," Reynaud said.

"Maybe we should go back."

"That's Nuncio's problem. You keep following those tracks."

"But . . ."

"That shooting's none of our concern, Obispo. Now, you ride on."

Obispo muttered a series of Spanish curses under his breath. He kicked his horse in the flanks and continued to follow Bone's tracks. Reynaud widened the distance between him and the Mexican, kept the muzzle pointed at Obispo's back, his finger curled around the trigger of his flintlock.

The tracks curved and headed into the mesquite forest. There was more shooting from the road, sharp cracks that carried on the evening air loud and clear. Obispo turned once as if to see if Reynaud was still following him. But he did not stop. Reynaud saw the woods ahead and wondered if Obispo would try to break away and lose him once they entered the thick mesquite. It was a chance he was not willing to take.

"Obispo, hold it right there," Reynaud said, just as the Mexican reached the edge of the mesquite forest.

"Eh?" Obispo said, as he pulled on his reins. He turned in the saddle and looked back at Reynaud.

"Do Bone's tracks go in there?"

"Yes."

"And, do you think you can follow them in this dark?"

"In the dark?"

"Yes, in the dark."

"No, I do not think I can see the tracks of Bone. It is too dark now."

"Then why were you going into those woods there?"

Obispo shrugged. "I do not know. You tell me to follow Bone. I follow Bone. To here. From here I do not know where he goes."

"He could be anywhere," Reynaud said.

Obispo turned his horse around slightly so he did not have to bend his neck to talk to Reynaud. He moved slowly and his gaze followed the muzzle of the rifle in Reynaud's hands as it moved with him. "Yes, he could be anywhere. I do not know where Bone goes."

"But you would take us into those trees, would you?"

"I follow the tracks."

"And what if you had lost them in there? Would you have told me?"

"Yes, I would have told you."

Reynaud gently brushed his horse's flanks with the rowels of his spurs. The horse took a step toward Obispo and halted. "Why did Matteo send you along with me?"

"I do not know."

"Yes, I think you do."

"He send me to help you."

"Obispo, you are going to tell me the truth, or I'm going to shoot you out of that saddle. Now, why did Matteo tell you to come with me?"

Obispo's moustache quivered as he wrinkled his face in a frown. Reynaud could not see his eyes, only dark holes in his square, high-cheekboned face. Small eyes, Reynaud thought, devious eyes, black agates chiseled into the skull. The eyes of a snake. He was close enough to see if Obispo's hands moved. One of them was very close to the large Spanish pistol sticking out from his faded red sash, and Obispo's rifle was jutting from its leather boot, within easy reach.

"I think that Matteo," Obispo said, "maybe he does not trust you."

"What makes you think that, Obispo?"

"I don't know. I think he just wants me to come along to see if you kill Bone. And Anson Baron."

Reynaud stepped his horse another two feet closer to Obispo. He held the rifle in his hand leveled at the man's belly. "And then what would you have done? Would you have ridden back to tell Matteo I had killed those men?"

"Yes, I think so."

"Obispo, you're a liar. Matteo sent you to kill me, didn't he?"

"I don't think so."

Reynaud knew Obispo was lying. Matteo would never have sent anyone along with him just to see if he carried out his orders. No, Obispo had been sent along for only one reason: To kill him.

"What were you going to do, Obispo? Shoot me in the back?"

"No, I do not do that."

There was no whining in Obispo's voice, but Reynaud could tell the man was worried, that he was getting ready to make a move. Obispo's voice was pitched just slightly higher, just enough above his usual register that Reynaud knew he could not wait much longer.

"I think you were sent to kill me. Now, isn't that the truth?"

"No. Matteo, he don't say nothing about killing you. He say just to watch you. Protect you maybe."

Now Reynaud knew for sure that Obispo was lying. Matteo would never send a man to protect him. Matteo had something inside him that was as hard and cold as iron, something mean and tough that was not quite human. Reynaud knew, and understood, because he had that same something inside himself. He had killed men before, and felt nothing afterward. He had felt nothing before he killed the men he had killed. He did not consider killing sinful or illegal, but right—his right, as a man. Matteo was like that, too. He had seen it in Matteo's eyes, heard it in his voice when he talked of his hatred for Martin Baron, for all the Barons. No, Matteo would not care if any of his men lived or died. He was not that way. But he would send one man to kill another. As Matteo hoped he, Reynaud, would kill the Barons; not because Matteo did not have the balls to do it, but because he wanted them dead, and it made no difference to Matteo who killed them, or how they died. When it was over, and the Barons were dead, he would not give them another thought.

"You are not going to kill me, Obispo."

"No. I am not going to kill you."

"But I am going to kill you," Reynaud said evenly, his voice flat as a cold iron griddle.

"But why? I have done you no harm, Reynaud. I do not know why you want to kill me."

"Because I don't trust you. Because I know Matteo sent you to kill me."

"No, Matteo did not tell me to kill you."

"You liar."

That's when Obispo went for his pistol. For a split second Reynaud's stomach swirled with a sickening fear. Obispo was fast, very fast. His arm whipped like a snake uncoiling and his hand blurred toward the butt of his pistol, like a shadow cast by some small quick animal. Regaining his senses, Reynaud did not hesitate. He squeezed the trigger of his cocked rifle and felt the jolt of the recoil and the muzzle belched an orange flame peppered with unexploded black powder. A puff of white smoke clouded his view, but he heard a grunt from Obispo and knew the lethal lead ball had struck home, probably in the Mexican's belly. He ducked, but there was no explosion from Obispo's pistol.

Fast as he was, Obispo had not been able to draw his weapon. When the smoke dissipated in the light breeze, Reynaud saw that Obispo was still in the saddle, hunched up and half doubled over, one hand clutching his midsection.

"*Maldita . . .*" Obispo muttered.

Reynaud rode up close to the wounded man, so close he could see the blood oozing through Obispo's fingers.

"I wish Matteo was here to watch you die, Obispo, you son of a bitch."

"Tu hijo de puta," Obispo gasped, his bloodless lips scarcely moving as he bit off each word.

"Curse me, you bastard, but you're dying like the dog you are, like you were going to make me die."

"*Chingate,* Reynaud."

Reynaud laughed. He grabbed the hair at the back of Obispo's head and jerked on it, pulling the dying man's head back. Then he leaned over and spit in Obispo's face. He released his grip on the Mexican's hair and slapped him hard across the chin.

"Do you think your curses do me any harm? I'll piss on your grave, you miserable *cochon.*"

Obispo tried to spit at Reynaud, but only caused more blood to gush from his stomach. His eyes glazed with the pain surging through him and he clenched his teeth as if to bite it off. He began to lean to his left and could not stop himself. He fell from the saddle and hit the ground on his shoulder. He rolled over, facing the dark sky above him.

"Another minute, ten, a half hour. That's all the time you have left, Obispo. I hope you take your pain with you, straight to hell."

"Tu hijo de mala leche," Obispo whispered.

"I'll leave you to your cursing and your dying. A pity you do not pray for your black soul."

Reynaud turned his horse away from the dying Obispo and looked up at the sky. He headed north toward the Box B, toward Baronsville. He did not see the man on horseback who emerged from the thick shadows of the mesquite and rode over to where Obispo lay dying.

"You are dying," Bone said.

"Yes."

"Do you have any money on you?"

"No. I left it with my wife."

"I will take your horse," Bone said.

"Take the horse. But shoot me, eh?"

"No," Bone said. "You will have to do that yourself."

"I am lying on my pistol. I cannot reach it."

Bone grabbed the reins of Obispo's horse and pulled on them to bring the horse in behind him.

"You will find a way, if you want to die quick enough," Bone said.

"You bastard. Are you going to kill Reynaud?"

"No. Somebody will kill him."

Obispo gagged and then went into a coughing fit. Bone rode away from him, to the south, toward the Rocking A, leading Obispo's horse.

As he rode away, Obispo tried to sit up. Blood spurted from his belly wound and he fell back. He gasped and tried to pull air into his lungs, but the breath he had breathed out was his last.

Bone heard a rifle shot from the road that cut through the mesquite grove. The sound died on the plain, and it grew quiet once again.

He looked up at the stars in the sky and thought of Dawn. He would see her this night, and they would ride away from the Rocking A and Matteo Aguilar and find another place to live and raise their son. He found himself hoping that he would see Anson again one day, that he would survive this night and live a long life.

ANSON HEARD THE muffled sound of a distant rifle shot. He froze for a moment as he scrambled to make sense of it. He turned to Peebo and whispered: "Did you hear that?"

"It was way off yonder in the mesquite behind us."

"Wonder who in hell it could be."

"You tell me, son."

"Well, we can't wait any longer. We'll probably lose a horse, but it's the only way I can figure."

"Why can't we just sneak through these here woods and go on by them?" Peebo asked.

"Timo, you tell him," Anson said.

"There are two men who listen," Timo said, "and they shoot good. They wait in the trees."

"You know these men?" Peebo asked.

"I know them. They are from my pueblo in Mexico."

"Maybe you are still friends with them," Peebo said.

"No, I am not friends with them. They kill my brother one day. Mens no good."

"Then I guess that's that," Peebo said.

"Looks like it," Anson said. "If we tried to make it across the road, we wouldn't get five yards. Juanito once told me sometimes it's best to meet the enemy head-on."

"This Juanito. He was a soldier, too?"

"No, and he wasn't talking about war or fighting, in particular. He was talking about problems in general."

"So he didn't really know about fighting and war. That right?"

"Juanito knew about a hell of a lot of things, Peebo. Now, you just shut up about him."

Anson did not question why he would think of Juanito at such a time. Juanito would have known exactly what to do in this situation. He would not be guessing as Anson knew he was doing. He had remembered that one thing Juanito had said, but he also remembered so many other things. Was this the best way to attack the enemy and escape? Probably not. Matteo's men were afoot. He and Peebo had two horses. But there were also three people for those two horses. Sure, they could backtrack and encircle the woods on the other side and escape with their lives; but that would leave Matteo's men alive and able to attack the Box B.

All those men would do, Anson reasoned, would be to wait for Matteo to arrive and then join him. Well, he wasn't going to leave them alive to fight again another day. He had come here to stop Matteo's advance on the Box B and he meant to do it—any way he could. If he had to lose a horse or both of them, he would, by the gods, shoot that man out of the tree and any others that fell under his sights.

"We're going to shoot our way through," Anson said aloud. "So get ready."

"What're you aimin' to do, exactly?" Peebo asked.

Anson explained. Timo said nothing. Peebo swallowed hard before he spoke. "Mighty dangerous," he said.

"We'll have to run like hell after we finish shooting as many of them as we can."

"And how are we going to get back to the Box B?"

"Walk, if we have to. Timo? *Listo?*"

"Yes, I am ready," Timo said in English.

"Then let's do it," Anson said. "I'll put my horse on the left, Peebo."

"That's mighty decent of you, son. But from the looks of it, it won't make no damned difference."

"It's our only chance. The way I see it."

"Okay," Peebo said.

The three men stood up, very slowly. Peebo and Anson got their horses and lined them up side by side.

"Reckon they'll go without leadin'?" Peebo asked.

"I'll lead my horse right up to where those jaspers are, then duck back. When I start running, you and Timo start running. Stay on that side of your horse and I'll come up behind you."

"You'll be right out in the open," Peebo said.

"Only for a second or two. Long enough, maybe, to drop that man up in the tree. Come on, before I start getting scared."

"Hell, son, I got enough 'scared' to go around. No sense in you gettin' it on your own."

Anson stepped in front of his horse and pulled on the reins. The horse balked. Then one of Matteo's men fired a shot and the ball kicked up dust in front of Anson. The horse stepped out and Anson started to run. He carried his rifle in his right hand. Peebo kept right up with him and Timo ran alongside, hunched over. Rifles barked and Anson heard the whine of lead. He saw flashes from the ground, but none from the man in the tree.

As the three men and two horses drew near the position of Matteo's men, the firing stopped. Anson could hear the metallic and wooden slide of ramrods and wiping sticks. He began to trot faster. A few yards away from the shorn tree, he saw the silhouette of the man sitting in it. A second later he saw the orange flash as the man fired a shot at Anson's horse. He heard the sickening thud of the ball as it struck the flesh of his horse's neck. The horse staggered and its front legs buckled.

Anson let the reins fall from his hand.

He dropped to one knee as the horse's hind legs skidded out from under it and the animal fell on its side.

Anson held the image of the tree shooter in his mind as he brought his rifle up to his shoulder. The afterimage of the orange flash still burned like a flower on fire in the forefront of his brain. He cocked the rifle as he drew it to his shoulder and dropped the blade front-sight on the man in the tree. He could see the Mexican pull his wiping stick as he lined up the rear buckhorn with the blade.

Peebo fired his rifle and Anson heard a man cry out in pain. Then there was another shot as Anson squeezed the trigger and felt his own rifle ram against his shoulder with the explosion of ninety grains of double-fine powder. He heard the flint strike, the whoosh of the fine powder in the pan and the full explosion, so close together they might have been a single sound and the air in front of him was filled with a cloud of white smoke that obscured his vision.

Anson did not wait to see if he had struck his target, but rose to full length, grabbed his saddlebags and dashed after Peebo's horse. Behind him, he heard a rustle and then a crash as if a body had landed on the ground. Then he heard a scream, followed by the staccato chatter of men speaking in rapid Spanish. Above it he heard one man trying to bark orders, shouting, in Spanish: *"Alla. Fuego, fuego."*

Anson was glad to see that Peebo was angling his horse toward the mesquite forest on the opposite side of the road. He saw Timo trotting close to Peebo, trying to reload his rifle on the run. Peebo was guiding his horse, almost gluing himself to its side as he ran with it.

"Timo," Anson said, "don't try and reload that rifle. Just run. Get to the woods."

Timo didn't answer, but he left his ramrod in the barrel of his rifle and kept his feet moving. Peebo ran a zigzag pattern and no more shots were fired as they reached the shelter of the mesquite. They went a few yards inside the forest. Anson stopped and turned around. "Hold up, Peebo," he said, as he drew his ramrod from the ferrules beneath the barrel.

"I'm goin' to get this here rifle switched over to caplock," Peebo said. "Lost a damned flint back there."

"You hit one of 'em," Anson said.

"So'd little old Timo here. He's a right smart shooter."

Anson poured powder down the barrel of his rifle. "See if anybody's comin'," he told Peebo.

"Timo, you hold this here horse," Peebo said. He rammed his rifle down into its boot and drew his caplock pistol. He ran to the edge of the mesquite and hunkered down to look across the road.

Anson finished loading his rifle and joined him as Timo began to reload his weapon.

"See anything?" Anson asked.

"Hard for them to hide, what with wearin' them white cotton shirts and trousers."

Anson saw blotches of white back in the trees on the other side of the road. Matteo's men were moving around. He heard the murmur of voices that rose and fell, just barely audible.

"They might be gettin' ready to come after us," Peebo said.

"They can't see us, can they?"

"I don't know. You dropped that jasper in the tree. Maybe one of them has owl eyes."

After a moment, Anson saw something move. The movement was odd and he couldn't determine what it was, at first.

"What's that?" Anson asked.

"Looks like one of them's waving a shirt at us," Peebo said.

"*Hola* . . . Anson Baron?" The voice carried from across the road.

"Sounds like he's hollerin' at you," Peebo said.

"Yeah. Wonder what he wants."

"Hell, answer him, son."

"I'm Anson. What do you want?"

"I want to talk."

"Walk over here," Anson said.

"You will not shoot me?"

"No. You come by yourself."

"I will come," the Mexican said.

There was a gabble of voices from across the road, men speaking in Spanish. Then, a man carrying a white shirt tied to a mesquite branch emerged out of the shadows and began walking toward Anson and Peebo.

"Looks like he wants a truce," Peebo said. "The way he's a-wavin' that there shirt on a stick."

"Shut up, Peebo."

Anson rubbed the edge of the frizzen with his thumb as he watched the man carrying the shirt wave it back and forth above his head. The man did not carry a rifle, but Anson could not tell if he had a pistol stuck in his belt or his waistband. One thing he did know. The shirt he was waving was not his own. This man was fully clothed in white cotton shirt and trousers. Anson could hear the scuff of his sandals on the road.

"Watch him," Peebo said.

"You keep an eye on those still over there across the road. This could be a trick."

"Yeah," Peebo said.

"I am called Nuncio," the man said, as he drew near. "I wish only to talk with you, Anson Baron."

"You come on," Anson said. "You carrying a pistol?"

"No," Nuncio said. "I leave the pistol and the rifle. I have no weapon."

Nuncio left the road and waded through the grass. When he was three yards away, he halted.

"Put down that stick," Anson said, "and walk over here with your hands over your head."

"I understand," Nuncio said. He threw down the stick with the shirt tied to it and then walked over to Anson, his arms outstretched, hands in the air.

"You speak good English," Anson said.

"I went to school. I am from El Paso."

"Peebo, see if he has any weapons on him."

"Hell, you can see he don't."

"All right, Nuncio," Anson said. "What do you want to talk about?"

"We wish to surrender," Nuncio said.

"Why?"

"We do not want to fight for Matteo anymore. My friends are tired and they have hunger and they have no sleep."

"Do they all want to give up?" Anson asked.

Nuncio nodded. "We are vaqueros. Don Matteo, he makes us march and he wants us to shoot and to kill. We do not want this no more."

"Do you have horses?"

"No. The horses, they are dead."

"What will I do with you if you surrender, then?"

"We will go with you, Don Anson."

"Do you have families?"

"No. Don Matteo, he do not want men to fight who have families."

"We are going to fight Matteo. Is he coming?"

"He is coming," Nuncio said. "He will attack the rancho of your father before the sun does the rising."

"You will have to come with us," Anson said. "We are going to walk to the Box B."

"We will come."

"I can't offer you any work. Not right away."

"We just do not want to fight for Don Matteo."

"Will you fight for me?"

"If you wish."

"Well, if you come with me, I will have to take away all your ammunition and we will carry your rifles and pistols with us."

"That is good. We will come."

"Call the others over here," Anson said. "Tell them to come one by one and each man count to ten before he walks over here."

"I will do this," Nuncio said.

"Anson, this doesn't sound like a good idea," Peebo said.

"Well, we can't leave these men here. They'd be at our rear. And when Matteo comes along, he'll probably shoot them."

"Better them than us," Peebo said.

"Nuncio," Anson said, "call out your men. How many are there?"

"We are only four left. The others, they are all dead, I think."

There was sadness in Nuncio's voice and Anson was touched. "I am sorry," he said.

"They were good men. Brave men. They were friends."

"I hope you will not try to pull a trick on us," Anson said.

"No, we do not play the trick. We will come with you."

"If you do, if you try anything, if you run, or if you slow us down, I will kill you, Nuncio. I will kill you and every one of your friends."

"I understand," Nuncio said.

"Jesus, Anson," Peebo said.

"Just shut up, Peebo. Nuncio, call out your men. You wait here."

"I will have Eladio bring my rifle and pistol."

"Tell them to unload their weapons and hold them over their heads—with both hands."

"I will do this."

Anson let out a sigh. He was taking a chance, he knew. But he believed Nuncio. He believed that Nuncio wanted to surrender and wanted to get as far away from Matteo Aguilar as he could.

Anson turned to say something to Peebo, when Timo came up behind them.

"You heard?" Anson asked Timo in Spanish.

"Yes."

"What do you think?"

"I think you do the right thing," Timo said.

"We're going to have to walk eight or ten miles. Timo, you take Peebo's horse and ride back to the Box B. Tell my father we are coming. On foot."

"That's my horse," Peebo said.

"Well, you ride the son of a bitch back, then. I don't have time to argue with you."

"Hey, hold on, son. I'll walk back with you. I just want to establish ownership of that there steed."

"Timo, get going," Anson said.

"I go," Timo said.

Nuncio called to the men across the road. Anson and Peebo waited, listening. Peebo cocked his pistol and Anson scowled at him.

Peebo could not see the expression on Anson's face, but he saw the movement.

"First law of Peebo Elves," Peebo said, "is 'Don't trust nobody.' "

"Fuck you, Peebo," Anson said, and turned to watch as the first man emerged from the shadows, his rifle uplifted over his head. In the pale light of the moon, in his white clothing, he looked like a wraith, a ghost lifting his arms in supplication.

36

THE SCOUT, A man named Pedro Castillo, one of two Matteo had sent ahead of his expedition, rode up on a galloping horse. Both horse and man were short on breath and it took Castillo a moment to compose himself enough to speak.

"What passes?" Matteo asked.

"We have found some dead men, Don Matteo. And we have found dead horses, as well. They are of the group you sent out with the Frenchman."

"All dead? Reynaud, as well?"

"I did not see Reynaud. That Tomaso, he is still looking for him."

"Nuncio?"

"I did not see his corpse."

"What of Obispo?"

Castillo shook his head. "I did not see the face of Obispo. Tomaso is still looking. There are many dead."

"Did you see the corpse of Anson Baron or any of his vaqueros?"

"No, Don Matteo. I did not see these men."

"What a pity. After you have rested a little, ride back and help Tomaso. Then you and Tomaso will wait for me."

"Yes. I will do that, Don Matteo."

"Did it look like a bad fight?"

"Yes. It looked like there was much fighting. You can still smell the burnt powder. The smell lingers in the grasses and in the trees. There are many trees there."

"I know."

"I will go back now to help Tomaso."

"Yes. Go."

Matteo watched Castillo ride off and disappear in the darkness. The moon made everything on the road ghostly, and every shape appeared to him as an enemy. He turned to the men following him. They were resting their horses and smoking their cigarillos. He had told them they could smoke when they stopped to rest and they were doing that. They were not talking because he had told them not to talk, even when they stopped. It was of no matter now. Anson Baron was not dead. He had not asked about Bone, but Castillo would have mentioned him if he had been among the dead.

But where was Reynaud? And Obispo? Had they gone after Anson Baron? Were they even now fighting, or had they all run off like dogs with their tails tucked between their hind legs? Or had Obispo betrayed him? He would not put it past Reynaud to make allies of both Bone and Obispo. That man had a tongue made of silk, a tongue that was double-forked, like that of a snake.

Matteo fished a cigarillo from his vest pocket, from the little tin he carried there which held the tobacco he bought in Mexico. He tapped the end of the cigarillo on the tin to tamp the tobacco tightly, and then he put the tin away and took a wooden *fosforo* and struck it on the brass of his saddlehorn. The match exploded in flame and he lit the end of the cigarillo and pulled the air through it until the end was glowing. The smoke bit at his throat and filled his lungs with a satisfying warmth.

"*Oye,* Don Matteo."

It was the voice of Dagoberto Santos, who rode behind him as his *segundo* on the march.

"Come," Matteo said.

"What passes?"

"Did you not hear what Castillo told me?"

"I heard some of what he said."

"Then you know there was fighting on the road ahead of us."

"Do you want to turn back?"

"No. I am going to fight Martin Baron and burn his house to the ground. I am going to kill him when the sun rises in the morning sky."

"Yes. You will do that, Don Matteo."

Matteo smoked and the two men were silent for some moments.

Santos wiped sweat from his forehead. "It makes warm, this night," he said.

Matteo did not answer. He was still mulling over in his mind what might have happened to Reynaud and Obispo, who were together and in charge of the men with Nuncio.

Santos tried another tack. "The Baron rancho is still far. We have much riding to do. It is good to rest here for some few moments."

"Dagoberto, I tell you this: I will not rest until all of the Barons are dead and my land is returned to me."

"Claro."

"You will not rest, either, my friend."

"No, I rest only now that we are here. We wait to ride on with you, Don Matteo."

"Where is Reynaud?"

"Eh? Reynaud? I do not know where he is, Don Matteo."

"I do not know, either. And Obispo. Where is he this night?"

"I do not know. Maybe he is with Reynaud."

"Maybe they are both in hell."

"Eh? In hell? I do not know. Are they dead?"

Matteo laughed, a dry, mirthless laugh. "Maybe they are dead. Maybe they are running like the rabbit, into the brush."

"Obispo is a man very strong. He would not run like the rabbit."

"No, he would not, Dagoberto. He would do what I told him to do, would he not?"

"I think he would eat shit if you told him to, Don Matteo."

"Yes, I think Obispo would eat shit if I told him to. But not Reynaud."

"No, not the Frenchman. He *is* shit."

Matteo laughed again, this time with enjoyment. "Maybe Obispo will eat him, then."

"Yes, maybe Obispo will do that."

"I am going to kill Bone, too, if I ever see him again."

"Bone? You would kill him? I thought he was your friend."

"I do not think Bone is my friend anymore. I do not trust him.

He should have killed the young Baron and come back to tell me that the young man was dead." Matteo drew on the cigarillo. He held the smoke in his lungs and it made him feel good for a moment.

"Maybe Bone will come and tell you that he has killed the young Baron."

Matteo exhaled the tasteless smoke and saw it shimmer in the pale light of the moom. "No, Bone will not come."

"How do you know this?"

"Because he would have been here already. No, he will not come, Dagoberto. I know he will not come."

"I do not know what to say, Don Matteo."

"Where do you come from, Dagoberto?"

"I am from Sonora."

"It is very dry and hot there."

"Yes," Castillo said.

"Did you ever fight in a war?"

"No. I have never known war."

"I, myself, have always admired the men who fight in war. I am interested in their thoughts. I am interested in their deeds."

"Yes, *Patrón*."

"What do they think when they go into battle? Do they think of killing the enemy or do they think of being killed?"

"I do not know."

"I wonder. I think there is something in man's soul that makes him unafraid to go into battle. I think the fighting man, the brave man, is not afraid to die. Do you not think that, Dagoberto?"

"I do not think of it."

"But what do you think about fighting with Martin Baron? Do you not wonder if you will be killed?"

"I think I will try not to be killed."

Matteo chuckled and drew another puff from his cigarillo. He blew the smoke back out quickly, through his nostrils and his mouth. He watched the gauzy smoke change shape and wave itself to nothingness in the slight puff of breeze that sprang up.

"How do you feel about killing another man?"

"If the man is an enemy, I will kill him. Then, I will not think of it."

"You are a good man, Dagoberto. Perhaps you are a warrior.

That is the way a warrior thinks. He thinks only of killing his enemy. He does not worry if he himself might be killed. Do you not think this is true?"

"Yes, Don Matteo, I think that is true. I do not wish to fight all the time, but there is a certain excitement to fighting, I think."

"Yes, there is a big excitement to go into battle. To know you are about to kill, to become master over another's life—I find that very satisfying."

"Yes. Such a thing would bring pleasure."

"Much pleasure. And life should be full of pleasure. I am most happy when I am fighting someone, or something. I am happy when I fight with the land to make it grow grass and food. I am happy when I fight the cows and put my mark on their hides. I am happy when I fight with my wife because I know she will lose and that I will win."

Castillo did not say anything. He drew a last puff of smoke from his cigarillo and threw its stub to the ground. Matteo chuckled to himself and finished his own smoke and tossed it into the air. It left a trail of sparking embers as it fell to the road.

"Do you know why I left some men back at the rancho—Perez and Domingo and Caudillo?"

"To guard your woman?"

"My woman does not need guards, Dagoberto. No, I left them there because I do not trust Bone and because I do not trust Reynaud."

"I do not trust them, either."

"Do you know what I told these men, Dago?"

"No, I do not know what you told them, Don Matteo."

Matteo smiled in the darkness and he was close enough so that Castillo could see the smile as Matteo intended. The smile was like that of a cat which has finally cornered its prey and is about to pounce. That was the kind of smile Matteo wanted to smile and if he'd had a tail, like a cat, it would be twitching.

"I told them to kill Bone if he returned to the rancho alone."

"They will kill him, then."

"Bone will not expect that, Dagoberto. They will kill him, yes, and I will feed his blood and his meat to the hogs."

Dagoberto shivered in the heat.

"Vamanos," Matteo said. "I am ready to be happy."

"What?"

"I am ready to battle. Let us go now, and the dawn will find us battling Baron as the warriors we are."

Matteo turned his horse before Castillo could speak and rode out ahead, lifting one hand to signal his men to follow him. Castillo barked an order and the column of men fell into double ranks, all silent, all with thoughts about what might await them at the dawning of the day.

Castillo felt a tightness in his stomach, for, after listening to Don Matteo, he, too, was thinking about the sunrise and wondering if the coming one would be his last.

37

DAVID WILHOIT WALKED out onto the road and stared up at the stars peppering the night sky like flung diamonds. They sparkled and blinked as if they were sentient, and the planets he could recognize pulsed with a glow of energy that seemed cold but palpable. He had become gripped with a stifling, smothering feeling of confinement while sitting hidden in the trees with Roy Killian and Al Oltman and now he began to breathe more evenly and naturally as he gazed at the limitless sky, his vision unobstructed by branches or leaves or tree trunks.

"Dave, get your ass back here," Roy called. "If somebody rides up that road, they'll spot you, sure as shit's brown."

"I need to get some air," David said.

"Air? There's plenty of air over thisaway."

"Give me a minute, will you?"

David heard Roy snort and he felt himself bristle. He knew that Roy didn't like him, but sometimes Roy truly got on David's nerves. Like now. And all evening, for that matter. David had stayed out of it, but Roy's constant needling of him over little, inconsequential things had begun to grate on his nerves. If Roy wasn't his wife's son, he might have told Roy to roll up his sleeves and prepare to defend himself. But Ursula doted on her unruly and often sullen son, and David dared not risk drawing her ire by openly criticizing Roy or calling him out to settle this ugly contention between them. So he had swallowed hard and kept his mouth shut, and endured Roy's not-so-subtle taunting as they waited out the night, listening for hoofbeats on the road, the familiar sound that never came.

"You measurin' the sky?" Roy said. "Whyn't you go get your damned surveyin' stuff and do it right?"

David walked over to the rope strung up across the road and pulled on it. It was tight enough, perhaps. If any riders came on fast, it might trip up a horse or two. He heard the rope creak on its moorings. He would have strung up a dozen or more. One lariat was not enough to tumble an army, and this one would break if enough weight struck it. He ignored Roy's taunting, as he had all night long. Roy Killian was a bully, and David knew all about bullies. A bully wanted attention and approval. Ignoring them made them mad, but once he decided to fight back, he knew he would be descending to their level. He had run into bullies all his life. Matteo Aguilar was a bully. Almost every boss he'd ever had was a bully at heart. A bully took pleasure in making someone else feel off-balance, ill at ease, defensive.

Ursula had said that she had raised Roy, but David couldn't fault her. No, Roy was probably the way he was because his father had been a rakehell who had abandoned his wife and son, a drifter who had lived by the gun and died by the gun. Jack Killian's shadow was over David's marriage to Ursula as much as Roy was a substance in it.

If only they didn't have to live in Roy's damned house. And those two women, Wanda and Hattie, they were enough to drive a man to strong drink. And Ursula was always putting a bug in Wanda's ear to marry her boy, and Hattie, too, for that matter. If David had been a jealous man, he would have resented all the attention those women gave to Roy Killian, but he was not. In fact, he was damned glad that Roy drew all the fire in that house—it gave him a measure of peace in the middle of a whirlwind.

He wished Roy would marry Wanda and then the house would get so small he and Ursula would be forced to leave and live somewhere else. Hattie, too, perhaps. But Roy was as wild as those mustangs David had seen running on the plain when he'd first come to work for Aguilar. Matteo had told him that the Mexicans, in the old days, had called this region "the plain of wild horses."

And, working with the Mexicans when he surveyed the land for Matteo, he had learned that the whole Rio Grande Valley was known by another name as well, one more fitting, perhaps. The name in Spanish still sent shivers up his spine: *"El llano de los muertos."* The plain of the dead.

There was death here on this plain, David knew. This was blood-soaked ground. He had found skulls when he set up his theodolite, and holes in the skulls, from arrows, from bullets, from lances. He did not know who the skulls had belonged to, white men, Apache, or Comanche, but they represented violence and death and no one had cared enough to bury the bodies of the dead. Their bones had been scattered by wild beasts—coyotes, wolves, and the like.

He looked up at the sky again and felt its peace descend on him. The plain of the dead was also a tranquil place at times, and he thought that it might be so always if man did not tread its wildness. This "war" with Aguilar was only a small speck on the broad land that was soon to erupt into a civil war that would sweep everyone up in its violence, pit North against South, friend against friend, blood against blood. Perhaps the entire United States would become one vast plain of the dead when it was all over. The thought of all that made him sick, and he no longer found solace in gazing upward into the endless reaches of the sky. He turned away from the taut rope and started walking back into the trees where Roy and Al were still waiting for their own little war to erupt on the Box B.

"Get enough air, Dave?" Roy asked.

David did not answer.

"Roy," Al said, "why don't you lay off the man for a while?"

"Aw, I'm just teasin' old David here. He can take it, can't you, Dave?"

"Oh, I can take it, Roy. Question is, what's the point in raggin' me all the time? Keep your mind off your own troubles?"

"What troubles?"

"I don't know. But you do."

"Now, what the hell's that supposed to mean?"

"Seems to me a man ought to know what troubles he has. I'm not a mind reader."

"No, you sure as hell aren't. You wouldn't like what's in my mind right now."

"I probably wouldn't."

"Well, just drop it, hear?"

"All right, Roy. Whatever you say."

The three men were silent for a time. David kept wondering when whatever was preying on Roy's mind would come bursting out of his mouth in a stream of invective.

Al stretched one of his legs, wriggled the toe of his boot. Then he did the same with his other leg, waggling his toe for several seconds. "Waitin's the hardest thing to do," he said. "Not knowin' just exactly what you're waiting for."

"You sound as if you've done this before," David said.

"Once or twice't."

"What were you awaitin' on?" Roy asked.

Al stepped in place for a couple of seconds, not making much sound with the soles of his boots. He leaned against a live oak and shifted the rifle from one hand to the other. It was still warm out, but he could feel the temperature falling slightly as the night drew toward morning. "I 'member one time," he said, "me'n Kenny Darnell was up on the Brazos, hidin' out 'long the river, waitin' for two jaspers what had robbed a feller over to Waco. They were a pair of mean sons of bitches and we heard they had a hidey-hole somewheres about and when they sobered up, they'd be comin' back." Al paused, wiped his mouth with a swipe of his sleeve.

"And did they?" Roy asked.

"We waited three days up yonder, with nothin' to bite on but hardtack biscuits and mean old jackrabbit jerky, and water in the river so salty you daren't drink a drop, and skeeters eatin' us alive and rattlesnakes slitherin' up by day and rats tryin' to gnaw on our boots ever' night."

"Sounds bad," David said. "How come you waited that long?"

"Oh, we figgered them two was comin' thataway, all right, and the longer we waited, the madder we got. We didn't have no warrants, but these boys had robbed an old couple in Waco and we knew they was mean as spring bears comin' out of hibernation, and one of 'em had beat the old lady because she begged 'em not to hurt her husband, which they did, the bastards, and we kept thinkin' of those two old people and what these old boys had done to 'em, so we waited, three long days and three nights."

"Did they finally come on by?" Roy asked.

"Me and Kenny was ready to wring necks by the third day out there. We commenced to arguin' and layin' into each other like two cur dogs. Then we got into a hell of a fight, with him throwin' the first punch and then me landin' a haymaker, side of his jaw. We was goin' at it when we hear someone hail us."

"Who was it?" Roy asked.

"It was them owlhoots. One of 'em said, 'You fellers mean to kill each other?'

"Me'n Kenny turned and saw them two killers standing up there on the slope like a couple of spectators at a prize fight. They wasn't suspicious or nothin'. Well, Kenny, he looks at me, and I look at him and then we stepped out and drew our pistols."

"You got the drop on them," Roy said.

"They were plumb caught with their pants down. We showed them our badges and they got these sad looks on their faces."

"So you had them," David said.

"Well, it wasn't over, by a long shot," Al said.

"What happened?" Roy asked.

"Before we could take them into custody, one of them asked us what we were fighting about. He said he was just curious. Kenny told him we was fighting over whether we should just kill those two on sight or run them into the hoosegow in Waco.

"Well, the other one got mad at that and went for his pistol. As soon as he did that, Kenny threw down on him and let fly a ball right into his gut. By then the other jasper was in a crouch and clawing for his iron, when I stretched my arm straight out and snapped the hammer down. My shot caught him high in the chest and he never did reach that pistol in his holster. He got the damnedest expression on his face and began to spit out blood. Just for the hell of it, when he was down on his knees and tryin' to catch a breath to curse me with, I shot him again with my .44-40 and blew half his arm off."

"What about Darnell?" David asked.

"Kenny, he didn't shoot anymore, but ran up the slope and laid the barrel of his pistol aside the head of the jasper he'd shot and asked him how he liked being beaten with it."

"And, what did the man say?" Roy asked.

"He said, 'Sweet Jesus, don't do that.' "

"Man, that was something," Roy said. "You killed them both, then?"

"I had to drag Kenny off of his man. The man's face looked like ground-up pork sausage. He was fair a bloody mess."

"He died?" David asked.

"Hell, he was dead a good two minutes before I got Kenny to quit."

"What about the fight you and Kenny had?" Roy asked.

"Oh, that was over. We had plumb forgot what we was fighting about and we were-out from facing down those two scalawags. We packed them on their horses and took them into Waco. The sheriff there stood 'em up on pine boards in front of the drugstore and put placards by 'em. Those two drew quite a crowd and we had a passel of free drinks at one of the cantinas."

Roy whistled long and loud.

To the surprise of the three men, there was an answering whistle from the road.

"Shhh," Al said, and bent low and leaned forward, bringing his rifle up to his shoulder.

Roy and David hunched down and aimed their rifles as well.

"Who do you suppose that was?" Roy asked.

"Be quiet," David said.

"Whistle again, Roy," Al said.

Roy's mouth was dry as sand. "I can't," he said.

"David. Can you whistle?" Al asked.

"I'll try." David whistled, but his mouth was almost as dry as Roy's. The sound did not carry far.

"Hell," Al said, and put a couple of fingers to his mouth and pursed his lips. His whistle was a loud one, piercing, and both Roy and David ducked as if they had been poked in the ears.

Then the three men waited for several seconds. Finally there was an answering whistle and they could hear men running up the road toward them, their footfalls heavy, as if they carried heavy weights.

"Here they come," Roy said, spotting two or three men emerging from the shadows in the distance, their silhouettes etched in moonlight.

Roy hammered back his rifle.

"Hold on," Al said.

"I got a bead on one."

"We don't know who that is yet."

"Hell, Al, you want me to ask 'em their names?"

"Just wait a second, will you?"

Then they heard another whistle.

"Those are Mexicans, I think," David said.

"Yeah, but who's that coming up behind them?" Al asked. "That was where that whistling came from."

"They're carrying rifles," Roy said.

"Yeah, but there's something funny about the way they're carrying them," Al said. "They don't seem to be expecting trouble."

"Yeah," David said.

Roy eased the hammer back down. He let out a breath and quickly drew in another one. He gripped the rifle tightly to keep from getting the shakes.

David felt his muscles begin to quiver and the rifle in his hands took on weight as if it had suddenly turned to lead.

Al licked dry lips with his tongue and kept a thumb pressed lightly on the hammer of his rifle, his index finger gently snugged against the trigger, ready to pull it slightly when he cocked, to muffle the sound of the sear engaging in the lock.

Then they all heard a voice yell in Spanish: *"Corren, corren"*—and the men on the road began to run faster.

"That's Anson's voice yonder," Roy croaked, his throat dry as a late-summer corn husk.

"Anson?" Al said.

"What?" David whispered, just before his teeth began to chatter.

"Andale," they heard Anson yell, and the running men loomed larger in the soft light of the moon, their figures limned with pewter.

"And there he is, with Peebo," Roy said, his voice scratchy as sand glued to paper.

"Well I'll be damned," Al breathed, and rocked back on his legs, letting his rifle-barrel dip from its aiming point.

"Anybody there?" Anson called.

Roy stood up. "Over here, Anson. Look out for that rope stretched across the road."

"Here we come," Anson said, and all of the running men turned and started toward Roy, David, and Al. "And right behind us, here come horses at the gallop."

Moments later Anson ordered the Mexicans to drop to their bellies as he and Peebo came up behind them as their legs were crumpling underneath their bodies. He and Peebo were out of breath, but they turned as they sat down in the trees and both pointed to the road.

"Aguilar?" Al asked.

Anson, still out of breath, nodded. Peebo gasped like a fish out of water and checked the lock on his rifle.

David sucked in a breath and looked up at the sky for a moment. The moon had turned into silver as a faint light from the east began to seep into the velvet of night, and from the direction of the Box B headquarters there came the early crowing of a rooster, and beneath it he heard the rolling thunder of hoofbeats pounding up the road just ahead of the breaking dawn.

38

MATTEO LOOKED AT the bodies of the dead men by the light of the mesquite torches. One of the scouts, Pedro Castillo, had lighted the mesquite branches at Matteo's command. The limbs were green and they crackled and made foul-smelling smoke. The leaves made the light brighter as they caught flame, and the trapped air inside the limbs sent jets of fire streaming through the flames and made a demonic hissing sound. Castillo thought it was a grisly scene, but he did not say anything to Matteo. The light flickering on the faces of the dead made their faces seem to move and assume grotesque expressions.

"They did not even cover up the bodies with stones and leaves," Matteo said to no one. And no one spoke to him about that as the two scouts sat their horses on either side of the bodies in the trees, holding their torches high above their heads.

The men behind Matteo stared at the lifeless bodies as if they were looking at dolls on display in a shop window, without expression, without comment. One or two held their stomachs with their hands as if trying to keep from vomiting. These were the young ones who had not seen much death.

"Do you see Nuncio here?" Matteo asked. "Do you see the face of Obispo?"

"No, *Patrón,*" Castillo said. "They are not here. We looked before you came to this place."

"Go over the tracks," Matteo said. "Use the torches. Tell me what happened. Tell me where the other men are, where they have gone."

The two scouts left the dead to shadows as they rode their horses over to the trail. They stopped by Anson's dead horse and waved their torches over the corpse as Matteo watched from where he sat his horse.

"There are no saddlebags," Castillo said.

"This is not one of our horses," Tomaso said.

"No, this horse has the B in the box. See?"

"I see."

The two scouts dismounted and began to search the road. They crossed it and walked into the fringe of the grass bordering the trees on the other side. One of them went into the forest and was gone a few moments. Then both of them examined a spot just inside the trees and they walked some ways down the road and back to their horses. They stomped out the burning brands and remounted. Matteo rode over to them.

"What did you find?" Matteo asked.

"One man, he walked across the road. He was with two men there, then he walked back. Then four men walked across the road and then three men and one horse met with them and they all went toward the Baron rancho. They are all gone."

"So, Nuncio and the others surrendered," Matteo said. Neither of his men said anything. "Do not try and catch them," Matteo said. "But you ride ahead and take care. If you see anyone, one of you ride back and tell me. We will go."

"Yes," Castillo said, and the two scouts rode off slowly as the half-moon climbed in the sky and made the shadows shift on their moorings like black cloth sliding almost imperceptibly at the invisible urging of gravity.

Matteo turned in the saddle and raised his hand. *"Adelante,"* he said, and spurred his horse into a walk. He marked the moon as it rose and mentally measured off the distance to the Baron ranch. A wise man, he reasoned, would have turned back at this point. A wise man would have waited for another time. A wise man would have counted his losses and started over under more opportune circumstances. But he carried the reasoning further: The man who waited never moved forward. No—this was the time. This was what he had planned for so long. Now was the right time. With Martin's wife dead, he would not be at his best. He would still be grieving and he, too, had divided his forces. Anson was somewhere ahead of him, probably on foot, or riding the horse so that he could guard his prisoners at gunpoint. Anson had lost men, too. Perhaps he himself was wounded.

Now was the time, Matteo thought, to get back the land that his family had sold too cheap, to reclaim what was rightfully his. Martin had no right to live on Aguilar land—land that had been in Matteo's family for generations; land granted his forebears by the Spaniards as land grants, for their loyalty and distinguished service to the crown.

The bitterness he still held for his family rose up in him as he thought of the way they had squandered their inheritance. But he had exacted revenge for their treachery and they were all dead, as Martin Baron and his son would soon be dead. Then he would be, once again, the largest landowner in the state of Texas, perhaps in the entire United States.

Matteo knew in his heart that he was destined to be a powerful man, and he envisioned himself with a large and magnificent hacienda, thousands of cattle, and vast riches, the wealth of a king, of a mighty sovereign. He lived with those dreams every day of his life as he had lived with them ever since he had been banished from the Rocking A by his family. He had come back from the land of the dead to claim his rightful property and he would never again let any man lay claim to Aguilar land—not Baron, not anyone.

As he rode at the head of the column, Matteo saw himself as a conquistador, a conqueror of all that lay in his path. He had been planning this for a long time and he would not let a few dead fools deter him from his divine mission. As he rode, he planned what he would do when he reached the Box B and how he would laugh to see Martin and Anson Baron die, and maybe he would let them die slow and watch their house being burned to the ground.

One of the men riding behind Matteo coughed, and the sound jarred him out of his reverie. Matteo frowned and looked up at the sky and saw that the moon had traveled some distance in its arc, and he breathed deep of the air, knowing his journey was not to last too much longer.

Two hours later Matteo halted the column and told the men to be ready to shoot. He drew his pistol and waited.

Castillo rode up, alone.

"What passes?" Matteo asked.

"We have heard something on the road."

"What have you heard?"

"We heard the noise of a horse and when I put my ear to the ground, I heard the noises of men walking and the horse walking. Tomaso is waiting for me to return. We are very close to the rancho of the Barons."

"Why did you not find out what was in the road?"

"I thought you might want to bring the men up and attack. Tomaso is waiting where I left him."

"Yes, that is a good idea," Matteo said. "We will ride up and see if Anson Baron is ahead of us. Just one horse, you say?"

"I only heard one horse. Many human feet. Then I did not hear them anymore."

"Good. We will ride up and see what you have heard."

Matteo and his men rode at a fast trot until they came to where Tomaso was waiting for them.

"Do you hear those ahead of us?" Matteo asked.

Tomaso shook his head. "No, I do not hear them."

"Let us ride after them. Be ready to shoot. Everyone—hear?"

All of the men grunted, made sounds of assent.

Castillo led the way, followed by Matteo and Tomaso. The men behind them rode in double file, their rifle butts braced on their pommels, their pistols loose in their holsters, within easy reach in their sashes. Some carried extra pistols on belts draped from their saddlehorns and a few had extra rifles in saddle scabbards. They all carried knives and plenty of powder and ball.

Half an hour later, Matteo ordered Castillo to ride ahead at a gallop.

"If you see them, come back quick," Matteo said.

Castillo spurred his horse to a gallop, and although his horse was tired, it gained speed and soon disappeared from sight. Matteo held up his hand and slowed his horse to a walk. Tomaso and the other men reined in their horses and many of them let out grateful sighs.

A few moments later Castillo came riding back.

"They are just ahead," he said, a trifle breathless. "I think I saw Nuncio. It will be light soon. We can catch them."

"Let us catch them, then," Matteo said, and once again he and the others put their horses to the gallop.

A few minutes later Matteo saw the men in the road. He also saw the rider, who turned in the saddle and saw them. He heard the man say something and then the men on foot started running. The man on horseback turned and Matteo saw the silhouette of his rifle. To his surprise, the man charged straight at them, leveling his rifle.

That's when Matteo noticed something odd about the horse. It was lame, and though it was trying to run, it faltered and stumbled and favored one foot so that it came on very slow.

Castillo turned to Matteo. "Do you want me to shoot him?"

"No, I will kill him. I want to draw first blood. You and the others go after those men. Do not shoot the man on the horse."

Matteo waved the other men on and they swept past him and raced toward the running men. The rider stopped for a moment and Matteo thought he was going to turn and chase after his men after they passed him, but he saw Matteo and spurred his horse. The horse could no longer run. It stumbled toward Matteo and the rider kept slapping him on the rump with his hand and kicking him in the flanks.

But the horse could no longer run.

Matteo raised his pistol and cocked it as the rider came on, the horse hopping along on three legs and trying to keep its balance.

"Matteo?" called the man riding the lame horse.

"I am Matteo. What do you call yourself?"

"Do you not know who I am, Matteo? Do you not remember me?"

"*Quien es?* Timoteo?"

"Yes. I am Timoteo. And I am going to kill you."

"Why? Because of your brothers?"

"Yes."

"You stupid fool."

Timo reined the limping horse to a halt and pulled his rifle to his shoulder.

Matteo heard the clicking sound as Timo cocked the rifle. He leaned forward until his upper body was lying on his own horse's shoulder. He raised his pistol alongside the horse's neck and took aim at Timo.

Timo was just about to squeeze the trigger when Matteo's silhouette disappeared. He hesitated, and in that instant he heard the spatter of rifle fire behind him.

Matteo heard the firing, too, just as he squeezed the trigger. His pistol bucked in his hand and spewed flame and smoke from the barrel. He saw Timo jerk and heard the splat of the ball as it struck flesh. Timo reeled in the saddle, but did not fall.

Matteo thumbed back the hammer on his single-action Colt's .44 and kicked his horse in its flanks. He rode up on Timo, looked into his glazing eyes.

"You did not shoot, Timoteo. Why?"

Timo opened his mouth and blood poured over his lips. His rifle fell from his hands and he leaned forward slightly as if doubling up from the pain in his chest.

Matteo put the muzzle of his pistol flush against Timo's temple as his finger curled around the trigger.

Timo shot a sidelong glance at Matteo. His lips moved, but no sound came out.

Matteo squeezed the trigger and the explosion forced the barrel of the pistol to jump upward slightly. The sound of the shot was muffled, but Matteo watched as Timo's head jerked sideways and came apart like a melon dropped from a great height. Blood sprayed out the other side and pieces of skull and brain matter flew outward in the pattern of an opened fan.

Timo, most of his head shot away, fell to the right and he tumbled out of the saddle and hit the ground with a dull and final thud.

"Bastard," Matteo said, and wiped the muzzle of his pistol on the rump of Timo's horse, which stood there quivering from the sound of the shot, dazed by the exploding gases so close to its ear.

Matteo calmly reloaded the two emptied cylinders of his pistol, to avoid accidental discharge from powder flash, greased the seated balls, and capped the two nipples. He looked up then at the sky and saw it paling as the half moon hung there, its glow softening to shadow as the dawn hovered on the horizon.

With the death of Timo, Matteo had accomplished two things. He had killed an old enemy, and he had let his men go into battle without him, as he had intended all along. Now he could view the battle from a safe position, from somewhere he could not be seen, and he could try and find Martin Baron in his sights and shoot him dead from a distance.

Matteo knew the layout of the Box B headquarters well. He knew every inch of the grounds surrounding the house and where the barn was, and the little houses of the vaqueros. He knew where he could hide and not be seen. And he knew how to ride away without anyone knowing he had ever been there.

Calmly Matteo holstered his pistol and drew his rifle from its boot. He checked the lock and poured fresh, fine powder into the pan. He blew away the top of the pile of grains and left a thin shadow at the bottom, enough to shoot fire through the little hole and into the main charge.

Then he turned his horse off the road and set his course to come up behind the ranch without being seen.

He heard the crackling sounds of rifle fire, and now it seemed farther away and he knew his men must have broken through the initial defenses that Martin had set up to defend his property.

Matteo smiled.

So far, he thought, all that he had planned was working.

39

ANSON PUSHED HIS saddlebags out of the way and turned to Peebo. Peebo narrowed his eyes and nodded.

"Was that Timo behind us?" Anson asked anyway.

"Yeah. Looks like he didn't beat us here."

Anson swore.

"No. My horse under him came up lame."

"He should have . . ."

"Yeah, I was thinkin' that. Too damned late now."

Anson looked back to the road and saw the riders coming fast. The first two horses ran into the rope that was stretched across their path and stumbled, faltered, then started to fall. Their riders hurtled forward, out of their saddles, and landed on their stomachs and lay still.

One horse fell on the rope, knocking it down. The other horse rolled over and further depressed the rope, so that it was no longer a barrier. The other riders, coming two by two, split up in a flaring vee and avoided striking the downed horses and men. One of the men who had been unseated, quickly grabbed up the reins and remounted one of the horses after it had struggled to its feet. The other rider pulled his horse to a standing position and ran to the opposite side of the road, pulling his horse after him.

Al took aim on the lead rider of the flying vee phalanx and led him two yards and squeezed the trigger. The shot went wild and Al cursed at the miss. Roy shot one of the horses streaking by and saw it falter, then collapse. Its rider hit the ground running and another rider snatched him up as he rode past. The fallen rider swung up behind him, and Roy's jaw dropped at this demonstration of agility and superb horsemanship.

Anson, Peebo, and David all fired their rifles, almost in unison, and one of the riders stiffened but stayed in the saddle. Then, while the five men were reloading, the riders coming up in the rear swung their horses toward them and fired their rifles at point-blank range before they veered to the right and drove their horses after the others.

Anson ducked when he saw the maneuver, and he reached out and pushed on Peebo's back to force him down on his face. Bullets whirred into their midst and he heard one strike flesh. He clawed for his pistol, but by the time he drew it, the last of the riders had swept on past their position.

Peebo got back up and Roy, who had ducked as well, sat up and started reloading his rifle. That's when Anson noticed that David was squatted next to him and seemed to be in trouble. He was crunched up, his arms flattened to his sides like tucked-in wings. His face was contorted into a rigid grimace as if he had been frozen by a sudden electrical shock.

"David," Anson said.

David looked at him with wet eyes that conveyed a look of pleading.

"Peebo, take a look at David here," Anson said. Anson touched David's shoulder, as if trying to brace him. Peebo put down his rifle and grabbed the other's shoulder.

"He don't look good," Peebo said.

"Did you get hit, David?" Anson asked. He bent down to look at his chest. He could see no blood. "Where'd you get hit?"

"Let's pry his arms back," Peebo said.

Al and Roy stared after the riders heading for the Box B headquarters, then looked over at Anson and Peebo. Al scooted over to squat in front of David as Anson pried his left arm away from his side.

"Nothing here," Anson said. "Peebo, did you check under his other arm?"

"Doin' it," Peebo said, and pulled on David's arm near the elbow.

David winced in pain and the blood drained from his face, turning it the color of putty in the stark morning light. He gasped as Peebo pried his arm farther away from his side, exposing the black hole in his rib cage. Anson leaned over to look at the wound.

"Got him in the bottom rib, looks like," Anson said.

"Maybe nicked his lung," Peebo said, pointing to the frothy bubbles of blood oozing from the hole.

"David, you've got to hold on," Anson said. "We're going to lay you down on your back and try to close up that hole."

David's lips were turning bluish and he did not answer.

"Roy, help us here," Anson said.

Roy crabbed over to hunker at David's feet. He laid his rifle down. The air smelled of nitrate and sulphur, and as the sun rose above the eastern horizon, the light spread from the treetops and eased down the trunks, erasing the shadows as it spread.

"Whatcha want me to do?" Roy asked.

"Pull real gentle on his feet while we take him down," Anson said. "Peebo, you ready?"

"Let's do it," Peebo said.

Al set his rifle down, the ramrod beside it, and scooted around to watch as Peebo and Anson pulled David backward to lay him flat on the ground. Roy pulled up on his feet and legs, then let them down after David's back was level.

"Tear his shirt where the ball went through," Anson told Peebo. "Give us some light on that hole."

Peebo grabbed the torn part of David's shirt and ripped it along the edges until it separated into two parts. Anson looked over at Al. "Got a canteen here? I want to wash that wound, see if I can't dig out the ball."

"Got it," Al said, and reached behind him. He handed Anson a wooden canteen.

They heard rifle shots over by the Baron house. They sounded like firecrackers, a rippling sound that crackled and popped in the distance.

David looked up at Peebo, who was staring into his eyes. "Bad?" he gasped.

"Don't know yet. You just grit your teeth, Davey boy, whilst Anson takes a look."

"It doesn't hurt," David said. "But I feel funny."

Anson looked up at the growing light and sighed. There was still a shadow over the wound, but he could see the hole. He reached underneath David's back to feel for an exit wound. He ran his hand back and forth and in a circle, but found no blood or other signs of another hole.

"Damn," Anson said.

"What?" Peebo asked.

"Bullet didn't come out," Anson said.

Roy crawled over to the side so that he could see David's face. He shivered at the sight of it. David was not breathing very well, he noticed. His chest did not move much when he took in a breath and his lips were blue, as if he had been eating berries. From his position Roy could see the wound as Anson poured water from Al's canteen over it, washing away the blood to reveal a clean black hole was that was turning purple around its circumference. He saw frothy white bubbles inside the hole after the water washed away.

All the unkind thoughts he'd had about David surfaced in Roy's mind as he watched Anson put his finger up to the hole. Roy wished he could take back those words now, but he knew this was not the time.

"David, we don't have any whiskey or anything," Anson said. "You want to bite down on something? A stick or a ramrod?"

"Why?" David asked, his voice feeble.

"I'm going to probe inside you for that lead ball. It's going to hurt like fire and then some."

"It doesn't really hurt now," David said. "Knocked the wind out of me. Felt like a slap."

"This is going to hurt," Anson said.

"I don't care," David said, and his eyes looked tired, Roy thought, tired and cloudy with pain, like the eyes of a deer he'd once shot, a deer dying from just such a gunshot wound through its lung.

If David died, Roy knew his mother would likely take it pretty hard. Even though he had no fondness for David, he knew his mother doted on him, put a heap of stock in him. Well, he didn't really hate David, but maybe he had been trying to stack him up against his own father, and David measured up right short against Jack Killian. And maybe he hadn't been fair with David these past months, not really giving him a chance or trying to be good friends with him. Now he was sorry, because it looked like David wasn't going to make it through the day, and it was going to be a mighty tough thing to tell his mother.

"What do you think, Anson?" Roy asked.

"About what?"

"Never mind."

"If I can get that ball out . . ." Anson said, and poked his finger gingerly past the opening in David's chest.

"I could go get Doc Purvis," Al said. "I think he's still in town."

"Be too late," Anson said. "Just be quiet a minute, will you?"

Anson touched fractured bone inside the wound and felt his finger swim in blood. David screamed and then went limp. His eyes closed.

"Jesus," Anson said.

"Might be a blessing to old David here," Peebo said. "He ain't goin' to feel much now."

"You shut your damned mouth, Peebo," Roy said.

"Hey, old son, I didn't mean nothin'," Peebo said.

"Well, you watch what you say about my stepfather."

Peebo shrugged. Al switched his gaze to Roy, studied his face.

Anson probed around inside David's chest. It was gruesome work, touching the spongy lung, the jagged edges of splintered bone, the slick hard slopes of organs he could not name. He drove deeper and made a circle with his finger, trying to find something small and round and hard. But everything he touched yielded to the pressure of his finger and finally he realized he wasn't going to find what he was looking for inside that bloody hole. Anson withdrew his finger and let out a breath as he rocked backward on his kneeling legs.

"I couldn't find the ball," he said. "It must be deep or in pieces."

"It could have gone any direction once it hit that rib," Al said.

"I don't know what else I can do," Anson said.

"Let me try it," Roy said.

None of the others said anything. They all looked at Roy as if he had lost his senses. They all knew that Roy and David had a bone of contention between them, and had never heard Roy say a kind word about his stepfather.

"He's in shock now," Al said, his voice soft. "You get to diggin' too hard and he might light a shuck."

"Well, we can't just sit here and let him die," Roy said.

"I can stop the bleeding, maybe," Anson said.

"Well, shit, if he's all tore up inside," Roy said, "what the hell good's that gonna do?" His voice was on the rim of hysteria and the others knew it.

"Old son," Peebo said, "he's just tryin' to help, Anson is, and you might want old Dave to be comfortable some before he goes."

"You sayin' he's goin' to die?" Roy said, glaring at Peebo. "You givin' up on him?"

Al scooted down closer to Roy. "Roy, you've got to face what's got to be faced. That ball hit a lung and as long as it's inside him, it's nothin' but a question of time. A wild ball like that can tear hell out of a man's innards."

"Damn you, Al. Damn all of you. I ain't lettin' David die."

"Nobody's lettin' him die, Roy," Anson said, as he leaned forward and started to tear off and stuff pieces of David's shirt in the hole to stop the bleeding. David's breathing was shallow and thready.

"He don't sound none too good," Peebo said to Anson, almost in a whisper.

"I know. I don't think it would have helped any if I did find that damned ball."

"What's that?" Roy asked, straining to hear what Anson and Peebo were saying to each other.

"Roy, I've stopped the bleeding for the time being," Anson said. "It's only temporary and it's all I can see to do right now."

"Let me see," Roy said, and scooted up to where Anson had been sitting. Anson moved back out of the way. He reached for his rifle and grabbed it up.

There was more gunfire from Anson's house. He started to recharge his rifle while Roy bent over and listened to David's breathing.

"I don't hear Pa's cannon," Anson said.

"No," Al said. "I was wondering about that."

"Me too," Peebo said. "Something's wrong."

They were all quiet then, listening to David's breathing, which had begun to falter. Roy was whispering something in David's ear, but none there could make out the words.

Anson resumed pouring powder down the barrel of his rifle. He nodded to Peebo, who slid away from David and picked up his rifle. In a few seconds he was reloading his own weapon. "Thanks for the flint, son," Peebo said. "Worked just fine. Now, if it could only aim the barrel . . ."

Roy sat up straight.

"I think David's dying," he said, and there was a whimper in his voice, a quaver the others detected.

Anson, Peebo, and Al avoided looking at Roy just then, as if they were embarrassed for him. Roy slumped and looked down at his hands. They were grimy from the black powder and the grease and he sucked in a breath to keep from choking up and crying right then and there.

David's eyelids fluttered open and closed several times. Roy leaned over so that David could see him. "David?"

"Ah," David said.

"Can you hear me?"

David's eyes remained open and Roy could see him trying to focus them.

"It doesn't hurt much, Roy," David said.

"David, I'm sorry I been raggin' you."

"No matter. Roy. You take good care of your mother."

"David, you're not going to die. We're goin' to get you a sawbones and fix you up. Doc Purvis is comin' out."

David opened his mouth and struggled to say something. He gagged and then started coughing. His face swelled and turned russet, and then the coughing stopped. His lips began turning blue once again.

"Purvis—he can't help me now, Roy. No hard feelings between you and me?"

"No, David. Never was. I mean I . . . God, just don't die, hear?"

David stopped breathing. Hie eyes widened and he looked up at the sky beyond Roy's face and he lifted one arm as if he were reaching out for something. He made a gurgling sound in his throat and then relaxed. His eyes closed, and when Roy leaned down and put his face close to David's mouth, he felt no air coming out.

David's arm fell back down and he lay still. His chest no longer moved and his face began to take on a pallid cast as the sun rose higher and the shadows shrank to isolated pools beneath the trees.

Roy doubled over and began to sob. His body shook and his tears fell on David's face. He cried for a long time as the rifles cracked in the distance, as if they belonged in another world and held no meaning for those gathered around the dead body of David Wilhoit as if waiting for Roy's tears to raise him from the dead.

Finally Anson cleared his throat to say something. But no sound came out and he looked at the others there, Al and Peebo, and finally at Roy, who was crumpled up but no longer weeping, and wondered if they had all been struck dumb at that moment and if only the rifles up at the Box B headquarters could speak in their crisp, sharp, lethal voices.

40

THE NIGHT HAD been long and nerve-wracking. The men were still restless and had moved around the past two hours more than usual, and Martin had heard them talking in low tones but hadn't been able to make out what they were saying. He sensed that they were faltering in their resolve to fight, and wondered if he should say something to bolster their spirits, help them find their courage.

The sky was paling ever so slightly, and he knew that if an attack was to be made by Aguilar and his men, it would not be long in coming. A sense of foreboding began to build inside of him, a blackness of the mind that the coming dawn could not erase with its spreading light. He wondered if the men would be able to act quickly enough to turn the wagon and if he could reload the cannon fast enough after he fired the first shot. So many doubts crept into his mind, like little snakelike tendrils with flickering forked tongues and blind eyes.

Martin saw the mist rising from the fields as the sun's streaming light began to blush the eastern horizon. He saw the fog float upward from the creek like a thick cloud and then unfurl to mingle with the mist under the delicate pressure of a light breeze from the southwest.

As the fog began to build and spread like some rolling carpet of cotton, he heard shots coming from down the road. Then, after a numbing silence, he heard more shots and the horrible scream of a man in mortal agony.

"Socrates, you and Carlos there, help me take these sides down. The rest of you men crawl under the wagon."

At first nobody moved, then Socrates walked over and Carlos Quintana followed him. The three of them began to unlatch the side panels and take them down, exposing the cannon on its bed, its brass barrel gleaming faintly in the dim light of the dawn. Martin climbed up onto the wagon. None of the men moved until Martin barked at them: "Take your positions. Now."

The men crawled beneath the wagon, and Martin heard them muttering to themselves as he picked up a small keg of powder and began to pour it into the hole. He had checked the load earlier and knew it was tamped down and ready.

"Lift the wagon when I give the word, and move right or left as I command, Carlos."

"I will tell them," Carlos said.

"Socrates, you find yourself a tree and stay behind it."

"Yes, suh," Socrates said.

Then they all heard the popping of rifles on the south road. Martin knelt down and took flint and steel and began striking sparks into a lead pan filled with fine wood shavings. One of the sparks caught and he bent down and blew it to flame. Then he took a long slow fuse and stuck its end to the flame. The fuse began to fume and spark as it started to burn. He had thirty feet of it and felt sure he could get off several shots. Near the muzzle of the cannon, he had set out cloth bundles of buckshot, pieces of metal, chunks of lead, and larger lead balls that he could ram down the barrel. The metal was seated on coarse black powder to act as the charge for each load. He had gone over the reloading a thousand times in his mind. It would be better if he had a helper but he knew it was something he had to do alone. He would be an easy-enough target if he wasn't careful. Two or three men would be too tempting for Aguilar's riflemen.

The light from the moon began to fade as Martin stood there with the burning fuse in his hand, listening to the rippling crackle of rifle fire.

"Men," he yelled, "get ready! Lift the wagon off its wheels."

He heard a scuffling underneath the wagon boards, the low sounds of whispered conversations. But the wagon did not move.

"Lift up the wagon," Martin said, in a loud-enough voice for all his men beneath the wagon to hear.

There was more talk and he heard scuffling sounds underneath him. "Get this wagon up off the wheels," he ordered again. *"Now."*

Then he heard a sound and turned to see the dim outline of a man standing beside the wagon. The others crawled out from underneath and stood up.

"We do not want you to shoot the cannon."

"Who is that?" Martin rasped.

"I am Julio Sifuentes."

"Julio, get the men back under the wagon and move this cannon."

"We do not want to do that."

"Why?"

"We have seen what the cannon does. We saw what it did to the Apaches. We do not want to see our brothers shot into little pieces like that."

"We are being attacked, Sifuentes."

"Yes, and we will fight. But we will fight our way. Not with the cannon."

Martin noticed the men all carried their rifles.

"So you're going against my orders, Sifuentes."

"We fought the Apaches for you. We will fight our brothers if they attack us here. But we do not want to see their bodies cut up and thrown everywhere like with the Apaches. We could not live with those thoughts for all of our lives."

"Well, I'm disappointed. Aguilar's men will be here any minute and we could have stopped them in their tracks with the cannon."

"The cannon does not belong here," Sifuentes said. "It is from a ship, and this is land that already has blood on it. Do not shoot the cannon. If you do, we will throw down our rifles and hide. We will not fight."

Martin saw that he was not going to win the argument. He looked past Sifuentes at the other men. For a split second he thought they might lift their rifles to their shoulders and shoot him if he defied them.

"Very well," Martin said. He lifted the fuse in his hand, then dropped it to his feet. He stamped out the sparking fuse and a puff of white smoke rose up and then dissipated.

"Bring me my rifle, Carlos," Martin said, as he sprang from the wagon bed. "The rest of you find cover and do your best. Otherwise Matteo Aguilar will win and probably kill you all."

The men scrambled for cover. Carlos brought Martin's rifle to him. It had been leaning against a tree behind the wagon where Martin had left it in case he had to make a run for it. He took one last glance at the cannon and thought: Caroline was right when she told me to get rid of the cannon. She hated the cannon and so do these men.

He should have seen it coming, should have seen the discontent in the faces of his men. But he had not. He had been thinking only of the four-pounder and the damage it could do, horrible damage, to Aguilar's men when they attacked. He had forgotten the horror of the Apache attack by Cuchillo and his braves. He had forgotten the mangling and the blood.

Now Sifuentes had reminded him of what the cannon could do. But he had already known, and so had his hands. The cannon was a useful weapon, a weapon of war, and this was war. Yet there was something different about this one. And there shouldn't have been. No one had protested his use of the cannon on the Apaches, but now that he was fighting Mexicans, the rules had suddenly changed. He knew there was a difference, but he did not know why. Were the Apaches so different from the Mexicans? What if they were being attacked by white men? Would the rules have changed again?

Martin wanted to ask Sifuentes and the others about this question. He wanted to know why they did not want to use the cannon, but were still willing to fight with rifles and machetes, and maybe even slingshots if necessary.

Martin's ruminations were cut short as he heard the rumbling thunder of hoofbeats beyond the barn, along the road. He knew the others had heard it, too, and he knew he did not have to issue any orders. In a few seconds they would all be fighting for their lives.

Martin cocked his rifle and braced himself against the tree. Then he saw them in the pale dawn light—two lines of riders breaking wide, one to come at them from around the right side of the barn, the others across the open toward the house.

The riders looked as if they knew where they were going. They did not shoot their rifles, but held their fire and they did not bunch up. He stopped counting at a dozen as one line disappeared from view and the other spread out and began twisting their horses in a zigzag pattern as if they had trained for this moment. It was both a beautiful sight and a terrible one, and Martin started measuring the distance from a rider he had picked out as he brought his rifle to his shoulder.

Before he could fire, Martin heard a shot. It came from an upstairs window of his home and he saw one of the riders falter and slump over in the saddle. But the rider did not fall, and kept coming. It was a long shot, but an accurate one.

Then he found his rider and led him and squeezed the trigger and felt the rifle buck against his shoulder as it spouted flame and smoke and blotted out the charging horsemen.

A split second later he heard a dozen rifles go off around him, and from the perimeter where his men waited behind earthen breastworks, and then there were shots from the house and he saw riders all around him, through the blossoming clouds of smoke, and all time stopped as Martin began to pour powder down the smoking barrel of his rifle.

And he heard the screams of wounded men and the yells of his own and he wished he had fired the cannon and ended it all as the battle swarmed around him and rifles crackled and popped from all directions and all the targets disappeared in the pall of white smoke that blinded and choked him as he seated patch and ball and jerked his ramrod free.

In that frozen moment of eternity, the battle broke over Martin and he felt all alone, with a terrible fear building in his belly that had nothing to do with his courage, but with all that he could not see and all that he could hear, as the peaceful world of the Box B exploded and screamed in his ears.

41

ESPERANZA'S HEART QUICKENED as she saw the distant rider, saw him multiply into two, then three, four, five, and then too many to count. They seemed to ride out of nowhere, out of the darkness and into the spreading misty light of the dawn. She knew who they were; she had been waiting all these long hours, her bladder full for the past thirty minutes, her stomach empty, her nerves taut as the strings on Lazaro's guitar.

She had sent Lucinda to Caroline's room to see what Lazaro was doing and if he was staying away from the windows. Lucinda had said she had to relieve herself, but would do that, then return. But she was not here now and her loaded rifle was leaning against the wall near another window.

Esperanza sat straight in her chair and cocked the hammer on her rifle as she scooted the barrel farther out the window. The riders were coming fast and she knew she would not have time to aim and shoot the first one. She picked the fourth man on horseback and moved the muzzle of her rifle until she saw the horse's head and then she lined up both front and rear sights. When she had the horse's head in view, she swung the barrel slowly to her left, trying to match the speed of its gallop, and when she had swung two meters she squeezed the trigger and kept the barrel moving as she had been taught to do when she was a girl shooting her father's old fowling piece.

She was not prepared for the explosion that made her ears hurt and drowned out everything but a steady ringing. She felt the rifle jerk hard against her shoulder and saw the smoke billow from the muzzle. The smoke blotted out all the riders and she did not know if her ball had found its mark.

The explosion had deafened her for a few seconds and then loudened in the empty room until her ears began to hum with a steady ringing as if a bell had been struck. The billowing white smoke mixed with the morning fog and she could not see if she had hit her target. Nor did she want to know. She slumped in her chair and pulled the rifle back inside to reload it. She sagged against the wall as rifles cracked outside and men began to yell and scream, her hands trembling and her body quivering.

Through the din she heard the door open. Still half-deaf, she heard the soft pad of sandals on the hardwood floor.

"Did you shoot an enemy, Esperanza?" Lazaro asked.

"I do not know. You should not be here. Go back to your mother's room."

Just then, rifles began crackling and Esperanza cringed at the sound, like bones breaking, and she heard rifle shots from the other rooms, so she knew the attack must be coming at them from all directions.

"I hear them," Lazaro said. "I hear them shooting. I wish I could see the fighting."

"You be quiet," Esperanza said and, almost mechanically, began to reload her rifle. "And stay away from that window." She saw him go to the window and start to lean out. "Get back. You might get shot."

"There is a lot of shooting," Lazaro said.

"I am trying to put powder in this clumsy rifle. *Callate.*"

Lazaro stepped back away from the window, but Esperanza saw that he was very excited. The ringing in her ears began to subside as she finished starting the patch and ball down the barrel of her rifle. She stood up and extracted the wiping stick from beneath the barrel. She tamped the ball and cloth down until they were seated and then poured fine powder in the pan and checked the flint to see that it was tight. She pushed the chair aside and stood at the window, looking out.

"Where is Lucinda?" she asked Lazaro.

"She had to go pee."

"She should be here."

"She will come. I think she is talking to the other women."

"Damn her," Esperanza said.

She heard a rifle shot and saw a horse stumble and go down. The rider was unhurt and landed on his feet. The horse kicked its legs for a second or two, then quivered a moment before it lay still. The rider threw himself flat on the ground behind the horse and took up a shooting position, using the horse for cover.

Esperanza aimed her rifle at him, but she could not steady or level the barrel and she knew she was trembling all over as if she had a fever.

She heard more shooting from inside the house and voices pitched high in exclamation coming from the other rooms, women's voices, and then she saw the man behind the house look up at her and turn suddenly and swing his rifle in her direction.

Esperanza uttered an oath in Spanish and leaned backward, hoping she would not be seen, but she knew it was too late. Her rifle barrel jutted skyward and she could not bring it down. It was as if she was paralyzed and then she saw everything in slow motion: a puff of white smoke drifting across the yard, a horseman racing toward the barn and crossing the path of another, two other riders galloping toward the front of the house, bent low over their horses' necks, and the man on the ground, taking aim at her. She saw, vividly, a tiny puff of smoke rise from the pan and a split second later she heard the report and saw an orange flame spew from his barrel and tear through a big cloud of smoke as white as cotton, and then the rifle she held stung her hands and began to fly apart. The stock splintered and she felt slivers of wood slash into her face and chest. Then she felt a mighty shock to her left shoulder and the impact stunned her for a moment so that she felt no pain.

Her rifle fell from her hands and struck the floor with a loud *crack* and then she spun to her left as the pain in her shoulder burned like a branding fire. She heard Lazaro cry out as she fell to the floor, dizzy from the shock of the ball and bewildered by her sudden fall. She hit hard and dancing lights spun in her head and she knew she cried out, but it sounded like someone else's voice because her neck hurt so bad now that she was sure it was broken.

"Esperanza, no!" Lazaro shouted, and she saw a shadow out of the corner of her eye and then he was bending over her and feeling her face.

"Help me," she croaked in Spanish, and then saw Lazaro rise up with blood on his hands, his face contorted in fear.

"Do not die, Esperanza," the boy said. "I will return with quickness."

Then she saw him run away and heard his sandals slapping the floor. She lay there dazed and in pain and wondered if she was going to die before Lazaro brought help.

I am breathing, she thought. I am alive. I have pain. As long as there is the pain, I am not dead. I must hold on to the pain, as my mother held on to her pain for so long.

Images of her mother emerged in Esperanza's mind. She envisioned her on her deathbed with the cholera, the rage of the fever that made her speak without sense, that made her cry out and curse God. That was when fighting such as this had been raging at the mission near San Antonio de Bexar, at the place of the Alamo, when Generalissimo Santa Anna had sent his troops to attack the small number of Americans. She could still hear the roar of the cannon, the rattle of muskets shooting, so many shootings, so many screams, and the bugles sounding like geese high in the sky. And her mother knowing nothing of the big battle, gave in to the pain and the fever drinking her water and her blood until her voice crackled like dry wood on fire.

She remembered her mother's eyes, glazed and open, but sightless and yet frozen as if she had been to hell and seen the flames there burning the sinners alive like they were cattle on a spit. She remembered bathing her mother's shriveled body with cool water and mezcal to keep the fever down and the lucid moments after the bathing when her mother would smile wanly and say that she hurt so bad she knew she must still be alive even though she had been with angels and had seen devils and thought that she must be in Purgatory, atoning for her many sins.

Her mother lived for many days, lived until they all heard the Mexican army band playing that chilling song, "El Daguello," and knew that all of the gringos in the mission were doomed. She could still hear the trumpets and the drums and then the cannons—so many cannons—roared, and she heard the charging Mexicans yell as they rushed the Alamo, and so many muskets firing and men screaming, until a deathly silence fell over the river and the plain and the city, and her mother gasped her last breath and slipped out of pain and life with a gentle sigh on her parched lips.

Before her mother died, however, she had said something to her daughter when they were alone that had stayed in Esperanza's mind and heart all these years.

"Daughter," her mother had said, "I am not afraid to die. I have never been afraid to die. It is the dying that is hard and a thing to be feared, for it is a terrible trial. Yet I know this is God's way and I am comforted by the thought. I know, because this dying is so hard, that I will not go to hell, nor to Purgatory, nor to Limbo. This is Purgatory, here and now. And I will pass through the flames of my pain and find eternal peace with God. Do not forget this when you come to the river. You will cross it, as will I, and I will be waiting for you on the other side."

She heard footsteps pounding up the stairs, voices echoing down the hall. A few seconds later the door to the room burst open and she saw people running toward her. First to reach her was Lucinda, who knelt down and clucked like a mother hen, chattered like a flock of magpies.

"Oh, Esperanza, what has passed? You are hurt. The doctor is here. Please do not die."

"Let me take a look," Doc Purvis said, and Lucinda moved aside.

Purvis set his little black bag down and squatted next to Esperanza.

"Lucinda, stay away from that window," Esperanza said. She saw Wanda grab Lucinda and pull her away from the window, and Hattie was there, and Ursula, who was holding on to Lazaro's shoulders. Lazaro was shaking all over as if he had the ague, and Esperanza wanted to reach out to him and take his hand to calm him.

"Well, I see you have some wood splinters that I can take out," Purvis said. "And let's take a look at that shoulder. Hmm."

Esperanza cried out in pain as Purvis ripped away the cloth of her blouse and touched the wound in her shoulder.

"I'm sorry," he said. "I can give you some powders for the pain. Doesn't look too bad. I don't see a ball in there. Must have hit a glancing blow. No bones broken that I can see."

Lorene leaned over the doctor's shoulder to look at Esperanza. "Do you want me to get some hot water, Uncle Pat?"

"No, I'll clean the wound with alcohol. One of you bring me a glass of water. Hurry."

"I'll get it," Hattie said, and ran from the room.

The firing outside continued, with shots sounding like pops or cracks, and sometimes they could hear the whine of a ricochet. Ursula pulled Lazaro down closer to the floor and Wanda and Lucinda squatted below the windowsill.

"I shot someone," Esperanza said, and crossed herself with her right hand.

"I think I did, too," Wanda said. "But there was so much smoke and dust."

"It's a terrible thing," Lorene said, "neighbors fighting like this. I don't see any sense in it."

"Matteo is a skunk," Ursula said. "I know. Me and Davey lived with him on his ranch. He's a mean person."

Purvis soaked a cloth with alcohol. The fumes made Esperanza gasp for breath and the others turned their heads away until the air cleared. Hattie returned with the glass of water and Purvis poured some powder in it, shook the glass until all the grains had dissolved.

"Here," he said to Esperanza, "drink this. I'll hold the glass. Can someone bring a pillow from that bed there? And I'll need help carrying her over there once I've cleaned her wound."

Purvis held the glass while Esperanza let the cloudy liquid flow into her mouth and down her throat. He made her drink it all and then Wanda handed him a pillow from the bed. He placed it under Esperanza's head, gently arranging it so that she was comfortable.

"Feel better?" Purvis asked.

"Yes. There is not so much pain now."

"Good. Now, I'm going to take these wood splinters out. You will feel some stinging. Then I am going to wash your shoulder in alcohol and put some medicine on it. Then you are going to bed and you are going to sleep."

"Yes, Doctor," she said.

"Is she going to die?" Lazaro asked.

"No, she's not going to die," Purvis said, and picked a pair of tweezers from his bag and began to search out the wood splinters embedded in Esperanza's face and chest.

"What's that?" Lorene said, standing up. "Downstairs."

They all listened. Purvis held the tweezers poised over a splinter.

"My god," Wanda said. "Mother, go and see."

"There's no need, daughter. They've set the house on fire."

Then they all heard it, the crackling of flames from somewhere down below, on the ground level of the house. Their eyes widened and their features became drawn with fear.

"Quick," Purvis said, "Lorene, you take this woman's feet and lift her up. I'll get the head. One of you get my bag and put everything in it. We must hurry."

"I'll help lift Esperanza," Hattie said.

"I will help," Lucinda said, and they lifted Esperanza up and started carrying her toward the door. Ursula packed Purvis's bag and then grabbed Lazaro's hand. She led him off, both of them stumbling to catch up to the others.

At the top of the stairs, the roar of the flames was very loud. A window cracked and as they descended to the foyer, they saw that the living room was filled with smoke. As they walked toward the front door, they saw flames shooting from the porch through the windows of the front room.

Soon all of them were enclosed in black smoke. And they all felt the heat rushing toward them. Lucinda screamed.

"We've got to get out," Purvis said. "Fast."

"How?" Lorene wailed.

The front room was snarling with flames and the walls bristled with fire that crackled and gulped oxygen and began to stream across the ceiling. The fire began to roar with its own terrible voice and the women began to cough.

Esperanza struggled in the grasp of those who carried her.

"Let me up," she said. "I will show you the way to get out."

And then the entire ceiling in the front room became engulfed in flames and they could no longer see the front door, nor any passage out of that place where they all stood frozen in fear and choking on the black smoke and weeping as their lungs began to burn.

One of the beams fell with a crash and scattered sparks in every direction. Hattie batted at her clothes to put out the tiny winking coals and Lucinda began to pray in Spanish.

"We are going to die," Lucinda said.

And Lazaro began to cry softly as the flames roared in his ears like the thundering voices of unnamed and unknown gods.

42

Ken Richman looked up from his drink when the three men entered the Longhorn Saloon. From their dusters, he knew they had ridden a long way, and from their faces he knew they were tired. From the looks in their eyes, he knew they were hunting someone.

The first man looked vaguely familiar to Ken, but he couldn't place him in his mind with anyone he knew or had met. The other two were slightly younger. They all carried rifles such as Ken had never seen before, shorter than the Kentucky rifle, but longer than the mountain carbines, and smooth, without flintlocks.

Nancy Grant, who was sitting with Ken, looked up, too, and stared at the three men, who stood there, just inside the batwings, surveying the large room. There were only two people at the bar, one of them Ed Wales, the other, his typesetter, Jim Callan.

"Who're they?" Nancy asked, looking at the big Waterbury clock on the wall. It was nearly midnight and she and Ken were both weary from a long day, their late-supper dishes long since cleared away.

"I don't know," Ken said. "But I'll find out."

He pushed his chair back from the table and stood up. The first man through the door saw him and strode his way. He was not a tall man, under six feet, but he looked solid under the duster, on the lean side, with a smooth-shaven face, dark hair that had grown long and had begun to curl a few inches from his shoulders. His eyes were brown and he had a straight nose, and bee-stung lips that were cracked as if he had not had water in a long time.

"You Richman?" the man said.

"Yes, I am."

"I was told to look you up. I'm Kenny Darnell."

"Caroline's brother?"

"Yes. I'm looking for Al Oltman. He said he'd be here."

"Did you know . . ."

"Yes, I know my sis died. Have you seen Oltman?"

"Bring your men over to my table and I'll buy you drinks. Al's not here."

Ken turned to walk back to his table. He heard Darnell's boots on the hardwood floor. He pulled another chair over to the table as Darnell waved at his men to come over. He sat down, and looked at Nancy Grant. She returned his frank stare and smiled.

"Ma'am," Darnell said. He touched a finger to the brim of his hat. "Kenny Darnell."

"Nancy Grant," she said.

"Sorry about your sister, Darnell. She had a nice funeral."

"Thanks." Darnell's men came up. He turned to them. "Boys, this is Mr. Richman and Miss Grant. Richman, shake hands with Dan Shepley and Jim-Joe Casebolt. Boys, you go on over to the bar and order what you like."

"The drinks are on me," Richman said.

"Obliged," said Shepley, as he shook Ken's hand. Casebolt just nodded and headed for the bar.

Richman signaled to the bartender. "What'll you have, Kenny?" he asked.

"Water would be fine." He leaned his rifle against the table, within easy reach.

"You haven't seen Martin, I gather."

"No, I knew Sis had died. Got a message from Oltman down to Corpus. I had other business. I haven't seen Martin much since he married my sis."

"You're a Texas Ranger," Ken said.

Darnell nodded. Richman lifted his hands and made a pumping motion to the barkeep. Then he held up two fingers and swirled them in the air. The barkeep nodded and took drink orders from Shepley and Casebolt.

"Did you come to Baronsville to pay your respects to your sister?" Nancy asked.

"Partly," Darnell said. "But I've got other business here as well." Darnell's jaw tightened and a muscle quivered next to his chin. "Where'd you say Al Oltman was, Mr. Richman?"

"Call me Ken. He's at the Box B. Martin is expecting an attack on his ranch in the morning."

Darnell's forehead wrinkled above his eyebrows. "You don't say."

"Afraid so. Do you know Matteo Aguilar?"

Darnell nodded.

"Matteo's got a wild hair up his rump about the land Martin bought from the family. Wants it back, I guess."

"Aguilar's plumb loco," Darnell said.

"I think you're right," Ken said. "Say, that's a mighty fine looking rifle you've got there. I've never seen one like it."

"It's a Spencer repeater," Darnell said. "A new make. Shoots right good. We got 'em from the army. I got one on my saddle for Oltman."

The bartender came over to the table, bearing a tray. He set a glass of water in front of Darnell, a whiskey at Ken's spot, and a glass of sarsaparilla at Nancy's place.

"Thanks," Ken said.

Darnell drank most of the water in his glass, wiped his mouth on his sleeve. Then he reached inside his pocket and pulled out an oilpouch. "Haven't seen a Frenchie in town, have you, Ken? Name of Jules Reynaud. From New Orleans."

"I've never seen the man, but I know who he is. He's in with Matteo."

"I know," Darnell said. "I'm just surprised he's still in cahoots with Aguilar. Them two mix about as well as fire and coal oil."

"Why do you ask about Reynaud?"

"In this packet here," Darnell said, tapping on the oilskin, "I've got warrants for both Jules Reynaud and Matteo Aguilar."

Ken, about to take a sip of whiskey, stopped the rising arc of his hand and the glass. "Warrants?"

"Reynaud's a slave trader and there's solid evidence he smuggled slaves out of New Orleans and drug 'em up to the Rocking A."

"Yes, I know. Martin took those Negroes away from Matteo and set them free. Some are living here in town, some are at the Box B, and Roy Killian has a couple, I believe."

"I don't care what happened to those slaves, Ken. I'm just going to put Reynaud and Aguilar in the *juzgado* for trafficking and stealing 'em."

"You've got your work cut out for you, Kenny."

"I aim to do it."

Nancy sipped at her sarsaparilla and watched Darnell in rapt fascination. "Are you married, Mr. Darnell?" she asked.

"It's Kenny, ma'am. And no, I'm not. Why do you ask?"

"Because you have a dangerous job and I would think a wife would worry about you."

"Yes'm, I reckon she would if I had one. Rangerin' takes up a heap of time."

"Were you and Caroline close?"

"Not after she got married; and a lot less after our folks died."

"How did they die?" Nancy asked.

"It wasn't natural. That's another charge on Aguilar and a separate warrant on him." Darnell patted the packet again. " 'Inciting Apaches to steal and murder.' "

"I didn't hear about that," Nancy said, looking at Richman. "Is that true, Ken?"

"Martin always thought Cuchillo was in Matteo's pay, and Anson says that Cuchillo's son, Culebra, is working for Aguilar. Says that Matteo gives him and his savages cattle and horses to make raids on the Box B. That's the charge. Apaches killed our folks, Miss Grant," Darnell said.

"Please. Call me Nancy."

"I'll go after Culebra after I put Aguilar and Reynaud behind bars," Darnell said.

"Are you going to stay a Ranger, or join the Confederate Army?" Nancy asked.

"I'm a Ranger, ma'am, till I die."

Darnell finished drinking his water. He put the oilskin packet back inside a pocket in his coat, and stood up.

"Well, if Aguilar's moving against the Box B, I'd best be getting on out there," Darnell said.

"But that's a long ride," Nancy said. "And you must be tired."

"I can rub some dirt in my eyes. We'll sleep when we can."

Richman stood up. "If there's anything I can do to help . . ."

"You keep an eye out for Reynaud," Darnell said. "Get word to me if you see him in town."

"I will."

"Is there a reward for him?" Nancy asked, looking up at Darnell.

"No'm, not yet. The ink on these warrants is still wet. But I'm authorized to bring him in dead or alive."

"And which would you prefer?" Nancy asked.

"It don't make no never mind to me which," Darnell said, tapping the brim of his hat with his finger. "Be seein' you. Thanks for the branch, Ken."

"You're welcome. When you come back, maybe you'll have whiskey instead of water."

"I might, at that," Darnell said. He looked to the bar. "Boys, let's go."

Casebolt and Shepley left their stools immediately. They picked up their rifles and followed Darnell out the door.

"My, what a surprise," Nancy said, after the batwing doors had stopped creaking on their hinges.

"Yes. I imagine Matteo will be surprised, as well."

"Maybe that'll be an end to poor Martin's troubles."

Ken finished his whiskey. The fumes burned his eyes and left them wet. He looked at the silent batwings, the darkness beyond.

"I keep thinking I ought to be out at the Box B with Martin right now," Ken said. "Helping him."

Nancy reached over and put her hand atop Ken's.

"No, you belong here," she said. "With me. I don't want you getting shot."

"I just hope Martin comes out of this all right. He's been having a run of bad luck lately."

"I know. It's so sad. Caroline dying and now this."

"I tell you, Nancy, I don't know why any man would want to run a ranch in this pitiful country. If it's not the Apaches or your neighbors trying to do you in, it's the damned wind or the rain or the hurricanes. I just don't understand why Martin ever left the sea to take up ranching."

"We all have our dreams," Nancy said.

43

THEY FINISHED COVERING David's body with hastily cut mesquite boughs. It was plain to Anson that Roy was shaken up at his stepfather's death. Roy was stumbling around like a man in a stupor.

"Roy," Anson said, putting the last bough over David's body. "Buck up. We've got to get to the ranch quick."

"Hey, I'm all right, Anson."

"I guess David's death hit you pretty hard."

"No. I can handle it."

"Bullshit."

"If you two are going to fight," Al said, "Peebo and I will walk to headquarters by ourselves."

"Come on, Anson," Peebo said. "Let's go."

"Roy?" Anson said.

Roy looked at the makeshift covering over David and doubled over for a minute. When he straightened up, his eyes were wet and he looked as if he was going to be sick.

"Just let me get my breath," Roy said. "Just give me a minute. You all go on ahead. I'll catch up with you."

"You don't have to come with us at all," Anson said. "It's not your fight."

Roy's face contorted at the lash of Anson's words, as if his head had been wrenched violently. He already felt bad about David getting killed and now Anson was laying into him. He felt as if he was locked inside some nightmare dream. He wished it could make all the hurt go away, wished he had never gotten into this fight in the first place. He wished David was still alive. And most of all, he wished he had not ragged on David so, especially right before he got killed. What in hell was he going to tell his mother? How was she going to take it? She might even blame him for not protecting David, and she might begin to hate him for hating David so. Everything was so mixed up and he couldn't think, couldn't move. He felt as if he was all torn up inside, as if he was raw and bleeding, only nobody could see any of it. It was all inside him, all tangled up and all mashed and twisted and cut up like butchered meat and he couldn't even cry, couldn't even pray, or curse, or get away from any of it. It was as if he were nailed down there by David's body, as if David's dead soul didn't want him to leave, but to stay there and die there with him for all the taunts and teasings and hatefulness he had bestowed upon him.

Roy looked askance at Anson. Anson had not moved, but seemed to still be waiting for him. None of this made any sense. David should not have died this way, should not have to lie there under a bunch of mesquite leaves as if he were just trash to be buried out of sight.

A volley of rifle shots spurred Anson to pick up his rifle. "We've got to go and help my pa out," he said. "Roy, you can stay here if you need to."

Al shot Anson a look of disapproval. Anson ignored him. He and Peebo started running to the road. Al turned to look at Roy. "Might be better if you come with us, Roy. You can't do any good here."

"I know. I—I'm just damned sorry I was so mean to him."

"It doesn't make any difference now. You can't help David none, and if you stay here and those Rocking A boys come back, we'll be cartin' your corpse to the graveyard. Come on."

Roy took a deep breath and shook his head as if to rid his thoughts of David. He stepped to a tree and picked up his rifle. "I'm ready," he said. "Let's go."

Al took off at a run, with Roy a few paces behind him. The two caught up with Anson and Peebo. They heard sporadic firing and the sounds grew louder and more distinct as they drew closer to the Box B headquarters.

"Sounds like a battle to me," Al said. "Lots of shooting."

"Yeah," Anson said, and gritted his teeth as he began to run faster. The rifle shots were not steady, but there were more of them, and he found himself counting out the seconds it took a man to reload a rifle. Juanito had said a man should be able to reload in twenty-two seconds while under fire, and Anson had practiced and practiced but he'd never been able to do it in less than about forty seconds.

He hadn't counted the number of men from the Rocking A who had passed them on the road, but he knew there were at least twenty or more, and maybe his pa had a couple of dozen, all told, up at the headquarters, and now it seemed like they were all shooting pretty regular and he knew how hard it was to shoot a man from a galloping horse. He knew his pa had cleared out the barn and stables and put the horses in a pasture out of harm's way. He kept listening for the sound of the cannon going off, but he never heard its roar and now, as his side began to ache from running, he was worried sick that something had happened to his pa.

"Look out," Anson said, as the barn came into sight. "Spread out and head for this side of the barn."

"Then what?" Peebo asked.

"Sneak around it and shoot anybody on horseback."

"What the hell happened to that cannon your pa lugged in from town?"

"I don't know," Anson said, and bent over to keep a low profile. He saw riders beyond the barn, but only briefly. They seemed to be riding in circles, or back and forth. He couldn't tell because they were too far away and were not in view long enough.

Al and Roy struck a path to the left of the barn and Anson turned right, with Peebo following him. Two riders came around the barn and Anson saw that they were reloading as they came, using the barn for cover. He stopped, took aim on the nearest one. Peebo stopped, too, and brought his own rifle to his shoulder.

"I got the one in the front," Anson said. "You get the other one."

"Son, I got him at the end of the pipe."

Peebo fired and Anson led his target and fired a split second later, and both shots missed as the riders spotted them and put their horses into a zigzag. Then the two riders raced around the right side of the barn and disappeared from sight.

"Damn," Peebo said. "I'm gettin' right rusty."

"I missed, too." Anson trotted toward the barn, spilling powder from his horn in his excitement, and lost track of how much went down the barrel. He reached the back of the barn and leaned against it to finish loading. "Sloppy," he said, knowing it had taken him the better part of a minute to reload, and his heart was pounding so fast he thought it was going to burst from his chest.

"Now what?" Peebo asked, as he leaned a shoulder against the barn. "I'm loaded. Are you?"

"Yeah, but I don't know if I poured fifty grains or two hundred down my damned barrel."

"Same here. I reckon I got enough to push the ball out the end."

Anson saw Al and Roy stop at the far corner of the barn. Al held a hand out to keep Roy back while he peeked around the corner. Anson smiled. He would not have to worry about Al. He knew how to fight.

"We ain't goin' to get much shootin' from back here," Peebo said.

"Follow me." Anson crept to the corner of the barn and craned his neck, staying low. He saw riders going in and out of the smoke, but none seemed an immediate threat. He stepped around the corner, knowing he was going to be without cover. Rifle shots popped and snapped like cracking dry tree limbs. He was surprised at all the white smoke. It clung to the ground, thick as clouds, mingling with the fog of morning, the dew evaporating as the sun struggled to clear the horizon.

Peebo came up behind him as Anson reached the other corner of the barn.

"We can't go into that smoke," Anson said.

"No, son, we can't. Want to try and make the front porch of the house?"

"We'll be walkin' into smoke."

"Make a wide circle around it, off yonder to the right. At the base of the slope. We can use the smoke for cover."

Anson thought about it. He had a rough idea of where the Box B hands would be and where his father would be with the cannon:

behind the house. Martin would have shooters inside the house. There was nobody in the barn, but anyone going in now, would be trapped. The slope Peebo was talking about lay almost directly perpendicular to the barn and house. The house sat up on a low hill, with trees all around it. If they could make it through the smoke to the base of the slope, then they could stay behind the smoke and make their way to the house. If they could get inside, they'd have cover and be able to help fend off Matteo's men.

"Sounds right to me," Anson said.

"Let's go, then."

Anson started running, straightaway from the barn, then began to angle left. He could hear Peebo's boots slapping the ground behind him. Bullets whistled all around them, but they knew these were wild shots. Anson ran straight into a cluster of smoke that hugged the ground and he coughed, gagged, fought for air.

Peebo, behind him, held his breath as long as he could and then began gulping smoke. Rifles cracked from within the dense cloud of white smoke and they heard lead balls ricochet and whine off somewhere out of sight.

Anson nearly stumbled on the sloping ground and he got his bearings as Peebo caught up to him. "This here's the bottom of that long slope."

"Yeah, I reckon. I figure the house is right over yonder. Sounds like most of the shooting's on the side and back of the house."

Anson listened. "Could be," he said.

"I wonder how Al and Roy are doin'."

"They'll do all right. Let's just worry about ourselves. Ready?"

"I'd like to see a target. We might want to go up this slope and see if we can't see down on the fighting."

"Hmm," Anson intoned. "Might be best, at that. That smoke is thick as pudding, but we ought to be able to see, if we get to higher ground."

"We'll also make better targets of ourselves," Peebo said.

Anson flapped his hand to blow smoke away from his face. Now they both heard hoofbeats; hoofbeats that signaled many riders still fighting, probably invisible to the Box B hands. It was eerie standing there in the smoke listening to the sporadic shots and the galloping horses and not being able to see what was happening.

"Well?" Peebo said.

"I'm thinking about it. We could maybe walk a ways up the slope, stay low and see what we can see. Can't see a damned thing from here. We'll be able to see the front of the house and the left side."

"Yeah?"

"And if it looks clear, we can run on down to the house and go inside."

"We'll have to yell to make ourselves known to whoever's inside. 'Else they'll likely blow our heads off, us chargin' in like that."

"Let's take it one step at a time. First, up the slope. Then, either pick us some targets if we can see 'em, or go on down to the house and get inside."

"Good enough," Peebo said. He started scrambling up the rise and Anson had to run to catch up. They did not look back down until they were well up the slope. Then Anson stopped and turned around.

Peebo saw Anson turn and he stopped and did the same.

Anson let out a sigh. Then he gasped at what he saw.

"Jesus," Peebo said.

With the sun at their backs, they had a panoramic view of the battlefield below. Amid the cloaking smoke, they saw riders shooting from the saddle at targets behind the house, hugging their mounts like Apaches and shooting from the hip. Then they'd race back into the smoke and reload.

"Look," Anson said. "There, over by the front porch."

Peebo turned his head to look where Anson was pointing.

"My god," he said.

Several men were pulling flaming torches from a fire they had built just beyond the smoke, and running up to the porch and tossing the firebrands inside the house. The front of the house was already blazing.

"Nobody's shooting at them, either," Anson said, as he knelt down and brought his rifle to his shoulder.

Peebo dropped to his knees and then slipped sideways to sit on his butt. He dug his heels in and braced himself as he prepared to take aim.

"Listen," Anson said. "I hear screaming. From inside the house."

"Let's start cutting down those murderin' bastards," Peebo said, as he lined up on the back of a man squatting by the fire.

Anson fired from the kneeling position at a man climbing the front steps, a torch in his hand. "I figure a hundred and fifty yards," he said, and squeezed the trigger. He saw the man pitch forward and drop the firebrand as he hit the top step.

Peebo shot and struck his man square in the back. The mortally wounded man fell face down into the fire and sparks flew upward like flung jewels.

The other men stopped what they were doing and turned to look up at the slope. Anson sat down and started to reload.

"They've spotted us, son," Peebo said. "A couple of them are going for their horses. We're going to be in deep shit pretty damned quick."

Anson finished reloading and saw the men clawing at their reins and grabbing saddlehorns. Then he saw the front of the house erupt in a wall of flames and, through an upstairs window, he saw the fire had spread to the upper story.

A great sadness washed over him as he saw his home streaming with fire and he knew that it was dying. He could hear the wood scream as the flames gathered momentum and raced through all the rooms.

But then the men who had started the conflagration were mounted and had turned their horses. They were riding straight toward him and Peebo, at least five of them, and there was no place they could hide.

Anson cocked his rifle.

Peebo cocked his weapon a second later.

The riders came on, driving their horses hard, and behind them the Baron house raged with fire and the front walls started to cave in as if they were made of paper.

It took all of Anson's resolve not to break down and weep at the terrible sight of La Loma de Sombra, the house his father had built, collapsing before his eyes as waves of flame swept over it like a terrible tide from hell and the smoke rose in a hideous column up to the blue morning sky like some ominous beacon that could be seen all the way to Baronsville.

44

MARTIN YELLED AT Socrates to take cover as the line of riders broke and rode in a wide arc on their position. They streamed out of the mist and the gathering fog like a swarm of hornets, and he was astounded not only by their horsemanship, but also their tactics. They seemed to have trained for just this moment. He aimed his rifle at one rider, only to see his horse cut sharply and change direction so that any chance for a shot was ruined.

Socrates scrambled under the wagon just as a lead ball kicked up dirt where he had been standing but a moment before. The other men were shooting, but Martin knew they were missing their targets. And as he bent low and ran to the side of the wagon to find cover, he saw one of his men grab his throat with both hands, his rifle hanging in the air for a second before it struck the ground, and the man's hands turned into bloody gloves and he gurgled a terrible sound before he crumpled and fell into a silenced heap.

The riders kept coming, singly and in widely separated pairs, zigzagging through the white smoke and the fog, and Martin saw that they were dead shots as several of his men were hit and fell down, out of action. He used the sandbags lining the wagon bed for support and was able to shoot an attacker out of the saddle, but when he started to reload, another came at him and he had to scuttle for cover.

He thought he heard screams from inside the house, and then heard another sound that he could not identify. He put them both out of his mind, for the moment.

He knew then that his cannon would have been useless in such a battle. There was no massed target for such a weapon. He ducked behind a tree and finished reloading, but no riders came at him and he wondered where they had gone. It seemed to him that the battle had lasted for hours, but he knew he had been fighting for only a few minutes. He heard shots from the other side of the house, but no more from the upstairs and he tried to think how long it had been since last he had heard shots from the upstairs windows. A long time. Too damned long.

He stood up and started edging toward the back of his house. He passed Socrates huddled behind one of the box elm trees, shivering with fear, his machete clutched tightly with both hands as if for support.

He saw movement out of the corner of his eye, and when he turned, Martin saw three riders following the fenceline. He saw them through the haze of mist and drifting smoke and the lingering fog of early morning. But the sun caught the riders and he saw they were not Mexicans. A moment later they disappeared and then he heard rapid firing from their direction and Mexicans crying out in pain, yelling in Spanish, and heard them trying to ride away from the firing on horses until the hoofbeats, too, died away.

One of the riders had looked familiar, but he could not place him. They all wore white dusters and looked like ghosts, and after he had reached the end of the house he thought he might have imagined them. He thought he might have imagined those, too, in the heat of battle. The mind could play tricks on a man, he knew.

Martin paused at the storm shelter, a mound of earth with a door leading to a cellar dugout. Caroline and the women often went there in dust storms or when the sky looked funny to them in tornado season. Caroline often went there to clean out the cobwebs and rotate the stored foodstuffs and water. Opposite, on the side of the house, was another door, an opening cut in the skirts he had put up to keep the cold wind out from under the house.

There was a trapdoor inside the house, in back of the stairwell, that would let them drop down underneath the house in bad weather and, if they hunched over, they could walk to that door and get to the storm cellar. The house was raised on blocks for air space beneath. He caught his breath there by the mound of earth and tried to push thoughts of Caroline out of his mind.

Quickly Martin ran to the front of the house along the back wall, and that's when he heard a sound that made his throat tighten with fear and roiled the bile in his stomach. As he turned the corner, he saw flames licking the front wall and spreading to the porch.

Flames licked at his face as he stepped around the corner. There was little fog where he stood, and no smoke. He saw a man toss a torch in through one of the front windows, then run back to the fire that was burning just in front of the porch. Other men were there, and their horses stood nearby, next to a large live oak.

Then Martin looked up and saw two men scrambling up the slope, up out of the smoke. At first he thought they were two of Matteo's men, heading for high ground. Then he looked more closely and saw them kneel down. A second or two later, both men fired. He saw one man at the fire, jerk and fall headfirst into the fire. Another man took a ball on the steps and fell.

Now Martin saw that Peebo and Anson were the men on the slope, but just then the other Mexicans abandoned the fire and caught up their horses. Five of them started charging up the slope after Peebo and Anson.

Martin spread his legs wide and took a bracing stance. He brought his rifle up quickly and brought the front sight down on the back of a rider pulling away to flank his son and Peebo. He squeezed the trigger and the man threw his arms straight up in the air as the ball caught him square in the back. His rifle went flying overhead and tumbled downward. The man clutched at his saddlehorn, but did not have the grip to hold on, and tumbled from the saddle.

Two of the riders turned to look back. Martin began to reload quickly, as one of them turned and trained his rifle on him. He tried to shut the man out of his mind as he poured powder down the barrel and dug out a patch and ball from his possibles pouch.

He heard screams and voices from inside the house that churned his blood, turned it cold. Then, there were poundings and crashes that made his heart squeeze into a knotted fist as he finished seating patch and ball. He looked up, and the rider was no more than fifty yards away, eating up ground fast as he charged straight at Martin.

Martin sidled to his left, shifting his position from complete exposure to a place behind a small elm that afforded only a minimum amount of cover if he stood sideways and flattened himself out. He brought his rifle up and steadied against the six-inch trunk of the tree and drew a bead on the advancing horseman. The Mexican reined his horse into a hard turn, then reined him over the other way in that familiar zigzag pattern Martin had come to know so well.

Martin followed his course, however, and just as the rider was pulling the horse over for another turn, he led him slightly and squeezed the trigger. The horse was less than twenty yards away when the ball caught the rider in the left lung. The impact twisted the attacker violently to the left as blood spurted from the dark hole in his shirt. His rifle slipped from his hand and clattered on the ground as the horse twisted in the turn and ran out from under the wounded man, leaving him to fall crashing to the ground. The smoke from his rifle blinded Martin to the other riders charging up on Peebo and Anson's position, but he stepped from behind the elm tree and batted the smoke away with his hands.

He heard several shots and saw puffs of smoke well up the slope, but he could not make out where Peebo and Anson were, at that moment. He began to pour powder down the barrel of his rifle as he trotted to a new position, but there was so much smoke around the house, and fog, that still he could see nothing happening on high ground.

The house was now in full blaze, and as he turned to look at it, the sidewall blew out at him. He heard a loud roar and felt the rush of furnace-hot air blast him even as the gust knocked him to the ground.

He felt searing pain as sparks and embers struck his face and neck and he started to roll out of the way, when he saw a fiery beam falling toward him. He dropped his rifle and lifted his arms to ward off the impending blow and then he felt a sharp blow to his head.

Everything went black as Martin lost his senses. Somewhere, far away, he heard someone yelling and something creaking and then there was only the silence and the blackness.

45

ESPERANZA STRUGGLED TO stay on her feet as she fought her way through the smoke and flying sparks. She felt weak from the loss of blood, giddy, and the heat in the blazing house was unbearable. Beams were falling from the ceiling, and sparks and jets of flame seemed to be shooting at her from every quarter. She threw her right arm up to shield her eyes as she fought through the choking smoke to lead the others, who were following her, to a place behind the stairwell.

"Hurry, you must hurry!" Esperanza shouted in English and she felt the others bunch up behind her and push her through the smothering smoke. The fire had not reached into the den, the kitchen, or the other rooms beyond the front ones, and she ducked under the stairwell and grabbed Dr. Purvis by the sleeve and pointed to the floor.

"What is it?" he said, his voice harsh from breathing smoke.

"Open," she said. "Quick, quick."

Purvis bent down and saw the trapdoor. He felt around for a handle as the heat intensified. He could hear the house collapsing, and the lick of flames on the ceiling was terrifying.

"There, there!" Lucinda said, crowding in. "The handle. Pull it. Pull it!"

Purvis found the countersunk handle and lifted up on it. The door opened upward and a blast of fresh air arose from the dankness of the ground below the house.

"Go down," Esperanza said, pointing her finger at the opening in the floor.

"No, you go down first," Purvis said. "Show us the way."

"I have much pain, much hurt."

"Go," Purvis said. "Now."

He gently pushed her and she squatted, dangled both legs over the floor's edge. Purvis held her hands and she slid off the flooring and down beneath the house. Then she crumpled to her right side and lay there whimpering in pain.

"Lorene, go down there quickly," Purvis said. "We don't have much time before the fire reaches us."

"Yes, yes," Lucinda said, and pulled Lorene toward her. She pushed the young woman toward the opening and Purvis helped his niece descend.

"Take care of Esperanza," he said.

"Take Lazaro," Lucinda told the doctor. "Help him down. He is blind."

"Yes, I know. Ursula, hand me the boy."

"Here he is," Ursula said, shoving Lazaro past Lucinda and Hattie.

Lorene reached upward for Lazaro as her uncle and Lucinda lowered him through the trapdoor. She was surprised at how light he was, and she eased him down. Esperanza took the boy's hand and led him away from the opening.

Wanda and Hattie were next to slide down through the trapdoor.

"Come," Lucinda said to Ursula. "I will be last."

"No, I'll go last, Lucinda," Purvis said. "Come on, Ursula. I'll help you down. It's not much of a drop."

"Thanks," Ursula said, and stepped up to him and looked down at the darkness. Her face was smudged and the doctor slapped out a small spark that had caught in her light hair. He smelled the odor of burning locks. "Thanks again," she said, and squatted down. She sat, and Lucinda took her left arm, Purvis her right, and she scooched herself over the edge and touched ground as Lorene helped steady her.

"Now you, Lucinda," Purvis said. "I'll be right behind you."

"Yes," she said, and sat down, swung her legs around and let them drop through the open space. Purvis got behind her and put his arms through hers as he bent down. He felt her weight as she pushed off her perch and then he slipped his arms free as Lorene and Ursula helped her the rest of the way.

Flames raced toward Purvis and he threw up an arm to shield himself from the blazing heat as a wall of fire slammed into the staircase and began eating at its structure. Tongues of flame curled around the steps and down underneath and Purvis knew it would only be a matter of minutes before the entire stairway was engulfed in flames. Then the entire staircase would come crashing down over the trapdoor opening.

Quickly he dropped to the floor and reached back for his medical bag. "Lorene, take my bag," he said. He reached down and put it into his niece's outstretched hands. "Watch out," he said. "Here I come."

Just then he heard a sickening screech and looked at the underside of the stairs. They seethed with writhing, serpentine tongues of flames that lashed at the wood, flames of blue and orange and bloodred hues, as if borne from some devil's pyre, some boiling-hot hell.

Purvis heard the terrible screech of the joints giving way and, just as he slid downward, the entire staircase, a mass of flaming wood, started to descend in slow motion toward him like some holocaustal gate slamming shut on souls destined for some eternal torture by fire.

As his feet touched the earth, the stairs crashed to the floor, sealing the exit, spewing sparks and firebrands and twisting, spinning coals down into the midst of them. Lucinda screamed and Lorene gasped as she grabbed her uncle's hand and pulled him out of the way just after the staircase landed with a solid thundering *smack* that echoed through the remaining downstairs rooms of the house. His clothes sparkled with coals and the smell of burning hair filled the dark underbelly of the house.

"Come quick," Esperanza yelled, and Purvis saw her running, hunched over, toward the back of the house. He and Lorene slapped at his clothes to smother the sparks eating away at the threads of his coat and trousers.

The ragged line of people, all bent over except for Lazaro, followed Esperanza as smoke filled the space beneath the house. Purvis saw glimmers of dull light at the end of the house, streamers leaking through the skirting in thin beams and shafts.

Then a door opened and light streamed in and he saw Esperanza dash through and turn to grasp Lazaro's hand and pull him outside. Then, one by one, the others bolted through the opening and, finally, he was standing outside, next to a mound that he saw was a storm cellar, and he was gulping air into his lungs and clinging to his physician's satchel with one hand and searching for a tiny spark in his hair that was burning into his scalp.

"Look," Esperanza said, "there is *Don Martín,* and he is hurt."

Purvis saw Martin stretched out on the ground, next to a burning ceiling beam, and he started running toward him. The others, all except Lorene and Ursula, who followed after him, stood there huddled next to the storm cellar.

He turned and yelled at them as he reached the corner of the house. "Get into that storm cellar, quick!"

Esperanza leaned down and jerked the door open.

"I'm not going down there," Hattie said.

"Oh yes you are, Mother," Wanda said, and pushed Hattie toward the entrance. Esperanza shooed the others inside just as flames began to shoot from the back wall. She looked up at it and saw that the roof was on fire and the flames were racing along the eaves, consuming the entire length of the slanted roof. Huge flames lashed out from the windows and, now, fire blazed beneath the house in that place they had just left.

"Get inside," Purvis called again, and then the entire wall began to explode and fall toward the place where Esperanza stood. Smoke spewed from every corner of the house and the engulfing flames swallowed everything outside in Purvis's line of sight. He could not tell if Esperanza had gone down into the cellar, nor if she had managed to close the door before the wall crashed over it and sparks flew into the surrounding trees like little winking messengers of death, airborne like fireflies, against the backdrop of billowing smoke.

"He's out cold," Ursula said.

"We've got to get him away from here," Purvis said. "Lorene, grab his feet. Ursula, you take him by the shoulders. I'll get him in the middle."

Fire raged so close, their skins began to dry out and turn hot as they lifted Martin from the ground. Quickly they moved away from the blazing house and the nearby trees. The burning structure roared and screamed like some dying thing, and when they got to an open place, away from the heat, Purvis stopped and released his one arm support for Martin and nodded for the women to let him down to the ground.

"Is he . . . ?" Ursula started to say.

Purvis shook his head. He looked at his niece. Lorene's face was covered with black soot. Ursula looked like some beggarwoman from the pages of Charles Dickens, her dress torn and black with smoke and soot, her face smudged with charcoal.

"I don't know," he said. "I don't know if he's dead or alive."

Purvis sat down next to Martin's body and opened his bag. Ursula and Lorene looked down at both of them as rifle reports sounded from every quarter.

And they knew that the battle was not over and that the killing had not stopped.

"I can't imagine something like this happening," Lorene said, shaking her head as if in a daze.

"Neither can I," Ursula said. "I never thought I'd see the day when neighbor fought neighbor with such meanness. Look at that beautiful house. It's ruined."

And then Ursula began to cry as the enormity of all that had happened swept through her senses like a harsh prairie wind laden with heat from the sun rising over them at that moment and peering down at them like some angry and merciless god.

46

MATTEO RODE BEHIND the adobe huts, well away from them so there was little chance of anyone hearing him pass by in the darkness just before dawn. His senses quickened as he rode past one and heard a baby crying inside. He stopped his horse and waited. He heard a soft crooning voice speaking to the child in Spanish and then the baby was quiet and Matteo rode on, halting his horse every few minutes to listen. A dog barked at him, then slunk away when he waved his rifle at it. No one came outside to see why the dog had barked. He did not see the curtains move slightly as he passed, nor the eyes watching him through the cracks in those curtains.

Fog arose from the creek and the fields and he knew the sun was coming up, although he couldn't see it. His timing was perfect, he thought. His men would start their attack on the Box B when conditions were just right.

He heard shots from the direction of the road, and then the rumble of hoofbeats. He passed the last adobe and started angling toward the Box B headquarters, in no hurry. He just wanted to find a good place where he could watch the battle undetected. He came to the creek which was masked by rising mist and fog, and crossed it; on the other side, a line of trees marked its route, and from within the treeline he could see the dim outlines of the barn and the house beyond.

He found a place where he could sit his horse and watch the house and yard. He had a fair view of the garden and a boxed wagon in back of the house, just barely visible. Or perhaps it was not a wagon, he thought. It could have been an outbuilding. There were trees around it, but he didn't remember ever seeing a structure in that place.

Back among the adobes, several women spoke quietly about the man that had ridden through, and two of those women knew that they had seen Matteo Aguilar. They knew he did not belong there but they were afraid, until one woman, Carmen Sifuentes, the wife of Julio, told them she would make her way to the house where her husband was and tell him what they had all seen. The other women said she was crazy and went back to their adobes and barred their doors.

From his position, Matteo could hear the rumble of many horses as they galloped up the road toward the house. As the fog thickened and rose, he saw a puff of smoke from one of the upstairs windows and a second later he heard the report. Then he heard more rifle shots and saw the white smoke burst into the fog, then mingle with it and stay close to the ground.

Matteo drew in a deep breath to quell the excitement that made his blood tingle and his heart beat faster. He could see his men riding as they had been trained to ride, encircling the house and grounds, reining their horses every few yards so that they zigzagged and presented difficult targets. There was a lot of shooting, but he did not hear the roar of Martin's cannon and he smiled, wondering if his men had knocked it out on the first charge.

He kept looking at the house, wondering when his men would do what he had asked them to—set it ablaze. He did not have too long to wait, although it seemed like much time had gone by. When he saw the first column of smoke rising to the sky, he knew his men had done their job, and after a few moments he saw the flames themselves, shooting from the front of the house.

As the sun rose higher in the sky, the fog began to roll off the creek and mix with the white smoke from the rifles and he felt secure in his position. So far, his men had not set the barn afire, and that began to worry him. He wanted to ride onto the grounds and see everything that Martin had built laid to waste. He wanted to see Martin dead, or on his knees, begging for mercy.

The firing died down and Matteo could see the Martin house was fully engulfed in flames. He smiled and ticked his horse in the flanks with his spurs. It was time, he thought, to ride in and claim victory. He checked his rifle and pistol as he rode out from under the trees and left the creek behind. He did not know that at that moment Carmen Sifuentes was speaking to Al Oltman and Roy Killian, telling them not only had she seen Matteo ride past her adobe house, but that she knew where he was at that very moment. Roy and Al were still near the barn, and they had taken their toll on those numbers of Matteo's men who had ridden past them unwittingly in their circular courses.

Roy told Carmen to go back to her home and that he would tell Martin and her husband about Matteo. She, as well as they, had seen the big house in flames, and she was weeping when she left them to return home.

Matteo rode toward the burning house, his eyes fixed on the column of smoke that marked its death, and on the flames that continued to consume the rear of the house. He did not hear any shooting and he was satisfied that he was the victor and that soon he would lay claim to all of the Baron lands and make them Aguilar property once again.

He rode to within fifty yards of the barn and along a pole fence that enclosed a corral, when he heard the click of a lock. His heart felt as if it had stopped and he lifted his rifle to swing the barrel toward the sound.

"Aguilar, you make one more move and I'll blow you clean out of the saddle."

Matteo froze, trying to recognize the voice.

"And if he don't do it, I will," another man said. "Drop that rifle. Now."

For a long second, Matteo considered his chances against two men.

Then, out of the smoke, he saw three men in dusters riding toward him. They all had rifles pointed at him. They rode out of the rising fog and the smoke and looked like ghosts in their white dusters.

Bewildered, Matteo remained frozen, unable to move or think.

And then he heard another click as another man cocked his rifle. The man was directly behind him where he could not see who it was, but he knew the man could be no more than two or three meters away.

"Matteo," Roy said, "I've got your sorry head in my sights and my finger's on the trigger. Drop your rifle and grab yourself a piece of sky right quick."

Matteo's heart sank and he heaved a sigh. He wondered, just then, if he wanted to live or to die.

47

Anson fired his rifle at one of the charging riders, then threw himself down and rolled, just as another rider fired at him. He heard the ball whiz past his ear and saw it plow a long furrow in the ground. He heard Peebo shoot as Anson grabbed the butt of his caplock pistol and drew it.

Anson moved again and heard two quick shots in succession. Peebo cried out and Anson, out of the corner of his eye, saw him twist violently to one side. Through the clouds of cotton-white smoke he saw one rider lean out of the saddle as if reaching for something just beyond his grasp. Anson cocked the hammer of the Colt's back and tracked one of the oncoming men. He squeezed the trigger and then stood up and shot the man again as he slumped in the saddle.

"Peebo?"

"I'm hit."

"Christ. I saw one go after Pa down there by the house."

"Your pa shot him, but look." Peebo, grimacing, pointed to the side of the house, which was exploding outward.

Anson saw a flaming beam fly out and fall right where his father was standing.

Two men lay on the ground a few yards away. Neither moved.

The third was still leaning outward, but his boot had slipped through the stirrup and he was caught there, a blood-rimed hole in his chest. Anson caught the reins of the horse and saw that the man was wheezing, blowing blood out of his mouth. His eyes were glazed with the frost of a dying man. His lips moved, but no sound came out, only bubbles of frothy blood.

"We got all three," Anson said. "You get hit?"

Peebo stood up on wobbly legs and Anson saw him holding his left arm. Blood streamed through Peebo's fingers and his face was contorted in pain.

Anson dragged the dying rider from his horse, and laid him on the ground. He cringed when he heard the man make a gurgling sound in his throat. Then there was a rattling as blood bubbled up and subsided with the man's last breath.

"Lookie over yonder, Anson," Peebo said, as Anson came over to see about his friend's arm.

Anson followed Peebo's line of sight and saw several of Matteo's men converging on the road, near the barn. Then, as they watched, one man lifted his arm, then dropped it, pointing toward the Rocking A. The riders followed him in single file as the leader put his horse into a trot.

"They're giving up," Anson said. "Going back. But I don't see Matteo with them."

"Did you ever see him?"

"No."

"Well, maybe that's him yonder with those men in dusters. And if I ain't mistaken, that'd be Roy and old Al riding with 'em."

Anson saw the riders coming toward the burning house, three men wearing white dusters, surrounding a dark, thin man on an Arabian, flanked by Roy and Al. Anson sucked in a breath. "That is Matteo. Damned if it ain't."

"We ought to string him up," Peebo said.

Anson turned and looked at Peebo. "Let me see your arm."

"Look all you want, son. It's just a blood wound. Ball took a little meat with it, but it's just a nick."

"Take your hand away."

Anson looked at the crease in Peebo's arm. There was a lot of blood and some ragged flesh, but Peebo was right: The ball hadn't hit bone.

Down near the house, which was collapsing rapidly under the onslaught of the flames, he saw people carrying his father away from the fire. He felt a tug at his heart, a sinking feeling in his stomach. He pulled out a bandanna.

"Let me put this around your cut, Peebo. I've got to get down there to see how my pa is."

"Do it, son."

Anson tied his bandanna around the wound on Peebo's arm. He tied a loose knot. "It'll soak up some of the blood. Feel like coming with me?"

Peebo looked at the dead men. The sun was full up and the fog wafting away in airy wisps on the flat. "Yeah. Let's go see about your pa. Can you hand me my rifle?"

Anson picked up both rifles. "I'll carry them, unless you want yours for a crutch."

"Sometimes you've got a real smart mouth, Anson. I ain't crippled. Not by a damn sight."

The two started walking down the hill. Roy waved at them and Anson pointed in the direction they were going. He saw the men turn their horses to circle the burning house and meet them at the bottom of the slope.

He looked at the house as the back walls began to shrink and fall in on themselves like sheets of burning paper. They crumpled and collapsed and sent showers of sparks flying into the air. The smoke column began to spread out over the sky high above them until it formed a thin gray cloud that would be visible for miles.

"Sorry about your house, son," Peebo said.

Anson could not speak. He was sick to his stomach, gripped with a sadness that could not be expressed in words.

And with the sadness a dread, heavy as an iron anvil, that his father might be lying dead on the ground. That was Doc Purvis kneeling over him, he knew now, and the women looking on, Ursula and Lorene, he thought, were like watchers at a deathbed.

48

THE WOMEN HUDDLED together in the storm cellar. Lucinda held Lazaro close to her, for he was trembling. They could hear the flames crackling on the wall that had fallen over the cellar door just after Esperanza had jumped down and closed it. They could feel the heat from the fire. Esperanza looked up at the door, an expression of anxiousness on her face. Her shoulder throbbed, but the bleeding had stopped.

"We're going to be burned alive down here," Hattie said.

"Listen," Wanda said. "I don't hear any more shooting."

"They have stopped the shooting," Lazaro said.

"Maybe it's all over," Hattie said.

"I hear voices." Esperanza crawled up the steps and put her ear close to the door. "Help me push the door open."

"Thank God," Hattie said. "I'll help. Wanda, come on."

Hattie pulled Esperanza away from the slanted door. She and her daughter pushed up on the door. It gave away and flapped open. Sparks flew as burning pieces of the fallen wall fell away, but the opening was clear.

"Go on, Mother," Wanda said. "I'll help Esperanza get out. Lucinda, bring Lazaro and follow me."

All of them stood outside. Hattie saw several people beyond the front of the house. She recognized Doc Purvis and his niece.

"Oh, there's Ursula, too," Hattie said.

"And some men on horses," Wanda said. "And I see Roy. Do you see him, Mama?"

"I see him."

The women and Lazaro started running toward the group of people. The entire sidewall of the house had collapsed and was smoldering. A burning hulk remained, still afire, and the chimney and fireplace in the front room were visible and still standing.

"It's just awful," Hattie said, as she looked at the wreckage.

Lucinda started to cry and Esperanza appeared stricken, her face drawn, her eyes glittering with dampness.

"Oh, there they are," Ursula exclaimed as everyone turned to look at the women and the blind boy running toward them.

Doc Purvis had just finished wrapping a bandage around Martin's head. The salve was already leaking through it, leaving a light-brownish stain. Martin looked like a wounded sheikh. Roy and Al were helping him to his feet. "You'll be a bit dizzy for a time," Purvis said. "That lump on your head will go down a lot slower than the dizziness will go away. Nasty blow, there."

"Much obliged, Doc."

Ursula looked around as if in a daze. "Where's David?" she asked, looking at Roy.

Anson stepped up and tapped Roy on the shoulder. "I'll take him, Roy. You go talk to your mother."

"Thanks," Roy said, slipping out from under Martin's arm. Anson took up the weight until his father was standing on his own.

Then Anson stepped away to look into his father's eyes. "Can you walk, Pa?"

"I can, but I'm not going to. Just let me stand here a minute and wait for this deck to stop pitching."

Anson laughed. "You're going to be all right, Pa."

Al gingerly released his hold on Martin, but stood close to catch him if he fell. The women crowded around to look Martin over and he grinned sheepishly at them.

"Doc, take a look at Peebo's arm," Anson said. "He's got a little scratch."

Purvis turned around and saw Peebo's bandaged arm. "Let me have a look," he said.

"Aw, Doc," Peebo said. "I've had worse from a dog bite."

Roy led his mother away from the group assembled around Martin. The fog had dissipated, and so had the smoke from the black powder explosions. The house still burned, sending more smoke into the air, along with fluttering ashes and vagrant sparks.

Sifuentes, Socrates, and several other Box B hands rounded the corner of the house and started walking toward the assemblage, big grins on their faces.

"Al," Anson said, "will you go back with me to get David's body and carry it here? And I left my saddlebags back there, too."

"Sure, soon's I talk to Kenny, yonder."

Martin took a step and turned around to look at the three horsemen holding Matteo between them.

"Kenny, I see you caught yourself a fox in my henhouse," Martin said.

"He's going to wear some stripes, Martin."

"Sorry about Caroline."

"Me too. I'll be back soon and we can talk about it, if you want."

"We're still looking for a Frenchman, name of Jules Reynaud. Have you seen him?"

Martin shook his head.

Al stepped out and walked up to Darnell. "Glad you got here, Kenny. You get the warrants?"

Darnell patted his coat and nodded.

"Howdy, Jim-Joe," Al said. "Dan."

"Is Martin there going to join us?" Casebolt asked, looking over at Martin.

"I'd say he's had a taste of war. Let me ask him."

Al turned to Martin. Just then, Ursula broke down and began sobbing. Roy had his arm around her shoulders and was saying something to her the others could not hear.

"David got killed," Al said, just loud enough for Martin to hear.

"Damn it all," Martin said. Then he looked at his men and they all took off their hats and hung their heads.

"You have a decision to make, Martin," Al said. "I asked you a question before this fight started. I reckon this is just a little taste of what civil war is like. We can put your neighbor in jail, but there's a lot more like him just waiting to take away everything you have. You can rebuild your house, but you can't bring David back to life."

Martin looked at the burning hulk of his house, then at Anson. Anson was trying his best not to cry. His mouth was knotted into a fist and he drew a deep breath and held it.

At that moment Ursula stopped weeping and turned to look at Martin. She caught his eye and nodded to him.

Martin looked at the blind Lazaro, then at Esperanza and Lucinda. They stood straight and they held their heads high and level. Lorene put her arm inside her uncle's. Hattie and Wanda, their faces smudged with soot, their clothes disheveled and unkempt, stared boldly at Martin, a noncommittal expression on their faces.

"You're right, Al," Martin said. "I can rebuild my house, and I will. And you asked me to join the Texas Rangers and I said I'd think about it."

"You did," Al said.

"Well, we had us a little war here. Matteo, you tried to steal my land and you burned down my home. And you killed some friends of mine—one at least. And you broke the law by smuggling slaves up here to the Rio Grande Valley. You meant to sell humans like they were cattle and profit from it. You're a thief and a scoundrel and now you're going to jail for what you've done."

Ursula and Roy walked closer so they could hear what Martin was saying. No one there said a word or made a sound.

Martin looked at Darnell and the other two Rangers, and drew himself up until he was standing as straight as the Mexican women.

"I thought about it when the shooting started. If there's going to be war—and I guess there is," Martin said, "then I'd rather be fighting on home ground with men I trust, men who have helped me in my little battle here. So, Al, my answer is yes, I'll join the Texas Rangers. But only on one condition."

"What's that, Mr. Baron?" Al said, suddenly formal.

Martin turned to his son.

"If Anson will stay here and rebuild what's been burnt and laid to waste and keep the Box B going. I want this to be the biggest and best cattle ranch in the country. Anson?"

"I'll do it, Pa," Anson said, and his eyes brimmed with tears.

"Then swear me in, Al. I'll join your Rangers right here and now."

A chorus of cheers erupted at Martin's pronouncement. The

three Rangers threw their hats into the air. Sifuentes and Socrates both grinned. Lazaro smiled, too, and clapped his hands.

Lorene looked at Anson and he looked at her. She smiled at him and he blushed.

Then Al walked up and shook Martin's hand. "You made the right decision," he said. "We're damned glad to have you with us."

"That goes for me, too, Martin," Kenny said.

Ursula pushed herself away from Roy and walked up to Martin. She put her arms around his neck and drew his head down. She kissed him on the lips. Everyone laughed and cheered once again.

"You're a fine man, Martin Baron," Ursula said. "The finest I've ever known."

Martin shook his head as Ursula stepped away. He turned to Anson.

"She's right, Pa," Anson said. "That goes double for me."

Martin's chest swelled with pride. He turned away to keep from choking up and he looked at Matteo, who was scowling and had not said a word. The two men glared at each other for a long moment.

And, then, Matteo lowered his head and slumped in the saddle like a man defeated and stripped of all honor before men much wiser and greater than he.